TREASURES ON EARTH

TREASURES
ON EARTH

Jessica Stirling

St. Martin's Press

New York

Library of Congress Catalog Card Number: 84-40739
    ISBN 0-312-81651-0
First published in Great Britain by Hodder & Stoughton Ltd.
First U.S. Edition
10 9 8 7 6 5 4 3 2 1

Contents

No man knows
Through what wild centuries
Roves back the rose.

Sir David Lindsay

PART ONE

Gaddy

ONE

Guarded Pastures

Raised by an icy wind that whipped through gaps in the bramble hedge a flurry of leaves danced before her into the tunnel beneath the oaks. Stirred by the blast, the trees flexed their boughs and, it seemed to Gaddy in her nervous mood, intended to bar the road against her. She was a strong handsome woman, no longer a slender slip of a girl, but the force of the wind shook her powerfully and made her blue eyes water and she lowered her body along the mare's back and clung with both fists to its tangled mane as she peered along the track.

She had heard how Pictish warriors, the true folk of the north, had forged this track long centuries ago when they stole south to storm the Roman forts in the hills above the Clyde. Since then many another highlander, some hardly less barbarous, had followed the route from the glens, driving cattle down from the wild free mountains into the lowlands' guarded pastures. Donald and she were part of that tradition. They had come into Stirlingshire out of remote Argyll every autumn for twenty-two unbroken years. Gaddy had no reason to suppose that the year of 1791 would be different, that on that November night her life would be turned upon itself forever.

For Gaddy Patterson and Donald McIver, the drove was one of many that patterned the seasons. In all they would travel near three hundred miles before the winter snows chased them home to the crofts of Ardelve on the bare backside of Ben Cruachan. In November, though, it wasn't black cattle they rattled before them. In November they laboured for personal profit not as hirelings of Lorne's wee lairdies or for penny fees from local cattlemen. The annual horse fair at the Thorn of Cadder on Glasgow's boundary was the magnet.

The Cadder fair was a modest tryst compared to Rutherglen or the swarming activity of Falkirk's marts where fifty thousand head would change hands in three days' trading. But Cadder was best for a man with healthy highland garrons to shift, those sturdy ponies which were the blood and bone of Scottish agriculture and the carting trades. After the fair, with the garrons sold, Donald and she would push on to other business, no less important. They would head down the valley of the Clyde towards Dumbarton, leading the mare, a bold-striding draught-horse, and her two-year-old colt, already strong enough to tip over a haystook with a flick of his tail. By long-standing agreement the mare would be covered by one of the Flemish stallions on the Edderly Estate where Donald's uncle was head horseman. The colt would be sold to the Edderly for seven pounds, the balance of its worth being taken for the stallion's services, an arrangement that had worked well for many years.

The mare was named Bracken, the colt Gallant. He pranced skittishly behind his dam, as if he sensed Gaddy's apprehension at turning on to private land.

"*Damn you to hell, woman*," Donald shouted. "*Bring them on.*"

Possessed by doubt, Gaddy continued to hold rein.

Once they trotted the garrons down the track and on to the hill pasture they would be foul of the law. From Perth, through Crieff and Stirling, public roads and attendant lands were considered to be the property of parishes and the lairds who owned the parishes. Fees were due, though to whom and in what score Gaddy had no notion. Donald had never paid for grazings and claimed he had no intention of starting now, law or no damned law.

"*Gaddy, do you not hear me?*"

The brooding hump of the moor was burled by whirling sleet which obliterated the village's outlying cottages. Tenants and labourers would be snug indoors. At the big house of Ottershaw only the horsemen would be out, grooming their charges in the sheltered stable-yard. Gaddy felt perilously alone. Tonight she pined for a family of her own.

Donald might share her bed but he was no husband to her. Still, she was used to desolate nights and to loneliness. Why should this one disturb her? Her mother, long since dead, had been blessed with second sight. Though Gaddy could not claim to spy visions in fire flame or hear voices in sea waves, a premonitory warning sang in her head like a note drawn from a taut fiddle string.

"*Come on, damn you, woman,*" Donald raged.

Still she could not bring herself to enter the enclosed track. Seated high on the mare's back, blanket and canvas for saddle, she clung bare-legged to its wet flanks. Her shawl clouted about her ears and the threatening wind straggled her hair. She was a tall, strong-boned woman of thirty-eight, with large hands and a shape of face that the herders in Ardelve called "chuffit-cheeked". She took the weather well, though in cold months she wrapped her legs in woollen strips to prevent chafing for she sat astride the mare as a man does, except in towns.

Donald lost patience.

"*Bracken*," he bellowed. "*Here t'me, Bracken lass.*"

What was it? Had there been a witch coven on the nearby hill? Did the stink of the unholy revel linger five days after All Hallows? Was that the source of her fear? Daft, Gaddy, the woman told herself. Stir yourself or Donald will whack you blue and black with the switch. She touched her heels to the mare's flanks and the animal dawdled forward.

The wind unleashed a fresh torrent of leaves and flung the oak boughs about Gaddy's head as she stooped under them. Bracken broke into a loping trot, the colt legging behind. She nosed for the open gate and surged up the muddy ramp. Gallant caught up with her. Donald jumped and quickly closed and roped the gate. They were in now, on Bontine's land, in Bontine's enclosure. Nervously Gaddy peered around.

Ewes sheltered under the branches which caverned the hedge. They rose with the garrons' arrival, blethered, and shifted away into the teeth of the wind. Bullocks were visible against the skyline before they kicked and thundered away over the fall of the hill.

The grazing was rough pasture, part of the shoulder of

the hill of Drumglass. Its slope plunged steeply from a conical summit down across the track, down across the Glasgow turnpike and through the gates of the Ottershaw parks right up to Sir Gilbert Bontine's front door.

Gaddy had laid eyes on Ottershaw House only once. Seven years ago Donald, the worse for drink, had tried to sell ponies there. He had been chased away by a couple of ploughmen. She knew of the Bontine family in the manner in which she knew of most landowners along the road, from tattle picked up around fairs and camp fires where drovers and packmen met. In the general opinion Bontine was no tyrant. He would not shoot you or toss you into a cellar for his smith to whip or even drag you up before the sheriff's man, unless for stealing. But Donald McIver had the unhappy knack of rubbing lairds the wrong way since he would not doff his bonnet to any man, even for the show of it. If they were caught it would mean trouble and loss of the sale at the Thorn of Cadder.

In the field, tussocks of coarse grass and thistle stalks stood out blind-white with sleet. There was a burn ahead, where tiny streamlets gathered off the hillside, and a bowl-like pool where the ponies could be watered. But there was precious little in the pasture worth paying fee for and there would be no justice in a charge of grass-stealing or hardly of trespass, though trespass it undoubtedly was.

Bracken followed the garrons along the hedge then upward across the slope of the hill, away from the belt of forest which sheltered the pasture. Gaddy could make out the garrons well enough and Donald's two dogs hugged low against the turf, silently snapping at the ponies' hoofs to keep them together.

Three hundred yards above the track were the remains of a wall and a hut of sorts. It had once been the home of an auld wife who had earned pick by scaring hares from the grazings before guns came into fashion, but she was long dead and the hut had no purpose but to shelter ewes. Even so, Gaddy would be glad to tuck herself inside tonight out of the cruel wind and away from disturbing fancies. It would cheer her to hear Donald ranting against the lairds, after they were settled and she had kindled a fire and boiled the pots. She would do the housekeeping while Donald tended the garrons and fed the horses from the meal sack. She would use some of her precious supply of tea tonight. Tea was Gaddy's only indulgence. She could not abide sma' beer, ale or spirits, though the drinking of "the lady's drink" was considered an affectation by the Ardelve crofters.

The garrons had found a chew of weeds along the exposed side of the wall and had strung out there, tails fluttering like pennants. Donald left them to it and went through the gap in the wall, preceded by the dogs. Gaddy let the mare follow, stepping daintily over half-buried stones. She reined the animal by the lee of the hut and Donald took the colt off the rope.

As he passed her, Donald muttered, "God, what ails you tonight, Gaddy Patterson?"

He did not expect a reply.

Gaddy slid to the ground. The wind plastered her skirts to her thighs and cloaked the shawl about her head. The pack-pony loitered close by, patient as a monument. Shivering and panting, the dogs waited too. Donald had not dismissed them. Dogs and horses were obedient to the highlander. He treated them well, better, oft-times, than he treated his woman. Gaddy approached the door of the hut enshrouded by a strange mingling of fear and excitement.

The hut had a rank sheep smell to it, dank as a sea-cave and pitch black within. But it wasn't the stench that appalled her. Lug and Birkie, brave full-grown mongrels and wise as sin, had backed away from the place, showing white teeth above curled muzzles, ears flattened and ruffs bristling.

Gaddy signalled, saying, "G'in Luggie. G'in, Birkie. Ga' awa' in." The dogs would not obey. Trembling, they remained pressed to the grass.

The mare snickered and stamped her hoof uncertainly. Big as he was the colt moved closer to his dam, rubbing his neck along her shoulder.

Gaddy said, "Donald?"

The man could not hear her. He had gone behind the wall to count the garrons while they cropped.

Gaddy took a deep breath and stepped forward.

Senses sharpened she detected a shape within the darkness of the hut, a pale, elongated shape which at first seemed to hang in the space above the dimpled black mud. It would be nothing terrible, of course; a flour sack, a scare-rag that a bairn had left. If she cried to Donald, he would stride past her and kick the thing and jeer at her imaginings.

Gaddy turned to the pack-pony and groped among the bundles wrapped to its back. She found the lantern in its oilcloth bag and the smaller bag that contained tinder and flint. Kneeling beside the wall, sheltering the box with her skirts, she struck a spark from the bluestone. She made flame in the teaze of wool and wood shavings in the tin. With a straw taper she transferred the flame to the tallow within the lantern, closed and latched it, and approached the doorway once more.

Cracked and slimy with moss, the lintel was hardly taller than her head. She stood beneath it and extended the lantern to arm's length.

It was no scare-rag after all.

Gaddy uttered a cry of horror.

A woman was sprawled across the floor of the hut, skirts screwed around bare, stick-thin thighs. Gaddy could see how she had pitched across the threshold and crawled into the shelter on her stomach. Spittled with sleet and mud, her fair hair stuck out like moulting feathers. She looked, Gaddy thought, like a young heron with its neck thrawn.

"Donald?" Gaddy whispered.

Birkie had trailed Gaddy into the hut and sniffed curiously around the stoup. The highland woman kicked out at the dog lest it defile the corpse.

"Donald, come quick."

Lug barked, relaying her command, but Donald cursed it and told it to hold its damned noise.

Gaddy inched forward, letting the puddle of light from the lantern settle on the dead woman.

She was hardly a woman at all when you looked close, hardly more than a girl, tall and angular with arms as thin as willow wands. Her right arm was crooked under her breast, a pillow for her cheek.

"Donald?"

Perhaps it was Gaddy's shout which induced response, a tiny plaintive mouse-squeak too faint and weak to be called a cry.

Gaddy fell to her knees, propped the lantern by the wall and drew back the girl's shoulder. The neck was limber and the head flopped. Sightless eyes stared into Gaddy's. She was fifteen or sixteen years old at most and, even with sunken cheeks and colour gone, pretty.

Gaddy swallowed the lump of pity in her throat. Gently she pushed the shoulder again. The body uncoiled and rolled on to its back.

There, pressed smothering tight against the girl's breast, was a baby.

"Oh, God! Oh, God!" murmured Gaddy Patterson and reached to gather the infant into her arms.

The Reverend William Leggat first came to Balnesmoor in 1772. The Duke of Montrose issued the presentation in his favour and he was ordained on the 9th day of June. Fifth son of a tenant farmer in Franklin, near Dunblane, he had attended school in Stirling and later the University of Glasgow. For three years after his graduation he served as tutor to the family of Mr Arbuthnot of Croal, near Perth. There he fell head over buckles for the daughter of the house, a haughty bitch named Isobella who clearly had her sights set on marrying nobility but, out of malice, almost drove the young minister mad with her strutting and teasing. So relieved was Mr Leggat to be free of the witch that he knelt before the altar of Balnesmoor old kirk on the eve of his ordination and took a private vow that he would journey no further in search of advancement and would be content with his lot as it had fallen him. He also vowed that he would not marry. The quest for a suitable wife might unwittingly lead him within range of another crocodile like Miss Arbuthnot and he did not think he would be able to survive such a trial of the flesh a second time. Celibacy, however, was a condition more easily promised than endured. By inclination, Mr Leggat was a loving man, though not particularly carnal, and his natural vigour soon found other outlets. No zealot, he avoided involvement in the quarrels which split the presbyterian churches. He based his ministry on sound doctrine, the teaching of the Catechism and the singing of metrical psalms. He was not without fervour as a preacher but he personified the new tolerance that had crept into the Church. He was, in general, liked for his moderation. By the time he had reached his prime he was much respected in the parish, not least for the size and abundance of his vegetable crops.

Some mean-spirited people muttered as how the Reverend seemed to spend more time labouring in the manse garden than he did in the vineyards of the Lord. But even the least magnanimous villager was forced to admit that he had done wonders with the ill bit ground that sloped away behind the manse, a plot once so peeled of feal and divot that not even thistles would grow there. Such profusion of fruit, flower and vegetable raised by a minister, folk said, surely attested to the Glory of God, and the value of regular dressings of manure.

The manse lay four hundred yards from the church in a cul-de-sac known as the Bonnywell, though the well itself was dry now and water was obtained from the west pump close to the Ramshead Inn. The front of the manse was screened by shrubs and an ivy-covered wall. It was a two-storey sandstone building with a slated roof and an ornamental brick chimney. Though the Bonnywell was at the quiet end of the village it also contained two lime-washed cottages, Bontine feus, which were leased from the laird by Mr James Simpson Moodie, handloom weaver and parish clerk.

James Moodie had two spinster sisters and a widowed mother to support, though with three pairs of female hands to "do" for him many a lad in Balnesmoor might have settled for a life of ease. Not James Moodie; he took his responsibilities seriously. The family lived in one cottage and worked in the other, spinning wool and weaving it into cloth. It was a tidy, well-packaged business which young James had inherited from his thrifty father. The loom was bolted to the floor close to the cottage's front window, ostensibly situated to provide light but also to furnish an unimpeded view of the manse.

It was close to six of the clock that Tuesday evening when the clatter of hoofs brought Jamie leaping from the loom board to the window. He peered apprehensively through the pane, wiped it with his sleeve and peered again.

Mother and sisters had heard the noise too and came running to Jamie's side.

"What is it? What's happenin'?" the elder girl demanded.

"Wait, wait 'til I see."

A rough-looking scoundrel in tattered clothing swung from off a garron's back. He flung open the manse gate and, hauling the pony behind him, stalked up the path between the trim little holly trees.

"Jamie, is it a robber, d'ye think?"

"The bearer o' ill tidings," said Mother Moodie profoundly. "I can tell."

"Do not judge, lest ye be judged," Jamie snapped.

Moments later came the faint echo of a fist pounding on the manse door.

"Watch. Watch close," said James Moodie. "See if she lets him in."

The housekeeper's lamp glimmered like an elf-light for half a minute then went out as the door closed.

"She did. She let him right in."

"Maybe he's a messenger wi' a letter," said the younger sister.

"Or a seedsman callin' for an order," said the elder.

"No seedsman would ride at such indecent speed," James Moodie said.

"Son, it bodes ill for somebody, I'm thinkin'."

"You're right, Mother," growled the weaver.

"Aye, but for who?" Mother Moodie said.

Curiosity burned like dry straw, not only in the women but in the weaver too. He was taut with frustration and anxiety. He kneaded his fists together, glancing from the window to the loom, then at his mother.

"I'll . . . I'll away over," said James Moodie. "I'll need t' see what's occurred."

"You canna go in your apron," Mother Moodie said.

"Lizzie, fetch my Sabbath breeks, and be slippy about it."

In fact the stranger had not been admitted to the manse by the elderly housekeeper, rather she had been brushed to one side by his haste. Now the old woman, gruff as a terrier, was threatening to send for aid if the stranger did not stand and explain himself. But the stranger had no intention of explaining himself to a servant. He had already stalked uninvited into the dining-room, drawn by the lamplight.

Mr Leggat had had a busy day. He had visited two aged worthies before dinner at midday and had spent the afternoon drilling bean rows in the dry ground by the north-west wall of the garden. Washed and groomed, the minister was seated at the supper table with a glass of loganberry wine, a copy of Young's *Farmers' Kalendar* open before him, when the drover burst in.

"Are you the minister?" the stranger demanded.

"Indeed. I am Mr Leggat."

"There's a woman dead."

Leggat was thin and fit, with soft, reddish hair and brown eyes, his hands as calloused and sinewy as a thatcher's.

Bristling with anger and injured pride, Mrs Sprott came into the dining-room. Mr Leggat held up a hand to her. "I will attend to it, Mrs Sprott, thank you." He addressed the stranger. "Where?"

"Up by the burn, on the Drumglass grazings."

"Who, may I enquire, are you?"

"McIver's the name. Donald McIver."

Mr Leggat had seen many of like type. He recognised the "regality of the road" in the grey wool bonnet, duffle coat, cord knee-breeks and thick rig-and-fur stockings ventilated by a number of holes.

"Are you, by chance, a cattle drover, Mr McIver?"

"That's what I am, sir. But it's garrons I have on this trip."

"Are you heading for Cadder?"

"I was, until we found the dead woman."

Mr Leggat's gentle manners hid a high degree of acumen. "Drumglass is part of Sir Gilbert Bontine's estate, McIver, as I'm sure you are aware. Why have you brought this sad information to me and not to the laird?"

"She . . . my . . . the woman told me t' find the minister."

"Would you have ridden on?"

The perspicacity of the question caught McIver by surprise. He gave a lopsided grin. "Aye, maybe I would. But there's a bairn too, an' the bairn's still breathin'."

"A bairn?"

"A suckler."

Mr Leggat got to his feet. "Mrs Sprott, hasten across the road and fetch Mr Moodie. Tell him to come at once. Oh, and where are my riding boots?"

"In the cupboard by the stairs. Are you ga'n oot with this ruffian? It'll all be a pack o' lies."

"It's no lie, mistress. I wisht it was," said McIver.

Before Mrs Sprott could move to do the minister's bidding there was a rap upon the manse's front door.

Mr Leggat grunted wryly. "Unless I am much mistaken, that will be Mr Moodie. Do let him in."

Minister and drover followed the old woman into the hallway and watched as she unlatched the door once more. Leaves rustled on the stone step and wafted into the hall, less deferential than the elder who, with neck craned and eyes popping, awaited an invitation.

"In ye come," said Mrs Sprott. "I was on my way for you. He'll have need of your protection, I'm thinkin'."

"Protection?" said Mr Moodie. "From what?"

In spite of his exalted position in kirk and community, James Simpson Moodie was short of thirty years old. He had whisked through boyhood and youth, however, and affected the air of a much older man. He dressed more like an Edinburgh lawyer than a country weaver and spoke in a "grand style" when he addressed the minister. He was shorter by a head than either the Reverend or the drover but thick-muscled and powerful.

"Excellently well-timed, Mr Moodie," said Leggat. "We must brave the elements, you and I. Be kind enough to fetch the horses from the livery and bring them to the gate. Also, if you will, call in at Mr Rankellor's house and see if he has returned from Stirling. If so, inform him that I would be obliged if he would rendezvous with me in the yard of the Ramshead as soon as possible."

Mr Moodie glowered at the drover, his curiosity not appeased. "What are you needin' the doctor for, Mr Leggat?"

"To attend a foundling."

"Would Mrs Campbell not do as well as the doctor?" said Moodie. "I could ride to Harlwood for her."

"A midwife would hardly serve our purpose or that of the poor infant – who is already born."

"Mrs Campbell comes cheaper than Mr Rankellor, much cheaper."

Mr Leggat sighed. "We'll discuss the payment of the doctor's bill later, Mr Moodie. As it happens I also wish Doctor Rankellor to be present in his capacity as sheriff-substitute. Now please do as I ask."

"I will, Mr Leggat. I will."

The elder turned and hurried out of the door and down the path.

The speed of his passage caused McIver's garron, which was tied to a little hazel tree, to whicker and stamp its hoofs all over the flower beds. Mr Leggat sighed again, seated himself on the stairs and pulled on his riding boots, which Mrs Sprott had drawn from the cupboard. She had also brought out a heavy wool coat, a knitted scarf, mittens and his travelling hat, all necessary to protect the cleric from the foul November air.

"Him – Rankellor – is he the sheriff's man?" asked Donald McIver.

"He is. By fortunate coincidence he resides in this parish."

"What are we needin' him for?"

"To settle the matter of responsibility," said Mr Leggat.

"Responsibility? We only went up there for water, damn it."

"Responsibility for the welfare of the infant."

Donald was not appeased. He fidgeted nervously while the minister made himself ready. He wondered what calamities Gaddy had called down upon him, what with ministers and elders and sheriff's men all dancing to her beck. Was it too late to cut and run from the ominous shadows of kirk justice and the law, to abandon his ponies, his horses and his mistress for the sake of freedom and a quiet life?

After all, Donald McIver reminded himself, he owed Gaddy Patterson nothing – and the poor pewling babe even less since it was like to die anyway, if not tonight, tomorrow.

"Come," said Mr Leggat, rising.

As if guessing what might be hovering in the drover's mind, he took a firm grip on the highlander's arm and led McIver from the manse.

Gaddy heard them swing out of the trackway into the field. Lug and Birkie, settled in a corner of the hut close to the fire, pricked up their ears and grumbled in their throats at the approach of strange horses.

Gaddy said, "Wheesh, wheesh, the pair of you," though the child in her arms seemed oblivious to the dogs or the looming presence of mare and colt by the door, where Gaddy had scattered oats to keep them quiet.

Where the garrons had strayed to Gaddy did not care. Her concern was for the morsel of existence which cuddled against her breast, too weak to grope in search of a teat and a taste of mother's milk.

Gaddy knew little of babies, except that they often died. In Ardelve, for instance, four out of every six did not survive a year, but were carried back to their Maker by croup, convulsions, or the flux. But Gaddy had delivered and nursed many calves and foals and was not entirely lost when it came to nurturing a young thing, though she was afraid for it, heartbreakingly afraid.

When found, the infant had been barefoot and bareheaded, wrapped in filthy swaddles of cotton stuff and knitted wool which had absorbed the wetness of the sleet. Straight away Gaddy had stripped the child to the skin. Donald had obeyed her instruction to fill a pot from the burn and light the bunch of dry kindling they had brought with them.

"It's a girl, Donald."

"Aye, it would be," Donald had retorted.

"Go now an' fetch the minister."

Donald McIver might be selfish but he was not altogether a brute. Besides, he had been quick to take Gaddy's point about the bother they would be in if they stole the child and were caught. Justice was still rough in Stirlingshire but on occasions the authorities could be uncommon thorough. They did not know to whom the child belonged or from what family the girl might be descended. So Donald drew the cadaver against the wall and covered it with the saddle blanket then took the pack from the garron, mounted up and rode back into the village to find the cleric.

The dry kindling did not last long and did not warm the pot much. Soon after Donald's departure, Gaddy was obliged to wrap the baby in a shawl and big blanket and lay it down while she went out and into the trees to rummage in the dark for dry sticks. Expert in foraging, she found them without straying far and was back in the hut within minutes. She broke and fed the sticks into the smoke then opened up the pack, found sugar and oatmeal and set them by, along with a wooden cog and a nice silver tea-spoon Donald had bought her from a pedlar once in a rare fit of generosity.

It was impossible to guess the baby's age. She was shrivelled and puny like a skinned leveret, lacking in vital energy. Under a cap of fine fair hair, her scalp was crusted. Her eyes exuded a yellow pus. She had no fever, though the cold was slow to come out of her. Gaddy hugged and gently rubbed her while waiting for the pot to steam. Age was important. If the bairn was very young then her stomach would reject anything except milk and Gaddy had no milk to hand. The baby had to be fed, and fed right soon. Gaddy prayed that the mite had tasted weaning saps and that her swollen belly would be able to digest oat gruel.

The burn water gurgled in the pot. Gaddy laid the baby down again, measured oatmeal with the tea-spoon, pinched in sugar from the canister and stirred the mixture until it thickened. She unearthed a clean kerchief and laid it over the wooden cog and poured the gruel through it, bagging the cloth and crushing it so that a milky substance dripped through to give body to the liquid.

All the while the baby lay motionless without a whimper, and the wind bellowed and brayed about the broken thatch and sleet refined itself into snow. Bracken and Gallant had come close to the doorway, huge against the speckled snow-light. Lug was on his feet, sniffing and whimpering at

24

the smell of the mash. To keep the dogs quiet Gaddy made a slosh of meal for them and tipped it, steaming warm, into their pan. Tails slapping, the dogs fell on it hungrily. Gaddy hoped that the baby would eat with as little coaxing. Cradling the infant against her shoulder, she took a dab of sweet gruel on the tip of her little finger and brushed it against the lips. There was no response. The bairn's eyes remained shut, not in sleep but in swoon.

Gaddy tried again. With the ball of her thumb she lifted the upper lip and touched the substance to gums and tongue. For a long moment it seemed that the child's natural instincts had ceased to function, then, to her enormous relief, Gaddy felt the little tongue stir and the gums close on her pinkie. The baby girned. It was the first sound she had uttered since the squeak an hour ago. When Gaddy removed her finger there was more girning, suitably petulant. Tiny fists closed on Gaddy's hair until the finger, larded with gruel, was reinserted. It was sucked clean very swiftly. Aye, Gaddy thought, she's thirsty as well as hungry. But she'll feed now and if her belly will hold and digest, she'll not starve, whatever else.

Gaddy was still patiently finger-feeding the baby when the thud of the approaching horses caused her to raise her head. She heard a man's voice, another answering. She was as dirty and ill-kempt as a bale of winter straw. But she would not disturb the baby's feeding to satisfy vanity.

"Through the gap, sir," she heard Donald shout. "There's the hut, see, wi' the bit light in it."

Disturbed by the arrival of strange animals, Bracken and Gallant thundered away. Donald would have a job catching them, though they might lure back later if he scattered more grain. Lug and Birkie had shaken off drowsiness and were bristling and snapping. Donald had sense to come first into the hut, grab the dogs and lead them out by their ruffs.

"Who's with you, Donald?"

"Men o' God, as your ladyship requested," Donald McIver grumbled. "Aye, an' a sheriff's aide."

If it had not been for the presence of parish luminaries, Donald would have welted her for putting him to so much trouble. He did not, Gaddy noticed, enquire after the baby's health.

She felt disappointed in her man, though he had never promised much and they had rubbed along fairly well for twenty years. But suddenly she saw Donald as a threat. She drew the baby against her, canting her shoulder to protect it until Donald went out and a stranger entered the hut, preceded by a big, bright oil-lamp.

"What's your name, woman?"

"Gaddy Patterson, sir."

"You're a highlander, are you not?"

"From Lorne, sir."

The stranger squinted at the baby. "Is the child taking sup?"

"She is, sir."

"What's in that cog?"

"Sweet oatmeal."

"Made with milk?"

"Only water, sir."

"Boiled water?"

"Aye, sir."

The man nodded and turned his attention to the dead girl under the blanket, swinging the lamp away with him.

The man with the lamp was broad-shouldered, of short stature, of an age with Donald. He had swart, sardonic features. He wore an old powdered wig with a cocky little queue jutting out at the back, a thick, greasy-looking topcoat with many epaulettes, and high, untanned riding boots. He reminded Gaddy of a coachman or, more like, a highwayman. The man did not deign to introduce himself but she gathered that he was the doctor and sheriff-substitute and that his name was Rankellor. Gaddy was fully aware of the power that Rankellor held, vested in him by the High Sheriff of the county. To hold office as a sheriff-substitute required no formal qualification, though the person must be "respectable" and willing to perform irksome and sometimes arduous duties. Doctors made good judge-substitutes, it was claimed, for they could dispense justice and medicine alike by the troy weight and, if necessary, purge the truth out of witnesses.

Two other men crowded into the hut. The taller had

reddish hair and a mild voice and manner. He came at once to Gaddy and, with hands on his knees, bent to inspect the baby.

"Is it a girl?"

"Aye, sir."

"Good. Good. Is she eating at all?"

"Aye, sir."

"Good. Good. By the by, I'm the minister. Mr Leggat."

"I'm Gaddy Patterson, Minister."

The Reverend Leggat gestured vaguely over his shoulder. "This gentleman is my parish clerk. Mr Moodie."

Gaddy nodded but the elder did not return her greeting, and instead glowered, sullen and silent, at the pewling bundle in her arms. Gaddy could sense his hostility. She did not need to earn it. It was enough that she travelled with a hire-drover. Moodie would be a settled worker. He would despise those who plied the road trades, with their fairs and trysts, inns and encampments. Mr Moodie peered past the minister for a moment, then grunted and stepped away to watch the doctor examine the corpse. The Reverend Leggat, drawn more to life than to death, got down on one knee beside Gaddy and asked if he might have a closer look at the foundling.

Gaddy opened the blanket and folded back the shawl.

"My, my! She is a poor mite."

"She has no fever, though," said Gaddy.

"How old is she, would you say?"

"I canna rightly tell, sir. Old enough to be half weaned."

"Ten months, perhaps?"

"No, sir. Six or seven would be my guess."

"I wonder if she has been baptised."

"I couldn't say, Minister."

"Was there no paper, no message in her clothes?"

"No, Minister."

Gaddy answered the minister's questions without guile or hesitation. She sensed that this man would do the baby no harm.

"Her eyes look so sore. Hasn't she opened them?"

"She'll open them when she's ready, sir. When I stop pokin' food into her mouth, most like."

"Try it," said Mr Leggat conspiratorially.

Gaddy withdrew her pinkie from the baby's lips and held it away. The baby grizzled in her throat then, like a nestling, opened her mouth wide. There was movement in her legs now as well as her arms, a gratifying strength of will that raised the girning into a yell.

The doctor turned from his grisly task across the hut.

Mr Leggat said, "Do you hear that, Harry? A joyful noise, is it not?"

"Too damned joyful," said Harry Rankellor. "There's not much amiss with her lungs, whatever else."

"Look, sir," said Gaddy.

"Ah-hah!" said Mr Leggat. "The windows of the soul. What a pretty blue."

The expression was hardly accurate for the baby's eyes were still gummed with pus but at least the glint of the pupils could be seen.

"Feed her again, do," said Mr Leggat.

Gaddy inserted the last of the gruel on her fingertip and the baby's eager lips closed on it, lids fluttering.

"You see," went on Mr Leggat, "if the child *has* been baptised into the Church, there will be a record of it and we may be fortunate enough to trace relatives."

"What if she's not traced?" Gaddy asked.

"She'll become a ward of the parish."

"What'll that mean, sir?"

"She'll be found a place within the parish."

"A place?"

"With a Christian family," said Mr Leggat.

"What if nobody'll have her?"

Mr Leggat pushed himself to his feet. "I'm sure someone will."

"But if they won't?" Gaddy persisted.

"She'll be cared for, never fear."

"Where, Minister?"

"Perhaps," the minister avoided an answer, "the mother has relatives who would be willing –"

"Where, sir?"

"Asylum will be found."

"The poorhouse?" said Gaddy.

"Yes," Mr Leggat nodded. "Yes, the poorhouse."

"I'll take her," said Gaddy.

"That may not be possible," said Mr Leggat.

"I'll take her," the highland woman repeated. "I'll look after her like she was my own."

"No doubt. But –"

Doctor Rankellor appeared like a shadow, interrupting the conversation at a fortunate juncture for Mr Leggat.

"What did you find, Harry?" the minister asked.

"No need to toll the bell, William," said Harry Rankellor. "There's no contagion that I can trace."

"God be thanked."

"Not a sign of typhus, cholera, pox," said the doctor, "nor of brutality or mortal injury."

"Did you locate the manner of her dying?"

"Without a cutting, William, I cannot. But I have no need to cut to give you a reasonable judgement. She died of starvation and exhaustion born of starvation."

"Was she with milk?"

"She was dry, or nearly so."

Mr Moodie had decently covered the corpse again and came now and stood with doctor and minister close to the small fire. Rankellor had placed the lantern upon the ground and its upward beam lighted the three men queerly, giving them a menace which the wisps of smoke accentuated. They looked, Gaddy thought, like warlocks.

Involuntarily she drew backward into the corner of the hut, the baby in her arms. She had been filled with dismay at the words the minister had uttered. Poorhouse. Workhouse. She had met too many starved and battered bairns upon the road, slaves of cruel masters, to put faith in parish charity. The kirk might "settle" the baby but it would be left to other less Christian hands to rule her future. She would be "sold", what other word was there? as soon as she could toddle. Sold into the coal-pits to push a barrow or hoist baskets or tug-tug-tug upon the rope of a trap until strain or dust or damp destroyed her.

Gaddy was only too well aware that children, however young, had to work for their bread. From an early age she had milked and carded, tramped wool, fed hens, lugged water and grain. But it was varied labour and never more than she could cope with according to her strength. And if sometimes there was not enough to eat, it was the same for all in Ardelve. But pauper girls and boys were no better than slaves, sold to the system as soon as they could toddle. She listened again, lips pursed. Crouched out of sight at the door Donald would be listening too. She knew only too well what Donald would say, how he would side.

"Can ye not deduce anythin' about her origins, Doctor Rankellor?" James Moodie asked. "I mean, it's not possible t' do that, is it?"

"Oh, I can make a stab at it, Moodie," said Rankellor.

"Where . . . where she came from?"

"Hardly that," said Rankellor. "She's about sixteen years of age, I'd guess, and she wasn't of the labouring class. Her fingers aren't calloused and her linen, though patched, is of the kind town servants wear."

"A runaway," said Leggat. "I wonder what she sought in Balnesmoor."

"She'll be a damned outcast," growled Moodie. "Runnin' away from her master an' not carin' where."

"I can say, with a degree of certainty, that she's been long upon her travels," said Rankellor. "See how her feet are torn and bleeding."

"Aye, so she's come far, from a far distance," said Moodie.

"Today," said Rankellor, "she came down from the moor."

"She wears no wedding band," said Mr Leggat.

"She'll have been thrown out when it was discovered she was with child," said Rankellor. "God knows how the poor creature survived at all."

"Are there no doubtful circumstances, Harry?" the minister asked.

"None, except that she was deserted by the man who put the baby in her."

"I fear he will never know how much she suffered," said Mr Leggat.

"Be that as it may, William, I suggest you have her interred without delay."

"Perhaps we can find a record of her somewhere," said Mr Leggat. "Will you write to the parishes tonight, Mr Moodie?"

"I will," said the weaver, thinly.

"In the meanwhile, let me examine the infant," said Rankellor. "She of the mighty bellow."

The infant made no fuss while the doctor palpated her limbs and studied her eyes and gums. "She's sound enough for somebody who has been deprived of nourishment. She's got several teeth already. Laudanum has been given her, fortunately in no great quantity. Perhaps it's as well that money ran out as well as milk or she might have been poisoned by ignorance."

"What can I do?" asked Gaddy.

"Leave matters t' your betters," snapped James Moodie.

Rankellor patted the woman's arm. "A teaspoonful of castor in a cup of penny-royal tea should speed the expulsion of poison and hasten the cure. I imagine she may be old enough to wean but a portion of milk must be included in her diet for a while yet."

Gaddy could smell the doctor, a dry odour, acrid as snuff, spiced with rum.

"But the bairn's not hers t' tend," said Moodie.

"Who better to tend it?" said Rankellor.

"The bairn's a foundlin' an' belongs to the parish."

"And what, may I ask, will the parish do with her?" said the doctor.

Agitatedly Moodie plunged into a reply, though the doctor's question had been rhetorical. "She'll be keppit until such times as the parishes to whose clerks I'll write on the matter declare they have 'no register', which should take two weeks t' be done."

"If nobody claims her, what then?"

"She'll be taken t' the orphans' chamber at the house at Judgehead."

"And you'll be rid of her?" said Rankellor.

"She's not my responsibility," shouted James Moodie. "I'm not t' blame for the system, Doctor."

"Might she not be put to a Christian family?" said Rankellor.

"Aye, but . . ."

"Why don't you take her in, Elder Moodie?" said Rankellor.

"Me? Why should it be me? I've no room. Besides, I canna . . ."

"In that case I respectfully suggest you find another home for her?" said Rankellor.

As Parish Clerk, Moodie must know how difficult it was to foster out orphans, particularly when there was no enticement, no charitable fee paid by the parish towards their keep. The poorhouse at Judgehead was the county's only institute for paupers, a dismal jail-like building run on a niggardly budget. There were more defectors from its gates than there were applicants for sanctuary; yet it was the place appointed for those snared by misfortune or born into sin, those who did not have the sense to lie down in a ditch and die. Rankellor had heard Moodie's advocacy of the principles of harsh charity in the past. But the elder seemed hesitant and spoke his piece without conviction.

"At Judgehead the child will be fed, clothed an' taught her prayers. That's all that any child needs."

"It's a living death, and you know it, Mr Moodie," said Rankellor.

"Don't send her there," Gaddy cried. "I'll take her and tend her, I promise."

"Better Judgehead than a drover's whore," said Moodie.

"Mr Moodie," intervened the minister, "that's quite enough, please."

"I must know the infant's safe," James Moodie said.

"May I remind you that the infant is not yours to dispose of," said Mr Leggat.

Moodie was immediately contrite. "Aye, sir. I spoke without due thought. The disposition is a matter for discussion."

Gaddy turned to the minister. "Give her to me, I beg you. I'll bring her up like my own."

"Have you children already?"

"God hasn't seen fit t' bless me with bairns."

"Harry," said the minister, "what do you say?"

"It's hardly a matter of the woman's fitness, moral or

substantial," said Rankellor, after thought. "Fine it would suit us all to let her adopt the child. Indeed, if the girl was older – six years, say – I'd have little hesitation in putting her into the care of a drover. It's a reasonable trade, and healthy."

"Please, sir. Please."

"But I must consider the tender age of the orphan."

Gaddy glanced past the doctor. She could see Donald looming in the narrow doorway, bonnet rimed with sleet, his bushy brows freckled. Hands on his hips and coat-tails thrust back, he was like a fighting cock taunted into temper and ready to rake with its spurs.

"Are you sayin' I'm not worthy an' God-fearin' enough to look after a bairn?" Donald rumbled.

"I'm telling you my opinion, according to precedent," said Harry Rankellor. "What's more, drover, I'll make no damned apology to you for upholding the law. Consider yourself fortunate not to be marched to Ottershaw and locked up. Sir Gilbert takes a dim view of trespassers."

"Take the baby, then," said Donald. "Take it and let us be on our way."

"*No*," Gaddy cried.

She sat down, sudden and heavy, in the corner of the hut, her arms wrapped around the infant. All of the men recognised that female implacability which each related to some girl or woman in their own lives, and which Elder Moodie multiplied by three.

"I'll go wi'out you," Donald threatened.

"*Go, then.*"

"I'll leave you here."

"Then it's here I'll stay."

Donald said, "Twenty-two years, Gaddy. Have you not been happy wi' me?"

"Half a wife, Donald, an' half a life?"

"What does she mean?" murmured Elder Moodie. "Half a wife?"

Neither Rankellor nor the minister answered him.

Gaddy said, "I always wanted a bairn. I never could have one. You told me, Donald, you wanted a child by me. Now God's given us what we asked for."

"Ach!" said the drover in disgust. "A damned foundlin'. Some other man's mistake. It's not what I was meanin', woman, an' damned well you know it."

"I want this bairn."

"It's her or it's me," said Donald McIver. "Choose."

"I'll bid you goodbye."

Donald McIver did not appear particularly dismayed. "So that's the way of it?"

"That's the way of it," Gaddy snapped.

"Wait, wait." Elder Moodie tried to catch the drover by the arm but McIver was too quick and too strong. Tearing himself from the elder's grasp, Donald stalked out of the hut into the wild, white night.

"Rash," said Rankellor. "Very rash."

Donald, it seemed, was already dismissed from Gaddy's thoughts. "If there are no other claimants, no family, will you put the baby into my keepin', sir?"

Rankellor sighed. "How will you support her?"

"By work."

"There's precious little work in these parts for an unwed woman with a baby," said Rankellor.

Mr Leggat said, "On the other hand, Harry, provided the child remains within the boundary of the parish . . ."

"It was meant, sir. Do you not see it was intended by Providence how I should be the one to come here tonight, to find the wee lassie before she died too?"

"Perhaps the woman's right," said Mr Leggat. "The ways of the Lord are, indeed, beyond our understanding."

From outside, in faint dwindling echoes, came the sounds of the highland drover angrily gathering the herd. He would drive the garrons and horses hard through the pitch dark and put over in one of the stances adjacent to the Thorn of Cadder. It would be an unlucky man, though, who would call Donald down to pay a road toll, though it would cost for grazing at the tryst, and no avoiding it.

Rankellor had no truck with those who saw the travelling kind as romantic adventurers. They came and went without consideration and hardly a mark of their passing, like the wind on the hill, like the wind that had blown the dead girl here, a ragged leaf plucked willy-nilly from the tree of life.

"Has he truly abandoned you?" the Reverend Leggat asked.

Gaddy smiled. "Not him. Donald'll be back wi' his tail between his legs ere a fortnight's out."

"What will you do until then?" said Rankellor.

"I'll bed right here," said Gaddy Patterson. "Me an' my new bairn."

The doctor snorted at the woman's naïve belief that love alone would succour the child. But he did not say her nay and gave her, thus, a chance to prove him wrong – together with a shilling to buy milk as soon as it was light.

TWO

Bread-and-Cheese and Kisses

In many parts of Scotland, high and low, sheep were already cast as enemies of the common man. Innocent though the beasts were they had become associated with beasts a damned sight less innocent, namely, absentee landlords. These grand gentlemen resided in London and conducted their Scottish affairs through stewards and agents. Dampened by Crown and law courts, the private wards of the noblemen were a thing of the past and a tail of loyal tenants was no longer an asset to a laird. In addition, rented tillage and the old run-rig system of farming were going out of vogue. Only high market prices had retarded the inexorable process of clearing and enclosing the land for sheep. In Balnesmoor, however, mixed farming and the enclosing of fields were established facts. There was no need for ministers to preach eviction as part of God's punishment for sin and claim that opposition to Divine decree was unpardonable sacrilege – not that Mr Leggat would have been party to such crass hypocrisy even if it had been the wish of the local nobility. Mr Leggat was sparing of the brimstone and averse to the Kirk meddling in politics. Besides, dyke-breaking and riots were unknown in the district. Even in Fintry, where folk were usually keen for a bit jab at the lairds and could foment a rebellion as fast as they could down a dram, there was no trouble at that time. Nonetheless, news of the happenings in France had disturbed Stirlingshire's ruling class and, however remote a citizens' revolt seemed from carse and strath, home-grown lairds were careful to preserve the *status quo*, a simple enough matter since sheep were already installed as natural fitments.

Sir Gilbert Bontine, for instance, was near as fond of sheep as he was of horses and would have increased the size of his flocks by several hundred head if it could have been done without more dyking. He was, however, a perfect type of the old *noblesse* to whom patience was not so much a virtue as a trait of character acquired through breeding. He could afford to wait. After all, in this quiet corner of Stirlingshire the family had lived for generations, enjoying the easy bovine life of small country lairds. The lands of Ottershaw and Balnesmoor had first been feued by a Marquis of Montrose in the early seventeenth century, and added to since. Now Bontine policies consisted of 2,200 acres of which 700 were in Ottershaw and the rest in Balnesmoor, 300 acres of the latter disposition given over to common grazing for the benefit of parishioners. The village, of course, belonged *in toto* to the Bontines, right down to the pig mews along the back of the Black Bull, a scurrilous howff which watered its ale and sold whisky which was run out of stills hidden in the backwoods of Aberfoyle, a spirit so coarse and fiery you could pick the bark out of it with your fingers and find your nails burnt brown in the process.

The mansion-house of Ottershaw had been erected in 1670. What remained of the original building was buried under an agglutination of wings and storeys staked on the west frontage by a handsome square tower. The main entrance, a circular-headed doorway, lay at the base of this tower. Above it, jutting towards the mountains of Loch Lomond and the home parks, was an oriel window of leaded glass. Behind this casement stretched a long, oak-panelled chamber, the so-called library. In this room Sir Gilbert sought refuge from the trials and tribulations of being father to eleven children, eight delivered by a first wife, now deceased, and three by a second wife who was very much alive. Sir Gilbert ate breakfast in the library every morning without fail and, if he was not riding abroad in the fields, took his noon dinner there too. Much of the business of the estate was conducted from the room, though it was no real sanctuary. Sir Gilbert was indulgent with his offspring, and children of various ages were forever barging in and out, like stirks on the rampage, chased by nurses and serving-maids. On that November morning, though, the laird was alone, for it was early.

The swirling wind of the previous night had dropped away and dawn was calm. A static, almost frosty mist blanketed the hills. Here and there sleet had banked and lain and the parchment leaves of the sycamores were varnished with wetness. Four roe deer grazed in the distance, smudges of rust on grey drapery. Pheasants strutted, stupid and arrogant, pecking the beech mast and venturing in scuttering little sallies among the ewes. It was the ewes that Sir Gilbert fondly studied as he supped his porridge and chewed his hot mutton ham. Sixty large Cheviots had been bought at less than a year from Tweeddale. Heavy, contented creatures compared with the tough Linton Blackfaces, they were reputed to be less hardy, which was reason enough for holding them in parkland, protected from the worst of the weather. He would keep them there the winter through and not put them up to the high ground until spring was well advanced. No labourers' cottages sullied the laird's view, no untidy farm buildings. Stables, coach-houses, dairy were all at the rear of the mansion. The home farm, where Sinclair the grieve held sway, was a quarter-mile away on a raised shelf of alluvial soil above the flood mark of the Lightwater, screened, all but its chimney smoke, by firs and beeches.

At first Sir Gilbert could not make out what it was that disturbed the shy roe deer and made them bound away into the willows on the river shore. He put down his fork and spoon and rose, rubbed the window glass with his coat sleeve, peered out into the mist. A sawing crake from a pheasant alerted him and the attention the sheep gave to a corner of the twenty-acre stretch. He peered with more concentration, wondering which of his servants had strayed off the path, or if Sinclair was abroad on some early bit of business. It was no man, though, who emerged from the trees. Sir Gilbert shoved up the lever and thrust open the casement. Cold wafted in on him, made the crackling fire in the hearth at the far end of the room seem brighter. But the laird, having been born to it, thought nothing of early-morning chill. He leaned his elbows on the sill and craned out.

The woman was walking straight towards the mansion.

She had the cut of a highlander. The plaid she wore was not caught by the corners in lowland style but swagged about her like a sash. Her skirts were kirtled up almost to the knee. Barefoot, she swished through the dew-frost as if it was new milk. Her shoes swung from a thong at her belt but she had no other pack or bundle, except the one she carried in her arms. Sir Gilbert did not have to strain his eyes to recognise that it was a babby.

If his eldest son, Randall, had been lolling round Balnesmoor as he used to do, then the laird might have suspected that the woman was about to lay a bastard grandson on his stoop. But Randall, a born reprobate, had been exiled to his Uncle Alexander's house at Marinwood in Kerry this past three years and Sir Gilbert doubted if the woman had walked across the Irish Sea to fetch trouble home to roost.

He shouted, "You there. Where do you suppose you're going?"

"To the farm, sir."

"This is private parkland, don't you know."

"I'm lookin' for the laird's man."

"Are you, indeed? What's your business?"

"I'm needin' to buy milk." The woman kept walking during the shouted conversation and was soon on the lawn between the narrow line of privet hedge and the steps up on to the terrace of flagstones directly beneath the window.

"What did you say?"

"Milk, sir. For the bairn."

"The dairy will sell you milk. Why do you require my man?"

"Are you the laird, sir?"

"Of course I'm the laird."

"I want a wee pick of land, sir, to rent."

"Land, you say?" Sir Gilbert scratched his earlobe. "Wait there. Advance no further. I'm coming down."

He put his feet into his shoes and snatched his feathered hat from the little table by the door and, leaving half his breakfast uneaten, galloped down the side stairs into the hallway where his head servant, Hunter, only half awake, was directing maids to various fireplaces and there was a general air of activity.

"Good morning, maister."

"There's a woman outside, Hunter."

"A woman, maister?"

Hunter had enough bother with the women under his charge within the house; nine in all, discounting the cook, who was answerable to nobody. Years of servitude had honed his instincts and he knew at once that he was not fairly to be held responsible for the woman outside, any more than he could be held responsible for tree-blight or bottle-fly or staggers in ewes. With a shrug, he opened the big main door and let the laird out, the cock-feather on his hat nodding fussily. The head servant followed to the door, though, and peeped out in time to see the laird going down the steps on to the lawn.

Hunter snapped his fingers. "Betty, tell wee Dougie to run an' fetch Mr Sinclair."

Betty went off to find the kitchen lad and deliver Mr Hunter's message and spread the word throughout the rambling corridors of the servants' hall that something out of the ordinary was happening.

Meanwhile Sir Gilbert and the woman met.

She did not quail from him, but highlanders quailed from nobody, though sometimes they were sly. This woman seemed the very antithesis of sly, however. She was frank and upright and met the laird's eye without the cold glint of hostility or cunning found in most vagabonds.

"Where's your husband?" said the laird. "If you wish to discuss a lease – and there is none vacant of this quarter, I might add – then you must discuss it with your husband." He paused. "I mean, of course, I must discuss it with your husband. You're not the one to discuss it with your husband. Or with me." He paused again. "Though your husband should be present."

"I have no husband, Laird."

"Oh-ho! So, to whom does the child belong? Your daughter, perhaps? You, I mean, aren't mother of the babby but you are mother to your daughter." He hesitated. "Grandmother to the babby."

"The baby's a foundling. Discovered last night up by the

burn on Drumglass, in the old hut, sir. Mr Leggat and Doctor Rankellor attended."

"Did they? Did they attend, do you mean, the birth?"

"No, Laird." The woman glanced at the mansion, at the man keeking out of the door. "The mother was dead, the bairn alive. Doctor Rankellor was sent for."

"Who sent for Harry Rankellor?"

"The minister did."

"Who sent for the minister?"

"I did, sir."

"Why did nobody deem it wise to send for the laird?"

"It was late after dark, sir, an' there was nothin' to disturb the laird for."

"Quite right. The laird could not have done much that Mr Leggat and the sheriff's substitute could not cope with, though I would have thought common courtesy demanded we inform the laird. They inform me. I am owner of the hut on Drumglass."

The woman suddenly offered out the bundle. "Do you want to see her, Laird?"

"See her? Why should I want to see her?"

"She was found on your land, sir."

"Is there something wrong with her?"

"No, sir. She's fine."

"How did her mother die?"

"Hunger, sir, of hunger."

"She wasn't one of mine," said Sir Gilbert, "was she?"

"I don't understand, sir."

"One of my parishioners."

"The minister didn't recognise her," said the woman. "Would you not be wantin' a wee look at the baby?"

Sir Gilbert was by no means averse to children. On the contrary, he had taken his turn at nursing his own infants and had sat up at nights fretting over their health many a time. He lifted the swaddled bundle from the highland woman's arms and looked down at the face.

"Seems sturdy enough," he said, instinctively rocking. "Has she a name?"

"I'll be callin' her Elspeth, sir."

"Elspeth. I was nursed by a woman called Elspeth, from

41

the Isle of Mull," said the laird. "You're not of that family, by chance?"

"I come from Ardelve, sir."

"On Cruachan?" said Sir Gilbert. "You're a long way from home."

"I came down with a drover. He went on to Cadder."

"Oh-ho!" said Gilbert Bontine. "Stealing my grass, eh?"

"Aye, sir."

"All the same, you highland drovers. No respect for the law. Do you have any conception of what it costs to grow grass? If I herded my sheep on to your croft and let them eat your barleymeal or the oats off your plate, you'd make a great fuss, wouldn't you?" He rocked the baby, the feather in his hat jigging. "Milk. Yes. She must have milk. But what's this about renting land?"

"I want to settle in the parish since Elspeth is the parish's ward."

"You'll run off, won't you? Back to your deplorable glen, after you have possession of her."

"This is a better place for her to be reared, sir."

"Well, certainly better than the inhospitable heights of Cruachan. But I have no vacant rents to offer."

The laird was still holding the infant, still casually nursing her.

Sir Gilbert had reached that vulnerable stage, with his fifty-fifth year fast approaching, when he would spawn no more. He was eager for grandchildren. Young Gilbert and Randall were the only two of an age to give them to him and neither of his sons, so far, had shown signs of wishing to wed. His daughter Sarah would soon be of an age to put on the marriage market, though, and the feel and smell of the babby in his arms stimulated his anticipation of coming events, of the sense of completeness he would attain when third-generation heirs started popping into the world. He would have aided this woman to obtain custody of the poor foundling if it had been possible. But he had spoken the truth. There were no available roofs to let at that period and he had no need of servants, the house and the estate being flooded with them.

"There's the hut, sir," said the woman.

"Hut? What hut? Auld Dame Peevie's hut? It isn't fit for pigs, woman."

"I'd make it fit, sir."

"What would you thrive on? You can't live on grass and water. There's precious little work to be found, with winter barking."

"I have four pounds an' eight shillings, sir, to see me through 'til the spring."

"Four pounds and eight shillings? How did you lay hands on such a sum?"

"I earned it honestly, sir. Saved it, over many years."

Though occasionally confused in the formation of sentences, Sir Gilbert was possessed of a Chinese mind when it came to calculating. He could add, subtract, divide and multiply with amazing rapidity and without the need to resort to counting stones or chalk on slate. He handed the baby back to the woman and stroked his chin with his forefinger.

"Bread at fourpence per pound weight, oatmeal at tuppence. Potatoes, cheap at sevenpence per stone weight, sugar at sixpence and milk various." He spoke at a gallop. "Average wages for a female hirer, one shilling and sixpence in the work week, or tenpence each day for an able-bodied labourer to keep his family. If we divide the difference between a labourer's wage and that of female hirer – three shillings – it gives you twenty-nine weeks, and a balance of one shilling."

"Aye, sir," said the woman, bamboozled.

"I suppose you'll offer me the shilling for rent?"

"What would the rent be, Laird?" the woman asked.

"How will you earn it," said the laird, "whatever it is?"

"By plantin' and sowin'."

"Seeds cost money."

"Three acres of the hill, sir, an' the hut."

"You'll be after my water, to lay claim to the burn."

"Behind the hut, sir, though I would want the drawin' privilege on the burn."

"How do you know the burn doesn't dry up, tell me that?"

"You would be unlike to have stock on a burn that dried, sir."

The laird was enjoying his conversation with the highland woman. It also occurred to him that he might profit by the woman's need. The parcel of land in which she had declared an interest was poor grazing and hard till and the hut itself was worthless.

Sir Gilbert said, "If you are willing to rent as stands, not to sting me for repairs, I might consider discussing a rent of the hut."

"How much would it be, Sir Gilbert?"

That she was taking on the burden of a lease for the sake of the babby was all too apparent. If he yielded to her request, if he made it possible for her to become a tenant in Balnesmoor, he would have little enough to lose if she failed.

"Arable or grazing?" Sir Gilbert said.

"Both."

"Both? Have you stock, then?"

"None yet, sir."

"Is it your intention to buy?"

"Aye, sir, in time. A cow an' some sheep."

"Sheep. I'm not having blight and blisters carried into my fields," said the laird. "It would be a condition of rental that all stock was inspected and approved by my grieve before you purchased it."

"I would agree to that, sir. What would the price be?"

"Three acres upwards from the rear of the wall at the hut?" said the laird.

"Aye, sir."

Sir Gilbert said, "Martinmas is next week. Most half-yearly rents fall due then. But some pay at Whit Sunday, in the May month. Some at Martinmas only, those who send fat lambs to market in the back end. If you occupy at Martinmas and pay at Whit, you'll have no spike above the ground, no payment in from whatever you can reek up out of yonder site, which will be deuced little. Are you still set on settling as a tenant in Balnesmoor?"

"Aye, sir, I am."

"Two pounds down," said Sir Gilbert as Sinclair appeared on the cinder path at the house side. "I'll let stand as fore-rent the balance, which is three pounds, all to be

44

paid in one year's time, at the Martinmas following this one."

"How much would that be, sir, next November?"

"Eight pounds, of course."

"And the length of the lease?"

"I won't saddle you with the burden of nineteen years," said the laird. "I will allow five. Nine, if you wish."

"Nine, sir."

"It's a great bargain, you have my assurance. In the vicinity of a village as prosperous as Balnesmoor, the accepted rental is from forty to seventy-five shillings each acre."

"But not for rough till, sir, surely?"

"Perhaps, perhaps not."

"Thirty-three shillings each acre for one year seems fair, sir," said Gaddy, turning as Sinclair approached.

Sinclair was a handsome man, tall, straight-backed, dark-haired. He could have had his pick of the girls of the parish but he had chosen to remain faithful to his tiny, shrew-like wife, Aileen, who had given him three brawny babies in as many years. Sinclair's father and grandfather had been grieves to the Bontine family and Lachlan had been bred into the job.

"Is it agreed, then?" said Sir Gilbert hastily.

"Aye, sir. It's agreed," said the woman.

The laird grinned and turned to his grieve who had paused deferentially within a yard of the couple. Sinclair's lean features were, as always, watchful.

He said, "Is there something the laird requires?"

"I've settled a lease, the rent of a field, Lachlan."

"Which field is that, Sir Gilbert?"

"On the side of Drumglass, east and north-east of the Nettleburn, with a rent of the old hut too, Dame Peevie's place."

"How many acres, Sir Gilbert?"

"Three; the woman requires a patch, no more."

"Is the woman alone?"

The laird took his grieve aside, whispered discreetly in his ear for a minute. Sinclair gave no opinion of the business that the laird had concluded. What the laird had done, though, was typical of small-minded, retrogressive, paternalistic landowners who cared little for modern developments in farming and never showed their nebs at the Harlwood Agricultural Improvement Society meetings, a body of which Sinclair was chairman. Privately, Lachlan Sinclair did not approve of the leasing-out of pockets of property, of carving up an estate. But he would utter no word of criticism against his master's decision, not even to his wife, who shared his confidence in most things.

When Sir Gilbert had finished giving instructions, Sinclair beckoned to the woman. "Come with me."

She glanced at the laird, less afraid of the landowner than of the grieve.

"Go with Mr Sinclair. He'll see to it that a paper is signed. We believe in putting things in writing at Ottershaw. He'll also give you a quart of milk for the babby."

The woman gave Sir Gilbert an awkward bow. "Thank you, sir."

"If you can't sign your name, make your mark," said the laird, "and have Mr Sinclair read the document to you first."

"Aye, sir."

"And have that infant properly baptised," the laird added, doing his duty by God and Kirk.

Then, with a wave of the hand, Sir Gilbert Bontine went back into the mansion to finish his breakfast.

In girlhood Gaddy had acquired many useful skills, a variety which had become alien to the run of folk in Balnesmoor where divisions of labour were well defined and a man or woman did only that which habit required of them. The close-knit members of a farming community tended to be jealous of the ruts which they and their forebears had carved, like the circular troughs worn into mill floors by the hoofs of wheel-donkeys. If you were born lowly then lowly you must remain. For the bedmate of a droving tink to aspire to the tenancy of Bontine property was an unthinkable affront to decency.

Gaddy was soon known in Balnesmoor. She did not skulk like a hermit in her ramshackle hut for, via the sheep-walk round by Coll Cochran's place, it was only a couple of miles to the main street and a quarter-mile more to the kirk. She would come, walking too fast for an honest buddy, the bairn fastened in a plaid on her back, her shoes bobbing on a thong at the broad, unfeminine belt she wore at her waist. It was soon learned that she was on the look-out for bargains, common things, old farm implements, rope and twine, sacks and boxes, anything she could scrounge, though she had the bawbees to pay for them and would not take charity. Though the good folk of Balnesmoor might give her short shrift along the road, they were, nonetheless, quite willing to relieve Gaddy of her money.

It was rumoured that she had earned a fortune on the flat of her back and, now she was knocking on in years, had come to Balnesmoor to whelk a few shillings from the hot, unfastidious, single labourers who lived in the bothies round about. It was also rumoured that she was agent for a gang of drovers who had picked the site on Drumglass specially and, with the foothold secured, would have it packed with scabby highland beasts before you could whistle, she wagging the right-of-entitlement in Sinclair's face if a word was said.

When the mother of the brat was buried the highland woman loitered by the wall while Mr Leggat read out the lesson and offered a prayer of intercession for the departed to find peace in Paradise. Doctor Rankellor and Lachlan Sinclair turned up. Mr Moodie stole time from his loom to attend, since it was his job to ensure that the sum of money taken from the poor's fund was not misspent; just the three men and the minister and her at the wall, keeking over, holding the bairn in her arms and crooning, since it was inclined to fret. A low, chalky morning it was, dark at noon, which was when Mr Leggat liked to do his burying. There was nothing to see except the shapes of the men and the woman by the wall and the kirk gable like a cut of old canvas hanging in the motionless grey air.

Six shillings and eightpence it cost the parish for the chest. One shilling and fourpence more for a mort-cloth. Mr Moodie's suggestion that the highland woman be compelled to pay the burial expenses was emphatically rejected

47

by Mr Leggat. There was an acrimonious meeting of the elders before Mr Leggat got his way and the parish buried the stranger on charity. Thanks to the Moodie girls there was plenty of gossip to pass from pump to dungheap, from drying-ground to common grazing, to keep sharp tongues wagging.

"But did she not have the bairn baptised?"

"Aye, sly bitch. Only when Mr Leggat insisted on it. Better twice accepted into the grace of the Lord, the minister said, than not at all."

"But she never went inside the kirk, did she?"

"Right to the font. She flinched when the holy water splashed her hand, so Jeannie Moodie told me."

"When was it, then?"

"Friday, the day after the buryin'."

"In secret?"

"Nine in the mornin'."

"Who stood for the bairn?"

"Rankellor."

"Yon Godless wight. Was Jamie Moodie there?"

"He had to be, had he not?"

"Was there only the one godparent?"

"Sinclair was the other."

"I'm no' surprised at Rankellor but I thought Sinclair had more sense."

"He jumps when the laird tells him."

"What name was the bairn given?"

"Elspeth. Elspeth McIver Patterson."

Balnesmoor was set on a straggling hill on the Glasgow to Stirling turnpike. There were thirty or so thatched cottages to start with, cottages which, but for their reeking lums, might have been mistaken for stables or hogsties, each with a dunghill, each with a pig or horse or cow tramping out back, a cart up-ended by its door, pools of squashy water where drains and gutters had fallen into disrepair, which, in the handle of the village, was nigh everywhere. Uphill, labourers' cottages rubbed shoulders with more substantial buildings, the lanes were better defined; some signs of limewash, a tack of curtains in windows, a glint of brass ornaments within; tradesmen and craftsmen, children, wives. In the square by the Ramshead Inn was a cobbled pump-stand. In the Bonnywell cul-de-sac the weavers' cottages crouched adjacent to the manse. The unostentatious kirk was saxon-spired, with two fine ash trees upon which, until ten years ago, the kirk bells had hung. Outwards Balnesmoor passed four biggish villas with sash windows at ground level and garret windows protruding from the slates, gardens guarded by gates and laurels. On down the road was Harlwood, three miles away. But Greenhead came first, with its sheds, workshops and smith-forge and the "office" where the Harlwood Flyer stopped, if Wattie McGowan could be bothered, to pick up mail for the city. The village's last outriggers were a muddy track up to the millstone quarry and four farms crouched like quail under the beak of the moor. Finally there was the crossroads, a four-armed sign – Harlwood, Balfron, Killearn, Fintry – separate roads drawing the adventurous on to the world at large or turning them back like a militiaman, saying, *No further for you, m'laddie. Go back where you belong*, a command which most of Bontine's folk were only too happy to obey.

Along that stretch and down by the cots at the Loup o' Kennart and in the back of the byres of the home farm, with Mr Sinclair's permission, Gaddy unearthed the tools she needed to begin work on her small-holding. She was filled with dismay at her nightly counting to discover that she had spent fourteen shillings in three days, plus two pounds she had paid over for rent and one shilling and tenpence for food and cloths. But she had the implements around her and, by the light of the sky through the hole in the hut roof, or by the flicker of the tallow candle after dark, she cleaned and sharpened them on a fine hard lump of whinstone she had fished from the burn, slippered by a drop or two of the castor oil she had bought for the baby.

Found wood and deadfall were hers by right. Sinclair had told her where willows grew along the Lightwater, clumps of coarse rushes in the water meadow. There was heather and bracken for strewing, enough of it up there, hardly a step from the hut, to keep her floor clean and her bed springy. If she could find good, dark hazel – white would do, though not as well – she could shape hurdles, for she knew how to split and weave to the posts. She would begin by making a hurdle door for the hut and a "maze" to baffle the cold wind then a better cradle for Elspeth than the old straw creel she slept in now.

Mr Leggat donated his expert opinion on the potential of the three-acre holding. Who would dare argue with a man on gardening matters when he had just delivered a cauliflower as large as a calf's head and a basket of sweet, unblemished pippins?

"Ah, nettles," said the minister. "Stinging nettles invariably mask good growing ground. If I were you, I'd snatch what days I can from the weather and turn over the nettle patch first of all. The land should be upside-down before the hoar frosts come."

"An' what should I plant, sir?"

"Nothing," said the minister. "Do all that you can to prepare for early spring planting. We will pray that March is dry. Do you lease the ground up by the moor's edge?"

"Between the ten posts which Mr Sinclair sank, sir. He measured it out exact, him an' two other men."

"I see. Well, if you can, do clear little patches into the bracken, for the soil there will be dark and fertile and ideal for potato beds, though you will have to give them much attention with the hoe later in the year."

"Aye, sir."

Gaddy salted away the information, adding it to her own untapped store of knowledge.

The site seemed so unprepossessing, shallow moss and moorish sort of land, with only a bottom ditch and hedge and the broken stone dyke. But in the minister's eyes it was an Eden in disguise.

"Unfortunately," said Mr Leggat, "it will prove impossible for you to do all this work unaided."

"Donald will be back to help me soon."

The cleric had his doubts but gave no sign of them to the woman.

Harry Rankellor, over dinner at the manse, was more outspoken on the matter. He declared that the drover would steer wide of Balnesmoor in the future and that the parish, and Gaddy Patterson, had seen the last of the man.

"In that case, how will she manage?" said Mr Leggat.

"In all probability," Rankellor answered, "she won't."

"She has taken on so much."

"Too much. It's understandable, however. Almost commendable," said the doctor. "I admire her spirit. Raw nature, though, is at the base of it. Consider her, William; a woman well past her prime by peasant lights, without children. How much of a godsend do you suppose that baby must have seemed to her?"

"A godsend indeed," the minister agreed. "But even with my best advice three acres of grassland cannot be tilled, planted and reaped of a harvest in a single year, sufficient to pay rent come next Michaelmas and leave a residue to feed them."

"How much did Bontine soak her?"

"Five pounds, with a stay on three."

"He should be drawn and quartered."

"No, that's unfair to the laird. The grazing alone would fetch that sum, close to. Besides, the soil is very good."

"Perhaps with four people to work it, and two of them with paying jobs to buy meat in the season."

"If the drover does not return, the woman will have to find, or be found, day work."

"Which," Rankellor pointed out, "will mean she has less daylight to clear and cultivate her own patch."

"She talks of buying stock; a cow, sheep."

"What a dream that is," said Rankellor. "Still, William, as you've seen fit to encourage her, I daresay you won't let her starve. It would not altogether surprise me if she went back to her own village with the child."

"No, Harry. I feel in my heart," said the Reverend Leggat, "that Gaddy Patterson is here to stay."

Rankellor grunted. "Have you had no news from the parish clerks as to the mother's identity?"

"Not a blessed word."

"A bastard, then, a poor bairn born on the wrong side of the sheets. Perhaps it's as well there was a highland drover and his whore in the vicinity, hm?"

"Indeed it is," said the minister.

51

"If the babe lives, I hope she has no cause to regret it."

"Regret it? Regret what?"

"The hand that destiny has dealt her."

"Come now, Harry, as a man of the cloth I do not subscribe to a belief in destiny, only in the mysterious workings of God."

Rankellor gave a twisted smile.

"Same thing, William," he said.

Lachlan Sinclair was careful to show no favour to Gaddy Patterson or the baby that went everywhere with her, like a part grown on to her body. He held a special position in the community, linchpin between landowner and land-holders, arbitrator of all disputes that affected the running of the Bontine estates. He lived by the law that what was right for the Bontines was right for them all. He was twenty-nine that November, a shade young for such a position but so sober and profound that nobody damned him for his youth. He had been lettered and taught complicated counting by his father and by "sitting on the bench" with the tutor that Sir Gilbert employed to teach his younger sons. Sinclair shone particularly in history, geography and Bible studies. It was not the fashion to invite grieves to become kirk elders but Lachlan Sinclair read the lesson once in a while, his voice precise, ringing and sure as if he was reading the Gospel according to Boll Weights and not God's Holy Word. And him so dark and straight at the lectern that the wee girls, and some of the not so wee girls, in the pews before him quivered and closed their eyes, flushed with suppressed desire, and prayed that they might be sent one like Lachlan Sinclair when their time came to wed. But none of the girls or women who worked under his charge ever made free with him for he would have frozen them stiff with his moral stare.

It was not on the laird's command that Sinclair had agreed to stand as godparent to the foundling. Sinclair regarded children as he regarded all young things, as products of husbandry, whether careless or not, and in need of nurture. Besides, he respected the highland woman, though he gave few signs of it, none that the cattlemen or horsemen or the women about the yards might pick up. Gaddy came down every two or three days for her quart of milk, for the weather was cool enough for the milk to keep. She endured the shunning that the dairy-hands dished out and paid no heed to the cackling of the girls who came to the doors to peek at her as if she was a monster with two heads. Sinclair, if he was there, made no fuss, nodded by way of greeting and did not address a word to her. He was watchful, however, and contrived to get close enough to have a glance at the baby. But business took Sinclair up to Coll Cochran's place quite frequently that season, for Coll was in dire straits. Watching a farmer struggle to save his patch without enough capital was like watching a man trying to bail out a boat with a corn-sieve. On the way to Coll's the grieve would ride out along the track through the oaks and look over the hedge at the Nettleburn to see how the Patterson woman was faring and what use she was making of the tools he'd sold her. What he saw, in those calm November days, did Sinclair's thrifty heart good.

No matter when he rode past she was hard at it, from before dawn until after dusk, taking time out from field labour only to cook for and feed Elspeth or tuck her up inside the hut for her afternoon nap. Sinclair was surprised at the range of the highland woman's skills. None of the work she did was quite perfect, not by the grieve's exacting standards, but all of it was satisfactory. If the farm servants at Ottershaw had seen how Gaddy drove herself, perhaps they would have been less resentful that she, a tink and a woman, had become a tenant of the laird. She was deft in hurdle-making, a craft hardly practised in Stirlingshire. She wove round hazel and stout ash branches into great limber rectangles on the simple frame she had constructed on the flat grass sward above the burn. The hurdles were to cover the breaks in the roof. Sinclair had not seen repair done in quite this manner before and he was intrigued. The hurdles were laid on the slope of the roof and bound with rope or willow strips, leaving a lapping eave to lead the rain off. All of the wood had been cut on the Lightwater bank and carried a mile uphill, armful by armful, and her with the baby happed to her back, too. Turfs lifted from the paths of the lazy-beds, she stacked by the foot of the wall until the hurdles were in place, then she built a step at the gable with some of them to give her a hunch on to the roof. Carrying four sods at a time, she climbed the step and crawled on to the roof and fitted and patted the sods down on the hurdles, going on and on with it, tirelessly, for four days.

When Sinclair passed by on the fifth day, however, he found the roof complete, a touch ragged but strong and solid, cross-roped like a croft thatch, with a top-dress of rushes and bracken straw and a purl of blue smoke rising out of the hearth-hole by the stone gable. It had taken her nine days in all. It would have taken a man and a laddie, under Sinclair's instruction, near twice as long.

From across the hedge Sinclair shouted, "Is the roof finished?"

"Aye, Mr Sinclair. It's snug enough for us."

"The weather will not last but another day or two."

"I can smell the change, sir."

"Have you enough firewood?"

"I can always find that, Mr Sinclair. I'll need to keep the place warm for Donald comin' back."

"Aye," said the grieve and rode on.

That night Sinclair came past again, for the track was quicker than the turnpike, and it was dusk and he was in a hurry to be back to Ottershaw to see to the horsemen who had been slack of late, feeling the winter come on and sleep around them. He paused, though, for a moment, to lift himself in the saddle and look at the Nettleburn, wondering. There was truth after all in the old saying, *What you own, owns you.* But Lachlan Sinclair had never seen anybody so quick to fall to the spell of ownership, to the thrall of the land. It might have been desire to have the baby for her own that first impelled Gaddy Patterson to forsake the life of a drover's woman, to sink a taproot here in Balnesmoor, but it would be the hill that would hold her and, by its intractability, perhaps, would destroy her as it was destroying old Coll Cochran, and him a farmer and man.

The night was shining, sharp and clear, with stars and a ringed moon. Sinclair sniffed the air, sensing the coming of the hard frosts now that the cloud had cleared. He shivered, thinking how cold it would be in the hut, with not even a bed to sleep on; yet, when he looked and saw the smoke against the inky sky and the flicker of the hearth-fire through the wattle door, he wondered if she would not survive after all, survive and prosper. Already, it seemed, she had made a home.

Gaddy bedded early, soon after seven. She ached with weariness and the unaccustomed labours of the day. She would be up an hour or so before daylight and had much to do tomorrow. Now she saw how easy the drover's life had been, if you could stand the wet and chill and brave the big winds in the glens and snow on the mountains; how it had been a lazy existence, ambling down after the beasts on foot or pony-back or perched on the mare, always moving yet never moving, as if the shires were only rooms that you strolled through, like an earl through his palace, not a quarter as strenuous as a farmer's daily round.

Carefully she smoored the fire, put the bucket of milk on the shelf she had built, along with the apples and cauliflower and the sheaf of carrots Mr Leggat had brought the day before yesterday. The shelf was to keep the mice from the food, from the meal bags and four tallow candles. In a dry corner by the hearth-side Elspeth was already asleep, turned on her side in the basket, only her nose and fist showing, sucking her thumb.

Gaddy crooned contentedly to herself as she unbuckled her belt and shed her outer garments, folded and laid them over the trestle by the fire. Fresh water in the pot, dry wood and the tinder-box put out on a flat stone. Today was over, tomorrow prepared for. The hut smelled warm, of soup, baked apples and wood smoke, mingled with the faint musky scent of heather brush mounded in the corner by the cradle; Gaddy's bed. The woman stretched, easing her shoulders.

She took off the bindings from her hair, rolled the coarse ribbons around her finger and put them also on the shelf.

Luxuriously she stretched again and fluffed out her hair with the palms of her hands then she blew out the candle and sank on to the heather. Crossing the plaid blanket over her, she cocooned herself within it. She used no pillow, resting her head on her arm, face close to Elspeth's, protect-

55

ing the baby with her body. Attentively she listened to the child's regular breathing then to the creak of the grassland as the cold gripped it. The Nettleburn trundled like a small iron wheel. An owl hooted, mocking itself like an echo in the track between the oaks. There was no whisper of wind now and all the fallen leaves were still.

Gaddy sighed. For the first time since he'd left, she missed Donald. She felt a faint, guilty desire to have his arms about her, the roughness of his body against her, to be wanted by him. She rubbed her breasts wistfully with the plaid, too sleepy to be troubled for long by need of the man. She closed her eyes.

Heretically, she wondered if Donald *would* return or if, with winter closing fast and the fair long over, he had trailed back to the crofts of Ardelve without her, back to his whiskery old mother and his fat wife and daughters and if, come spring again, he would seek out and seduce another girl to take on the road with him as he had done when she was young and had never known a man.

In the creel Elspeth stirred.

Thoughts of the drover drifted from Gaddy's mind. Opening her eyes she studied the little face behind its sucking fist, features formed by soft firelight and dusky shadow.

"There now, m'luckie. There now, m'love," the woman murmured. "Nothing to be feared of when your Mam's near. Sleep now. Sleep well."

And Elspeth did.

THREE

A Friend in the World

The dog days of November and the Christmas month were scarred by bitter weather. Bone-hard frosts succeeded flurries of snow. The summits of Dumgoyne and Drumglass smoked with spindrift. On the moor lonely cattle died and wedder-flocks scattered far and wide in the struggle to find crop. Labourers and lairds, weavers, wives and cattlemen alike shivered inside as well as out for seditious draughts whistled under every door, no matter how well fitted. In Gaddy's hut on the Nettleburn there was no escape from the cold. Slow, voiceless frosts ate through the ground into her legs, made her stomach cramp and head ache. Blizzards flayed her cheeks, raised blains and blisters, chapped her lips, hacked her fingers and stung the hollows of her nose so much that she cried with pain. Fain would she have hugged the fire all day, happed in plaids and shawls like an invalid. But the water bucket was empty and the wood near gone and eight pounds owing in rent hung over her head like an icicle waiting to drop. One Martinmas was not so far after another that she could afford to pamper herself, no matter how severe the weather. But dyking and fencing were impossible. Stones were welded to the earth, twigs without sap. She could not line potato beds in ground like granite. It was all she could do to brave the numbing cold to find firewood and draw water from a hole smashed in the burn. Every other day she stumbled down to Ottershaw to buy milk or waded through snowdrifts to the village for barley-meal or a candle or a twist of salt. Every night she counted the money in her purse in dismay at how fast it was dribbling away, penny by penny, and no progress to show for it.

By the beginning of the Christmas week Gaddy realised that she would never turn eight pounds rent out of three acres of hill grazing, let alone make enough profit to keep them for another year. Locked in solitude by unrelenting ice, she brooded on the foolishness of striving for independence. She had been so desperate to obtain custody of the God-sent child that she had ignored Mr Leggat's gentle warnings and Doctor Rankellor's pointed admonitions. She felt no rancour towards the laird, though. After all, she had begged Sir Gilbert to give her the lease and had been delighted by his eagerness to grant her wish. She could expect no more from the minister, the laird, the doctor, however. Opportunity was not enough; nor hard work, nor love. In six short weeks weather had changed everything.

Planting would be late, the first crops late. Prices would be high. Seeds would cost a king's ransom. Her notion of buying a sheep or cow with the proceeds suddenly seemed laughable. She would hardly be able to afford to buy an egg, let alone a hen. She had been more secure on the road with Donald, wintering in lodgings in the old croft in Ardelve with her duties prescribed by habit, known and accepted as the "second wife" of wild Donald McIver. Donald had taken her as casually as if she had been a meadow flower, plucking her from a cluster of young girls who lived in the glen by Cruachan to go on the road with him on the hire droves of spring and early summer. Damned be the man who would deny Donald the right to satisfy his appetites. Damned be Donald's lawful wife who had cheated him by turning thick in the head after bearing her fifth child. The idea of taking Elspeth back to Ardelve did not tempt Gaddy. The crofters would convince themselves that the baby was Donald McIver's bastard and would ensure that the baby did not starve, even if Donald cast her off; yet she would be a slave there too, trapped by need. Now that she had tasted independence, Gaddy would not settle for bondage to the ill-knit clan who would give her sup but no compassion. In finding Elspeth Gaddy had also found release from the domination of instinct, from the idleness of thought which was the lot of the women of Ardelve. Purpose brought new passions. Mind as well as heart must be used in their governing. But impatience gripped her as never before. Frustration with the enduring cold turned quickly to a kind of rage. Now she understood the anger that possessed the menfolk of Ardelve, saw why men gathered in inns and dram-shops to drink themselves stupid. It was done to release rage, to annul the impotence of being. Small creatures they were, helpless against the north wind and the sullen snow-laden sky. When she waded through the powdery drifts of a morning and saw the Lomond peaks etched against leaded cloud, it was hard to sustain hope; and this but a month into winter and many more months to come. At first she tried to cheer herself with the notion that Donald had lingered on at Edderly with his uncle, that he would return at any time, mounted on the mare, jingling silver in his pouch. But hope soon waned into wistfulness and wistfulness into anger, anger into resignation. Only Elspeth kept Gaddy on an even keel.

The child waxed under care, glowed brighter in Gaddy's heart the bleaker her prospects became. Gone were the sicknesses which had marred the bairn. She was active, demanding and responsive, so well fed that she cared almost as much for the manner of supping as for the food itself. Sometimes she would make a game of it, spewing out the ruby pap of stewed blackberries or the honey-yellow cream of mashed turnip which Gaddy had so carefully prepared. She would jerk her mouth away from the spoon, then waggle her tongue. Her bright eyes would roll mischievously and, to draw Gaddy on, she would open her mouth wide, only to close it again as the spoon approached once more. Gaddy was never cross with her. It seemed natural that Elspeth should tease to find out where she stood in relation to the world, if it would bear her with humour or with cant. She thrived in the dry cold, wrapped up so loose and thick that she resembled a large fir cone. She had corn-dolls and a rag ball to play with and a windmill with turning sails which Gaddy made out of a pine block, a nail and two shaved slats. She had also laid claim to Gaddy's silver teaspoon which she used as a drumstick and to suck when her gums were hot, for she had cut several teeth and more were crowding. Long before Christmas she was crawling vigorously about the hut floor and out on to the hard mud at the door. She would probably have waddled like a hedgehog across the pasture to the ditch if Gaddy had not brought her back. To protect the inquisitive child from the dangers of the open hearth it was necessary for Gaddy to construct a little pen, lined with straw and a blanket, to pop Elspeth into while she fetched water or wood. Incarceration made Elspeth howl but Gaddy fussed over her when she returned and the little episodes of desertion appeared to do the child no harm. All in all, with the days shaped around her welfare, Elspeth gave Gaddy no cause for concern. If only her plans had been progressing without impediment, if there had been money coming in, Gaddy would have been happy. But money was going out, progress of the Nettleburn patch had ceased and the hard weather showed no sign of easing. Gaddy could not think what to do, how to save what remained in her purse and spin it into the growing season.

It was Lachlan Sinclair who brought Gaddy the proposition. The grieve rode up the slippery track from Ottershaw on a grim, blood-shrinking Monday morning about a week before Christmas. He carried a skinned rabbit and a round of red cheese, the first gifts that the grieve had ever made to Gaddy, except for the new shilling he had pressed into Elspeth's palm on the day of her Christening, a handsel demanded by tradition. Somebody a little more versed in the ways of the lowlands might have regarded the meat and cheese as a bribe but Gaddy did not understand how much disturbance an eviction would cause to the grieve or how it generated an undertow of ill-feeling among other Bontine tenants who subsisted close to the knuckle. Baubles of icy snow dangled from the garron's belly-hair and fringed its well-shod hoofs as Mr Sinclair walked the pony cautiously across the strip of open ground between the track gate and the hut. He wore a jacket of coarse tweed, an Inverness bonnet pulled over his ears, his boots laced tight about his shins. In spite of the cladding, his face was ashen with the cold. He envied the woman her rotundity and the glow which exertions with the chopping knife had engendered, for he interrupted her in the act of hacking up a birch branch. Like a lambkin, Elspeth was penned in the hut doorway, peeping at her mother through the weave of the hurdle. Lachlan Sinclair was not much of a one for small talk. He came directly to the point.

Coll Cochran was crippled with rheumatics and in sore need of a labourer to thresh grain for daily feed since he had cattle stalled about the place and more starving on the hill.

"Why does he not hire labour?" Gaddy asked.

"He cannot afford to hire labour," said Sinclair.

Bill-hook hanging in her hand, breath in a great pale cloud before her face, Gaddy said, "Is there nobody at Ottershaw to do the work?"

Sinclair said, "Ottershaw pays a winter wage to its labourers. They would rebel at being asked to work for it off the estate."

"What does Mr Cochran do in the season?"

"This past four years," Sinclair answered, "he has employed a tink or raggy-johnnie, somebody who will work for a woman's wage."

"Is he so hard-pressed?"

"Since he lost seven parts of his herd to red-water disease he has been very hard-pressed."

"Have the Cochrans no children?" Gaddy asked.

"A daughter, married to an Eskdale shepherd. Three sons, all of whom left Balnesmoor to make livings for themselves elsewhere. One, I heard tell, was driving a dray for a brewer in Edinburgh. Of the others I know nothing. Coll doesn't talk of them."

Wind ribboned the moor's breast with silken snow but the trees, even the evergreens, had no life in them and remained motionless. Gaddy sucked her under lip.

"I have my own acres to tend," she said.

"In this weather?"

"Aye," said Gaddy. "How d'you know I can thresh?"

"All highland women can thresh," said Sinclair. "Besides, you can do no worse than a good-for-nothing who would fill his cuffs with the wheat and steal more than he left for feedin' the kye. Most day-labourers think threshin' can be done without attention."

Gaddy murmured, "An' leave ten pecks per bushel in the straw."

61

"He'll pay you, Coll will."

"How much?"

"By the piece."

"In what amount?"

"Two pence per day," said Sinclair. "He can afford no more."

Gaddy swished the bill-hook and brought up a scoop of the dry snow on its point. She studied it for a moment then turned from the waist and looked to the distant mountains, to the great pyramidal summit of Ben Lomond blanched against the harsh sky. It might be weeks, months, before winter relented and a wind change brought rain.

"I'll go tomorrow."

"Go today," said Lachlan Sinclair.

Misfortune had dogged Coll Cochran all his born days, though there were those in the parish who would have put the origins of his ill luck down to marriage to Etta Cleghorn. She was cross enough for any man to have to bear without the burden of debts his father had accumulated and a grizzling old mother and two grizzling sisters, twins at that and twenty years his senior, whom Coll had dutifully sheltered and endured until death had claimed them.

By dint of hard labour, frugality and self-denial Coll had cleared off the parental debts and had dragged the farm at Dyers' Dyke into some sort of profit. But Dyers' Dyke was cursed, as Coll himself was cursed, and the damned laird should have paid poor Coll just to occupy the place. It was not that the till was bad or the grass inferior or the buildings in poor repair, just that the acres seemed impregnated with evil vapours so that one disaster followed another without rhyme or reason. Grains withered, cattle pined, turnips, cabbages and potatoes developed spot or worm or root-thread. There was hardly a season without some tale of woe to tell about Coll Cochran and his sad old patch. Even those farmers to whom a dirge was the sweetest of music, who raised moaning to a fine art, had to bow to Coll. But Coll never took advantage of it. He was seldom heard to complain about his lot. Etta was never heard to do aught else.

The sons could not get away from their mam and that

fiendish farm fast enough when they were grown. The daughter, dainty and delicate as she appeared, had her mother's tongue and disposition and was no loss, really, to her Dad when a shepherd from Eskdale made his bid for her at a spring fair in Ayrshire in the days when Coll had still done much of his own selling, before the laird screwed tight on manorial privilege. The fact was that Coll had gone down into Ayrshire with cattle and the daughter in the hope of being rid of the lot. Coll had given a good, healthy little heifer out of his herd to compensate for the years of misery that would lie ahead for the love-sick swain.

After his daughter's departure, Coll was left alone on the farm with only his wife for company – and red-water disease, black quarter, wort poisoning and the wet cough. He dwelled in a haze of drenching fluids and Glauber's salts with the skinning knife, burial spade and quicklime bucket never far from hand. Within the house too old Coll had to thole the continual odour of sickness, though the beasts were a damned sight less voluble about their ailments than Etta who had more symptoms than you could find in all three volumes of Buchan's *Domestic Medicine* and spent every waking hour describing them in detail. Vials and jars and blue-glass bottles, herb packets and pill-twists littered the shelf above the hearth. Hand-bellows and clyster tubes hung on the bedroom wall. There was even a special little mule chest which contained Etta's own chamber pots and a long joyned table upon which she kept "her samples" ready to thrust upon Doctor Rankellor should he be persuaded to call upon her yet again. Even the patient Coll finally lost his wool at this grisly museum and insisted that Etta keep it covered with a length of cheesecloth, a demand with which Etta complied, though she found such callousness in a husband hard to bear and took to bed in consternation with a severe and noisy gripe.

Coll was only too willing to hire the highland woman as a day-labourer. He let Sinclair talk him into it, however. He did not wish to admit that he was attracted to Gaddy Patterson.

Coll had had Gaddy much on his mind since their first meeting, when he had given her the old foot-plough from the byre, a tool with which his great-grandfather had broken sod on the hill behind the Dyke. From the instant that Coll had clapped eyes on Gaddy, he had wanted her. It was an odd attraction to come on so quick, in a community in which relationships took years to ripen and be recognised. Quite properly Coll did nothing about Gaddy Patterson. He had no opportunity to press friendship, no time to make opportunity. But he thought of her, strong and calm, with a low purling sympathetic voice and a way of listening with her head tilted in concern. He thought about her constantly as he ploutered about his chores in that cold, cold month, with his knuckles swelling and joints turning to stone and the beasts roaring and stamping in their hunger.

There had been a time, long years since, when he had thought of Etta so, when he had dreamed of Etta by him in the yard or in the byre. But he could remember only the echo of the feeling and not its satisfaction for it had never been satisfied. Etta had never been one for doing more than her share, even when times were at their hardest; none of them had, not the boys and not his genteel, airs-and-graces daughter. It was as if they all blamed him for the deprivations which they suffered and resented the fact that father failed to provide them with luxuries as well as necessities.

Gaddy was the first stranger Coll had encountered for many a long day. He no longer drove cattle to market or bought at fairs. He took monthly Communion from Mr Leggat but was not a regular kirk man, since he could not afford to sacrifice a morning's work for worship. Thank God Balnesmoor was not a strict parish and was far too pragmatic to "observe" a day of rest. Once in a blue moon Coll would stroll down to the Ramshead for a can of ale and a crack with his neighbours but he had no extra cash to spare for regular visits to the inn. To escape from Etta he took his ease out of the kitchen, about the yards or up on a rock on the edge of the moor with the village and the valley of the Lightwater spread before him. Skylark and peewit, kestrel, tit and crow were companions enough for Coll Cochran while he puffed his stubby clay pipe and, without rancour, contemplated his past and his future and let his mind be soothed by wistful longings, though by the year of '91, at the age of fifty-five, dreaming, like everything else, required more effort.

The qualities in Gaddy Patterson which so rankled with James Moodie were the very ones that Coll Cochran found appealing. Her roundness, her glowing health, her stolidity, the ambience of freedom that clung to her like musk. Coll would have paid a crown to have her company at Dyers' Dyke; but tuppence was Sinclair's estimate of the rate for the job, and he needed somebody to thresh the grain since he could not do it himself.

She arrived about one of the clock. Coll, on the lookout, saw her approach. The bairn was wrapped against her in a wide tartan plaid, a dash of colour in the charcoal landscape, one catch of movement in the stillness. Coll had decided how he would act – restrained. After all, he reminded himself, he was the paying master and she the hireling. For all he really knew of her, it might be her intention to rob him, pilfering as much grain as she could carry before he caught her. Times were hard with her too, according to the grieve. He greeted her brusquely and led her straight to the barn where he had laid out the wheat.

The barn was large, too large for the paltry stock he carried and for the harvest he reaped. It was achingly cold within the vaulted building and the air was white. He showed Gaddy the day's breakings, gave her a choice of flails. In the high days of farming at the Dyke he would have had forty beasts stalled and more on the hill, four or five day-labourers threshing here. But everything had shrunk, including profits, though he had harvested quite well that autumn on the strips he could afford to sow himself. The bothy was empty, byre stalls nearly deserted. Turnip piles had pride of place in alcoves that had once troughed fat swine. He had more space than he knew what to do with but neither the men nor the means to make more of it.

"Where can I put the baby?" said Gaddy, as she removed the shawl and plaid wrapping from about her body. "It's too cold to keep her here, an' there will be a wheen o' dust."

"I'll take her into the house."

"You'll not leave her to hurt herself?"

"My wife'll keep an eye on her," said Coll.

65

Gaddy handed over the child who, parted from her mother and given to the silver-haired, hard-handed man, quite naturally set up a great wail. Holding her tight with his forearms Coll clucked and chuckled and Elspeth quieted, though she cried again when the man carried her out of the barn.

Coll was glad to get indoors, for the afternoon vapours had eaten into his joints and they ached sorely. Etta was seated by the hearth, a bowl in her lap and a masher. For an instant Coll wondered if this was some new diversion she had found for herself, if she was in process of preparing a balsam or a plaster, then he recognised peas and par-boiled potatoes and realised that she was only making a pudding for supper.

"See who's come to visit us," he said.

Etta Cochran expressed no pleasure at the company of the brat. At that stage she could not possibly have guessed what strange thoughts reeled in her husband's head. She merely resented the attention the child stole from her.

"There's milk an' a bap in the cupboard," Etta snapped, grinding peas into dough in the bowl.

"I thought you might . . . I've the byre to see to, Etta."

"If you must employ a female t'do your work," said Etta, "don't expect me t' be a nursin' maid. I've enough to occupy me with housekeepin', Coll Cochran. With my stomach moiled as bad as it is, it's lucky I'm able t' keep for you at all."

He should have anticipated Etta's reaction. Now, by having the straw made by Gaddy Patterson and Etta being thrawn about the bairn, he would lose the day's light. He would be required to waste precious oil in the lantern to do the mucking and strewing, as well as feeding the ponies in the black of evening.

The kitchen was hardly cheerful. The fire under the brick oven needed wood to give it heart and the fire in the hearth, though adequate to toast Etta's knees, was blocked by her big wooden chair and the tray with the mixing bowl on it. The light from the room's slot windows was stagnant. He must make the best of it, though. He would tend the bairn himself in the hope that Etta might relent. He turned his

face to the child. She was active and bonnie, blue eyes
swimming with tears. She had the knack of breaking your
heart without effort, not riling you with fractious demands.
Doris, his daughter, had been just the same when she was
a wee thing, instinctively playing up to menfolk. Most lassies
did. Coll chuckled. Because his hands were crooked and
might frighten her, he touched the tip of his nose to Elspeth's
brow and did his imitation of a startled duck.

Tears ran but the sobbing ceased.

He dabbed her with his nose again, and quacked.

"Donkey!" Etta exclaimed.

"Hee-haw! Hee-haw!" said Coll Cochran.

"Muckle great fool!" said Etta without warmth.

But the donkey imitation proved popular with his audience. Coll repeated the performance and soon had Elspeth
giggling.

Let the time pass, Coll decided: I'll use the oil and brave
the dark and if I keep at it perhaps I'll not feel the cold.

Appeased by the muffled *thwack-thwack-thwack* of the flail
from the floor of the barn across the yard, by its good strong
yielding rhythm, Coll Cochran carried the bairn to the
cupboard to find her milk to drink and a bap to chew,
leaving Gaddy Patterson to her threshing and his wife to
her sulk.

There was little enough to threshing once Gaddy got used
to it again. Dyers' Dyke was no Ottershaw. Its requirement
of grain and straw could be filled by a couple of hours on
the floor. For the first week, however, Gaddy trudged home
each evening like an old crone, back and arms aching and
hands raw. She could see why Coll's ailment kept him from
the work. A firm but flexible grasp upon the rod was
required. Gaddy quickly mastered the rhythm and left few
full grains in the straw. To her candid way of thinking, she
earned her tuppence honestly. When she got back to the
Nettleburn she had too much to do to dwell on arithmetic,
to count her money. Thus the job relieved her nagging
anxiety and gave purpose to the winter's days.

Elspeth was well cared for while Gaddy toiled amid the
chaff, though whether by Coll or by his wife Gaddy could

67

not be certain. She had not yet clapped an eye on the mysterious Mrs Cochran, except as a shape by the door or a face at the window. The wife seemed to be as shy and retiring as the husband was amiable and out-going. It mattered not to Gaddy. While the land remained beset by black frosts and snow there was nothing she could do at Nettleburn and was as well selling her labour to a gentleman like Coll Cochran.

It was not surprising that Gaddy failed to comprehend Coll's desperate plight at first. To Gaddy, Coll was half roads to being a laird. He could read and write, owned stock and dwelled in a spacious farmhouse. Coll appeared to be "comfortable" compared to the crofters round Cruachan or the labourers who hung about the yard at Ottershaw.

On the eve of Christmas, Gaddy threshed a double portion. Coll presented her with a piece of fat pork and a treacle cake and gave Elspeth a painted wooden duck which he confessed he had bought from the carpenter at Greenhead because he had not the dexterity to make the toy himself now. Elspeth recognised the effigy which pleased her so much that she addressed Coll in squawks and little gabbling quacks which Coll seemed immediately able to identify, as if man and child had devised a secret language. But even on Christmas eve there was no sign of Etta Cochran. She did not venture to the kitchen door to offer a seasonal greeting. Convinced that the woman was indeed an invalid, Gaddy's sympathy for Coll increased.

A visit to the kirk on Christmas morning, however, put things into a true perspective. It was there on the pave by the gate that Gaddy and Etta Cochran first came face to face. The wife ignored the highland woman with a toss of the head and a sniff loud enough to be heard in Harlwood and Gaddy was left with the feeling that she had made a mortal enemy, worse by far than Elder Moodie.

Most of Balnesmoor's presbyterian population turned out for the Christmas service at eleven o'clock in the morning. The men were fortified against the rigours of an extra-long sermon, many readings and the singing of psalms, with breakfasts of meat and ale. The women were trigged out in best bonnets and cloaks with, here and there among them, a pelisse of sarsenet or velvet to which feathery flakes of snow clung like additional ornaments. The kirk itself was full to overflowing. The elders spent the duration of the service leaning against the wall, arms folded, or paraded solemnly up and down the side aisles during the singing, to show themselves off and keep their circulation going. The crowd in the church, its excitement and general surge, created an evangelical atmosphere, rather than one of sober, nodding piety. Reverend Leggat was in his glory, enjoying every moment of the celebration of the Saviour's birth. The nobility, wealthier farmers and their families were in box-sided pews on the west side, properly separated from common folk but on display, nonetheless. Social divisions in the parish were observed throughout the pews, up to the wives and children of the "humble" cottars in the gallery.

Gaddy, with Elspeth in her arms, was one of a ruck of mothers of young children gathered under the stern brow of the pulpit. On this day Mr Leggat would not permit the little children to be shuffled off to the cold hall adjacent to the kirk, but welcomed them, red-cheeked howlers included, and adjusted his pitch to project over the bedlam below. In deference to the needs of children, and to bladders rendered sensitive by the excessively cold weather, the minister clipped his Christmas sermon and excised a couple of less relevant readings and managed to keep the service as brief as conscience allowed, so that the doors were open and the congregation flooding out by a quarter past one o'clock, Gaddy among them.

Mr Leggat, in the modern manner, stood by the kirk door flanked by his elders, to shake hands with those that wished it, giving each and every one a blessing for the day.

Over the bonnets of the ladies of Harlwood, who flocked around him, Mr Leggat called out, "Are you well, Mistress Patterson?"

"Aye, Minister."

"And the child?"

"She's fine, Minister."

"Merry Christmas to you."

"An' to yourself, Mr Leggat."

Though Sinclair and his wife had been in kirk, the grieve

had gone to attend the carriages for Sir Gilbert and his family, and Harry Rankellor had whisked his wife away to the Ramshead where there was hot spiced wine and a privy.

The folk of the parish dispersed on foot, by garron and in chaise and cart. All you could see for a quarter of an hour were beaver hats and bonnets along the cul-de-sac and down to the Bonnywell. Craving a little company, Gaddy loitered too, wishing that somebody would give her a nod, though, knowing the dour nature of the villagers, she did not expect it. She began to walk away from the kirk gate, Elspeth in her arms.

Snow was lightly falling but the cold had eased. Piled above the village the hills were bleak against the sky. She lived up there, now she thought of it, higher than anyone in the parish. She went down the lane by Murphy's store and found nobody there, except at the entrance where the lane joined to the inn yard. She heard him call out her name.

She turned.

Coll came towards her. He did not seem old now and walked spryly, though he kept his hands in his pockets. He wore a brushed-tweed suit, gentleman's shoes with buckles and a felt hat with a fan of pheasant feathers in it. His silver hair stuck out on all sides and Gaddy had an urge to tidy it. She felt a wave of affection towards him for crying after her, and wondered where he had hidden his scowling wife.

"Gaddy?" He stopped by her and peeped at Elspeth who reached out her hand to grab the pheasant feather. "Gaddy. I had hoped t' ask you to have supper, but . . . ."

"I've eggs an' cheese an' cake, Mr Cochran."

"Plain fare for Christmas."

"It's nearly dark, anyway. No weather this for jauntin'."

"She'll . . . Etta will have nobody to the house, not even at Christmastide."

"It doesn't matter," said Gaddy.

But it did matter.

Coll searched her face with such hurt in his eyes, not physical pain but a terrible biting loneliness, that Gaddy hoisted Elspeth on to her shoulder and turned the child away from the sight of it.

Coll had no need to say more. There would be no merriment and no love at Dyers' Dyke that day, or any day. Coll was not the prisoner of random misfortune. He was shackled to a wife who despised him and had caused him to build walls around their barren relationship. But Coll had been reminded, if he had ever forgotten, that outside the walls of his marriage there was wildness still, a romanticism of the blood, earth and instinct, however mellowed by age and his own gentle disposition. Startled by the insight and its implications, Gaddy flinched. Celebrations, monuments of the year, the earth's unvarying ceremony of seed time and ripening and harvest must be extra hard to bear for a man who had mastered only the lineaments of life and not its sources, who had bound himself to labour in resignation, who considered himself in control even of failure.

How undramatic the setting was. Moist flakes dithering out of the sky. Rich odours released by the moisture and faint warmth that had come about noon, the smells of smoke and cooking cabbage, dungheaps and stews and collops. But the gesture was big for Coll Cochran and the tawdry homespun setting of Murphy's lane had no space to accommodate it completely.

"Come an' visit me," said Gaddy. "At the Nettleburn."

"I've the horses –"

"I'll keep the fire lit an' a lantern in the door."

"Will you mind?"

"Come – when you can," Gaddy said. "However late it is."

"We'll talk." Coll Cochran admitted a need that would have been incomprehensible to most men in the parish, men to whom communion with a woman not their wife meant carnality, the impress of crude pleasure, not sharing. "We'll just talk for a while."

"For as long as you like, Coll," said Gaddy.

For long enough conversation was all there was between Coll and Gaddy Patterson. But it was conversation of uncommon intimacy and had, from the very first, a closeness which both woman and man found addictive. Neither had experienced this sort of sharing before. Piece by piece Coll unravel-

71

led the disappointments that had carded his soul like wiry thorns. Finally he told Gaddy that he was inclined now and then to wish for an early death. What was there left for him? Etta had chased away his sons. Lettered though they were, not a word had been heard from them in years. Even Doris did not write now. She might have been in America not Eskdale for all the hope he had of seeing her or his grand-children.

Coll told Gaddy of the farm's failure which in the parish equated with failure as a man. He had not over-reached himself, had not been greedy or profligate or lazy. He had worked like a Trojan to keep his head above water, to manage as his father had managed. But inch by inch the comfortable security that his father had built up slipped away from Coll. He could not rightfully take his place as his father's son, portly and affable and a pillar of the village. His father had juggled a series of debts, secret owings and long-term borrowing which his "name", his outward bluffness, had kept unclaimed for three decades or more. But with his father's demise, the creditors lost their faith and claimed in the notes at once and he, Coll, had had to squeeze the land for all it was worth to settle the bills, to pay for his father's respectability.

"If it wasn't for Etta I'd let it all go," said Coll. "I'm skinned to the sinews. Sinclair says he'd look for a loft for us and a job of some sort to keep me going. But Etta, God, the shame of it would kill her. How can I do that to her?"

"What if you went to another parish?"

"I was born in a cottage in Kennart, two miles from here. Etta was born in Harlwood. What parish could we go to now where we would be taken in?"

"If your wife loves you, Coll, she'll go with you, wherever it is."

"She wouldn't starve," Coll said, evading the issue. "I would strew dung for a carter before I'd see that happen."

"How much is owin' on Dyers' Dyke?"

"Three terms' rent. Sinclair will stand no more. I can't in honesty say I blame him."

"If you had fat stock . . .?"

"The stock's lean as a ship's biscuit. Though I have the

fodder, the cows haven't taken well."

"Where does the bull come from?"

"Ottershaw. Sir Gilbert leases me a bull. It's a good animal with well-bred blood. No, it's a thing to do with the Dyke. If I was more of a kirk man, Gaddy, I would think it was a curse called on me by God."

Coll could say it without fear of ridicule. Though Gaddy was no farmer, she had lived her days on the knife edge and accepted that a man need not be a failure to fail at what he did. She told him of drovers who had slaved for years, to lose all that they had in one bad buy. She spoke of stealthy disasters which had overtaken cattle traders whom everybody considered as secure as the Royal Bank. Coll listened but was not soothed.

Through January and into February the cold lasted. There would be a day here and there when the air would warm and the snow begin to melt and the Nettleburn would plash loudly and wisps of rain would sift across Drumglass to give the farmers hope of a thaw but, within the week, the sky would be lacquered with cloud once more and the cycle of polar winds and snow would begin again.

Gaddy came early now to Dyers' Dyke. She got through the threshing well before noon and turned her hand to other tasks. She mucked and strewed the stalls and stables, carted hay and feeding dooks out to the cattle that Coll had unwisely left on the moor. The poor brutes had congregated at the birch wood which bordered Short's farm, on the nip of the moor towards the stone quarry. They would not leave the shelter of the trees and had taken to gnawing bark like deer, so desperate for crop were they.

"It's too late, Gaddy. I canna bring them in now."

"There's three gone already, Coll. You could round them and stall them for the rest of the winter, fatten them for a spring sale."

"The feed won't last into March."

"Aye, but it will."

Coll shook his head. He was not being deliberately stubborn in sticking by his decision. There was a kind of fatalism in it. He had put the fate of the herd on the hill into the hands of another power, hung it on a sudden turn in the weather. But the nights, from eight or nine until midnight, which he spent at the hut on the Nettleburn, consoled him, deadened him to the inevitable loss of Dyers' Dyke. The simple thatched dwelling perched on the slope of the hill was as warm as a cave of the earth. There was always a fire, a soup pot on the hearth, blankets and plaids about, a candle lamp to welcome him.

"Does she know you come here?" asked Gaddy.

"No, no. Och, no. She imagines I'm at the Black Bull."

"Does she say nothing?"

"She sleeps like the dead." Coll shrugged.

If Etta guessed that he was seeking solace with the hireling she kept the lid of indifference screwed down upon her suspicions.

God knows, Coll could not have managed without Gaddy during the thirteen weeks of white weather. It was the worst spell in living memory, so hostile that even the sports which usually cheered the winter days had been abandoned. Ponds and lochs stood bare of skaters and those who loved to swing the curling stones. Even the bairns had quickly wearied of the novelty of snowballing and sliding and sucking icicles. Now they were full of coughs and colds and girned at their chapped hands and knees. Coll could not have adequately attended to the cattle on his own. Sure as death, he would have lost most of them if it had not been for Gaddy's efforts. She seemed to bring energy to Dyers' Dyke, to replace his lost vitality. In the byre the cattle even had a trace of sleekness.

"Cold never killed a thing," said Gaddy. "It's lack of nourishment that brings sickness. Wet weather's worse for hoofed animals."

If it had not been for Etta, Coll would have taken Gaddy on as his labourer, just as if she was a man. She was a better hand than many a man he had employed in the past. But Gaddy was a danger to him: she tempted him. She offered him the luxury of companionship and, having tasted it, he would have done anything, however rash, to hold on to it. The woman gave his existence base and centre.

Came sun, splitting the blue-grey cloud, came rain and the burns gushed and the rivers swam with mud and winter's debris. Tassels on the hazel tree and the russet stalks of coltsfoot in the damp, black soil behind the dungheap told Coll that the winter was over. Within his body, like sap, the blood moved and sharp pains stitched his joints and brought mobility in compensation.

Coll said, "You'll be workin' on the Nettleburn now, Gaddy."

Gaddy said, "In a day or two."

Still she came to Dyers' Dyke, though, every morning, up through the rain and over the mush, no longer carrying Elspeth in a shawl but holding the child by the hand if it was dry enough underfoot. Coll was about early, watching from the byre door for the woman's appearance, giving her a wave and a shout of greeting, for the farmhouse was safe behind the gable and Etta could neither see nor hear him from there, nor mark the fondness in his voice. But if his wife was out in the yard feeding the hens, or if she had gathered her strength sufficiently to begin a wash in the big wooden trough, then Coll would say nothing until Gaddy was close, give no sign that he was filled with pleasure at the sight of her.

"I see Mr Short's begun to break the field," Gaddy would say.

"Short's o'er hasty. It's too soft for the horses yet."

"Mr Leggat tells me I should till for potatoes."

"When did you see the minister?"

"Yesterday. He came in the afternoon."

"It's true, what he said," Coll would say. "It's time for tillin' grassland. I'll not expect you tomorrow."

"Tuppence is tuppence," Gaddy would say.

She left early, after the threshing was done. Coll knew that she was going back to her own small farm to labour further, to slit the thick turf with the blade of the foot-plough and turn it over. Hard work for a woman. Already she had marked the lines of the plots by the hut and up on the border of the bracken, reaping down the sodden brown stalks and erecting posts for fences. One telling was enough for Gaddy. She remembered everything that Mr Leggat had imparted before Christmas, all the recommendations that Coll had made during the dark winter evenings. Methodically she put them into practice. The money she had earned from Coll, that portion diligently saved, would buy seedlings. When he went to the Nettleburn of an evening now, Coll was obliged to tread carefully between the soft black loam of the rectangular lazy-beds which extended from behind the wall and across the shoulder of the burn. He found Gaddy less lively, sleepy after her double share of manual labour and with attending Elspeth, who grew sturdier with every passing day and had found both her voice and her legs.

For Coll the spring was marred only by the approach of Whitsun. He had not enough in his iron box to meet half of the debt due to the Bontines. Sinclair was aware of it and, having written off the Dyke, came no more to spur Coll on. By selling the stock down to the last beast, he might discharge his debts. But then he would have land with naught to feed upon it and not enough to buy another herd for fattening for the autumn. He might till it all, slave at the plough behind his team of horses. But horses would have to be fed and rested, and seed corn bought. After a period of concentrating on solutions, Coll's brain fagged and he gave himself over to dreaming of Gaddy, of a life even simpler than the one he lived now, mysteriously and innocently free of the burden of the farm and of Etta, free to settle with Gaddy and grow root crops and raise a few head of cattle on the manageable plot that she had leased.

Etta was aware of her husband's desperate plight. Surreptitiously she had counted the savings in the iron box when Coll was out. She had been dependent on her husband for so long, however, that she had lost the habit of fretting about the farm. Faced with the possibility of eviction, she could not raise a spark from her imagination, could not believe that Coll would allow it to happen. She trusted him to save her home without her aid.

It was Gaddy Patterson who, busy as an ant with her own plot, evolved a plan that might save Dyers' Dyke for the Cochrans.

Gaddy had been associated with drovers all her adult life. Some of their quickness of mind had rubbed off on her. She had learned at first hand certain tricks that drovers used to cull income when accident or disease struck, how they could make an extra effort and accelerate the pace of trading to cover a slump. But in the early spring there were few fairs at which to sell cattle. Cattle fetched their price in the autumn, with the three great trysts at Falkirk and a late one at Doune to bring out bankers, breeders and buyers from all corners of Scotland and England. Graziers who had barely survived the winter were, therefore, open to exploitation in April and May. Many were forced by hardship to sell quick for ready cash, for a handful of silver and a note of promise. Most banks now recognised such notes, but that was damned small comfort for a grazier who owned a sheaf of them come season's end, for the banks would not always accept responsibility for payment, that, in the bankers' view, being a matter of honour between buyer and seller.

Graziers and breeders around Balnesmoor were reluctant to deal with drovers or sell their stock in small parcels. They preferred the "old system" and in the spring sold cattle on the ground to the laird's man at a fair price per head. Later in the summer Sir Gilbert would have the herd steered to Falkirk and sold by a reliable agent. Sir Gilbert took the risk, price up or price down. Though the laird was not given to exploiting the complexities of the trade, which was part of its fascination, the Bontine estate invariably made profit. For many years, apart from the drove to Ayr to find a husband for Doris, Coll had been happy enough to follow local fashion. There was, however, no agreement which bound a tenant to sell his stock to the laird. A man was free to find a buyer for his beasts anywhere he chose and at any time. If Coll Cochran could not meet his overdue rent come May, though, whatever stock he had at grass would be knocked down to the laird in payment of the debt. Unlike Gaddy, Coll did not understand that with the snows still thick in the passes of the highland glens wintered cattle from lowland byres would be at a premium, not just with summer graziers but with meat marketers and purveyors.

Gaddy had not forgotten the exhilaration of on-the-spot sales, when circumstance had been turned into guineas by a drover's quick thinking and glib tongue. Once or twice Donald had even sold a herd before he'd bought it when a purveyor's need was great and the quality of the beef hadn't mattered. She had watched, admiring and amused, while the drover did his deals and had learned, without being aware of it, how such transactions might be contrived.

Selling cattle, lean and shaggy off the hill, ran counter to Coll's conservatism. Even so, Gaddy raised the matter with him and, in the end, with Whitsun only three weeks off, had his agreement to let her sell his herd in Dumbarton, not at the marts but directly to the butchers who, after the long cold spell, must be crying out for carcasses however scraggy. Dumbarton was an easy drove. Starting before cock-crow, the pair of them could manage it in half a day's ride.

Uncertain, Coll nodded agreement nonetheless.

Gaddy pressed him no more. He had given her his trust. He had little choice. It was risk all, or lose all. Gaddy knew that it was Coll's future and not her own that she would be staking in the back streets of Dumbarton.

FOUR

The Wedding by the Loch

In late afternoon Coll cut out the stotts, bullocks approaching their prime. He penned them by twilight in the yard, where they stamped and splattered round the hay dooks and water trough and coughed and clacked and roared well into the night, in high excitement. Everything else was ready for an early start; the little cart, ponies, the sacks of feed that, on Gaddy's instructions, Coll had rustled down from the loft. In the byre, close to calving, were three cows. On the hill remained nine stirks and four heifers, crop of matings with the Bontine bull. There were no champions in the lot that would take the road to Dumbarton, though they were heavy enough for pure West Highland, and would drop as carcasses at close to three hundred pounds avoirdupois by Gaddy's reckoning. In hue the herd was mostly black, with some dun and two banded; small-headed, barrel-like, their pot-bones well covered, their stubby horns a waxy green. Men who knew cattle would not be deceived by the patchy condition of their coats, would size up their worth as beef and would pay not less than six pounds and five shillings per head for the parcel, so Gaddy said. Coll was not convinced. In the gathering month of April, before Whitsun rent fell due, the laird's man would offer five pounds to tenant graziers and the promise of three more for fattening before the lift in the back end. It had always seemed fair. Of course, Sinclair saw to it that the beasts were fit to put on over summer. He paid no cash for sickly kye and had little interest in heifers in which the home-farm abounded. But extra profit of twenty-five shillings turned on each stott, with nineteen to tally, and summer grass left light, would pay off the arrears on Dyers' Dyke and go far to cover the year ahead.

Slow and patient, bound to traditional ways of doing things, Coll could not believe that deliverance could be so easily achieved. He was afraid of taking his stock away by himself in the fore-end of the year, with calving not yet started. He was afraid of novelty, of what Lachlan Sinclair would say when the cattle were missed; and missed they would be since Sinclair could scan a field from a mile away and tell how many thistles had been chewed. If such fat pickings were to be made through direct dealing why had Sinclair not brought the matter to his attention? Why had the members of the Harlwood Agricultural Improvement Society not mounted an examination of the system? Pondering the unvoiced question Coll could only conclude that it was a system which involved over-much risk. It occurred to him that a drover's woman might be less shackled to convention than Bontine's factor. Could it be that Sinclair was well aware of the additional money that wintered stock might fetch if driven to the right place at the right time? Tenant Cochran could not bring himself to doubt Sinclair and, by implication, the lairds of Ottershaw, to shed the habit of thirty years of bondage. No more, though, could he deny his faith in Gaddy Patterson.

Tormented by doubt, Coll slept not one wink on the night before the drove.

There was another reason for anxiety; Etta.

Etta shunned him. Not only would she not wish him good fortune with the venture, she would not lift a finger to aid him, though he carefully explained the need for it and how, if what the highland woman said was true, they would be free of debt and, for once, have their noses in front. Etta would have none of it. It was not that she argued a case for not going to Dumbarton, she simply refused to address words to her husband. Happed in a shawl of bilious green wool, she hugged the fire all afternoon and evening, rising only to relieve herself, not to cook or serve. She had a tea-kettle and a pan of gruel, an array of vials on a stool by her heel from which she poured drop by drop a wicked concoction of medicines, spooning them into her thin lips with apparent relish.

"What are you doin' to yourself, Etta?"

No answer.

"What's that you're takin' now?"

No answer.

"Are you ailin', dear?"

No answer, apart from a twitch of the shoulders and a forced cough.

Coll no longer kept account of her battery of herbs and potions, acquired from packmen who, passing word of mouth of Wife Cochran's infirmities, beat a regular path to her door. But Coll recognised the tang of squills and the astringent odour of ether clouding the hearth. He ate by himself, cold fare, taken at the table by the window away from the fire, his head averted from the monumental picture of misery that occupied the ingle. She was still there by the embers when Coll took himself to bed.

It was after midnight when he hauled himself restlessly from under the blanket and went in search of her, found her asleep on the broadshelf in the little back room where, in days long gone, the boys had bedded.

"Etta? Etta?"

It was no sham sleep. She was dead to the world, purling like a milk-fed calf, the pure clean whiff of ether all around her like a halo.

She was still snoring when Coll stole out of the house at four o'clock in the morning to gird the pony and load the two-wheeled cart, to wait expectantly for Gaddy and the bairn to appear out of the darkness and for the day's adventure to begin, a day's adventure which, for Coll Cochran, would never really end.

Luck, if it comes at all, may appear in the strangest imaginable form. If superstitious folk are daft enough to ascribe to a clover leaf or horseshoe the properties of conferring a bonnie turn to fortune then there should be no difficulty in accepting that it was something other than coincidence that steered Coll Cochran's cattle off the High Street and into the shambles of buildings that clustered under the great rock of Dumbarton where two gentlemen, Mr Spruell and Mr Wallace, had, in adjacent galleries, blocks and cleavers parched for want of fresh-killed meat.

Individually Mr Wallace or Mr Spruell would have carved lumps out of the guileless farmer and his lady. Between them, however, in competition not collusion, the fleshers of Ossian's Close would cut their own throats to spite each other in a rivalry notorious in the town.

Dumbarton was a spot neither beautiful nor picturesque, not at all in harmony with the magnificent surroundings of river, moor and mountain. Seen from the Clyde it was a mere aggregate of huddled dwellings chequered by the timbers of ship-riggers and the nets of salmon fishers, topped by the reeking cones of glass and chemical works. Its mean little docks and bow-legged harbours were dominated by the mighty rock which, huge and weather-worn, shadowed Ossian's Close for eight hours out of every ten. The Close itself was hardly more than a vennel, with beams like gibbets and a gutter down which bloody water washed whenever it rained.

It was not by accident that the fleshers had adjoining premises in this least salubrious part of the burgh. Since childhood the couple had been engaged in a bitter feud. Neither intended to let the other out of sight until disgrace or death removed one or other from the scene. At the age of ten Mr Spruell and Mr Wallace had each been apprenticed to the same cattle butcher and, from that long ago day, had fought up and over each other, hock by hock, rib by rib, to attain dominance in the hoof of the market.

Mr Wallace was a coarse-muscled, bearded man, jovial and loud and venal. He took his bachelor pleasures in a tavern called the Celtic Earl and in the rooms of the newly-founded Salmon Club along with other gentlemen of sporting bent. Most of his Salmon Club cronies were well-to-do and it was to these wealthy carnivores that Mr Wallace sold best table beef and mutton and from them that he received contracts for slaughtering. He was liked for his hearty good nature and admired for his skill with fowling-piece and fly-rod. By the gallus lassies of Leven's print-fields, Mr Wallace was admired for other attributes as well, but these were not bragged about in company unless the whisky had been flowing free and the conversation had become mirac'lous. Mr Spruell, on the other hand, was a wee polished-marble pillar of the church; the ancient kirk on High Street, quaint, begalleried and filled to the doors with old nobility, from whom William Spruell received patronage in the form of orders and commissions. Mr Spruell seemed awful small for a man whose trade was wrestling stotts to the ground, sawing bone and tearing gristle. But he was deceptively strong and very dexterous with his dainty hands. He could slice veal thin as a leaf even when it was raw, and made the best mince-collops in the shire. His wife was a giant beside him. She had given him seven children in the course of the years, all as dry and neat and sand-buffed as their daddy, and just as virtuous. It was Mr Spruell, quick of eye as he was of hand, who spotted the Cochran herd first.

The forenoon had been fine and bright with a scudding breeze ruffling the Firth and little cutters sliding smoothly this way and that across the mottled brown waters, and the flags on the staff that crowned the wall of the castle standing out snapping-stiff. There was air about and a feeling of spring and everything would have been as fine as the weather for Mr William Spruell and Mr Bob Wallace if there had been work for them to do. It was not that they hadn't customers. Mr Stirling of the print-fields was awaiting a side of beef for a Saturday dinner party; Lady Fream had requested sixteen pounds weight of mince-collops; the Celtic Earl had an order in for steak-bits to bake into pies, and Doctor Pierce wanted a sirloin. Mr Spruell and Mr Wallace could hear their clients' voices clamouring like ghosts in the empty galleries. And suddenly there were cattle, bullocks on the hoof, three days before the weekly cattle market on the Broadmeadows where there would be naught to bid for in any case except sick cows and stirks the wind could blow over, this being the time of dearth, though try telling that to Lady Fream.

Each of the fleshers employed a boy. One was enough for the volume of business, and they could always hire a sack-hand come the back end, and often did. But on that spring afternoon the boys were idle too and, not sharing their employers' animosity, were round the back of the sheds playing chuckies for farthings. Mr Spruell stood, as usual, with arms folded neatly over the breast of his canvas apron, keeping an eye on Mr Wallace, who, smoking a cutty, sat on a box repairing a split fly-rod with glue and thread and in turn keeping a silent eye on his neighbour. But at the clatter of hoofs the pair were suddenly, frantically active.

Heads twisting, eyes darting, the puffs of smoke from Mr Wallace's pipe coming thick and fast, the fleshers of Ossian's Close ran in search of the source of that welcome sound. Mr Spruell, being nearer the Close, saw the glorious sight of nineteen head of black and banded stotts coming down the vennel at the half-gallop. He spread his arms as if to catch the kye, tilted his chin and muttered a prayer of gratitude to God for delivering the meat unto him. But Mr Wallace had other ideas. When he caught sight of Willie Spruell in that position, he had no need to spy the beasts for himself. They could only be in one place, the Close, and heading, by the increase in sound, towards the river, towards the wide open doors of the galleries. He ran, waddling, through his shed, with his short-apron pressed tight against his thighs and, plucking up a cleaver from the block, shot through to the tethering ground at the back, yelling, "*Iain. Iain, here, lad, here,*" to alert his assistant to opportunity. He veered right through the narrow lane and into the Close proper. By God, the kye were nearly on him. Confronted by the sight of a burly butcher wagging a blade, they reared and kicked into such a state of confusion that the woman in their midst was near knocked sprawling and the light two-wheeled cart with a pony in its shafts and a gaunt-looking farmer on its board dunted into the rump of the last leaping beast and projected it forward. Mr Wallace waved and shouted and stood his ground, and Mr Spruell, aglare with fury, came haring up the Close shouting that the herd was his as he'd seen them first. The herd, of course, belonged to neither of the fleshers. But they were used to doing business in a rough-and-ready manner and there would be time to skin the grazier or drover or whoever owned the beef when the beef was safe and secure on the premises.

It was Iain and Malcolm, the boys – one brown and oval as a hazel nut, the other like a pole with ears – who bunched the cattle and got them into the narrow lane and, opening and closing gates like drilled militiamen, split the herd into two pens at the rear of the galleries in the tethering ground. Meanwhile Mr Wallace and Mr Spruell bellowed at each other out in the vennel and the wifie and the mannie from the cart, though choked and breathless, held each other by the arms and, for some reason which neither of the butchers could fathom, laughed and laughed and laughed.

Laughter was far from James Moodie's lips when, having settled his mother to his place at the loom, he slipped out of the rear door of his cottage and set off on foot for Dyers' Dyke in the hour he allowed himself for dinner.

He wore his workaday clothes but had topped them off with a gravat of fine black wool and his grey suede gloves. In the breast of his jacket he carried his boxed Bible. Prayer and the reading of the Scriptures were daily habits to which the Elder paid attention, though his devotions could not be said to be heartfelt or unduly prolonged. If there was no hint of humour on Moodie's face, there was a certain wry pleasure in his breast, for he had been summoned on a matter that made much appeal to him and restored his belief that he was arbiter and sinew of conscience for the parish, attentive in those areas where the minister was most remiss.

Inquisitiveness was so much ingrained in James Moodie's nature that he regarded it as a virtue, a talent begging to be put to the service of God and the ill-wights of Balnesmoor. Alas, he had graduated to office too late and in a parish saddled with a minister like Mr Leggat, a moderate of such tepid orthodoxy that James Moodie was often tempted to lay hands on the mealy-mouthed chanter and shake him like a riddle under which all the chaff of rational, charitable forgiveness fell through. If the folk of Balnesmoor and district could not discriminate vice from virtue then the minister of the parish, aided by his trusted elders, should be prepared to undertake the labour for them, thus delivering them from sin and assuring for them eternal felicity.

Upon the mottled fly-leaf of his wooden-boxed Bible, a gift from his late-lamented father, were inscribed the words,

All worldly things stand on two lame legs, uncertainty and insufficiency, and therefore are not to be depended upon.

Moodie senior had not been educated in penmanship; Jamie had no notion who had set down the phrase for his father, nor could he understand why his father had neglected to identify the source of the quotation. Even so, Jamie used the miniature text as a kind of personal catechism, an answer without a question, without fully understanding its meaning or its implications. James Moodie was devoted not to doctrine but to courts, committees and assemblies in the tradition of the great John Knox, the Scottish Messiah. Moodie collected all manner of misdeeds and minor scandals, let them ripen in his memory to feed, in due course, his image of a God-fearing servant of justice and to strengthen the notion that the elect were relatively few and that he, of course, was one of them in spite of his own dark secrets.

On that fresh bright March afternoon, with the scents of the moor heady in the nostrils, Mr James Moodie walked with head bowed and mind fixed on the matter that had brought him out of the village and up to the high farm. If the woman who had summoned him, by a note slipped under the cottage door, had been younger perhaps Jamie's consciousness of the spring day would have been tweaked and his blood would have stirred with anticipation of another sort. But Mrs Cochran was far too old for Moodie, and far too ugly. He was her confidant, as the Patterson woman was Cochran's confidante, and he enjoyed the relationship for the control it gave him over the family at Dyers' Dyke. Moreover he perceived that there might be advantage to it, that he might eventually turn it to his own purpose.

The farmhouse door stood ajar.

"Mrs Cochran. It's the elder."

A croak invited him in.

She was seated by the hearth, clean-dressed by Balnesmoor's standards but ailing. Moodie noticed, however, a soup plate on the drainer and egg-shells in the slop bucket. He doubted if Mrs Cochran was ill enough to need to fast for better health. Solicitously, Mr Moodie seated himself on the stool to her left, pretending that he thought her too

86

feeble to stir herself in welcome. She stretched out a hand and he took it in both calloused palms.

"It was fell good o' ye to come so hastily, Mr Moodie," she quavered.

"A cry o' need must be answered promptly by any person o' Christian conscience, Mistress Cochran. What is it that troubles you?"

"He's gone away wi' her."

"Eh?" Mr Moodie sat up.

"He's gone away wi' the highland bitch."

"Elop . . . I mean, run off?"

"To Dumbarton, so he claims."

"Dumbarton?"

Moodie put a hand between his knees and dragged the stool closer. He glanced behind him at the door. A hen peeked in at him, clucking, but the elder's scowl sent it fluttering back out into the yard in alarm.

"What have they gone t' Dumbarton t' do, Mistress Cochran?"

"Sell our cattle."

If Mr Moodie was disappointed by her answer, he gave no sign of it. He had learned by experience that even the most willing confessor had to be coaxed a bit. Speculative intimacy drew him even closer. The woman smelled sharp, not sour; of alcohol and aromatic herbs, he thought, not being overly familiar with ether.

"The pair o' them went away this mornin'."

"What about her bairn?" said James Moodie. "What about Elspeth?"

"Went too, in the cart."

"How many cattle?"

"Nineteen head."

"Does Sinclair know of this?"

"Nobody knows but him an' her. It was her put him up to it, I tell you. He'd never have done anythin' so daft if it hadn't been for the spell she's got on him."

"Spell? Has she worked spells in your hearin', Mistress Cochran?"

"Turned his head, I tell you, Mr Moodie. I am beside m'self. Worn an' sick unto death wi' it all. She has led him into the ways o' temptation, right enough, just like you predicted."

"Uh-huh, uh-huh, uh-huh!" murmured James Moodie. "So it was her suggestion, them goin' to Dumbarton together. How long since they left?"

"Before daylight."

"How did you get the note to me?"

"I . . . I dragged m'self out."

"Uh-huh, uh-huh! Now, Mistress Cochran, tell me this, if you can – when will they return?"

"He says tonight."

"Uh-huh! I'll believe that when it happens," said James Moodie. He patted her arm. "Sorry, Mistress Cochran, the thought slipped out. It must have entered your head too, though?"

"It's a fair crack t' Dumbarton town," said Etta, as if relenting in her suspicions and beginning to consider giving her sinner of a husband the benefit of the doubt.

"Havers!" said James Moodie. "I could walk it three times over in a daylight span. I'm afraid, Mistress Cochran, that if the pair o' them do not return, it'll be from their own choosing an' not the weight o' miles between here an' Dumbarton."

"Aye, you're right, Mr Moodie."

She began to cry.

For a moment, Moodie was nonplussed. He had had women weep all over him before now, some a good deal younger and more attractive than Etta Cochran; hers was not the first "confession" that Mr Moodie had promoted, the errant ways of Coll Cochran were not the first to be catalogued in his sympathetic ear. But there was something about this wife's tears that touched Moodie. For a few brief seconds she seemed vulnerable. He patted her hand, then her shoulder. She turned against him and shed the shawl and hugged herself against his broad young chest, enveloping him in that sharp-sweet cloud ethereal.

"There, there now, there now," Moodie mouthed out of habit, as he had done when his sisters were young and fractious and he had had the tending of them. The woman hugged him tighter. James Moodie was afraid. It was all he could do not to thrust her away. "There, there, there, there."

"What'll I do? What'll I do, Mr Moodie?"

Moodie opened his mouth, gaping like a fish out of water. No words came. He could hardly breathe. He struggled to utter advice, a mutter of platitudes, anything to be released from the dark imaginings that had taken hold of him.

He fell backwards and the stool coggled and he slipped to the floor, his arms stuck out. Robbed of dignity, at her feet, he stared up at Etta Cochran in a kind of horror as if she had been responsible for humiliating him, for opening his heart to the realisation that there was more to life than ambition and security. He scrambled to his feet, sucked in a lungful of air, and towered over her.

The Bible, still in its box, had found its way into his hands and he held it out before him as if to ward off a devil.

"P . . . p . . . pray, Mistress Cochran," James Moodie said. "Pray that it does not come to pass."

His advice did not satisfy her.

She rose; the very act of releasing her body from the chair by the hearth suggested new-found determination.

Holding the Bible to his chest, Mr Moodie backed away. But her fingers closed on his forearm, delaying his retreat into the open air.

"What if it does come t' pass?" she demanded. "What then, Mr Moodie?"

"I . . . I . . . I'll see to it that she's punished."

"What about Coll?"

"Him too," Moodie promised, then, in passing doubt, added, "If that's what you really want, Mistress Cochran."

Slug-trails of tears still marked her cheeks but her eyes were dry and fierce. He saw hatred there, bitterness and a naked lust for revenge. It frightened him.

"Aye, faith, that's what I do want," Etta Cochran hissed. "Punishment."

James Moodie swallowed. "So be it. If the pair o' them don't return to Balnesmoor tonight . . ."

He left the sentence unfinished. He was uncertain as to how he could guarantee the sort of punishment that Etta Cochran had in mind. He could recite chapter and verse of kirk processes for private admonition and public censure but he lacked the power to destroy. And it was destruction that the woman craved. He glimpsed things in the farmer's wife that disturbed him, passions that lay below the petty, titillatory appetites of most parishioners, the wheedling sins that an elder could enjoy and which, in the working of them, would not contaminate his soul.

"We'll . . . we'll say a wee prayer, Mistress Cochran."

Stepping back, and with one eye wide open, Elder Moodie rolled out a dozen platitudinous phrases, asking God to bring succour to this wronged wife; not peace but strength of will. That done, the elder hurriedly took his leave.

The afternoon was still fresh and bright and James Moodie felt blessed by the open weather as he strode down the track away from the brooding farmhouse. He felt almost as if he was passing out of a valley of shadow, a place clouded by suffering and betrayal where a man might stumble and lose himself. At the back of his mind was the thought that Etta Cochran might be exaggerating, that there might be no other reason for the farmer and the highland woman to be off together than the selling of cattle.

But he doubted it. Oh, aye, he doubted it.

To James Moodie's way of thinking, innocence must never be assumed. Experience had taught him otherwise.

It boiled down to one stott. Which stott did not matter. If they had droved eighteen instead of nineteen perhaps the buyers would have been satisfied to take even portion. But that odd beast worked the trick. It proved that all Gaddy had heard about the fleshers of Ossian's Close was not exaggeration.

In Mr Spruell's pen were ten animals.

In Mr Wallace's pen were nine.

"I spied them first, Bob Wallace, so ye ken fine well they're mine."

"Damned if I ken anythin' o' the kind, Spruell. He who finds, keeps."

The young apprentices had done their best for their employers and, fair used to this sort of thing, had seated themselves on the pen spars to enjoy the fun. The bullocks were calm enough, steaming and snorting in unfamiliar surroundings but glad to be hemmed in, not rolling forward between hedges or houses. Coll had taken position in the corner, where the posts of the pens met, as if to remind the maddened butchermen that he was still the owner of nineteen head and that nobody had yet thought to make offer to him for anything.

As they shouted, the butchers inspected the cattle, each in his own pen, walking through and round them, craning over a rump or saddle to howl at the rival, so loud that you would have thought the pair were separated by the width of the Clyde and not by four or five yards of muddy ground.

"I'll have the pick o' the beasts at any rate," Spruell shouted.

"Pick? Pick? By God, you'll be lucky t' have any at all," shouted Wallace. "I wouldn't sell you one if you an' your brats were starvin' on the strand, Spruell."

Nineteen beasts were too much for one flesher to cope with; there was ample beef to share between the pair. They could have put their fat heads together and fixed a price and cut Coll to the bone on the herd but that tactic did not occur to them. The magical appearance of beef on the hoof in a period of dearth, the unexpectedness of it, had temporarily stunned the butchers' commercial instincts.

Inspections complete, Mr Wallace and Mr Spruell gravitated to the division of the pens and, gripping the rail, glowered speculatively at the other man's share of the spoils. Gaddy knew that the pair had calculated the state of the catch to the pound-weight and waited, a little tensely, for shrewdness to temper avarice.

"I'll give ye four, Bob Wallace," said Spruell, magnanimously. "I'll select the four, though."

"For that," returned Bob Wallace, "Ye'll have none."

It was then, without prompting by Gaddy, that Coll stirred himself. He sauntered to the middle division of the pens, passing behind Mr Wallace, and, without so much as a glance at either of the butchers, lifted the top rail. He set it down on its end and lifted the second rail. Cattle milled and churned, backing away then clubbing towards the farmer, herd fever strong in them or the hope of water and leisurely cud.

"What the devil d'ye think you're about?" demanded Bob Wallace.

"Movin' my cattle," said Coll.

"Out of my pen?"

"I never put them there," said Coll.

"Into *his* pen?"

"An' out of his pen into the road," said Coll. "And on the Broadmeadow."

"The Broadmeadow?" said Mr Spruell.

"To crop 'til Friday."

"Friday's not market day," said Mr Wallace.

The butchers had come together at last, flanking the farmer and the half-gap in the railing, Mr Wallace blocking it with his belly and nudging the inquisitive cattle back with his elbows.

"I've a buyer comin' down from Inver –"

Coll was not permitted to complete the falsehood.

"Buyer?" snapped Mr Spruell. "I'm the buyer, sir."

"My apologies, gentlemen, for any stramash caused," said Coll. "Come, Gaddy, we'd best gather an' go on."

"You brought them *here*," said Bob Wallace.

"They ran," said Coll.

Gaddy could hardly suppress her laughter again. She hoisted Elspeth into her arms and hugged the bairn tightly. For a sombre chap from Balnesmoor who had no truck with market-men, Coll was acquitting himself well. Donald McIver could not have done better.

Unctuously Mr Spruell placed his hand on Coll's shoulder and, as if conferring a blessing, said, "I'll pay you five pounds per head, as they stand. Siller to honour the sale; a note for the balance on the bank to be collected tomorrow."

It said much for Mr Wallace that he even let Spruell finish his bid.

"Six," Bob Wallace said. "Six pounds for lean cattle is generous."

"Six pounds an' five shillings," interjected Mr Spruell. "For the nineteen head."

"Mine for six pounds an' eight –"

"Six pounds an' twelve shillings."

Coll's tongue darted to his lips but he kept his gaze flat

and disinterested as he shifted the middle rail. Mr Wallace put an arm around the necks of two steaming bullocks, like an uncle demonstrating fondness for a pair of scallywag nephews. "Six an' fifteen shillings."

The stotts tossed pettishly but Mr Wallace held them.

Gaddy realised that the extravagant bids would not be liable to be met. Ossian's Close was not the Royal Mart. Neither of the quayside butchers had that sort of capital in the spring season. They were not bidding now, but boasting, carried away by enmity and the spirit of competition. That one odd bullock kept them going. Eight pounds was a high-season price for fat cattle and, even with beef scarce on the hooks, the fleshers of Dumbarton could not turn profit on carcasses bought at more than a hundred and fifty shillings each not even with hides and hoofs and horns to sell in turn.

"Eighteen."

"Seven pounds."

They were bidding with money that they did not possess for cattle that they would have to graze for months, costing more in grass feed. She had not quite believed Donald's tale of the lunatic butchers of Dumbarton. At best she had hoped for small favour, not this. She began to feel apprehensive again.

"Seven an' five."

"Seven an' eight."

"An' nine, damn you, Spruell."

"One hundred and fifty shillings, sir. It's a handsome offer for winter stotts."

Coll raised himself on toe-tip, rocked, arms folded over his chest. "How will I be paid?"

"Silver down, an' a note for the balance," said Mr Wallace.

"A note for how much?"

"The balance." Mr Spruell had insinuated an arm around Coll's waist, as if he intended to lead him straightway to a chest full of coin.

"You've made me a tidy offer. I've no complaint about the sum," Coll said. "Only about how I may collect it."

"From the bank, man, from the bank," said Wallace.

93

"The Bank of Scotland. *My* bank. On *my* note of hand," said Spruell.

Disengaging himself from Mr Spruell, Coll said enquiringly, "A note of hand for the best part of one hundred an' fifty pounds?"

Immediately Mr Wallace released the struggling bullocks.

"How . . . *how* much?"

"To be exact," said Coll fluently, "the total on the table's one hundred an' forty-two pounds and five shillings."

"You'll get no better, sir," said Spruell.

"Aye, but an offer won't buy corn seed," said Coll. "Only coin'll do that."

"My word's my bond," said Spruell.

"Damn it, man, I'm good for every farthing," cried Wallace. "Ask anybody in these parts. Ask Sir Peter Stirling, if you doubt me."

"Are you promisin' me a hundred an' forty-two pounds with payment in full by tomorrow mornin'?" Coll said, glancing first at Mr Spruell and then at Mr Wallace.

"Give or take a day or two," said Mr Wallace.

"A three-month's the accepted term," said Mr Spruell.

"I require payment at once."

"Damn it, man, that's not the manner in which business is done."

"I'm not fashed t' do business here at all," said Coll, shrugging and turning away.

"Wait."

"Hold on."

It must be now or it would be never. At any moment the butchers would begin to retract their wild offer of a hundred and fifty shillings for each beast in the herd. They were used to buying fat cattle in small parcels of four and five and had, Gaddy supposed, got whirled up in that sort of calculation. Gaddy assumed that the men would have drawing accounts with the Bank of Scotland but, being the sort of tradesmen they were, would not have limitless credit.

"Nine head," said Coll, "totals sixty-five pounds, five shillings."

"Divided?"

"That's what I've a mind to do," Coll admitted. "Split my herd betwixt the pair o' you. Equally."

"What about the odd one?" said Wallace.

"Half it down the middle," said Coll.

Cheeks flushed with suppressed laughter, Gaddy quickly carried Elspeth away from the pens into the vennel.

The "dividing" of that poor old stott would provide more girning and grousing opportunities; it would be worth its weight in sanguinary argument to the quarrelsome butchers.

"Me, I'll take the hindquarters," piped in Mr Spruell.

"Damned if y' will," shouted Mr Wallace.

Gaddy returned to the cart where the pony in the shafts and the pony on the tether behind the tailgate waited, patiently chewing the forks of hay that she had thrown down for them from the sack. She mounted the board and set Elspeth beside her, holding the child steady with one hand as she snicked the reins and expertly brought the cart round in the narrow close and pointed it back towards the High Street, as if Coll was committing an act of robbery and she was making ready to gallop away with the spoils.

One hundred and forty pounds; Donald had never turned so much on spring cattle in all his years as drover and dealer. She felt proud of herself for having snatched the faint opportunity. Proud of Coll Cochran too for the manner in which he had conducted the "auction".

The Dyke was safe now. Sinclair would have his back rent. Bontine's coffers would swell that wee bit more. And she would see to it that Coll acquired at least a dozen handpicked stotts to crop the summer pasture, giving him more beef to sell come the back end of the year. She felt glad for Coll. She was smiling when he stalked round the corner from the pens with the two little bags of silver in one hand and the long paper billets in the other, holding them up for her to admire like new-caught trout. He climbed up beside her. She tapped the reins and the pony moved off.

Elspeth clung to Coll's thigh, hugging him. Ahead the hills were dappled by the slant of the evening sun. The great rock of Dumbarton was stark in wine-red and brown shadow as they cleared the walls of the Close. Coll shook the coin bags to make them jingle then, without haste, leaned across the board and kissed Gaddy on the cheek.

"The daft, dizzy johnnies bought betwixt them after all," he said. "Sixty pounds more than Sinclair would have paid. Sixty pounds."

He threw back his head and laughed aloud, something Gaddy had seldom heard him do before, as if he had thrown depression and inhibition to the winds that fluttered off St Patrick's Quay.

"Forty-two pounds, five shillings in silver," he tolled the leather bags between finger and thumb again, "and a pair of notes, each worth fifty pounds."

"I pray that pair won't go changin' their minds."

"How would it be possible, Gaddy? I've signed promises an' they have my cattle."

"Even so," said Gaddy. "I'm thinkin' we'd best be at the bank office when it opens its doors first thing tomorrow."

Coll said, "Stay in Dumbarton?"

"It would be daft to make the same journey twice."

"Stay over the night?"

"Aye."

"Where would we lodge?"

"I'm sure we'll find a barn or byre-shed."

"No," said Coll. "No."

Gaddy's heart lurched with disappointment.

She had no reason to suppose that Coll's correctness and sense of honour had melted along with his worries about Dyers' Dyke. After all, he had a wife at home. Etta Cochran would not rejoice in the saving of the farm if it meant that her grievous hold on her husband had been loosened, even for the space of a single night.

"No draughty barn or byre-shed for the likes of us, Gaddy," Coll declared. "We'll find ourselves an inn. This night we'll share as fine a supper an' as soft a bed as money can buy."

"Coll, when we get home – to Balnesmoor, I mean . . ."

"Devil take Balnesmoor," said Coll and, reaching across her, tweaked the traces to make the pony pick up speed.

The calf, with a soft flax rope looped above its fetlocks, came out easy after all. The cow gave a final heave to be quit of the birthing and there was the new creature, all slippery in its dismembered sac. Sinclair had hardly had to pull at all, though he had liberally coated goose-grease over the calf's cantle. The chaff-sheet which he had spread was awash with bladder-water but Sinclair paddled in it regardless to wipe viscid fluid from the calf's mouth and nostrils.

"I'll give it a bit straw-wipe, Mr Sinclair," said Etta Cochran.

"No." Sinclair's tone brooked no argument.

An uncomplicated birth, as this had been, could be handled well enough by a woman. But the old school of cattle-wifies had queer ideas; wiping the calf with straw was one of them. Wiping only agglutinated the hairs and prolonged the drying process, giving rise to chilling. The liquor amnios evaporated quickly enough in the air and left the soft hide dry and warm.

"Is it no' breathin'?" Etta Cochran bent to peer over Sinclair's shoulder.

"It will, it will," said Sinclair. "Give me a modicum of room, if you please, Mistress Cochran."

Reluctantly the woman shuffled back from the chaff-sheet.

Though the calf appeared to be dead, Sinclair had felt its heart beat and knew that all that was required was to inflate its lungs. He ducked his head and, hoisting the calf's neck in the crook of his arm, opened its mouth and blew steadily and forcefully into it, sufficient encouragement to cause the creature to gasp and come alive. A moment or two later it gave a blathering roar, blubbered and struggled to rise in the world.

Sinclair untied the rope then lifted the calf and carried it suspended, head up between its forelegs, to the littered crib which Coll Cochran had had prepared and ready. Straw would keep it warm and its mother could attend it in comfort. Sinclair swished away the chaff-sheet. She, the wife, could wash it later before it got too stiff. He inspected the cow. The dangling placenta would come away with pressing in a couple of hours. She seemed healthy and happy, like the calf. She had calved before, last spring, producing then as she had done now a sturdy little bull-calf to add to Cochran's herd. The cow dunted past the grieve

97

to get to her boy-bairn. Sinclair ran his palm gently along her flanks, smiling with his eyes.

Calving in a byre was easy work and safe. God knows, Highlands did well enough on their own. Coll Cochran had obviously attended the cow patiently during the difficult weeks of pregnancy. He could not understand why Etta had jittered out of the byre to summon him so urgently in the bare hours of dawn. She had come herself right to his cottage and battered on the door so loud it had wakened the whole family. She could have gone for Sim Wanlock, who lived closer to the Dyke and was the best cattleman in Balnesmoor. She could have gone to Smith's place too; Smith was an easy-going loon and would have walked over hot coals to help a beast in calf. But she had come right to him, to the grieve.

Sinclair had been fully occupied this past three weeks. Winter had left its legacy in crumpled hedges, uprooted trees and a scantness of grass that had caused him to delve deep into the feed stores for cattle and sheep alike, even to purchase barley and oats at an exorbitant price to keep the horses strong. Ploughing was behind, ditching almost untouched. Calving on the Bontine estate was byre-done and came in earlier than on the tenancies, who had the bull late. Even so, the Bontine home-herds had been swelled by nineteen bull-calves and eleven heifers. The curse of slinks, calves born dead or shed unformed, had been surprisingly light considering the conditions. All over strath and carse, though, cows were faring badly. They were malnourished and strained by the thaw-mud, aye, and ill-tended too since the gospel of good husbandry and careful management had not spread as it should have done.

Busy or not, Sinclair had learned that Coll Cochran had taken nineteen head of lean beef out of his grazings and away down the road towards Dumbarton. Sinclair had also discovered that the Nettleburn hut had been closed. Its door was barred with a log, a pile of brushwood mounded against it to keep hares and deer from entering in search of food. It had even come down to him – through his wife who had it from Hunter's wife who had it from the younger Moodie – that Coll Cochran had ridden off in the cart with Gaddy

Patterson. But Sinclair had been obliged to set gossip to one side until he could establish for himself just what was what, and what was brewing up there on the bleak farm at the edge of the moor. For that reason he had personally gone to "assist" Etta Cochran in the calving instead of sending a cattleman.

Sinclair had seen Coll's cows. He knew that they were well fed and comfortably bedded and would drop close to the last day of the month, two hundred and seventy-three days being the term, though a majority of Highlands ran six or eight days late. It was unlike Coll to leave calving cows in critical phase, with florid udders, enlarged milk-veins and excitable. Etta Cochran had been a farmer's wife for long enough, though, and in the days before she fell sick had buckled to. She was not stricken with amateur panic. Fine well she knew that the cows would calf, all things being right, naturally and normally. But Etta, it seemed, had lost all self-reliance. He had been summoned, Sinclair realised, not to deliver a bull-calf but to be incorporated into some captious, premeditated intrigue.

From the facts already in his possession, Sinclair deduced that Gaddy Patterson had persuaded Coll to drive stotts to market. With fat cattle at a premium and no grass yet to relieve the tenants north and west of the Clyde, there was no telling what Cochran might receive for his beasts. While the laird would gain the rent arrears due on Dyers' Dyke, he would lose profit on the sale of Cochran's stotts. The laird, of course, had no lawful claim on Cochran's cattle, unless as payment of debt; but tradition was on the laird's side, and tradition had been flouted. Sinclair was torn between grudging admiration for Coll Cochran's boldness and concern at the setting of a precedent that might catch and spread about Balnesmoor like a moor fire.

Sinclair checked the other cows. They showed no signs of immediate drop and were content enough, tonguing quietly in reply to the motherly sounds from the nearby stall where the new-born calf was being licked and nuzzled.

The work had taken but an hour and it was now only about seven o'clock. On any other farm in the Lennox, Sinclair would have been offered hospitality, breakfast or a dish of tea or a stoup of ale. But he expected nothing of the kind from Etta Cochran, and nothing of the kind was what he received.

"I thank you for what you've done, Mr Sinclair."

The laird's man wiped his hands and forearms on straw. He would wash when he got back to Ottershaw.

"He should've been here t'do it himself," Etta Cochran said. "It's an ill tenant who'll neglect his cows the way he neglects his wife."

"The beast could have calved without assistance."

"How could I be sure o' that, Mr Sinclair? An' him gone for three days with never a word."

Like James Moodie, like everyone in the village, Lachlan Sinclair did not wish to tarry in the woman's company and be an audience for a bitter tirade against Coll. But he had come here, in person, for the purpose of gleaning information and he brought the subject directly to the point, asking, "I hear tell he's gone to Dumbarton to sell cattle?"

"It doesn't take three days to sell cattle. He's with her."

Kitchen-maids and fine ladies might play the game of wink and hint but that wasn't for Sinclair.

"How many head?"

Etta Cochran told him.

"She'll be dealing for him," Sinclair said. "She's more used to it than Coll."

"He should've sold to the laird."

The woman's face was contorted with slyness. She was prompting him to agree with her low opinion of Coll, to side with her in hatred of Gaddy Patterson. Sinclair would do neither. It was to be *informed* that she had dragged him to the Dyke, not to birth the bull-calf. Let her get on with informing him.

"Three nights," said Etta. "Three nights with the high-land woman."

It was on the tip of Sinclair's tongue to explain that Gaddy Patterson would be a damned sight more comforting a companion on the road than most women, and more useful too, but he kept silent.

"Went to Dumbarton."

"Why are you telling me this?" Sinclair asked.

"It's the laird's business, is it not?"

"No, it's not. The laird is not concerned."

"It's Sir Gilbert's beasts . . ."

Sir Gilbert's profit, maybe, but not Sir Gilbert's right. If he had been strung up by the hams over a roasting pit, Sinclair would not have voiced his heresy aloud, not to Etta Cochran, not to anyone. Beneath the carapace of loyalty that protected his doubts like a tortoise shell, there was a streak of radicalism in Lachlan Sinclair that, if he had been born without favour, would have turned his energy rogue. He too might have waved the cap of liberty as the peasants in France were doing and have fought the Tories on their policies of repression. He understood by his reading what movements there were throughout Europe and believed, compatibly, that advancement did not end with the chair at the Harlwood Improvement Society.

Balnesmoor was not London, however, or even Edinburgh. Mutters of revolution and threats of war were not common talk on the lips of the people hereabouts. One tenant farmer whose head had been spun in the right direction by an easy-going woman from another kind of society was hardly a threat to Ottershaw or the good order of the estate. Like Etta Cochran the jacquerie of the Lennox lands would be dragged into scandal rather than reform, swayed by tattle from any depth of thought. God knows, they had enemies enough without engendering enmity among themselves. But that was the way of it, and Lachlan Sinclair, his education notwithstanding, was out of that stock of honest, petty servants who put their own position above all else. She, the wronged wife, had no thought at all for implications. He, the laird's man and the iron fist of Ottershaw, had no connection other than fancy with the revolutionary sentiments that he read of and silently cheered.

It was not defiance but desperation that had sent Coll Cochran out with Gaddy Patterson on the road round the marts. Aye, if ever persuasion came under the banner that the highland woman bore, even he, happily married and true to his lot, might find himself lured away from narrow paths into a new sort of righteousness.

Though Sinclair gave no answer to Etta's question, he

showed his impatience and displeasure plainly, scowling and shaking his head. He had never had sympathy for this acidic woman, in whom feminine wiles and anxieties had curdled under strains much less severe than those to which other marriages were subjected. As far back as he could remember, Etta Cochran had wanted for little. If she had lost Coll to Gaddy Patterson – a turn which was, in Sinclair's opinion, very doubtful – then she had but herself to blame. Marriages, like growing ground, had to be attended and carefully nurtured if they were to weather the seasons and remain fruitful.

If it had been Etta's intention to recruit him as an ally, she lacked the wit to cajole.

Abruptly she snapped, "*You* brought her here, Lachie Sinclair."

He would shelter no guilt about that action.

He snapped back, "Aye, woman, to do what you would not."

"An' what would I not do, tell me?"

"Help him."

"Help him that never lifts a finger to help me?"

"He feeds you, keeps you clothed and warm, puts a bloody dry roof over your head . . ." Sinclair modulated his anger. "Just what more do you expect of him?"

The answer was ugly, too frank to be uttered aloud.

In Etta Cochran was born the assumption that her sex justified all, an aspiration towards gentility that he had observed in many women in Harlwood and Killearn, a kind of self-love that excused any demand that a woman might put upon a man, that reduced marriage to a system of deals and payments.

How long was it, Sinclair wondered, since Etta Cochran had put her arm about her man's shoulder and told him in a loving voice that she respected the value of his labour? Years, probably. It was fine when the man was strong and bore the brunt of circumstance with pride, then he could take the weaknesses of women in his stride, carry the load for both. But there were times that came to all men, all but the brutes, when there was need for solicitude, for caring and for tender expressions of appreciation. Let the kirkmen jabber about love and sin; to Lachlan Sinclair, educated and disciplined, neglect was the cardinal vice.

Blazes take her, he would not be dragged into petty rage like a dead twig into the millrace. He could shelter behind his position and his rectitude, pretend indifference when, in his heart, he felt compassion for Cochran and admiration for the highland woman who had built much out of little and, it seemed, would effortlessly impart that knack to Coll if he had a mind to learn this late in the evening of his life.

Spitting out the words, Etta Cochran said, "She'll *not* have him. She'll *not* have him. I'll see them both *damned* first."

And you with them, or in their place, Sinclair thought.

Besides, if Coll had it in mind to bed with another, then Gaddy it would be for she was easy and loving by nature, fashioned by the droving life and not the hems of a village or town.

Though his arms were not yet dry, Sinclair pulled on his jacket and planted his brown bonnet on his head. He gave the bonnet a deliberate, formal tug to show Etta Cochran that he was half-way to being a gentleman and stood above her quarrel.

"How long did you say they have been gone?" he asked.

"Twice I told you; these three nights."

"In that case," said Sinclair, "I fear it's too late."

"Too late for what, pray?"

"Damned or not, she has him already."

It was just such an objective opinion that Etta Cochran had hoped to draw from the grieve, witnessed by his reputation and authority.

She let out breath in a long moaning sigh and hugged her arms to her breasts under the ragged shawl.

Sinclair realised that he had erred but could not fathom how to redeem himself.

Touching the bonnet once more, he said, "Good morning to you, Mistress Cochran."

She made no reply.

She had no more to say to Lachlan Sinclair. He had given her what she desired; confirmation of her martyrdom.

The rest would not be her doing, but God's.

* * *

103

Conviviality was in short supply in the black-rock glens that fissured the flanks of Ben Lomond. There were few hospitable houses and no inns at all, save one that Gaddy had heard of but had never visited. It was peculiar to realise that they were only fourteen miles from the main street of Balnesmoor, for the great lift of the mountains, cloaked still with heavy snow, made Inchbuck seem like another country and the tacksmen of Montrose who dwelled there as alien as American redskins. Even those parts of the wide-spread parish that joined to Balnesmoor were less familiar to Coll Cochran in nomenclature and contour than the city and the towns south and east along the turnpike. He might have been a thousand miles from Dyers' Dyke, not a mere seven hours' drive away with the cattle that Gaddy had hand-picked from the mangy steadings that clung to the loch shore.

Thirteen bullocks had been selected and paid for, one here, one there, on a troll through Balloch into the hard country. Here the wind leaned cold and strong, the hill grazings below the snow skirts were bare and ptarmigan and hares were still grey. Grey too were the farmers upon whom Gaddy called. They seemed as glad to enjoy an hour of human company as they were to receive the guineas that Coll counted into their eager palms.

Breeders from the south would have scoffed at the dealing. In this remote parish, though, wintering of stock and the buying and selling of it was not done to an intricate, hard-fast system. Need called the tune. Many of the beasts had been on short rations since January and, without exception, the survivors of the hungry months were in low condition. From the runs through the straw-yards Gaddy picked raw-boned stotts, ones in which the skeleton seemed large in comparison to the weight of the flesh. Such animals would soon fill out on the Dyke's summer grass and would put on full weight by the autumn. Handling told Gaddy if the skin was over-thin or over-tight. She groped for a hide that was mossy and mellow under her fingers. She inspected the tails thoroughly, for a thick tail with a hairy tuft at its point indicated that the bullock was of strong constitution. Coll was no mean judge of cattle but even he could not match Gaddy's breadth of experience. When she slapped a particular stott on the rump and said, "Aye, we'll take this chap," Coll meekly dug into his pouch and produced the four guineas or five that the bargain had been struck upon and paid them over without argument.

In this manner, working a zig-zag course from steading to steading, Gaddy and Coll replenished the Dyers' Dyke stock at a cost of less than sixty pounds. What amazed Coll, when he viewed the new herd on the track, was that it was so "level", the beasts all of a uniform size, as if they had been bought pedigree.

Droving the made-up herd was tricky and Gaddy aimed for no more pace than two miles in the hour. She walked ahead, Coll snecking the cart behind, tapping strays into line with a willow switch. Snug in a meal sack on a basket-seat, Elspeth rode beside him, chattering at every new sight. They let the bairn down to toddle off her restless energy at every opportunity, had her petted and fed tidbits by farmers' wives while business was being done in the straw-yard or out on the hill. And Coll never let dab that Elspeth wasn't his child or Gaddy his wife and did not correct folk when they called her Mistress Cochran.

Two nights had been spent in low, miserable inns. Coll's boast that they would sup like kings and sleep in linen sheets had not been realised. Gaddy knew better than to put up at one of the grand inns that had sprung up around Dumbarton. Drovers, like tinkers and packmen, would not be made welcome there, and ingrained thriftiness led her to known haunts. The inns she chose had grazing but few comforts, were hardly more than pits of cheap whisky where sup was rough and beds even rougher. It worried Gaddy not at all and even Coll, who was inclined to hygiene, took the discomfort in his stride. He was consoled by glasses of mulled wine, a tipple of which he was fond, and by the bulky money-pouch stuck down his breeks where no rascal could steal it, short of murder.

If they had made the turn and come back along the loch shore that cold evening then it would not have happened. But Elspeth was chilled and Gaddy keen to find shelter and a fire and, prompted by a memory of packmen's stories, had pulled the herd behind her to the Inn of Inchbuck where, by sheer chance, they stumbled on a soldier's wedding.

Inchbuck was no place at all; a bridge over a gushing burn, a small sad farm hidden behind alderbrake. The inn was set in a fold in the bracken-covered hill above the lochside track. It was nothing more than a long low steading, kitchen and cowhouse knocked into one apartment, with stabling in a separate outbuilding and a green sward in front, the lawn protected by banks of wild rhododendron which would not burst into flower until May or June. But smoke purled from its chimney, lanterns glowed in the tiny windows and the desolation of the mountain was cheered by the skirl of bagpipes and the chirrup of fiddles. Skeins of dancers wove patterns in the green spring gloaming while the wide-open doors gave a glimpse of the men and lassies within. Small boys capered about in excitement and little girls played games of hankie-tag. Old men and women, ancestors of the bride, sat on a bench and smoked their pipes and supped bumpers of hot toddy that were passed to them through open windows.

Gaddy stopped, reluctant to intrude; but the herd legged past her and broke on to the lawn's edge and, after kicking, soon dropped to crop the sprigs of dry grass on the verges. Even if Gaddy and Coll had decided to retreat, it was too late. A tall, tall man – far taller than Coll even – came louping towards them with one arm upraised.

"Come awa' in an' welcome," he shouted.

Abandoning their games the boys and girls flocked after the host to stare at the strangers. The set of the dance broke. Gaddy turned questioningly to Coll who had got down from the cart and, with Elspeth in the crook of his arm, was leading the pony forward.

"Have ye come far the day, then?" the tall man asked.

Familiarly he put his arm on Gaddy's shoulder. He had been liberal with whisky for his guests and had matched the best of the parish's drinkers cup for cup. His bonhomie was boozy but no less sincere for that.

"McAlpine, I am," he declared, still with his arm round Gaddy. "An' if you're drovers you're doubly welcome, since my auld father was a drover in his youth, afore he settlit in these parts. Frae Skye he came. I travelit wi' him many a time when I was wee."

McAlpine was landlord of the Inchbuck Inn. It was his daughter Margaret, the eldest of four, who was that day being given away to a handsome young soldier from the garrison at Inversnaid. McAlpine obviously approved of the match though a less tolerant man would have drowned his daughter in the loch before he'd let her wed into the military.

These last dozen years the garrison at Inversnaid had become but a ghost, a tarnished token of military order. A poor handful of NCOs and enlisted men, bossed by scape-grace subalterns, suffered like transported criminals the lonely exile of life on the remote loch shore. Now that law and order had come to the glens, the function of the garrison was almost a memory and, with war in France looming large, the last of the regular soldiers would soon be shipped out and 43rd's black watch changed no more to the cry of ospreys and the roaring of Lomond's stags.

The host of the inn at Inchbuck had always made the soldiers welcome and offered them the cheer and comfort of his hearth and kitchen. McAlpine was a coarse, irrepressible man, too large in his generosity to suit some of the folk of Buchanan parish but friend to many. He had the victualling of the Inversnaid mess, such as it was, and had turned quite a bit of silver out of it. He was happy enough for Margaret to wed her gunner, since the lad was a Scot and canny and would take the girl, pretty though she was, off his hands for good and all.

Within five minutes the new herd had been chased to graze on a dribble of hay and chopped turnips in a hedged field behind the inn and Gaddy, Coll and Elspeth were being toasted by half the company and pressed to consume their body-weight in hot comestibles. Seated at a broad pine table with their backs to the hearth, they were served for a minute or two by the willowy bride and her dashing, kilted groom, a lad as generous and out-going as his father-in-law.

Food was of a variety and richness the like of which Gaddy and Coll had seldom tasted; broths and hotch-potch, shoulder of lamb, chine of beef, pork ribs, spit-roasted fowls, trout perfectly smoked and seasoned, cheeses of several hues and textures, and a huge crumbly round of bride's pie which, stuffed though they were, it would have been inexcusable not to sample. Wine flowed freely, as did ale and whisky. In a corner of the ingle-nook three sophisticates conducted experiments with copper pans and a tray of spices, concocting potions of wondrous fragrance and subtle sting. Seated on Gaddy's lap, Elspeth was fed broth followed by flakes of chicken specially broken by the host's good wife. Finally, armed with a horn spoon, Elspeth discovered how to sup from a cog of sweet brose thick with honey and cream and, as Gaddy soon deduced, quite liberally laced with whisky. Bright-eyed and flushed, the bairn created a stir when the cog was whisked away from her. Rising to her knees, she beat time to the fiddlers' reel and wiggled and waggled merrily, just this side of tipsy.

"Don't fret yourself, Gaddy," Coll said. "She'll whisk up like a rush light and, in a quarter hour, be a sleepy wee stump."

Coll was anxious to be among the spicy pans steaming on the hob and, excusing himself, left Gaddy with the bairn. Gaddy did not grudge the man his pleasure. She had spied something that teased her fancy too. A big tea-pot was going the rounds in the kitchen place. She carried Elspeth on her arm and, on the pretext of thanking the bride's mother for her hospitality, insinuated herself into the circle of tea-drinkers.

"It's a right royal herd ye have out there," said a small stout woman with jet-black hair coiled into unsuitable ringlets. "Are ye for the market?"

"We're buyin', not sellin'."

"Your man, is he a drover, then?"

"He's a grazier," said Gaddy.

"Tenant?"

"Aye, on Bontine land, by Balnesmoor."

"'Deed, I've a cousin in Balnesmoor, marrit on to a Murray. Perhaps you'll have her acquaintance. She's named Mary, like I am m'self."

"I'm not long settled there, truth t'tell," said Gaddy.

They were perceptive, these steading wives. With little

else to do for social diversion, they had raised gossiping to an art unsurpassed even in the Lennox villages.

"Marrit late, eh?"

"Aye," Gaddy admitted.

"Bred late, too," said the jet-haired woman, then, to take the vinegar out of her remark, added, "an' sicca bonnie bairn. Chookie, there's a lovely wee chookie-love," and tickled her forefinger against Elspeth's earlobe.

The child responded with a great glowing smile which drew a chorus of *aaawwws* from the assembled ladies and conveniently diverted the progress of an awkward line of questioning. But Gaddy detected sleep swimming in her daughter's dauntless blue eyes and, finishing her tea, cradled the child to her breast and began a gentle, incidental rocking that would cause Elspeth to nod off.

The distractions of the pipes' wail, the stamp of brogues on the earthen floor, the yells and yelps of the dancers who had moved indoors from the darkened green, the belly-roars of laughter from the boozers and all the rest were, for Gaddy's foundling bairn, but a lullaby, passing as steady and rhythmic as sea-waves on a golden strand. With never a flicker or start she cuddled snug in her mammy's arms, with her thumb in her mouth, sucking contentedly on the taste of Atholl Brose.

Three truckle beds in a back room were quilted with blankets to shelve the younger children, those, like Elspeth, who had fallen sound asleep. There were five of them and a very young baby, shored by pillows. A low wood fire in an iron stove kept the room warm as a womb and two young girls, inn-servants, sat on stools, chatting *tête-à-tête* and nibbling on hazelnuts from a basket between them; their job was to look out for the sleeping bairns and leave the mothers free, for once, to enjoy themselves.

Gaddy bedded Elspeth down, stroked her hair soothingly, then returned to the main rooms where rowdy games had replaced dancing. The whole company, including groom and bride, were involved. Coll and his fellow imbibers had found the perfect mixture and, pots in hand and wreathed in happy smiles, were dispensing the hot spiced wine to anyone who cared to try it, handing out glasses and cups to those who passed by in the big, noisy circle of a chain-dance. In that formation, packed under the rafters, spilling out into the kitchen, they played *Silly Auld Man* and *Pen the Ram* and a kissing version of *Babbity Bowster* as a result of which many of the young lads and lassies vanished from the assembly to search for romance among the rhododendrons.

There was more feasting, more drinking, then with midnight approaching and energy flagging, there came the final performances; a sword-dance done by the groom's friends, a mime of the New Milkmaid which was very comical, and to end, a rendering of *Cameron's Lass* by the bride's younger sister. She was a thin, pale child who sang so sweet and mellow that Gaddy could smell the August grasses and hear the sigh of the south wind in the glens of Cruachan. She felt her eyes mist with tears. She leaned on Coll. The melody rose sad and vibrant. Young folk were drawn from the bushes, auld wives from the ben and hard-bitten boozers were lured from their cups to listen in wistful silence to the plaintive song from the girl in the white gown who, like Cameron's lass, seemed too frail to be long for this world. When the song was over there was a stillness in the inn, broken at length by the stamp-stamp-stamp of the piper's brogue on the flag at the door as he struck up *The Blythesome Bridal*.

The bride and her soldier groom had slipped away to make ready. They were setting out on a journey that night, fulfilling an old tradition of Inchbuck. Coll and Gaddy rose with the others and followed bride and groom out of the inn to be led by the piper along the track to the lochside.

There was no curl at all on the water and a sixpenny moon stood above the shoulder of the mountain, marbling the snow. After the heat and confinement of the inn, the cold clear space seemed to isolate folk, separate them one from the other, as they walked cautiously, two-by-two. Even the very old followed along the path lit by young men with pitch-torches, and the moonlight was bright enough to show them the way to the shore. Margaret, the bride, wore a full black cloak sewn with a red lining over her gown. In her arms she carried a new round loaf, a jug of good ale and a cannikin of fresh milk. She walked very tall by the side of her gaudy young husband in his swaggering kilt.

"Where will they go, this hour of the night?" Gaddy enquired of the woman behind her in the line.

"Across to the islet of Inchbuck. McAlpine has a wee steadin' there. It's been attendit with a fire an' clean linen an' water on the boil. Tomorrow, they'll need to be back at Inversnaid. But tonight they'll be alone."

The islet, only a few hundred yards from shore, seemed to float upon the water like a clump of wool. A lantern had been set in the steading window to guide the couple. The boat was a high-gunwaled craft with two stout oars. It was held afloat at the water's edge by Margaret's brother and a sergeant from the garrison, bluff men but solemn. Groom and bride climbed into the boat and the soldier settled himself at the oars. A lantern was placed in the stern. Margaret sat with her bundle in her lap, face towards the prow, as the men pushed the boat into deep water and Kenneth, her husband, bent and tugged on the oars. The piper played a haunting tune that Gaddy had not heard before, half triumph and half lament, while the boat drew across the loch. The company waited on the pebble shore until the boat-lantern came to rest against the outline of the little isle, and went out. The pipe-tune rose clear and loud across the silvered water, then, abruptly, ceased. By tree-track and lawn the guests wended back to the inn, quiet enough except for a bit of giggling and a guffaw or two from those too young and lusty to understand that there was more to love and life in marriage than bodies bouncing on a bed.

Toddy was waiting, tea too; but soon the wedding guests began to take their leave. Tomorrow – today – they would be up at dawn to face the unrelenting labour of the steadings, indentured to byre and stall, flock and herd and the uncharitable master of the land.

While Coll patrolled the herd, Gaddy collected Elspeth from the back room. Lifting the sleeping child into her arms, she carried her to the loft by the north gable where the inn-keeper's wife had dressed a bed for the travellers and a wooden cot for the bairn. From below, Gaddy could hear revellers laughing; six or seven men had gathered round the hearth to make a night of it. But the loft, reached by a stair through a trap at the far-back of the kitchen, was secluded. Gaddy put Elspeth down and rocked the cot until the bairn settled, then she carried the candle to inspect the bed.

It was big enough. Its bolsters were inviting, its blankets thick. She turned it down and found it clean.

She glanced at the open trap.

If Coll did not sleep here, where would he sleep?

She unbuckled her broad leather belt and unwrapped her skirt, unbuttoned her bodice and undressed to her shift. Like a swimmer taking to the sea, she plunged into the icy bed and pulled the blankets up to her chin. She felt small, small as Elspeth, in the low, partitioned room. She soon warmed, though, warmed into wakefulness and wistful need of him. She wanted him to lie by her through the night hours of that strange, fulfilling day. But she would not ask it. She sensed that he must come to her, that it must be his wish and his will that would cause it to happen. She heard footsteps on the stairs, the creak of the trap, the thud as he lowered it on its rope, closing off the inn kitchen.

"Gaddy, Gaddy, dear, are you asleep?"

"No."

On the islet of Inchbuck the young bride would be clasped in her husband's arms, lost in the awkward joy of inexperience. She would be mad in love with the novelty of her freedom and of being needed. But Coll was not a boy; nor was he like Donald McIver who would have taken her roughly, noisy with drink and thick with pride. Donald would not care who she was or what they had shared that day or in years past, the history that held them together.

But Coll Cochran cared, cared too much perhaps.

He blew out the candle.

She heard him undress. She felt the blanket lift and his cold legs dunt against her calves.

"God!" he said, with a choked sort of laugh, "You're as warm as new bread, Gaddy."

She found him with her arms and folded his lean, sinewy body against her. He smelled of spiced wine. He shivered when he touched her. He disentangled his arms and blew

on his fingertips considerately before he placed his hands
on her breast.

She waited, needing him, patient though for his response
to match her own. He twisted, cowled the blankets over his
back and lifted up her shift. His gnarled, calloused hands
were gentle upon her breasts, his mouth loving. She lifted
herself against him, one hand upon his back, pressing him
tenderly against her until he no longer needed restraint, nor
heeded it, and Gaddy's warmth became heat, and ardour,
like love, was shared.

Conscience tweaked Coll as he approached the farmhouse.
He had been around Dyers' Dyke for half an hour, settling
the new herd to its pasture and grooming and feeding the
ponies. He had done these chores first, before approaching
either house or byre. He was as keen to see the calving cows
as he was to meet Etta. Gaddy had left him at the road-end,
had gone off with Elspeth to the Nettleburn. Perhaps the
highland woman too was ashamed of what had taken place
between them. Coll had not talked of it on the drove from
Inchbuck. Now, at a minute or two after three o'clock, he
approached the door of the farmhouse.

It was significant that Etta had not come out to greet
him. He expected her to be sulking. But he noticed that a
freshening east wind unravelled a spool of woodsmoke from
the chimney-head and flapped at laundered sheets and
blankets on the drying line; noticed too that the tack of
curtain on the windows had been washed and the glass
wiped over. He unlaced his boots and took them off at the
door, for the step had been white-clayed.

"Etta?" he called.

He went into the kitchen.

Pans bubbled on the hob. The hearth was swept, the
room tidy. The aroma of mutton broth expelled the sickly
odour of medicines.

"Etta?"

She came out of the back room with an expression of
pleasant surprise on her face; and her Sabbath dress on.
She had washed her hair and re-curled it, she presented
such a picture of wifeliness that Coll's conscience tweaked

again, like a gripe. Perhaps he had frightened her by staying away so long. If only she had listened to him, had sympathised with his need to turn profit. She came forward, smile fixed. She turned her cheek, offering it for a kiss, something she had not done in fifteen years.

Coll put his muddy boots by the fire to dry.

Outside, the wind was stronger, bustling about the yard and whisking a few grains of chaff through the open door. He almost expected Etta to chase them away with a broom. Instead she drew out a chair at the table, at a place set with spoon and fork.

"You'll be hungry after such a lengthy drove?" she said.

"Aye."

He took off his jacket and hung it on a chair-back and warily seated himself. He could hear the rustle of her bombazine overskirt, a garment that had not been out of the moth-proof chest for a decade. For reasons he could not explain, the sound made the hair on his neck rise.

She put soup before him, served in a plate, not the usual wooden bowl.

She broke bread for him.

Coll picked up his spoon, paddled it in the soup, made himself eat as if nothing at all was the matter. He felt queer, though. It was as if she, Etta, had not only guessed what had taken place but had been there in the loft of the inn at Inchbuck, disguised as a moth or a spider, watching. Coll coughed, keeking at the woman out of the corner of his eye. He had intended to be silent, making no outward show of guilt or apology. He had decided not to give her the satisfaction of ignoring him. He had not expected this treatment, however. It disconcerted him greatly.

"I . . . I bought new beasts. Good stock, Etta."

"So I see, so I see."

Her brightness was unnatural, frightening. Coll paddled in the soup again then blurted out, "We sold the stotts in Dumbarton for a tidy profit. We'll be all right now for a year or two. Back on our feet."

"Mr Sinclair was here."

"What did he want?"

"Just to see what was what."

She turned, a plate of boiled mutton steaming in her hands. She gave him a simpering smile, raddled with loyalty. "I told him I didn't know where you'd gone or when you'd be back."

"What did he say?"

"You never can tell what Sinclair's thinkin'."

"Aye, but did he *say* anythin'?"

"No. Where were you?"

The question was supposed to be off-hand. She held her head back, wreathed in steam from the slop of flank mutton.

"Dumbarton, then up by the loch lookin' for strong stotts."

"Did you have a long drove today?"

Coll tucked into the soup, eating quickly. He spoke with his mouth full. "Aye, from Inchbuck. We . . . we stopped there yesterday night. We had cattle to see. Fine beasts, though not many. Stayed at the inn."

He would have embellished, would have yielded to the spell that seemed to draw confession from him. Strenuously he resisted, withholding all mention of the soldier's wedding. Instead he fished in his pocket and brought out the leather bags, unlaced them and tipped guineas out on to the table. "See."

"My, my!" Etta commented. "My, my!"

He wanted out, wanted to be away from her unctuousness, her cloying insincerity. He loathed it worse than he loathed her spite. He had grown too used to despising her. The new, loving wife was a turn she could not sustain with conviction. He left the coins by his hand while he finished the bread and broth. The empty plate was replaced by boiled mutton. He cut into the meat in haste, forking lumps into his mouth, chewing. He made no more attempt to fan her enthusiasm for the results of the drove. The guineas lay as neglected as crumbs upon the table by his hand.

"How're the cows?" He glanced round.

She was standing with arms folded under her breasts, head cocked, a little disturbing smile shanking up the corner of her lips.

"No calves yet?" he said.

"Aye, the one."

"Queenie?"

"I took her milk just an hour ago."

"Took her milk?" Coll dropped his fork and got to his feet, the chair scraping on the stone floor. "Has she o'er much, is that what you're –"

"It's dead."

"The cow's dead?"

"Daftie," said Etta. "The calf."

"But . . . but how?"

"Mr Sinclair calved her, an' it seemed fine." Etta paused. "It just died."

Coll dragged his boots from the hearth and stuck his feet in them. He strode out of the kitchen to the byre. Damn him for his patience, he should have come here the instant the herd was behind the hedge. It was not that the calf was crucial to his accounts now – a week ago the loss of one bullock would have been disastrous – but he hated losing an animal, especially one that should, by all the laws of husbandry, have been born alive and thrived. Queenie was a healthy cow. He had tended her with great care. He slowed as he entered the shadow of the byre and walked slow to Queenie's stall.

She was tethered, comfortable enough, with a slack bag and pink udders. She turned her head as he came to her hind end and looked back along her flank. Though he was not fanciful when it came to dumb animals he imagined that there was reproach in her brown, long-lashed eyes.

"Aye, lass. There, lass," he murmured.

She lowed softly as he stooped to inspect her underparts. He saw nothing untoward and, stepping back, glanced round to find the calf.

It was stretched on a bank of mouldy hay in an alcove at the byre's end, tethered, Coll noticed, by a length of rope around its foreleg. He could see the tracks where it had been dragged from the crib. Queenie groaned and rattled at her bites as he knelt to examine the calf. He stroked its soft hide and muzzle. Why had the creature died? Its belly was tight with milk, its rump was clean, its mouth free of obstruction, its neck glands normal. There was no reason why it should have died, no reason at all.

He massaged it with his palms.

The long body and legs were still pliable. The cadaver had not yet begun to stiffen. It could not have been dead more than a few hours.

Sniffing, Coll leaned over the corpse.

The odour about the bullock's muzzle was pungent and unmistakable.

Ether.

Coll scrambled to his feet. He turned for the byre door, shouting, "*Etta. Etta.*"

She stood in the blustery light of the doorway, the bombazine overskirt flapping, the beady, brittle smile still on her lips.

Furiously he stalked towards her; then stopped.

No, damn her, he would not give her satisfaction, would not acknowledge her wickedness, would not admit that he knew how the calf had died and the reason for it.

"Aye, dear? What is it?" his wife said innocently.

"Fetch me my skinnin' knife."

"What was it happened?"

"Nothing," Coll Cochran said.

FIVE

Black Cattle

Balnesmoor boasted no regular midwife for there was no woman in the manse, spouse to the minister, to force the pace of progress by paying for one! The laird and his ladies could not have cared less about the breeding habits of the peasants, having enough to concern them with their own. Unintentionally, however, the Bontines and their kind advanced the state of natal care in the parish, for the fecundity of the landowners meant that Harry Rankellor had to keep in tune with obstetrics whether he wished it or not.

Fortunately Harry Rankellor did not agree with the opinion of many of his fellow physicians that childbirth was an indelicate and disagreeable branch of medicine best left to the other sex, nor did he put up divisions of rank when it came to exercising his skills. He gave the same gruff attention to a cottar's wife as he did to a Bontine lady, though he charged a much smaller fee, or none at all.

Give help when needed, was Rankellor's motto, otherwise let Nature take her course; keep the leeches in the bottle and the purgatives in the box. In the heat of summer, though, carrying a child could be both tedious and difficult and, since women worked as hard as men at hay-making and harvest, many terms were aborted in the stubble or behind the whins. Rankellor could never decide, no matter how he pondered, whether it was stoicism or ignorance that drove the women so, or – and this was more in keeping with the cynical side of his nature – was it greed to take gain while the sun shone, the few mean pence that the hired work paid in season?

One day in late August she came to the back door, by the kitchen. He could see, when called by Purvis his cook, that she had come across the moor from the Nettleburn and not by the village streets. She was known to travel thus, up where other women never went unless there was work, by paths which men avoided unless they were poaching. She had the child with her, Elspeth, her body lengthening, the chubbiness of infancy gone from her limbs. She walked straight and swinging for a wee thing and evinced no shyness when he, hands on hips, stooped to admire her. Complexion fair, hair thick, eyes blue and clear; she would be a beauty when she reached womanhood – he would stake a hundred crowns on that — provided she did not grow too tall and gangly. But now she was the picture of a sturdy, pretty country child, an endorsement if ever there was one for the benefits of uncontaminated air, regular nourishment and not too much coddling.

He asked the Patterson woman what he might do for her; his eye told him that it was not the child that was ailing.

Gaddy opened her hand and showed him a one-guinea note, one of the old issue printed in two colours, thumbworn around the edges. He was surprised. He had heard from Leggat that there had been business done with cattle for Coll Cochran and had learned that the Nettleburn, as well as Dyers' Dyke, was a thriving rig after a fair spring and fine June weather. Even so, he was a trifle put out to be offered a banknote by a woman to whom, a bare ten months ago, he had doled out a charitable shilling.

"What's this for?"

"You, sir. I'm needin' a doctor's advice."

Purvis was hovering, ears waggling. He ushered the woman and child through the kitchen and into a panelled corridor that led to the gun-room.

It was a gun-room no more; he kept his pieces and rods in cabinets in the library. The ground-floor chamber was now used for occasional consultations, mainly emergencies caused by accidents, and for storing drugs and chemicals. Rankellor acted as his own apothecary, though grinding, measuring and mixing was done by Robert, Purvis's eldest boy. Wooden shutters were kept half-closed for sunlight damaged some chemicals and botanical preparations. Rather than bother the boy to open them, Rankellor lit a lamp upon the cluttered table. Through the slip of window glass sunlight streamed down upon garden and moor. It seemed odd, at noon, to be in here at all, since Rankellor was by habit a night-time worker.

"Well?"

She told him, eyes down, what she thought had happened and why she had taken the original step of calling on a physician.

"I assume," said Rankellor, "your drover returned one dark night, half-drunk, and begged forgiveness in your bed?"

"Drover, sir? Och, you mean Donald. No, no. He never came back this way at all," said Gaddy Patterson ingenuously.

Rankellor was irked by qualities that he had previously admired, prodded – he would admit – by the proffering of that damned large banknote. She was so abominably assured. She did not patronise him, of course, as the wife, say, of young Gibert Bontine did, all lofty and haughty in her sickroom finery. But Gaddy Patterson was of low class and the assurance she evinced lay in sources other than that of privilege or wealth, the banknote notwithstanding. She was not even ashamed of her foolish pregnancy. There was a kind of heresy here which disconcerted the doctor.

A pregnancy it was, however; Harry Rankellor had no difficulty in establishing that fact. He required no trappings of modesty to do his work, no sheet draped like an Arabian tent over his head and the lady's abdomen, no scowling female relative in the room to ensure that decency was not betrayed, and none of the usual euphemisms for bodily functions. When he asked direct questions the highland woman gave him direct answers, without blushing evasions.

"What age are you?" he asked.

"Thirty-nine years."

He nodded. He put several questions about her menstrual periods, considering the possibility that fullness in the breasts and cessation of regular bleedings was a sign of termination, rather than conception. His examination, though, put that possibility out of the basket.

She was long in the tooth for a primigravida but strong-boned and in excellent health. She had, she said, weathered the sicknesses that had accompanied the first weeks of the condition. She made light of discomfort. She had been driven to seek his advice only by pain, and worry for the child in her womb. She had felt the baby kicking. Rankellor took little heed of this statement. From experience he knew that many sterile women who desired a child imagined a quickening. Nevertheless, the absolute signs were there. Foetal heartbeat came positively through the bell of his "trumpet". He could palpate the foetal parts. Gaddy Patterson was into her fifth month, probably the twentieth week.

Rankellor instructed the woman to rise from the dorsal position. This she did with alacrity. Elspeth was by the window, seated on a wooden stool. She had watched her mother's unusual contortions with serious concentration but had seen nothing that might shock her. Gaddy Patterson had, indeed, addressed a few quiet words of comfort to her adopted child while the doctor conducted his examination.

Rankellor poured alcohol on to his hands and laved them. His puffed shirt-sleeves were tied above his elbows. He let them down.

"Aye," he said. "It's as you suspected."

"The pain . . .?"

"You're not as fat as you look," said Rankellor, reassuringly making a jest out of it. "The abdominal wall . . . you understand?" Gaddy nodded. "The wall of membrane, tissue and muscle is thin so the baby's floating comfortably in its sea of liquor. I can feel it there, push it about like a cork." Rankellor elected not to add anxiety to anxiety, though he was not altogether satisfied with the mode in which the baby was presented. "The stitching pain is naught but bubbles of gas pushed against your ribs. You've no bleeding, no bleeding at night?"

"None, sir."

"The birth will occur about Christmastide."

"Aye."

"You must be careful not to over-strain yourself in the interim."

"I've work that must be done."

"Do it with as much ease as you can. Do not, woman, lug sacks or heavy turfs up and down that damned hill or

somebody'll find you lying dead with a ruptured stomach."
That should be enough to put the fear of God in her,
Rankellor thought. "I would also advise against eating
green vegetables, since you do have a touch of the bloat."

She nodded. She had smoothed down her dress and skirts
and fastened her bodice. In spite of the warm weather she
was well muffled up, a sign that she was willing to respect
the mores of the village. Harry Rankellor knew of women
who, when pregnancy was confirmed, would not leave their
rooms, let alone their houses, as if the condition was shame-
ful, like leprosy or a syphilitic canker. The antithesis of those
overly modest ladies were the cow-wives and pickers who
would waddle to the rigs, with bellies hanging as brazen as
brass, and tackle a full quota of hard-hoe or binding with
only a suck at their tobacco pipe or a pull from an ale
bottle to deaden discomfort. He could not imagine Gaddy
Patterson behaving thus. She would surely want this child
as desperately as she had wanted the foundling. She would
care for it as she had cared for Elspeth. According to
Leggat, though, the Nettleburn patch was demanding and
strenuous.

The Bank of Scotland note was on display again.

"It's far too much," said Rankellor.

"I'll need to pay, sir, lest I need to come back."

"Can you afford it?"

"I have some money put by."

"How did you acquire money?"

"From Mr Cochran. I earned it by work."

"Old Coll? He's the father, is he?"

She did not answer him. At least she had some sense of
propriety. Rankellor was relieved. He did not like the idea
that she had been bestowing her favours indiscriminately
about the hill farms. He could understand why old Cochran
might want her. Etta Cochran's whining would shrivel any
man's parts like frost does swedes. If Rankellor's wife had
been as interested in Balnesmoor gossip as she was in the
doings of Edinburgh society then perhaps he might have
heard a whisper of what had been going on at Nettleburn.
But his informant was the minister and sometimes Mr
Leggat could be incredibly naïve.

"Very well, I'll take your pound note. For it, however, I'll see you safe through your term."

"But you're a man?"

"Would you prefer to have some filthy auld wife from Harlwood or Balfron pawing at your belly and wrapping the poor slippery mite in docken leaves to ward off witches?"

"I can attend . . ."

"However it is done in Ardelve," said Rankellor, "it's not done slackly in my parish, not if I can help it."

He plucked the banknote from her hand, folded it and placed it upright in a jar of pipe tapers. He had a considerable liking for money and would not misplace the note. He also had a sense of duty and would do for her more than he had promised. Besides, he was somewhat concerned about the mysterious stitching pain. She was not the sort of woman to complain unnecessarily. In four or five weeks' time he would have a better idea of how the baby lay and if there was the likelihood of mis-presentation. Lusty though she appeared to be, at near forty years of age the woman would need his ministrations if labour was to be trouble-free and the baby born unmarked. Perhaps, though, it would be best if the babe was "lost" before completion? The notion that that was why she had come here crossed his mind. He discarded it. He had a vivid recollection of that night last November when Gaddy had pleaded for the foundling. Mothering instinct was strong in Gaddy Patterson, he would stake his reputation on it.

"Does he know; Cochran?"

"No."

"He should be told. I mean, damn it, he'll see for himself in a week or two, especially if he . . ." Doctor Rankellor left the sentence unfinished.

Gaddy Patterson said, "I'll tell him soon."

"Who'll tell his wife?" said Rankellor bluntly.

Again the highland woman gave no answer. She summoned the child from the stool by the window and took her hand.

"It'll be very hard on you, raising two wee ones *and* working the ground," said Doctor Rankellor.

He might also have told her how bastards were discarded

from the community of Balnesmoor. Bairns were conceived on the wrong side of the blanket with depressing regularity, indeed they were, but the results were shushed-up or patched over. If the girls were young and not too ugly they would be found husbands from the pack of herd-lads and day-labourers or, if there was no help for it, rushed out of sight to spend a year or two slaving for a relative a decent way off from the home place.

"I'll manage," said Gaddy Patterson.

Was it possible to survive on dreams and determination? Was that even a fair question to ask in connection with this woman? It seemed that she cared for money and survival in more than rudimentary terms. She had a confidence in her own being that was rare in the stratified realms of Balnesmoor. Besides, he had known many a rascal and black sheep prosper in spite of ranting ministers and the reading of texts proving evidence to the contrary. Rankellor did not regard Gaddy as an evil influence, but she puzzled him greatly.

She nodded her head, happy enough it seemed. She repeated, "I'll manage fine, Mr Rankellor."

He showed her to the kitchen door and out into the garden.

He watched as she steered Elspeth over the stile and on to the sheep-track that meandered down from the moor. He watched for a long time while the figures of the woman and her bairn became smaller and smaller. But Gaddy Patterson did not, as field women do, become one with the land. Even against that vast warm counterpane of heather-hag and bracken she retained a peculiar individuality.

Taking off his wig, Harry Rankellor fanned himself with it. He must have a word with Leggat. If trouble brewed because of this turn of events the minister would bear the brunt of it, through Etta Cochran and that champion of the righteous, James Moodie, both of whom, Rankellor guessed, would soon become obsessed with sin.

Coll had never fully understood before what a deal of difference money could make to a man. Without money, in that summer of the year of 1792, he would have been up against it with a vengeance, in debt not only to the laird but in debt to conscience too. It was not conscience about his treatment of Etta that pricked him but vexation about Gaddy. He was torn between the essential duties of the farm and his desire to be with her, to share her struggle down at the Nettleburn, a patch which, without logic, Coll had come to regard as a burden that she maintained as much for his benefit as her own.

Money, though, made all the difference. Without it Coll would have been tossed about like an old shirt worried by a collie. He used some of the money to remove the strain of decision. Since Gaddy would take little from him, except the fees which she earned by labour, Coll was obliged to repay her by sharing his time with her. No misery this; he wanted to be with her and the bairn every minute of every hour. Time spent on his own place, and particularly about the farmhouse, seemed like a penance.

After he had paid off the overdue rent, he purchased seed and poultry and quantities of certain chemical substances which Sinclair recommended as being beneficial to sour ground. He installed two levels of pipe drain and paid for a new ditch. He paid for a section of hedge to be constructed at the whinfield gap – and he hired an able-bodied young man with sound credentials. Docherty, from Fintry, would carry out the heavy work throughout the growing months. At long last Coll had got ahead of himself. With Docherty to do the general farm work, Coll had energy to spare. He used it to pay his debt to Gaddy Patterson.

Each evening, when the business of the Dyke was done or Docherty could tend it unsupervised, Coll set out for the Nettleburn with a wrap of tools across his shoulder and his pipe in his mouth, to "dig in" with the woman on her rented patch. He trimmed the hut, built stalls of wood, set shelves, and erected a neat boxed bed under the renovated beams. It seemed to take no time at all to do the wheen of jobs that needed doing, whether on the land or the dwelling, for Gaddy was with him, turning the foot-plough or loading the sled which the pony would pull away. Root crops were in on time, pea-rigs and beans too. Bracken was cleared and stones removed from sheltered grass. Coll bought her two she-goats and, through Sinclair, acquired six hens and a fettlesome young cockerel which went daft home-making in a roost Coll had built around a broad-boled oak. Gaddy accepted the gift of livestock without much demur for, as Coll persuasively pointed out, at least the steading now smelled like farm. Her reluctance to accept gifts from him stemmed from the fact that she encouraged his love-making and did not wish to seem to demand payment for it in any shape or form. She gave herself to him out of love, not calculation.

To touch her, to hold her in his arms, to lay himself against her soft, strong body heightened in Coll the feeling that he had been summoned back from the brink of the grave to discover some blink of pleasure that had eluded him not just in middle years but throughout his life.

Etta had rapidly reverted to her usual pattern of behaviour after that single, insulting exhibition of wifeliness on the evening of Coll's return from the drove, with the calf lying poisoned in the byre. Because of Gaddy, though, it seemed but a skiff of time from March to mid-summer and beyond with the Dyke in fine order, the Nettleburn taking shape, and the aches and pains thawed out of his body. Coll cared not what his wife thought of him, or Sinclair, or any of the long-nebs and kirk-buddies in the village. He was a changed man, and glad of it. So changed was he that he heard Gaddy's astonishing news without fear or panic, envisaging perhaps some ideal Eden in which he resided for the best part of every day up on the hill with the highland woman and the two bairns, the Dyke ticking over, and Etta locked by her own choice in an eternal sulk.

Gaddy had chosen the moment; they were together in the dusk on the sward above the burn. The first owl was calling in the tree-tunnel and the last of the rooks flying home high, high overhead. Coll had his pipe in his mouth and held Gaddy's hand in his. In the hut, Elspeth was fast asleep. Even the lively little she-goats had settled on their long tethers, folding themselves down for the night. On the shoulders of Drumglass, the ewes of Bontine's hill flock summoned their lambs to them, their baa-ing calls rolling soft across the slope like balls of thistledown.

Gaddy came right out with it.

"Coll, I have a child in me. Our child."

It was as if he had known, though he hadn't. If he had thought of possible consequences of his loving he had never spoken of it. But it must have occurred to him, farmer and cattle breeder, that his virility and his love might quicken her barrenness. It was, after all, a thing to do with the body, less mysterious than the heart or the soul, and more predictable too.

"Are you sure of it?" He puffed his pipe, still holding her hand as if she had announced nothing more startling than the fact that one of the hens had begun to lay.

"Aye. I've seen Doctor Rankellor."

Now he reacted, turning his head in sharp inquiry. "The doctor? Are you sick?"

"No," she said. "But he was the one who told me."

Coll smiled indulgently. "Did you not know for yourself, Gaddy?"

She saw the humour in it. "I could hardly believe it."

"By God, the tongues'll wag now."

"Is that all you have to say about it, Coll Cochran?"

He put the pipe aside and drew her to him down on to her knees on the grass like a little young swain pledging his troth, not a man as aged as he with a woman as heavy as Gaddy. Facing her, he placed his arms about her waist.

"I'll build a crib for it."

"Time yet, Coll. It'll not be here 'til December."

"Are you frightened?"

"What way should I be frightened?"

"It'll be your first, will it not?"

"Aye."

"Late in the day, Gaddy."

"Is it too late, do y' think?"

"It wouldn't have happened if it'd been too late."

She snuggled herself against him, head on his shoulder.

"I'll put by for the winter," said Gaddy. "That's what I'll do. I'll have wood in the store an' fodder for the chooks an' goats, for us too. It'll not be any bother, Coll. Not in December when it's quiet."

He knew then that she was different, set apart from the

flock, where so often the imminence of a child was treated as a dour inevitability, something brought down like a curse upon sinners. He thought of his sons and daughter in their infancy; of Etta, who – even she – had shown a stir of love with the first born but had lost it soon with the thankless task of tending. "Thankless" was Etta's word. It was as if his wife had been drilled into thinking that it was *she* who must be thanked, not Providence, for bringing that small form of deliverance. How he had loved them when they were young, revelled in their dependence on him. It was poverty and poor ground which had sapped his strength and his hope, turned them away in their adulthood. Poverty and rain, poor ground – and Etta. With Gaddy there was no cycle of inevitability. She stood apart from it.

In the hut a candle burned, set safe in a little circlet of stones. With the coming of twilight he could smell the land gathered around that solitary glimmer, see the shapes of the white she-goats like ghosts collapsed upon the grass. It dawned on Coll that he had fathered again and differently. For a moment, awareness of mortality possessed him. He gave an involuntary growl, like a dog dreaming.

The grizzled old gods of anxiety plucked at him, girning.

She would be forty years old when the bairn was born. He would be fifty-five. By the tally the child might be orphaned before it was old enough to fend properly for itself. He struggled not to think in plain arithmetic terms. But if it was a lad – ah, then he would be keen to see the boy settled on Dyers' Dyke, to have the hill farm handed on, all flourishing.

As if she guessed what troubled him, Gaddy linked her arm in his and led him back across the field to the hut.

"There'll be two of them," she said. "Elspeth an' the new one. If anythin' happens, they'll have each other to lean on, Coll."

"I was just thinkin' . . ."

"Don't," she said.

". . . what Etta will say."

"It'll be my bairn, not hers."

"Come now, Gaddy," said Coll. "She's still my wife."

"I'm your wife."

"Aye, in all but name."

"I need no name."

No name might do for Gaddy but the truth would not go away. In the ledgers of the law and the kirk, Coll Cochran had a name already, whether he liked it or not.

Purposefully he pushed melancholy aside as they stooped into the hut, into the firelight and candle-glow, and closed the door on the darkness.

Coll did not inform his wife that Gaddy Patterson was carrying his child. Etta was unapproachable on any level and Coll's head full of plans that he wished to bring to fruition before he committed himself to revelation and the nightmare of wrath that would surely follow. Those few who knew the truth did not share it with the community. Rankellor, Leggat and the wily Sinclair were privy to the secret, each in his own way galled and disappointed at Coll Cochran's temerity; yet none of the three stalwarts cared to broach Etta. Long before October, there was a conspicuous bulge about Gaddy's belly which only an exchange of skirts and broad belt for a shift-like garment kept hidden. Somehow, though, Gaddy's pregnancy remained unannounced and did not become public until the autumn.

It was many years since anyone in Balnesmoor had been denounced to the congregation but there were still those in the pews who could remember how stimulating Sabbaths used to be and how the prospect of hearing a catalogue of moral crimes, followed by a scalding sermon, had fair sharpened the week. Over the spout of the pump, in the reeking atmosphere of the inns, behind drawn curtains and closed doors of cottages, however, screeds of misinformation were perpetrated by the imaginative upon the curious. Much of it was "genteel" but much was so disgustingly ribald that it became separated from the sturdy highland woman and the lean, stooped farmer who became in turn as disembodied as characters in bawdy verses and sniggering songs. If it had been known that *she* was big with *his* bairn, speculation would have taken on an edge. Everybody would have waited to see what the other *she* would do and how *he* would worm his way out of that murky corner. But the folk of Balnesmoor had far more to occupy them in August and September than whisperings and speculations about Gaddy, Coll and Etta Cochran.

Labourers bore the brunt of the compound character of the season. Securing the harvest demanded the participation of every man, woman and child in the parish whether on small, penurious plots or swagged across Bontine's exuberant fields. Bands of reapers and binders, paid by the piece, were imported to bolster the local forces and, after dark, the inns hopped with hard drinking and carousal. Gaits and stooks and pillars of straw sprang up along the strath and, in spite of a phase of weary weather, the ground was shorn by scythe and sickle, acre by interminable acre. On the hill and in the parks the ewes were drafted and the tups brought to them. Sir Gilbert was never far from the sight of his darling flocks, spying on their matings, his guns racked up until that important business was complete and he could get away after grouse and partridge with an easy mind. In weavers' cots looms clacked incessantly, for spinning-wool and fine strand were plentiful after the July shearings, and the Moodie sisters were out upon the roads at all hours, collecting and delivering. In the manse garden Mr Leggat, brown as a mulatto, slaved to fill the vacant slots from which early crops had been removed. He had no time and, in truth, no inclination now to call on Gaddy Patterson who, by all that he had heard, was not only pregnant but prospering.

Meetings of the Harlwood Agricultural Improvement Society were suspended in the summer months. They would not resume until the autumn sales were over and the nights came early over Drumglass and Dumgoyne. Besides, there were not daylight hours enough for all Sinclair had to do and he saw precious little of his wife and sons. Autumn was a peculiar time for the animals, with a tendency to disease; sheep to hepatitis, calves to quarter-ill and horses to colic. Sinclair spent much of the day examining and doctoring or urging the grooms and cattlemen to caution in the lull between harvesting and the gathering of cattle for the Falkirk trysts. It was on this point that the laird's man and Coll Cochran clashed horn to horn.

Coll's hand-picked herd flourished well on the grass of the Dyke and, as Gaddy had promised, had strapped on beef at several pounds per day. Never had the Dyke produced such desirable beasts, fat and glossy and dew-muzzled. Coll had decided that he would winter only a small herd this coming year and try, with Gaddy's aid, to make enough capital to see the Dyke through until the spring. Then, as before, he and the highland woman would take to the road and buy grazing stock in March, by which time the baby would be old enough to travel with them. But first came the trysts, the three great sales of Falkirk, which attracted English dealers by the score and at which Bontine's agents would sell the Balnesmoor herd in one parcel, unless prices could be bettered by a split.

The Falkirk sales were accommodated on a 75-acre common at Stenhousemuir, held on the second Tuesday in the months of August, September and October. In August there was, by comparison, but a pickle of cattle, much of it local. In September the range was shared with sheep and many horses. But in October, when the highland drovers teemed down from the north and eager buyers from the south, near half a million pounds in sterling would be floating free. Most of the cattle were beasts intended for wintering but there was a sincere and separate market for summer fatstock too. It was into this more specialist ring that Coll intended to toss his little herd. He had, however, neglected to tell Sinclair. When the Bontines' cattle buyer, a wrinkled kernel of a man named Wardrop, with cunning brown eyes and fingers as thin as earthworms, turned up at the Dyke to count heads and shell out the standard eight pounds per beast, willy-nilly, Coll packed him off with a flea in his lug.

Sinclair was up on his gelding post-haste, with a face like phizz. He came late and caught Coll on his way over the gate at the Nettleburn with Gaddy and the little lass waiting by the post to welcome him.

"What's this, Coll Cochran?" Sinclair shouted from the saddle.

"I'm visitin' a friend."

"About the cattle."

"I'm sellin' my own herd this year."

Coll's stoop was gone, shoulders were square, jaw thrust out. He held the pipe like a little dirk, jabbing with it, irked perhaps at being delayed in his pleasure with the highland woman, though, as Sinclair could see, she was well filled out now with the bastard child. Though the night was fine and warm, Sinclair was scratchy with fatigue.

"What about the winter?" he shouted, still fighting the horse and setting up a violent stour of dust from the track.

"I've enough to winter, Mr Sinclair. They'll winter fine an' be all the better for it. I might be in the market for some heifers, though."

"We had a bargain, Cochran."

"Bargain? I remember no bargain – Sinclair."

"Why did you not take green money in the spring?"

"I'd no need of charity."

"What about all those years when you were glad of it?"

"Aye, what about them?"

He had one hand on the gate, standing proud as if he and not Sir Gilbert owned moor and hill and all the land you could see with the naked eye.

"Have they to count for nothing?" said Sinclair.

The woman was behind him, holding the girl by the hand. He could see by the earth on her smock that she had been hoeing the potato runs which she, with Cochran's aid, had ripped out of the bracken and which, by the foliage, would yield a top crop in October.

Coll said, "What will your man, what will Wardrop recommend you pay me?"

"Eight pounds."

"I can make twelve or thirteen. Wardrop'll have told you how handsome the beasts are, and how fat."

"On the laird's good grass."

"On *my* grass. I'm tenant not bondserf, Mr Sinclair."

Sinclair got the gelding steady at last, up by the gate, the horse's flanks heaving as if it had caught the full tilt of the rider's annoyance, though Sinclair's voice was calm again and his face almost without expression. The woman did not move or utter a word, yet Sinclair had the sensation that there was a communication between her and the farmer, that it was her voice he was hearing through the man's mouth.

"I'll let them go with the laird's herd for eleven pounds an' ten shillings," Coll Cochran said.

"Sell them yourself."

"I presume –"

"Presume what you like, Coll Cochran. I'll not bargain nor allow any agent of Sir Gilbert to bargain. The arrangement has never failed before. I'll not have you makin' mock of it now."

"Mock? To put my own work into my own pocket? It's not me that makes a mock. It's –"

Sinclair interrupted him. "What if you make less than you think?"

"I'll suffer the loss."

"And the estate will suffer you beggin' an extension on the rent come term-time?"

Coll leaned his body into the field-gate. He had no evident anger in him, only an assurance that made him seem in all things, even age, Lachlan Sinclair's equal. "No, Mr Sinclair. I'll beg no more. I'm free of your dung-hawk now an' I'll not let you rake me into the pile again, damned if I will."

"Coll Cochran," said Sinclair, "you are mad."

"Mad? Fesh, Lachlan, I've only just turned sensible," said Coll. "All it took to let me out was *this* much extra silver." He held up his hand, thumb and forefinger pinched together. "This much. There was no trick to it after all. A single breath of capital an' I got sparks where before you'd only encouraged smoulder."

"I warn you, Coll, be careful how you meddle."

"Are you afraid others'll follow my example?"

"By God, but you're cocky. Nobody hereabouts envies you anything, Coll." Sinclair swung the gelding in full circle and dragged it closer to the gate. Towering over the couple, he pointed his willow switch at Gaddy. "That woman's not your wife. You'd do well not to forget it."

"Is that intended to be a threat, Sinclair?"

"I've more to do with my time than threaten fools," Sinclair said. "I'm givin' you a last and final chance, Coll. Nine pounds sterling for each sale beast in your herd."

"Unacceptable, Mr Sinclair."

Lachlan Sinclair would not humble himself or besmirch the standing of his masters by haggling with a love-stunned old man. He dug his heels into the gelding's flanks and rode off, dipping and canting his body to avoid the hanging oak boughs, late-summer dust clouding behind the mount.

Coll leaned out to watch the grieve's departure, then, still gripping the spar, laughed harshly. "Aye, that'll show him. He'll not tamper wi' my independence any longer."

Gaddy put a hand on Coll's arm and he turned quickly, suddenly concerned, anxious for her opinion of his stand against the grieve. She gave none, however, though her silence seemed like affirmation. In Gaddy's eyes there was evidence of the pain that had gripped her several minutes ago, a sudden stitch that stretched like a hot wire between the bones of her hips and that did not diminish much below a hard tense ache.

Coll did not notice her pain, though, for he did not look into her eyes. At that moment he was wrapped up in himself, too arrogant to pay anyone much heed, not even Gaddy to whom he owed it all.

It was a lowering grey day with flicks of rain carried on the wind, enough to grease the site at Stenhousemuir with surface mud, though the common was rugged and moorish and protected by thick banks of broom. The drove along Carron Water through the hills of Fintry and Kilsyth had been no pleasure jaunt like the trip to Dumbarton. It had cost Coll a stiff horn-fee at two new toll gates too, though the road was a far cry from being a turnpike. Gaddy, Elspeth and the farmer had spent a miserable night huddled under a canvas in the cart on a patch of scant grazing leased from the Grahams' factor and a long haul from the tryst. They were up before daylight, however, and hoped to reach the sales before noon.

Latterly it was slow going. Knots of cattle and sheep milled at every bridge and bottled up at the spittal by Den Lodge.

Coll's enthusiasm waned when he first cast eyes upon the bedlam of the tryst itself. It was a sea of sheep, cattle and horseflesh with new rivers feeding it from all directions. The road from Stirling was a heaving flood of wet hides, red, black and brindled, spilling sluggishly into deltas of open ground for leagues around the sale rings. The noise was like thunder out of hell, audible for ten miles around, a hoarse suspiration of accumulated sounds that seemed to hang like fog on the wind. Now and then the fluctuating roar would be pierced by the fierce bellow of a bull driven mad beyond endurance or the sickening scream of a dog trampled under-hoof. Fourteen head of fat cattle seemed a puny offering to make to this Moloch.

Though he had been to many a bustling market, Coll had never seen anything to compare with it. He felt quite frightened as he steered the cart after his string of cattle with Gaddy, bravely taken to foot, bunching them tight with a stick in each hand, shouting like a harridan at anyone who barred their progress.

On the ridges of neighbouring farmhouses, perched on stacks and clinging to the few trees that wide-bounded the common, herd-boys tried to spot and separate their parcels of cattle among the bushes, shouting and gesticulating to men on the ground who, often with snarling dogs to add to the panic, flailed into the broom with crooks and staves to thrash out the strays. Pack-horses and carts were tethered in a ragged oval between the waiting herds and the paths that ran like spokes into the hub of the show rings. Stalls, bankers' booths and sagging refreshment tents were ranked in lanes congested with dealers, their women and wives. The stench of beer and cooking meats mingled with dung and urine, thickened by smoke from camp fires and braziers.

At last Coll was forced to abandon the cart. He tied the nervous ponies, fore and aft, to stakes hammered into the ground. He flung them corn but knew they wouldn't settle and prayed they wouldn't tear their traces or drag the cart on to its side. Theft too was a possibility, he supposed, yet he had no alternative but to leave the cart, for Gaddy had wended on, leading the string, and he had lost sight of her in the crowd. Hurrying, he picked up the herd threading a route among wicket sheep-pens.

Several minutes later Gaddy turned them into a narrow

haven behind a long grey-green marquee where beasts should not have been. Had the leasee of the site, an Edinburgh brewer, caught them he would have stampeded the herd, though Coll had no way of knowing it at the time. Empty barrels and extra trestles were all that the space contained but Coll was nervous lest the cattle catch their hoofs on the tent ropes and break their legs. Gaddy checked them though, sticks fanned, her voice rhythmic enough to draw the bullocks' attention and hold them comparatively still. Soon they began to crop the waves of dry stuff that backed the tent, and snout about for green grass. Coll had Elspeth in his arms. For once, the child was fractious.

"I'll take the bairn."

Relieved, Coll handed over the child who quieted a bit in her mother's arms. It was not good for Gaddy to carry the girl for long. She had enough to contend with, with her bulk and the weight of her stomach which, this last week, had grown large. She was red-faced and breathless, Coll noticed. His concern for her increased his anxiety and his desire to be out of this brawl.

"How d'we get them to the buyers?" he asked.

"We bring the buyers here," said Gaddy. "So long's nobody spots us, they'll be fine where they are."

"But how d' we know who'll be interested in fatstock?"

Gaddy grinned. "I'll awa' an' bell our wares."

"What's that you say?"

"Shout," Gaddy explained.

"Is it always like this?"

"It'll be worse come Thursday."

"God, I hate it."

"Then you'll never make a drover, Coll."

"What'll I do?"

"Keep them from tramplin' down the tent. I'll be back soon."

With Elspeth slung on her hip, Gaddy went round the end of the marquee, leaving Coll to look out for his beasts.

In truth, she was quite relieved to be on her own. She had a purpose additional to that of crying for a buyer. It was better if Coll did not learn of it. Besides, the farmer's abhorrence of crowds did not chime with her excitement.

Like Donald McIver, she thrived on the clash and confusion of big fairs and gatherings.

Safe away from the cattle runs, in the avenue of pitch-booths, she put Elspeth down.

"Hold tight to Mammy's hand," Gaddy instructed her daughter.

Walking at a pace to suit the child, she started along the field to find the stance where horses were sold and trade done in highland garrons.

It was one of the clock or after. It would fall dark by six, though mechanical salesmen and pedlars of seed, tools, dogs and drink, jugglers, acrobats and fiddlers, tobacco vendors and purveyors of hot food would light their stalls with torches and lanterns and, if the rain did not worsen, would entertain the crowds for most of the night.

Pennants fluttered and huge dolls made of straw, dressed in plaids and tartans, nodded from their ropes above cloth-iers' benches. A massive brown bear, chained but un-muzzled, ate a loaf with its paws, legs spread out and its back against its stake just like a great gross ploughman taking his dinner. Elspeth's eyes popped. She clung to Gaddy to make her stop and the bear, champing away, peered over its paws at the child and gave her a throaty growl by way of greeting which made Elspeth jump. Gaddy reassured her and they watched the bear stuff bread into its maw for a minute or two until a boy with a barrow laden with clocks distracted the bairn and they followed him as he pushed his load, all chiming and tinkling, to a cart where his father had gathered a crowd by sticking lighted tapers into his mouth and blowing out blue flames. In a more leisurely frame of mind Gaddy would have allowed her daughter to view these wonders but she had only so much energy to spare in her state of pregnancy and moved on, pulling Elspeth gently behind her.

She could tell by the smell where the horse sales were taking place. Soon she heard the familiar whickering of ponies and the flathering neigh of draught horses. She led her daughter to the open front of the tent within which the dealers gathered. Clouds of tobacco smoke and whisky fumes veiled the men within. The babble of voices was deafening, a medley of dialects, from Skye Gaelic to guttural Yorkshire jabber and the sing-song accents of Fenlanders and men from the Broads.

Lifting Elspeth, Gaddy entered the mouth of the tent and craned to scan the throng. She saw hats of drab stuff and beaver, flat-tops, broad-brims and bowl-crowns and many blue bonnets, fists gripping whisky cups raised above heads, and all sorts of weathered faces, old and young, lumpy, frank, sly and brutal, and among them, at last, one that she recognised.

"Callum," she called out. "Callum."

The packmen, for that was Callum McSween's trade, turned and looked in her direction. Bawdy remarks were exchanged as McSween came towards her, toting a glass of whisky in one mittened hand.

"Ach, Gaddy Patterson, is it yourself then?"

"Aye, it's me."

In his fifties, Callum McSween had always been jovial. He peered at Gaddy from under heathery brows. "Bonnie as ever, m'luckie. What's this?"

"M' daughter."

"Do ye say now? Aye, by the look o' ye, Gaddy, ye're makin' up for lost time."

"Is Donald here?"

"Donald? Do ye mean McIver?"

"Is he here at the tryst? Have you seen him?"

The packman brought his mouth to the rim of the glass and sipped whisky. He wiped his stubble chin and his eyes turned sly. "Has Don'l got this t' answer for?"

"Is he here?"

"Aye, somewhere about. Come back wi'out ye, lassie. Droppit home in December, if I recall. I heard tell ye'd desertit him. Is that a fact?"

"They're not his bairns," said Gaddy.

"Far o'er bonnie t' be any o' yon brute's makin'. Aye, aye," said Callum in sympathetic agreement. "Here, lass, I've a spool o' fine silk ribbon in the pack wid suit the hue o' the wee lassie's hair, aye, an' a set o' pins t' go with it."

In Ardelve and on the road Gaddy had always enjoyed Callum McSween's company. Now, however, she could not abide his heavy, foetid breath or the leer in his rheumy eyes. When he reached to pet Elspeth, Gaddy drew away. The packman sensed the slight and stiffened.

"Have ye a man, then?" he said.

"Aye, I've a man."

"What'll ye be wantin' wi' McIver? Ye're no' in any state for a tumble."

Gaddy's revulsion was growing by the second. She stepped back into the open air. Behind the packman the gang of kindred spirits egged him on.

"Has Donald ponies with him?" Gaddy asked.

"Aye, aye," Callum McSween answered. "But . . ."

Gaddy turned and hurried away. She was appalled at her reaction to a man she would once have called a friend, like a dozen other companions of the drove roads.

Callum McSween was doing what he had done for thirty years and would do until the day he fell down and died. There would be nothing left after him, no mark upon the world he had inhabited. With sudden insight Gaddy saw that it was from that fate she had escaped. She had seized upon a half-chance to turn her life from the feckless destiny of men like McSween. Her search for the drover had been but a whim, a bit of a need to show off how she had blossomed in Balnesmoor, to rub Donald's nose in the fact that there was a man who had sired a child and made growth in her body. She wanted Donald to see how she had not only survived but had flourished, and to suffer a pang of regret for all that he had neglected to do for her. But suddenly it seemed unworthy of the status she had gained from Coll. She was of the village now, not the croft, a creature of the hearth not the camp fire. She drew Elspeth to her, and tarried, unsure of quite where the ale tent lay with Coll and the herd behind it.

And then she saw him.

He had a string of garrons, fewer than usual for the time of year. There was no sign of a mare, only the pony-string. Donald had been bawling at them and, with his face turned towards her, his jaw opened and the shout stilled on his lips. He recovered quickly from his surprise. With a swagger he came over to her. She saw the dogs, Birkie and Lug, tear out from among the hoofs and, crouching, pin the pony-string. She saw too, even before Donald spoke, the girl, a lithe girl with brown tangled hair and bare brown legs clasped round the garron's wet belly. At most she was seventeen. She would have been bonnie but for the bone-broken nose which had set badly and squashed her nostrils wide like a piglet's. She was saturated and sat shivering without any sign of interest in the lively surroundings.

"By God, Gaddy, you'll not be tellin' me y' found that one under a bush," Donald roared.

Before Gaddy could resist he had locked his forearm about her waist and was patting her stomach as if she was a mare in foal. His familiarity repelled her. Made timid by the stranger's loud approach, Elspeth whimpered and scrambled to hide behind her mother's back.

"Sonsy as ever y' were, m'luckie, damned if you're not. Far too damned sonsy for me in that pretty state."

If Gaddy had hoped to confront him with evidence of her prospering life and wring even a droplet of remorse from the man with whom she had spent so many years she was doomed to disappointment. Donald was more arrogant than ever.

"You canna match yon wee thing, except for weight." He waved his arm in the direction of his new mistress. "Found her in Dalmally in need o' a good strong man t' look after her. Her name's Janet."

"I'm pleased for you, Donald."

Unlike McSween there was no drink on Donald's breath. He managed to be fiery and aggressive even when cold sober.

"The bloody mare died on me. Her an' the foal. Died o' the cold in Jan'war. Lost one o' my lads too, the youngest. Carried t' his Maker a month syne. A mercy, since he'd been ailin' sore all winter." The death of a son caused no catch in Donald's voice. He bawled that information too as if boasting of it. He went on, "I dealt wi' the Logans. Got a herd from them for good money. I'll have a new mare in a year or two, you'll see. I'm promised a female foal off the Edderly when I have the fee."

She listened distantly, without interest, while he shouted news at her. He was not oblivious to her condition or to the presence of the child in her arms but such matters did not affect him. If he had paused, caught breath, said that he had missed her or that he had even spared one thought for her in this last eleven months, she might have lingered. But she drifted away from him, just drifted, while he danced beside her, filling her ears with the garbage of *his* life, *his* deals, *his* idiosyncratic concerns.

She wanted to be rid of him, to be back with Coll, and yet as he cried at her Gaddy felt a soft curl of pity for the drover.

"I've a fine herd o' garrons here this year. Top price, top price for them. Money in the bag. No need for me to take t' the southern tracks this season. You'll not be seein' me in the likes o' Balnesmoor."

"I'll need to away, Donald."

"She bides in your loft, her, Janet, in your auld blankets." He hesitated then put his questions diffidently, his eye turned towards the refreshment tent, as if he was thinking of drink and not of her. "Who put it there? Was it the minister? Did y' bed the cloth, eh?"

"A farmer."

"Not yon sly wee kirk elder, eh?"

"He's a farmer."

"What brings ye here to Falkirk?"

"I'm sellin' fatstock."

"How many head?"

"Fourteen."

"No market for fatstock," Donald announced. "Waste o' time comin'."

"We'll see," said Gaddy. "Donald, I'll have to go."

"I'm not keepin' you."

She glanced up at the girl on the garron's back. Her head was canted and she was staring at Gaddy through lank brown locks, staring stupidly, without comprehension, spit dribbling from her mouth – a daftie with a broken nose.

Donald did not have to shift his gaze to know what Gaddy had seen and recognised.

141

He was silent, sullen, ashamed.

Whatever Gaddy had hoped for from the meeting it was not this.

Gently she said, "I wish you good luck, Donald."

He nodded, lids heavy, lips slack.

"I'll need –" she began.

"Go," he said. "Away back t' your damned farmer."

Obediently Gaddy hurried off.

She would never see Donald McIver again. Whatever circumstances contrived for her, with Coll's protection or without, the roads back to the crofts of Cruachan were closed. She would, she must, lie on the bed she had made for herself in the parish of Balnesmoor.

Elder Moodie knew he was chancing his arm. He had only recently heard rumours that the highland woman was with child and had not dared substantiate the truth by consulting Etta Cochran. He was mortally afraid that he would be the harbinger of the grave and wounding news and would thus personally suffer the first wild wave of Etta's wrath. He was well aware, as was half the village, that Gaddy Patterson had louped off on another cattle jaunt with old Coll Cochran and he had pored long over his edition of *Forms of Process in the Church of Scotland*, and had even had his mother copy out certain relevant passages, to help him concentrate his mind on a decision to proceed without further delay.

One paragraph in particular encouraged him to take the bull by the horns that very Tuesday night.

"Yet," the book stated, "when no sufficient evidence by testimony can be mustered, pregnant presumptions, such as suspicious frequenting in her company, of being *solus cum sola in loco suspecto*, in suspect postures and suchlike, which he cannot disprove to the satisfaction of the kirk-session, may so lay guilt upon him as to show that there appears no other way of removing the scandal but his appearance to be publicly rebuked therefor."

The line of Latin, which he did not quite understand, convinced James Moodie that law and precedent would support him in his petition to the session and would provide a cudgel with which to beat the liberalism out of the Reverend William Leggat.

"Suspect postures"; how James Moodie's imagination fondled that judicial expression, though it wasn't quite as titillating as *solus cum sola.*

Armed with Minute Book, Ledger of Accounts, volumes of kirk procedures and the digest of quotations which his mother had sewn into a thin sheepskin wrapper, Elder Moodie arrived in the session room at the back of the kirk at a quarter past six. He secured a seat at the end of the long table from which position, directly opposite the minister, he might spread influence over the other three elders.

Water-glasses, wax candles and dark curtains drawn over the one window made the session room as official and secret as a man could wish.

In due course the other elders arrived. Mr Parry and Mr Dewar came together, having stopped off at the Ramshead to oil their vocal chords with a wet of whisky. They were followed by the Reverend Leggat, washed and shiny after his labours in the garden; finally by Mr Symington, breathless and rushed as usual. Moodie's fellow elders were in the mature tradition of fitness and Godliness which the call to the office required. Only Jamie Moodie's zeal had rattled him up the ladder in treble-quick time and enabled him to dominate the older men.

Significantly none of those present were tenant farmers. In the last decade, trades people and craftsmen had infiltrated the sanctum of the kirk and, in Balnesmoor at least, had supplanted rustics in positions of power. Mr Parry was a seed merchant with shops, under the management of his sons, in Stirling and Dunblane as well as Harlwood. Mr Dewar was a stone-cutter, plasterer and builder with eight men in his employ and never a chisel or slate in his plump hands these days. Mr Symington was an agent for an assessor of land, a mysterious occupation which seemed to involve much measuring and the co-operation and respect of the landed gentry of the Lennox. Any of the three could have bought and sold Jamie Moodie, though none of them would have dreamed of mentioning it in the weaver's presence. Mr Moodie was recognised as a craftsman in his own employ, though he owned little except the loom and a couple of shelves of books inherited from his father.

The session was constituted with a prayer from Mr Leggat.

The prayer was duly entered in the Minutes, otherwise, *ex facie*, the meeting would not have been considered regular. Business proceeded without a flutter, dealing with incomes and out-goings, the appointing of plate-elders and other matters essential to the spiritual advantage of the parish. Recent entries to the registers were read aloud, births, marriages and deaths, then, with the Reverend thinking of getting away home to his supper and bed, Elder Moodie threw a torch into the hayrick and set the evening ablaze.

Elder Moodie's opening statement was unequivocal.

"It has come to my attention an' has raised in my breast the deepest concern that a member of this parish an' of this very congregation has committed an act, or acts, of considerable moral depravity, to wit," said Mr Moodie, in full oratorical flow, "adultery with a woman other than his wedded wife."

"D'ye say now, James?" put in Mr Parry who had somehow missed the wafting gossip about Coll Cochran of the Dyke. "Who would that be?"

"The party guilty of this scandalous offence against God an' Nature," James Moodie embarked on his reply soberly, "is by name Coll Cochran."

"Dod, now how did he manage that!" exclaimed Mr Parry.

"Lasciviousness knows no barriers of age," said Ian Dewar. "I'd heard tell something of the sort was going on. I commend Mr Moodie for bringing it to our attention."

"Who might the woman be?" said Mr Parry.

"The woman," said James Moodie, staring up the table at the minister, "the woman is a drover's wench of mature years who came into this parish as a mongrel an' was welcomed by certain gentlemen of standing; a gesture of sound Christian intention, I've no doubt, but one which, in retrospection, seems a wee bit ill-considered in the light of the obscene behaviours which have materialised since."

"Sure ye can't be meanin' the Patterson woman?" said Mr Parry.

"Aye, he means the Patterson woman," said Mr Dewar.

"You never let dab t' me about it, Ian."

"I did so. I told you –"

"Gentlemen," interrupted the Reverend. "I am aware of the situation to which Mr Moodie alludes."

"Aye, Minister," said Mr Symington, "There's no' much dings past your lugs, right enough. I take it you've interrogated the sinners?"

If Peter Symington had been rehearsed by Mr Moodie he could not have framed the question better to suit the purpose of embarrassing the minister.

Mr Leggat hesitated.

Elder Moodie's gaze bored at him like an awl.

"I . . . er, no. In point of fact, I did not care to give an excess of credence to the sinful aspect of the relationship."

"Oh-aye, Mr Leggat, but you did *know* of the relationship?" said Ian Dewar who, like James Moodie, disliked the minister's moderate approach to parish government.

"I knew of *a* relationship."

Moodie was busy writing, pen flying fast as a swallow from page to ink-stand.

"A relationship with this drover wifie?" said Mr Parry who was only pretending to be naïve.

Mr Leggat studied his elders. All except Moodie were in the evening of their lives, in late fifties or early sixties. Dewar was a notorious tippler, red-cheeked and with a bulbous nose, a miser who treated his workers abominably. George Parry was a thick-set, self-satisfied fellow, bald and smoothly plump, generous to charity but not to his sons who had no share in his thriving business and stuck it out only to protect their inheritances. Peter Symington, as thin and fussy as an old spinster, had the dank eye of a conspirator and would be, without doubt, Moodie's apostle.

"Cochran employed her on his farm in the beginning of the year," said Mr Leggat. "It was Sinclair who made the introduction."

"Cochran, then, was seducit," Dewar stated.

"Gentlemen, I question if this matter is publicly censurable," said Mr Leggat.

"The highlander's an unmarried woman," said James Moodie.

"I know she is."

"The Form of Process is unequivocated an' clear as day, sir."

Mr Leggat knew what was coming. He sighed and stroked his chin and wondered in his heart if perhaps the kirk-session were right and he had somehow committed an indiscretion by taking the woman so readily into the bosom of his kirk.

James Moodie flicked open the parchment wrapper and read aloud in his best big Bible voice. "When an unmarried woman is known to be with child . . ."

"With child? Dod, there's a turn up," said Mr Parry.

". . . the same gives ground to a kirk-session for a process against her, an' after she is cited, she is to be interrogate who is the father of that child; an' in this case, where there is a child, whereby there is an undeniable scandal, the keeping secret of the father a ground of greater offence, an' of suspecting many innocent persons, if she discover not the father she is to be looked upon as contumacious an' cast from the circle of the Christian parish forthwith."

"Yes, James, I'm familiar with the Form," said Mr Leggat.

"But the father's not in doubt," said Symington. "It's Cochran. Everybody knows she went away wi' him to the cattle sales. She's away wi' him at Falkirk tryst right this very night."

"Besides, he spends nights in her hut at the Nettleburn," said Ian Dewar. "We could find a dozen eye-witnesses to attest to that."

"Will she *confess* who the father is, though?" asked Mr Parry.

"She can hardly deny it," said Symington.

"She might," said Dewar.

"Then we'll confront her with Cochran," said Symington.

"She's 'confrontit' him once too often by the sound of it," said Parry.

Mr Leggat, slapping his palm on the table, said, "Enough

146

of this libellous speculation. May I remind you, Mr Moodie, that the Forms of Process also stipulate that all matters relating to adultery and the getting of child are first to be dealt with by private treating, in meekness, charity and seriousness. Did you not think to write down *that* passage?"

"Minister," said James Moodie, "the eyes of the community are upon us. We've delayed long enough. She's with him e'en now."

"Selling black cattle," said Mr Leggat. "That's what she's doing with Coll Cochran."

"You don't sell cattle in the dark, sir."

"She has her child with her," said Mr Leggat. "Her first child, the foundling."

"Exposin' the poor wee bairn to scenes of uncleanness," said Moodie.

Mr Leggat got to his feet. "Very well, Mr Moodie, let us have it on the table. What particular form of punishment would you have me call down on Cochran and Gaddy Patterson?"

"It's not for us t' say, Minister," said Parry.

"It's a matter for much discussion," said Symington.

"After we ascertain *all* the facts," said Dewar.

"Out with it," said the minister angrily.

"Cochran must be rebuked in kirk, and make due promise to commit no further sin on pain of excommunication," said Elder Moodie.

"And the woman?" said Mr Leggat.

"Sent out of the parish," said Moodie.

"We are not empowered to do that," said Mr Leggat. "We are not court judges that can sentence her to transportation."

"Perhaps not, Mr Leggat," said James Moodie. "But we *can* redeem the children. That much *is* within our power."

William Leggat was aghast. "Redeem the children?"

"The first bairn was a parish foundlin'. We can take her back into parish care at any time of our choosin'," said James Moodie. "If we believe the second child's in moral danger we can even –"

"How can you sit there and make such wickedly cruel suggestions?" shouted Mr Leggat. "Without an appearance by either party, without giving either of them an opportunity to repent?"

"I'm statin' what it's within our power to do."

"Old Cochran this month," said Ian Dewar silkily. "No saying whose bed she'll be creeping into next month."

"There's a wife," said James Moodie. "A good, honest, God-fearin' member of our kirk. Is she not deservin' of the protection of this session?"

"I cannot believe my ears," said Mr Leggat. "Is it possible that we are crying for blood?"

"Hardly that, Mr Leggat," said Parry. "Hardly blood."

"To take away the Patterson woman's children would be an offence against all principles of charity, of Godliness. It would be downright pagan. I will not be a party to any process which might lead to such a conclusion," Mr Leggat cried.

"Then the whole matter must be took to the Presbytery," said Elder Moodie.

"It's Mr Leggat who must do that," said Symington.

"But if Mr Leggat won't do it," said James Moodie, "then we may accuse the minister of collusion in scandal an' take the case to the Presbytery ourselves."

"Hah!" Mr Leggat said. "So that's it? I am to be challenged by my own kirk-session and disgraced before my peers."

"Did you not give the woman place in the kirk?" said James Moodie. "Can you deny you baptised the bairn?"

"I will not deny it," said Mr Leggat. "What's more, I would do the same thing again tomorrow, without a qualm."

"We have uncovered uncleanness an' exposed the filthy behaviour of two sinners," said James Moodie. "Will you not act, Reverend Leggat, as the kirk commands you t' act?"

"The kirk does not command. God and Jesus do not command," said William Leggat, in a fine-drawn, positive tone. "Neither the woman nor the man are evil."

"Meaning?" said Ian Dewar.

"I will arrange the outcome of this matter in privacy and with discretion," said Mr Leggat. "With compassion too, gentlemen, since there seems to be a sad lack of that Christian virtue in this room tonight."

"Without recourse to the Presbytery?" said Ian Dewar.

"It is not necessarily a Presbytery affair."

"How many times did you, Mr Leggat, visit the woman at her dwellin'?" said James Moodie.

"I . . . I . . ."

"Did you make her gifts, personal gifts?"

"I took her fruit; foodstuffs. For the child."

"Did y' not visit her a dozen times or more?"

"Great Heavens, Moodie! Are you suggesting that I had carnal relations with this woman?" Mr Leggat slumped down in his chair, shaking his head in incredulity.

"I'm suggestin', with due respect, Minister, that you'd do well to abide by what we tell you."

Few folk, certainly none of the Balnesmoor elders, had ever seen such an expression dash the Reverend Leggat's features. Mildness was gone; in its place was a scowl of such contorted rage that Parry and Symington quailed before it.

"I am not on trial, James Moodie," Mr Leggat cried. "Nor will I be a tail wagged by the likes of you. Any of you. You are servants of the Church, as I am. Yes, oh, yes, sin *is* serious business but it does not only have to do with carnal things. What you are doing, James Moodie, is sinful too. Why do you want me to persecute the highland woman?"

"She's an influence for evil," said James Moodie, not daunted by the minister's splenetic outburst. "She must be excluded."

"It isn't Gaddy Patterson that you have your knives out for. It's me, is it not? Hence this threat of arraigning me before the Presbytery, of making a dreadful scandal where, as you well know, none exists."

Ian Dewar said, "But there is a scandal, sir. The woman has seducit the husband of a good wife and has gotten herself with child by him."

"That I admit," said Mr Leggat. "I have every intention of dealing with the offenders, man and woman, and of following the process laid out for our guidance. But mark what I say, Mr Moodie, I will not see two infants torn from their mother and tossed into parish care just to satisfy your thirst for righteousness. Nor will I publicly humiliate a man whose life has been nothing so far but an arduous travail. No, gentlemen, I'm not so jealous of my own reputation that I will immediately bow to your petty desires."

"Be that as it may, Mr Leggat," said Moodie, "as elders elect of this parish it is incumbent upon us to protect the spiritual an' moral wellbeing of –"

"Stuff and nonsense! I'm weary of your silly word-plays, Moodie, particularly as the word 'love' doesn't seem to have a place in your vocabulary."

Spots of colour burned on the minister's cheeks. It took an acute effort of will to bring his temper under control. He noticed, however, that Moodie had been so distracted by the vehemence of the argument that he had ceased writing in the Minute book. If a verbatim report appeared in that record now, Mr Leggat decided, he would charge Moodie with deliberate falsification. At root, it was a lame manoeuvre. Moodie had sufficient basis of truth in his call for reprimands to create terrible upheavals in the parish and within the presbytery.

William Leggat was not afraid for himself. He feared for Gaddy Patterson whose weaknesses had somehow become strengths and whose strengths these hypocritical petty men saw only as vices. Sermonising would not bring them round. He needed time to negotiate a compromise between his duty to the parish and his illogical wish to protect folk who, if not innocent or blameless, did no hurt to God. If he had to pick a person to publicly reprimand, better it be Cochran's wife. Vaguely he understood what motives stirred Moodie to badger Gaddy Patterson. Moodie wanted the woman in his power so that he might sneer at what was good in her and dull that which was lively and bright, to sour the sweetness of a love he could not share and therefore could not tolerate. Moodie's "goodness" was stained by selfishness. He wanted respect, position and power instead of affection. He was not alone in that perversion of human need.

"We will conclude with prayer," Mr Leggat announced.

"Conclude? We haven't finished, sir," said Ian Dewar.

"For this session, Elder Dewar, we *have* finished."

"Bow your head, man," advised Mr Parry.

"Wait," said James Moodie. "What decision has been reached, Mr Leggat? Particularly in respect of the child?"

"No decision, Mr Moodie. I will, I give my Christian word, examine and explore the possibility of charges with the man and woman in question. I will discover the truth and then, and only then, will we consider what it is best to do for the community, for the sinners, and decide if they are truly fugitives from God's grace."

"When will this be done?" Symington asked.

"On the couple's return to Balnesmoor."

"Without delay, Mr Leggat?"

"Without delay, Mr Moodie," answered the Reverend. "Now, Mr Moodie, will you kindly bow your head?"

"I will, Minister, I will," said James Moodie who might comply in deed but never, ever in kind.

Indeed the couple in question had the stoop of fugitives during their return from Stenhousemuir, though more from rain than any spiritual failings.

It had not gone easy for Coll and Gaddy, though in the end profit had been good. No keen and reputable buyers had answered Gaddy's call on Tuesday afternoon so the herd had had to be moved to a ring site and Coll had had to dig into his pouch to pay the fees. But on Wednesday morning, after another sodden night in the cart, Gaddy had gone out into the crowds and had found a clutch of butchers and victuallers to whom, in little parcels, the herd had been sold at a low price of thirteen pounds rising by twenty-eight shillings for the last pick of the beef. In all the taking was £206. 7/- which, after deduction of tolls and fees, left Coll with almost £190 on the sale. It was better by far than he would have done with Bontine. Considering that it was his second take of the year, he was delighted with it. Satisfaction was diminished, however, by the rain and the long plod along the Carron Water, with Elspeth, nose running and a cough tickling her throat, crying in Gaddy's arms. Though Coll was used to wet work, it seemed to leech the pleasure of the trip. He wanted only to be home again.

If he had known what was waiting for him there, Coll

might have snitched the pony round and headed south with his mistress and his foster bairn and his purse of money and never have returned to Dyers' Dyke.

It was closing in to dusk before the cart wheels sucked out of the muck and on to the stones at Main Street's end. Over Drumglass cloud swirled low and October rain fell like a muslin curtain. Early lights blinked here and there in the mansions and the cottages as wearily Coll guided the pony along the familiar route towards the road-end that curved up to the Dyke.

Gaddy and he had spoken hardly a word to each other, not even during the short rests that they had taken along the road, more for the ponies' sakes than their own. While he had Docherty to attend the evening's chores, Gaddy would have to feed hens, see to the goats and light a dead fire from scratch before she could begin supper. It would have been a nice thing if he could have taken her back to the kitchen at Dyers' Dyke, to have had her fed and warmed there and for Etta to find a linctus among her stock of medicines to soothe the child's throat; a daft drover's dream, of course.

"Coll," Gaddy shook his elbow.

His eyes had been trained on the pony, seeing only the road unrolling. Now he glanced up.

"What is it?"

"See."

Elspeth had fallen asleep, tucked under the shawl that Gaddy had wrapped around her, her head resting on her Mammy's swollen stomach and her feet on the seat. Her nose ran and her eyes were rheumy and she breathed through dry, parted lips. But it was not Elspeth to which Gaddy called his attention.

They were coming out of the cottage doors, leaning through the low windows, under dripping eaves. Women. Children. Old men.

"What . . .?"

"I don't know, dear," Coll muttered.

The cold in him now came from a source other than his sodden clothes and sopping feet. He hunched his shoulders, drawing his head in protectively even before the first clod thumped against the cart board and made the pony rear in the shafts.

"God, what was that?" Coll looked left and behind.

It was the wife of a labourer. He knew her name. Jessie Stewart; a red-haired shrew of a woman in her early thirties who had given birth to nine children and managed to save only four. She had flung the clod of earth. Even as Coll turned, she flung a stone which struck the bed of the cart and skited along it and, with most of its impact gone, bounced against Gaddy's back.

Instinctively Coll shouted aloud, "Stop that," and smacked his whip across the pony's crupper. The trailing pony was struck by tag of kail, the root-rind thick enough to sting.

Gaddy sank to her knees, back braced against the board seat. She drew her shoulders like wings over Elspeth who had wakened and was crying in fright as the cart lurched across the street and made the corner and went down the hill, Coll shouting in alarm, "Get back. Get awa', all of you."

The commotion drew other cottars' wives to their doors and the cart had to run a gauntlet of flung garbage. It was not only the flying cabbage roots and fistfuls of clay that made the man and woman on the cart flinch and cower but the hate-filled cries of "*Whore. Bitch. Drab. Out wi' her. Out. Out.*"

"Coll, Coll, why are they doin' it to us?"

"Christ in His Mercy!" Coll said. "They've found out."

Coll gave no further explanation. He dragged the rein and sawed the cart into the gutter of Main Street and ran it hard round the corner into the dirt road that straggled up the hill to the track through the trees.

The crowd did not gather and follow, though their jeers trailed them through the opaque grey air for a quarter of a mile or more.

The violence of the outburst shook Coll as much as it mystified Gaddy. The guineas in his purse did not seem suitable recompense for peace of mind and did not add up to payment for his good name. But when he stopped the cart by the shoulder near the field gate and saw the pain in

Gaddy's face all concern for himself evaporated. He took her in his arms and held her and vowed silently that however much it cost him and however bitter the community's show of indignation he would not repent. He would fight them, all of them, for Gaddy's sake and for the right to choose his own road to perdition.

He took Elspeth and held her secure while Gaddy clambered down from the cart.

"I'm comin' home with you," Coll said.

"No, you mustn't."

He managed a grin, wolfish and not without courage.

"Why not, Gaddy?" he said.

"What'll they say?"

"I don't care what they say," Coll answered. "Anyhow, it makes no matter, dearest, not now the secret's out."

She hesitated then nodded and, leading the pony, steered the cart through the gap in the thorn hedge and up towards the Nettleburn.

Coll had made his choice.

SIX

One Foot in Eden

Sin was taken seriously in Scottish parishes. Balnesmoor was no exception. The outburst of violence against Coll and Gaddy had been spontaneous and genuine. While certain God-fearing folk tished and tutted out of concern for the souls of the sinners and believed that punishment would follow the breaking of Holy Commandments as surely as night followed day, the majority gave vent to their feelings for the pure malicious pleasure of it. The physical attacks were not continued, however. Coll tried to carry on as if nothing had happened. In this he was aided by Gaddy who kept close to the Nettleburn and no longer risked walking to the village; and by Etta who, fully informed of the calamity, waited quiet and sly for James Moodie to fulfil his promise and bring down judgement on the pair.

William Leggat spoke in private with Gaddy and with Coll. He was nonplussed by the woman's indifference to public humiliation and he did not have it in his heart to warn her, then, of Moodie's threat to separate her from her children. The minister was even more put out by Cochran's refusal to admit that it was any business of the kirk how many women he chose to support, provided he had the wherewithal which – shaking his purse – he damned well had.

Meanwhile the elders were having a rare time consolidating their position of power, with clandestine suppers and "urgent" meetings in the upper room of the Ramshead in which the ale and expressive Christian sentiment flowed freely and never a prayer was to be heard.

Peter Docherty, the Dyke's hired man, fared best out of it. While the labourer was as mute as a post while up at the farm or around the bothy, he let rip to his companions in the Balfron Inn. Not only could he tell the whole tale but he could imitate to perfection the characters involved, from Coll cocking his leg over the mistress to Etta wrapping herself up behind locked doors in case anybody got a keek at her precious body. Etta's chastity became more of a joke than Coll's infidelities. Gaddy came in for least criticism. The boozers of Balfron were earthy men and sensed in Gaddy a scale to match their own.

Conversations with Harry Rankellor shed a more oppressive light on the scandal. Mr Leggat was the recipient of the doctor's confidence.

"Hold your water, William," Rankellor advised. "God, or Nature if you prefer it, might solve the problem for you."

Asked to explain himself, Rankellor went on, "I fear that the woman may not bear a living child."

"She seems robust to me, Harry," said the minister.

"There's pain and, I fear, a displace in the womb."

"Can you do nothing for her?"

"I'll do what I can, of course," said the doctor. "But if the babe does not live, would that not absolve you from further action?"

"I don't quite comprehend."

"God's punishment."

"Oh, come now, Harry!"

"I'm no theologian but I do understand the mental processes of the average peasant. If that ill thing does come to pass, and you obtain a promise from Cochran to be discreet, then the affair will fizzle out and the villagers will squander their malice elsewhere."

"My elders, Moodie in particular, will press –"

"What Jamie Moodie needs," said Rankellor, "is a lively companion for his bed."

"Harry, really! I can't see what that has to do with it."

"Our Jamie is a man full of passion in a house full of women. His humour is dark and his blood troublesome. But he will not admit it. I do believe, William, that the benighted chap has convinced himself that needing a mate is in itself a sin."

Mr Leggat said, "I believe he has found outlets for his need. He is, one cannot deny, a hard worker both at the loom and for the kirk."

"Tolerance has its limit, William. Ask Coll Cochran if you doubt me. He is illustration enough, to be sure, of what may happen if need is too long suppressed."

"I am an unmarried person too, please to recall."

"Now, now, don't sulk. You're a different kettle of fish, William. You willingly forsook the dubious pleasures of matrimony for the sake of your vocation. Moodie's vocation is not so yielding."

"Why does he wish me to persecute the Patterson woman?"

"Out of jealousy, perhaps; or out of a reluctance to confess that he is attracted to her."

"I find that difficult to believe."

"Attracted to her liberty, her freedom."

"She has lived a harder life than Moodie, I imagine."

"Ah, yes, William," said Harry Rankellor, "but she has *enjoyed* it."

"She enjoys the child, Elspeth, certainly."

"She has so much love in her. I think that's what Moodie resents."

"And I think I must disagree. Jamie would never fall as Coll Cochran has done."

"Precisely," said Harry Rankellor. "Moodie is mad with himself for not being able to 'fall', as you put it."

"I can't condone this way of thinking."

"I'm making no judgement on either man," said Rankellor. "I'm just pointing out that the heart has more dark nights than the month of December."

"What shall I do about it, Harry?"

"Delay," said Harry Rankellor. "Allow the woman peace until the bairn is born."

"I don't know if the session will permit me to delay much longer."

"Are you frightened of the Presbytery?"

"I'm frightened of the parish, of what will happen to the parish if I'm transferred."

"Where would you be put?"

"Oh, I wouldn't be 'put' anywhere. But I would lose my flock. I could not abide that."

"Thank God I'm a saw-bones and not a man of the cloth," Rankellor said. "Look here, William, if Cochran refuses to make confession of contrition before you and the kirk session, if he won't mend his evil ways by giving up the woman, warn him that you'll have no alternative but to admonish him in public and deny him Communion."

"It's against my grain to take such a step."

"It's the only step that'll appease your elders and satisfy the congregation, is it not?"

"I'm afraid that may well be the case."

"Inform the session you'll commence the process in January. Make some feasible excuse for the delay. But not a move until January, William."

"Why?"

"I told you why."

"Because the babe may not live?"

"Nor may the woman," said Harry Rankellor.

If there had been quantities of ice and snow or if the accident had happened after dark then Gaddy would not have survived and Rankellor's cynical predictions would have been borne out. But whatever God or destiny had in store for the good folk of Balnesmoor depended not only upon Gaddy Patterson's continued presence among them but upon the survival of the girl child in her womb. Two things saved Gaddy; daylight and soft weather.

Through the short days of November and the early part of the Christmas month Gaddy had succumbed to the drudgery of life on the Nettleburn. Each span of twenty-four hours seemed an age. Each simple chore incurred pain and exhaustion.

It was not just the weight of her belly that slowed her movements but a loss of inner quickness. She could not help but believe that the bairn inside her was already dead. There were no little stirrings now, only killing knife-pains, pains which seemed sometimes to be in her mind and not her body, pains for which there were no consolations, not even Coll. Least of all Coll, perhaps. He had become apprehensive of her and she in turn sealed her lips and denied him the truth, though it was plain in her drawn face and crabbed waddling walk that all was not well.

When he asked her, in dread of a true answer, she would tell him, "I'm fine. I'll manage," again and again until neither the farmer nor Gaddy believed it and the litany became a mockery of courage and optimism.

She could not sleep in any position. Lack of proper rest sucked her reserves. She had no thought for what was going on in the village and wished no talk with the minister or even with Coll about the "scandal" that centred around her. She had joined another company. She believed that she was damned and took to brooding about what would happen to Elspeth when she was gone.

Birthing held no mysteries for Gaddy but the workings of nature within her had no rational explanations and she overlaid them with superstitions. She saw herself, in the nook by the wood fire in the cave-like hut, as an altar and the stillborn babe a sacrifice that the kirk, not God, had demanded from her. She was not "sensible" at all in the first eight days of December. Coll, though he came faithfully, never stayed long. He found excuses to be away again, preferring – even – Etta and the familiar miseries of the kitchen at Dyers' Dyke to facing the woman he loved in helplessness.

Elspeth offered Gaddy her only tether, something to cling to in the last weeks of the pregnancy. Even when she was burned up by self-pity and sorrow, slumped under the weight of pain, she drove herself to present a steady face to the child. But she was not altogether sure that she did not hate Elspeth when the child's quite ordinary demands called for effort beyond that which she felt she could make.

"Mam, Mam, Mam." Even the words shot through Gaddy. "Mam, Mam, Mam. Chookie-chookies i' the corn. Mam, Mam, Mam. Spill-milk. Mam. Mam. Mammy."

Coll took up the potato crop and put the best of it into a dry store on a deep shelf beneath the eaves, which was the best he could fashion for it. He bought the small ones for cattle food for the Dyke and paid Gaddy in provisions. He pitted the rest. Even in November Gaddy struggled to give him assistance. But it tired her so badly that Coll could not bear it and came and did the work up by the moor's edge without announcing his arrival, leaving Gaddy in the hut. He racked a great quantity of kindling, brought down a brewer's barrel to fill each day with water drawn from the burn. When that was done, and the interior of the hut as cramped as a locker, there was no more he could do but take Elspeth for "wee walks" to allow Gaddy to rest for an hour or so.

Rankellor made his calls with an appearance of casualness. He dropped by in November and again early in December. He came tramping down off the moor, a fowling-piece under his arm, a spaniel leaping and snuffling at his heels, his game-bag empty. That the visits were not quite so off-handed as they seemed became evident when the doctor produced his listening-trumpet and proceeded to sound Gaddy's heart and stomach.

Rankellor provided words of encouragement and cheer. On the second occasion he left her a box which contained a dozen dough-like pills of laudanum which were to be chewed one at a time in case of need. Gaddy buried the pills in the sod of the moor as soon as Rankellor was out of sight, lest she gave in to the temptation to take them. Even so, there was a part of her, part of the "old" carefree drover's lass, that was thankful for Rankellor's attentions.

If she had consumed even one of the laudanum pills Gaddy would have put her relief down to that. But she had taken nothing, except a little oat gruel and a dish of tea, when she found that the pain had gone away. For the first time in weeks she was entirely free of it. Its disappearance worried her. She put Elspeth out to play in the yard and undressed. She seated herself on a little nursing-stool before the smoking fire. Her breasts were heavy, milk-thickened. As she looked at the great steep slope of her belly, she could see just below her chest-bone a pulsation of the skin. In fascination she watched for a moment then gently kneaded her stomach, seeking out the familiar ache with her finger-tips. There was no trace of it now.

She dressed again then leaned her shoulder against the hut wall and closed her eyes. Now that the nagging stitch was gone, her eyelids became instantly heavy. For almost the first time she felt as if the heavy, mutinous belly belonged to her and was not some strange, separate entity that had been wished wickedly upon her. She felt a glow of hope, of excitement grow out of the relief from pain.

"Mammy. Mammy."

She opened her eyes. "I'm here, sweetheart."

Elspeth appeared at the door. She no longer wore small clothes. She had a little skirt kirtled up about her calves and her feet and legs were bare and, as always, stained with mud. Though it was December the day was quiet and calm, with motionless, unthreatening cloud banded across the hills of Argyll. Gaddy smiled at her daughter.

The child had round eyes and a breathless air of wonder, which was common to her these days when everything seemed magical, even the most ordinary events in the enclosed world of the Nettleburn.

"What is it?"

"Tottie."

Tottie was the name of one of the white goats.

"What about Tottie?"

Lips pursed and hands fluttering, Elspeth made her explanation as best she could.

Tottie, it seemed, was on the roof.

Elspeth was learning about jokes too and had played many a good one on her weary mother.

Gaddy struggled to her feet and listened. There was no revealing grin on her daughter's face, however, and she could hear the crackle of the young she-goat's hoofs upon the thatch, a dry bracken coverlet which she had laid over the sod. A dribble of moist dust pattered into the half-loft where the potatoes were kept. If this original event had happened yesterday Gaddy would not have known how to cope. It would have broken her into tears of anger and frustration. Today, though, with the nagging pain gone, she saw the humour in it and, laughing, went out of the hut with Elspeth and walked round on to the slope.

It was a mystery how Tottie had got on to the roof. The hut, though, was not quite upright and seemed from certain angles to slant back into the rise of the hillside. A bit of a trot and a scrambling leap, ungainly but strong, might have taken her there.

"Tottie, *down*. Tottie, *down*. *Bad* lassie. *Bad* lassie," scolded the little girl, waving her arms as she had seen Gaddy and Coll do when they were herding.

Tottie was cropping at some tough delicacy she had found among the litter, secure enough now that she had attained the heights. The gnawed rope trailed from her neck. The other goat, Marigold, was on her feet at the tether's end watching with considerable interest and envy, *meh-hehing* quizzically. Talking to a goat, as Gaddy had recently learned, was like asking a stone to roll over of its own accord. Goats were as thrawn as schoolboys and could pretend to be deaf when it suited them.

Elspeth had a notion of what might be done. Lifting a twig, she hurled it with all her might at the goat on the roof. The twig had no force behind it and fell harmlessly short.

"No, love," said Gaddy. "Don't throw things at Tottie."

She had no wish to frighten the animal and cause it, perhaps, to fall off the roof's edge and break its legs. Livestock, even goats, were too valuable to risk in accident. Would it be possible to leave Tottie where she was until Coll came? Tottie answered the question. The goat's forelegs crackled through bracken-straw and turfs. She extracted her hoofs with difficulty then in a tantrum bucked. If she turned flighty she might crash through the roof.

Gaddy waddled down to the back of the hut, telling Elspeth to stay where she was. The child was excited, chattering. Gaddy moved the rustic ladder, made of rope and pine wood and only four rungs high, from against the gable and propped it against the wall. She was not unconscious of a certain danger in what she was doing but, with independence strong in her again, she undertook the task as best she could. Picking her way up three rungs of the ladder, she pressed her belly against the stages. She had a stick in her fist and snecked and slapped the roof slope with it, calling out to the she-goat. Sensing discipline, the goat turned her rump to the woman and cropped some more.

Laboriously, Gaddy pulled herself closer to the ragged

eaves and, with her head over the edge of the roof, tapped the stick against the root of Tottie's tail. The effect was explosive. Tottie pranced and butted, then, on hind legs, danced stiffly round and, with a jabbing motion like a pugilist, bounded over Gaddy's head. Forehoofs clipped the highland woman on the head. Unbalanced, she swayed backwards. The short ladder yielded to gravity and, with Gaddy under it, crashed to the ground. The she-goat, uninjured, crashed away into the heather.

Lying on her back, the ladder resting on her stomach, Gaddy saw Tottie's departure out of the tops of her eyes. Though the distance from eaves to ground was only five or six feet, she had had no protection against the dead-weight of the fall. She was winded and shocked and, as she discovered a moment later, bleeding.

Above her, a little way off, Elspeth was transfixed, less in horror than in amazement. Grunting, Gaddy pushed away the ladder. She lifted her upper body from the waist, flapping her arms like fins. Her legs had no feeling in them. For an instant she feared that she had cracked her backbone; then the pain began again, sudden and breath-taking, scalding across her abdomen into her pelvis.

She cried out. Tears squirted into her eyes. She clutched the grass with her fingers as if to hold herself on a spinning wheel. She twisted and locked her elbows as the pain tore across her, and remained half-upright, refusing to swoon. Through tears, she peered at her bare thighs. Her skirts had ruckled up in the fall. She saw blood dapple the white skin.

She sucked in a hollow whistling breath.

"El . . . El . . . Elspeth. C . . . come here to Mammy."

The bairn did not stir. Her amazement had turned to fright.

Gaddy tried to move. Blood trickled on to the grass between her knees. Pulsations low in her stomach, an ebb and flow of pain contracted her muscles. Each expansion brought a stab of pain like a blade made of cold iron.

Gathering air into her cheeks, calm-sounding and hardly above a whisper, she said, "Elspeth. Go to Daddy Cochran's house. Go to the farm."

"Mammy? Mammy?" Elspeth put her thumb in her

mouth. Her nose was running. She tucked her left hand between her legs, knees turned inward in an attitude of awkward coyness.

There was no time for cajolery.

"Go to Daddy Cochran. You know the way. Through . . . through the far gate an' along the track. The way we've always gone."

"Wi' you, Mammy. Wi' you, Mammy."

"Mammy's hurt. Go an' fetch Daddy Cochran."

Elspeth sidled closer. She needed comforting. She came towards her mother, though, as if she feared a blow. Seeking a token of reassurance she put out her hand.

She was hardly more than two years old and the Nettle-burn and the track to Dyers' Dyke were hostile and infinite. It was not that she did not understand Gaddy's instruction; she could not bring herself to leave her mother. In the child's mind, now, the route to the field gate by the oaks bristled with monstrous dangers. Still, she sensed the urgency and desperation in her mother's voice and, perhaps with some innate portent of the future at the sight of woman's blood, stuck her thumb deeper into her mouth, turned and made for the distant field gate under the oaks.

Twisting her head, Gaddy watched her daughter depart.

Another strand of anxiety wove itself into Gaddy's fear, worry for the safety of the bairn. Elspeth would not have to climb or cross water, be liable to encounter stray beasts that might trample her. But the Dyke was a long way off for small, unformed legs, though Elspeth was used to walking. Under the gate she would go, on to the track, along the track to the fork by the high thorn hedge and on to the lift of the lane from which the farmhouse could be seen, even by someone no taller than a thistle. Potential dangers spun persistently in Gaddy's brain, topped by pain. The pain had become spasmodic now. The flow in her lap no longer seemed like liquid, more like dry sand, as if life was running out of her grain by grain.

On the hut roof a pair of carrion crows had alighted to pick over the broken turfs, crabbing like cripples, their beady yellow eyes on the woman below who, weakening, lay back upon the grass and stared unmoving at the sky.

* * *

The lentil broth was dumped down without ceremony. The stuff was thick enough to stick to your ribs, though, and in it floated dods of boiled potato to give it substance. A strip of boiled beef steamed on a plate. There would be but a scrape off it to flavour brown bread for the three of them. Even so, Docherty had eaten worse many and many a time. He had worked on farms where the dinner was so scant you wondered by one o'clock if you'd eaten at all.

There would have been no word of conversation during the meal if Docherty had not been at table. As it was, Coll talked only with his man and Etta addressed herself to neither. That particular forenoon, in fact, Docherty was steering the conversation. He was fishing to find out if Coll intended to keep him on. Winter was a lean time and, since Mr Cochran had so few head of cattle on the ground, Docherty was doubtful if he would be drawing his shilling much longer.

It was Docherty's ears that first picked up the unusual sound. Crouched over his bowl, spoon dripping, he stopped his jaw moving and lifted his head. The kitchen door lay ajar, for there was no wind. No bird or beast had made that noise.

Saying nothing, Docherty put down his spoon and rose.

The Cochrans watched him, puzzled, as he went to the door and, cocking his head, listened intently.

"What d'you hear, man?" Coll asked.

"I thought I heard a bairn cryin'."

"It'll be a callin' cat, like as not," said Etta.

"Nah, nah. Listen."

Coll too came to the door and both men went out into the yard.

"I hear nothin'," said Coll.

Docherty lifted his hands and grinned sheepishly. There was nothing in calf so neither man was drawn to the byre or the field. They had turned back into the farmhouse when Docherty stiffened.

The gable of the byre cut off sight of the road to the village and it was a wonder that the sound was audible at all. It was low and breathless and rode on the still forenoon air like the creak of a cart axle.

165

"There it is."

The labourer clumped across the yard and round the corner and squinted down to the fork in the track where the path from the Bontines' woodland cut into the lane.

He shouted, "Boss, come here quick."

Minutes later, Coll swept the stricken child up into his arms and listened as she blurted out her imperfect account of the accident. He required no detail of embellishment. He had gleaned enough information to prompt him to immediate action.

"Ride down to Rankellor's," he told Docherty.

"I'll run it faster, boss."

"I'm away to the Nettleburn. Somethin's happened."

"Is it . . . is it her time, Mr Cochran?"

"If it is, it's too damned early."

"What about this wee one?" said Docherty. "Will ye leave her wi' the mistress?"

Comforting Elspeth with pats of his large hand, Coll hesitated. It was natural to leave her at the Dyke. There would be no place for her down at the hut if things were as they seemed. Even so, some instinct prevented him taking the bairn back to the kitchen, leaving her alone with Etta.

"Take her wi' you. Leave her wi' the servants at Rankellor's house. They'll look after her."

"Are ye sure about that, Mr Cochran?"

"Hurry, man, hurry."

"Aye, right."

Sobbing, Elspeth was transferred to the labourer's arms to be carried across the moor path to the doctor's house.

Harry Rankellor was well aware what sort of delivery he would be required to make when Gaddy Patterson went into labour. Breech presentations were not uncommon. Certain adroit and daring midwives managed to turn the baby during pregnancy but he had no experience of that technique and was reluctant to try it.

Nature was dealing the drover's woman some devilish cards: prematurity as the result of a fall. He spurred the horse faster, the game-bag slapping against his rump and his wig and broad-brimmed hat slipping about on his head.

Cochran was with her when Rankellor arrived. The old farmer was terrified at the sight of the blood-streaked watery liquors. The farmer, who had birthed in his time hundreds of calves, should have understood the signs. Mercifully, though, Cochran had not tried to move the woman, though he had lifted her head and shoulders from the damp ground and cradled them in his arms. A glance was sufficient to tell Harry Rankellor what was what. The situation was not irredeemable by any means. He was brusque with Cochran, more like a depute-sheriff than a doctor.

On Rankellor's instruction, Coll pulled up a section of wicket fence and on it the men transported Gaddy into the hut.

With him Rankellor had brought two small lanterns and four wax candles. He dumped these items from the bag, along with two silver flasks which contained French brandy and Scotch whisky. Having removed his coat, he untied the ribbons of his shirt, furled up his sleeves and secured them above the elbow. He had hairy, muscular arms and sinewy wrists.

With Coll's aid the hurdle was propped by the foot-end on the box bed and Rankellor issued instructions to the man who, like it or loathe it, was condemned to act as midwife for the next several hours.

"Light the lanterns. Use the new candles. I can do fine without smoke. Build up the fire to draw heat. I need boiled water, tempered with a touch of cold, at the ready. Give me my knife from the bag there."

"Knife?"

"Are you deaf, Cochran? I'm not going to skin her. If you're qualmish about this business, do what I ask then wait outside."

"Has she . . . has she thrown the bed?"

"She's not a damned ewe, man."

"Is she dyin'?"

"Get on with your work."

For a moment, before the prolonged process of delivery began, Harry Rankellor's cynicism caused him to wonder if Cochran's question was entirely without self-interest, if the farmer did not, in one compartment of his heart, wish for the poor woman to pass decently to her Maker. She had served Cochran well, one way and another, but now, come what may, she would be a bother and a burden to him.

Contemplations on love did not enter into it as far as Rankellor was concerned.

Cochran looked glum.

"The knife, the knife."

Cochran found and passed it.

Rankellor cut the bands that held Gaddy's skirt to bodice and began to disrobe her. She was conscious but unhelpful, mute and gasping like a whale he had seen once on the sands at Portobello in his student days, a poor, panting creature out of its element, scuttled by its bulk. He loosened all that he could, lifted her hip and unwound the heavy skirt. He furled up the undergarment and, in the same motion, placed bridged fingertips upon her upper abdomen.

Coll, eyes squinched shut, extended the bright little lantern.

By its light Harry Rankellor confirmed his diagnosis. It was exactly as he had suspected. The mortality of the child now depended entirely upon his skill.

Already the membranes had ruptured, their dilating force had been lost. He had prepared for the infant's resuscitation. A warm bath, hot cloths and a wipe of whisky were ready, or soon would be. Incomplete breech; the legs of the baby were extended, thighs flexed on the abdomen, a position that would lead to complications. Some midwives would have fastened on the trailing leg and hauled the shoulders and head into a straightness, killing or maiming the child. Even with the membranes broken, patience was the order of the day for an attendant. Rankellor resisted the temptation to bring the legs down. He would not do so unless impactation or arrest occurred.

It would be a slow and painful labour for the Patterson woman. She would need all her strength to endure it. Already blobs of sweat stood on her brow. With his handkerchief Rankellor dabbed away the perspiration. Her colour was not encouraging, blue tinged, the eyes sunken. He had not lied to Leggat. He was afraid for the woman's life.

"A wee push now, just a wee push."

He dared not hasten the progress of the breech by traction but he encouraged the woman's efforts by mild fundal pressure.

The light flickered. Rankellor glanced up. Coll Cochran was trembling.

"This will take many hours," the doctor said. "Put the lamp there on the post and go outside. Smoke your pipe. I'll call when you're needed."

"Is there nobody else? A woman who could . . .?"

"Is it not your child, Coll Cochran?"

"Aye, aye, it is."

"Besides, what woman would come on short call?" Rankellor said. "Your wife, perhaps?"

"I'll be on the stoup."

"Very well."

Labour lasted from noon until after midnight.

Only after the buttocks appeared did the doctor turn the woman across the bed. Hours more passed before the feet finally showed, accompanied by a great shrieking cry from Gaddy. Even then it was far from over. Rankellor's task had only just begun.

Fortified by occasional nips from the silver flask, the doctor rubbed his hands and forearms with a block of pure beef suet and slid his fingers inside. He lifted out the infant's feet and, strenuously urging Gaddy to effort, held them. Another shrieking contraction ejected the little creature as far as its umbilicus.

"Give me the warm cloth."

Coll, who had been summoned by Rankellor's shout, did so.

Rankellor wrapped the visible portion of the baby in it and supported it in his left forearm. He wriggled his fingers and brought down a loop of the birth cord, held it and counted the pulsations. At least the damned cord *was* pulsing. He continued to pinch it gently to prevent it being torn as Gaddy thrust again. Her pulse was quite thready, her breathing ragged. She had almost ceased to sweat and a chill had invaded her limbs. She was far gone, battered by effort. Rankellor talked to her sternly, while he noted the position in which the infant's upper body was lying. He felt the next rapid contraction while he was within, an

169

involuntary spasm that Gaddy hardly seemed to notice.

Between Rankellor's finger and thumb the faint throb of blood in the birth cord died.

"God and Jesus!" Rankellor exploded.

Everything urged him to haste. He restrained himself. He had read in certain progressive texts that it was ill-advised to expedite delivery by traction on limbs and body; there was more danger here for the mite than from asphyxia. Ten minutes was not too long for the child to survive unimpaired with the cord compressed. He must not hurry unduly, though he must not waste an unreasonable amount of time.

The baby lay half on his forearm.

"It's a girl, Cochran, if you're interested."

Coll Cochran grunted. He was sitting in shadow away across the fire, an unlit pipe clenched in his teeth, his eyes fixed on Gaddy and on the ill-formed, wrinkled length that hung between her thighs.

Passing his right hand up the wall of the vagina, Rankellor searched for the baby's arms. They were still above the brim, the vagina packed and narrow. At this crucial stage Rankellor could not afford to be indecisive. He drew down then lifted upwards, manipulating the infant's body. He passed his right hand over the little shoulder and wormed his index finger into the elbow. He must exert no undue force or he would fracture the delicate bone. Cautiously he rotated the child's body and, in a rush, felt the shoulder delivered. He brought the arm down slowly, folding it across the ridge of bone.

Gaddy was passive, almost stuprose, breathing in a series of rapid and disturbing coughs which made the final delicate stages of extracting the infant's head doubly difficult.

On his feet now, the pipe dropped on the straw, Coll watched in fascination as Rankellor rotated the baby's shoulders and, in spite of pelvic contraction, brought the infant fully out of the vagina.

Seconds later, with its airways cleared of matter, and a drop of neat whisky rubbed on its gums and across the base of its spine, the baby gave a twitching shudder and began to breathe.

"Hot clothes. Quickly."

Coll gave the doctor the wrappings.

"Here." Rankellor handed the swaddled child to the farmer and turned his attentions to Gaddy.

She betrayed no sign of interest in the new-born babe. She was almost unconscious and terribly weakened by her ordeal.

The child, premature by twenty days, was not out of the wood yet, not by a long chalk. Her skin, tender and bright red, hung in unattractive folds. She weighed, Rankellor reckoned, no more than three pounds. She must be kept warm and away from fevers though she evinced a sufficient evidence of vitality by her pewling to give the doctor hope that with care and good management she might survive the first threatening weeks.

For the time being, though, Rankellor had done all that he could do.

Cochran still stood with the infant in his arms, rocking it.

On the bed, turned and eased out, Gaddy Patterson was breathing more regularly. Some of her pallor had returned. Rankellor pitched a few more logs on to the fire. Fortunately the weather was kind, with no breeze and only the merest touch of night frost.

"Are you goin', Mr Rankellor?" Coll said.

"I'll return tomorrow."

"But it's . . . she's so frail. How can I . . .?"

"The babe will feed, I expect, in six hours or so. If there's no sucking response, try her with a drop or two of warm, boiled water. Your woman will be able to feed her. With help."

"She looks so ill."

"No," said Rankellor. "Not ill. Utterly exhausted. Don't fret yourself, Cochran. I won't abandon either the child or the mother. But there's nothing I can do that you cannot. Keep the infant warm, and allow the woman to sleep."

"I should . . . I should be gettin' home."

"*What!* For what reason must you go home? To celebrate the event with your wife, perhaps?" Rankellor spoke sharply. "It is your bounden duty to stay here as long as this woman requires you. Ah, but you say, it isn't man's work. You should have thought of that long ago, Coll Cochran. You must stay here at least until the woman is well enough to attend to the needs of the child. And there's the other, the little girl. She may pass a night or two at my house, I daresay my wife can put up with it, but I've no intention of being saddled for long."

As he spoke Rankellor put on his coat and gathered the tools of his profession into the game-bag. He left the flasks until last. He unstoppered one and sniffed at it, passed it to Coll.

"Here, you may finish what's left. It's whisky. I'm not wasting best French on you."

"Thank you, Mr Rankellor."

Coll lowered his head and contrived to tip the flask and quaff its contents. He returned the container to Rankellor who dropped it into his bag.

"What's wrong with your face, Cochran?" Rankellor demanded.

"I . . . I don't know what I should feel."

"Feel?"

"Glad, or what?"

"My God!" The doctor shook his head incredulously. "My God!"

"I suppose I should be happy."

"Of course you should be happy. It's a live girl child. She may not see New Year, Cochran, but be thankful to me, as well as Divine Providence, that she completed her journey into this harsh world. At least it's a beginning."

"Aye," Coll Cochran said. "A beginning."

It took Gaddy many weeks to recover her strength. If it had not been for Coll's hiring of an auld wife from Blanefield neither she nor the baby would have seen Christmas.

The auld wife was a cantankerous, seal-whiskered widow who made no bones about the fact that she would have preferred to be home in her own favoured cottage and had taken on the task of nursing "the leddy", as she called Gaddy, only from sore need of money. She had raised nine children of her own, had been a nursing maid to the Stewarton family and considered herself, even now, far too well-placed to be serving an "unweeded woman" in a sod-roofed hut. But what Mrs Boyle did, she did well and her manner was gentler than her tongue.

It galled Gaddy to admit a need of the old woman's help, to watch the crone performing tasks that she could not do for herself, bringing water, breaking kindling, stirring pots and dressing Elspeth who had returned from her sojourn in Rankellor's house spoiled and fractious.

The baby absorbed all Gaddy's attention, particularly in the first month.

It seemed that Anna, as she had decided to call her daughter, could not ingest breast milk. Gaddy had to stroke off a small quantity from her full breasts into a china egg-cup and mix it with half part of boiled water, then feed this to the infant by means of a glass tube with a black rubber bladder on the end, drop by drop by drop.

It took so much care, so much patience, that the first week after the birth went by for Gaddy like an unpleasant dream, washed as she was by weariness and a great leaden heaviness in her body. While she was glad enough to turn over to Mrs Boyle all other tasks, she would not permit the old woman to attend Anna and, shaking herself out of sleep, heaving herself out of bed, did everything for the baby that had to be done according to Doctor Rankellor's instructions.

Rain came and squalls of wind. Cold sleet slapped at the thatch. Gaddy saw the weather in glimpses as a prisoner might see the sky, when she went to empty the chamber pot or, in due course, to visit the earth closet some yards from the hut. For the rest, it was all Anna. She was wrapped in the puny baby with an intimacy that was all-consuming.

Elspeth was not much taken with her sister. The upset in the tenor of her little life was difficult to bear. Even at two she realised that now she would have to share the measure of attention. She consoled herself by being winsome to Mrs Boyle who gave that approach short shrift. Tears and girning fits came next.

Gaddy petted her elder child in the intervals between feeds. She understood how Elspeth must be suffering and tried to make amends. But there was little time for play.

Coll might have shared this aspect of parenthood with Gaddy, but Coll came infrequently now. Gaddy could not blame him. With an auld wife, a sickly mother, a fretful girl and a puny baby packed into the hut where would a man find a whiff of comfort? She worried, though, worried because for the first time in her life she had been weakened beyond will and made dependent upon others.

As the days mounted into weeks, however, Anna filled out. Slack folds of skin became smooth and she learned to suck full milk from the breast.

On the Tuesday between Christmas and New Year, Rankellor made a final visit. He hefted the baby in his hands as if he was weighing a salmon while she squalled crossly and Elspeth watched from a corner with an enigmatic smile on her face.

"Small," Rankellor pronounced, "small but full-formed. Keep her clear of wet and chills. Don't over-feed her in the hope of making her grow faster. It'll do her no good. How about yourself? Can you get about yet?"

"Well enough."

"Have you a good quantity of milk?"

"I have, sir."

"Well, don't neglect yourself," the doctor said. "I'll not be calling this way for two or three months. I'm off to Edinburgh to undertake a term's teaching at the College and to enjoy a little civilised company for a while."

"I canna thank you enough for what you've done."

"I was paid for it, remember," said Rankellor.

He had not told Gaddy the truth. Certainly he had a term's instruction to do at the College of Medicine but he had applied for the position. He preferred to be out of Balnesmoor during the next few months, to avoid being involved in the quarrel that had sprung up between Leggat and the elders. He had delivered the bastard child, all Balnesmoor knew that, but he saw no reason why he should be cast as a sort of Satan when there were others in the parish more qualified to take on the role. He did not feel duty bound, in this event, to support the minister, friends though they might be. He left Gaddy Patterson and the

174

squawling baby with an infinite sense of relief and rode his carriage out of Balnesmoor the following morning happily enough.

If Coll Cochran had had a carriage and a post in a distant town, he too might have forsaken the highland woman and the village at that juncture.

It was not to placate the fiddle-faced elders nor out of a late-discovered obligation to Etta that he restricted his visits to the Nettleburn. For the time, he was lost. He felt as if he had walked a thin plank across a deep chasm and got stuck in the middle. He found it hard to think of the little red wrinkled creature in its cocoon of shawls as his daughter. The only positive thing the farmer did was to assign Peter Docherty to a full twelve months' employment, and pay him his hiring fee. He had skittled through a fair bit of silver in the last nine months but had much to show for it and still a piece of chink on the side to set against the eventuality of a rainy day or, as seemed more like it, to act as a bulwark against the wrath of the elders led by James bloody Moodie.

The minister brought a handsel gift of russet apples in a basket and a little woollen shawl which he had commissioned from the pins of his housekeeper.

Mrs Sprott did not approve of the likes of Gaddy Patterson but she approved of Jamie Moodie even less and knitted the tiny garment with all the skill at her command. She, and she only, knew that Mr Leggat had already decided on a course of action.

"They'll need to be chastisit, Minister," Mrs Sprott had reminded him; as if he needed reminding.

"I'm aware of that sad fact."

"He'll not repent to the session, will he?"

"No. And if he did, the session would insist that he transgress no more and I can't see Coll Cochran agreeing to give up his friendship with Miss Patterson."

"Particularly since she's made money for him."

"I doubt if his motives are mercenary."

"He's a farmer, Minister," said Mrs Sprott, whose husband, while he lived, had been just that. "I never knew a farmer yet that didn't have a mercenary streak in him."

"Perhaps," said Mr Leggat. "But Cochran is not the real object of Mr Moodie's spite."

"Mr Moodie fair needs put in his place."

"Yes, but the village is behind him."

"Aye, there's folk in this village would do well to remember the words writ in the Old Testament, in the twenty-third chapter of the Book of the Exodus."

Mr Leggat could not bring to mind all the ordinances in the chapter for he was more drawn to study of the New rather than the Old. He allowed Mrs Sprott her little moment of triumph.

"What words are those?" he said.

Smugly, Mrs Sprott quoted the ninth verse; "*And thou shalt not oppress a stranger: for ye know the heart of a stranger, seeing ye were strangers in the land of Egypt.*"

"Most apt, Mrs Sprott. Unfortunately I doubt if any of our flock would admit to 'knowing the heart of a stranger' since they have never felt themselves to be strangers anywhere, let alone in Egypt."

Even so, the following Sunday forenoon James Moodie found himself faced with the first dozen verses of the Book of Exodus as his portion of the reading from the Word of God. Even the weaver could not summon up the effrontery to put a rasp of warning in his voice as he uttered the words, "*Thou shalt not raise a false report: put not thine hand with the wicked to be an unrighteous witness. Thou shalt not follow a multitude to do evil; neither shalt thou speak in a cause to decline after many to wrest judgement.*"

But, because of the text or in spite of it, Mr Moodie and the three other elders confronted the minister that same afternoon and demanded action.

Slow-grinding though the wheels of a kirk-session might be they could not be checked forever.

"Is it not a fact that the child has been born?" said Mr Parry.

"A girl child, yes," said Mr Leggat.

"An' has the father been acknowledged?" said Mr Symington.

"Yes, she has acknowledged Coll Cochran as the father."

"An' does the aforementioned Coll Cochran deny that the child was sired by him?" said Mr Moodie.

"On the contrary."

"An' has Coll Cochran been informed that he must succour the child?" said Mr Dewar.

"He freely accepts the incumbent responsibility."

"But does Coll Cochran faithfully promise to renounce and recant from the ways of wickedness an' have no further truck with the woman?" said Mr Moodie.

"He has not so agreed," said Mr Leggat.

"In which case, Minister, since it's a known fact Coll Cochran has not forsook his indulgence in episodes of carnal pleasure with this drover woman an' has indicated to yourself that he will not do so to restore his good name in the eyes of the parish and of God –"

Mr Leggat could brook no more of Jamie Moodie's claptrap.

He interrupted, "I will cry him to shame from the pulpit, Mr Moodie."

"When?"

"Next Sunday."

The four men muttered and nodded, glanced in satisfaction at each other as if they had scored a profound and lasting victory over evil.

"And what if he's no' there?" said Ian Dewar.

"He will be cried three times, as is the form," said Mr Leggat.

"And then?" said Mr Symington, who wanted to hear the dire sentence from the minister's lips.

"I will withhold Communion," said Mr Leggat.

It was the following day, Monday, that the clergyman took himself to see Gaddy, bearing the little gifts. He found her in excellent spirits, out of bed and dressed but cleaving to the shelter of the hut and never far, he noticed, from the warmth of the fire.

After duly admiring the new arrival, Mr Leggat asked if he might have a word privately with Gaddy and the auld wife, grumbling, went out to replenish the water butt.

Gaddy held the tiny baby so lovingly that Mr Leggat, for all his resolve to be direct and firm, hemmed and hawed a deal before the woman, realising his nervousness, brought him to it.

"Is it the session, Mr Leggat?"

"I'm afraid it is."

"Is it a public rebuke they're wantin'?"

"It is indeed."

"I'm not mindin' that."

"The rebuke would be made against Coll."

"He'll put up with it," said Gaddy.

"But, if he does, he will have to . . . have to make a profession of repentance, which means not . . . not committing the same acts of uncleanness again."

"It wasn't unclean."

"Gaddy, Gaddy!" said the minister. "He'll be obliged to give you up. Not to see you again, or communicate with you."

"How can that be, him livin' just up the road?"

"Believe me, Mr Moodie and the other elders will keep close watch."

"Will you not baptise Anna, then?"

"What?"

"I'll need to have her baptised."

"Oh, no," said Mr Leggat. "My elders would never stand for it. Gaddy, how can I make you understand that in the sight of God you have sinned with Coll Cochran? I've refrained from making a thorough investigation into the facts – I don't believe in digging about for every detail just for the sake of it – and neither you nor Cochran have denied it. But you *have* sinned. You have committed fornication and he adultery and it *is* a great scandal and quite indecent and I *must*, under obligation, take some action."

"How will I get her baptised?"

"In this parish, or any other parish in the Lennox, baptism will not be possible until the scandal has been removed."

"It'll be a bit late in the day –" Gaddy began.

"Do not, I beg you, treat this matter lightly."

"That I'll not do."

"It seems so to me. Have you no contrition?"

"I'm not sorry, Minister, if that's what you're meanin'."

"But Coll Cochran is lawfully married."

"Aye, well, it doesn't seem to me that it was made in Heaven."

Suddenly Mr Leggat detected an iron-hard strand in the highland woman's character. He might have remarked it before, put it down to determination, but now he saw it as selfishness. She sat there like some pagan Madonna, the infant against her breasts, the first child standing beside her, presenting such an earthy, resolute picture that Mr Leggat felt daunted by it. He was also angered and spoke with an unusual degree of force.

"It may not matter to you that you will be debarred from partaking in the worship of Christ and from the sustaining power of Christian community, but it will matter to Cochran. I fail to understand why such a person as Coll Cochran has cut himself off not only from the kirk but from the sympathy of the laird and the grieve and from all his friends in Balnesmoor."

"He has no friends here. The laird never cared about him. Is he to bear the burden all his days, Minister?"

"God will –"

Gaddy allowed him no entry into sermonising. "I'm not claimin' Coll's mine. What he does is for him to decide. But I want my bairn blessed."

"If you have so little regard for the establishment of the Church, why, in God's name, do you feel so strongly about baptism?"

"I do, that's all."

"It can have no meaning for a person of your calibre."

Mr Leggat spoke the accusation softly, deliberately baiting the woman.

"It might for Anna," Gaddy retorted.

"If the pair of you sincerely repent of your –"

"Why's all this happenin'?" said Gaddy. "I took the bairn nobody wanted. I've brought her up right."

"You're confusing issues. You also took another woman's husband to your bed."

"She'd stopped takin' him to hers. In the eyes of God is that not a sin?"

Mr Leggat got to his feet. "You're dreadfully confused. I

179

see, however, that no amount of talking will bring you to your senses. I must warn you that the matter may be taken out of my hands, may become more than a local concern. My elders wish me to address it to the Presbytery. Do you know what that is?"

"Aye, the Kirk itself, the rulin' body."

"They will deal with you and with Coll Cochran much less leniently than I will."

"What can they do?"

Mr Leggat hesitated. He was a half generation too young to have witnessed the full power of the Presbytery of the Church of Scotland in action. But he had read accounts of the punishments meted out and the zeal with which certain reverends pursued those who had sinned in the flesh. He was unsure of his ground, however. He would give Gaddy Patterson a scare, though, and with little enough compunction; some sentiment in him had dried up. She was challenging even his moderate views with attitudes deliberately defiant.

"They may take away your children."

"They canna." She was not, as yet, dismayed. "They canna do that, Mr Leggat."

"If they believe that the children are in moral danger, yes, I believe they can. You are not married. You have had carnal relations with a man who is married. Neither of you will repent or forswear the relationship."

Still Gaddy showed no sign of panic. "I'll not let them."

"You cannot prevent it."

"I can steal them away," Gaddy said. "Hide them."

"Out of Balnesmoor?" said Mr Leggat. "How will you support them? Are you not dependent on Coll Cochran for the best part of your livings?"

"I could . . . I could find the means."

"Is it not easier, Gaddy, to give him up?"

"Not if he needs me still."

"This stubborn attitude is very unwise."

"Aye, Mr Leggat, that may be, but I never claimed to have much wisdom."

"For the last time, Gaddy, will you come to the kirk with Coll Cochran and make confession of your sins before the congregation and offer signs of true repentance?"

"I can't."

"Do you mean that you won't?"

"If you won't baptise my Anna, I canna obey your kirk."

"That is plain ridiculous," said Mr Leggat. "After all that we have done for you."

"You've been very kind, Mr Leggat, an' I give you due thanks for it. But that's an end of it. I've nothin' to be sorry for, an' I won't pretend. What Coll does is up to Coll."

"You will become an outcast, do you realise?"

She closed her eyes and shook her head, then, opening the lids, looked straight into Mr Leggat's face. "It's not bein' cut off from the kirk an' the folk o' the kirk, shunned and stoned, that makes a person an outcast; it's not bein' loved."

"God loves everyone who obeys His commandments."

"Aye," said Gaddy. "God loves the sparrow – but He gave the sparrow wings."

"Gaddy, there's no more I can do for you."

"Baptise my bairn."

"No more," said Mr Leggat. "Not even that."

It was early for her to be out and about but she fed the baby and put her down warm to sleep in the old basket crib with Mrs Boyle to look after her, then took an ash stick and went out across the field to the gate, saying nothing to the auld wife as to her destination or her purpose.

She found Coll in the pasture a quarter mile from the farmhouse, strawing by the hedge where feed racks would be set out when the snow came. He had brought out a few leaves of hay for the beasts that were there and they had remembered enough to trail in from the distant alderbrake and from over the gully to munch the tidbits and low and bellow crossly at the farmer for being neglectful of their welfare. There was grass enough still, though, to keep next spring's stotts muscular and the calves and heifers had more byre-room because of the mild winter up to that January afternoon.

It took Gaddy a while to struggle along the track – her legs did not seem to belong to her yet – but when she saw

Coll she straightened and tried to get a bit swing into her step and left the ash stick hidden by the hedgerow.

He greeted her warmly enough and made a fuss of her appearance there, expressing surprise. But she could tell that he was shy now and that the trust of a month ago, and the heartfelt communion between them, had been undermined.

She enquired about the herd, the farm. He answered her questions with a customary mixture of boast and gloom, the skein of all farmers' conversations.

"Mr Leggat called on me," Gaddy said.

"Aye, he was here too."

"In the house?"

"He cornered me in the hay-shed."

"Did he tell you?"

"He did that, in no uncertain terms."

"He won't baptise Anna."

"I canna blame him for that."

"I want my bairn taken into the bosom of the Kirk."

"Easy enough," said Coll, with a shrug. "Present yourself to the gang of elders, tell them what you did with me an' how you're sorry for it an' will never do it again. Then they'll be magnanimous an' Leggat will announce that we've been forgiven, an' in a month or two he'll pour the water on Anna's brow."

"I won't do it," Gaddy said. "But I want you . . ."

"Want me to what?"

"Do it."

"*What?*"

"Or I will go. We'll not see each other again, not in the dark, Coll, or in the light."

"I'll have none o' that talk."

"Could you not do it?"

"No, I damned well could not."

"Then," said Gaddy, "I'll leave from Balnesmoor."

"Where would you go now, saddled with two wee bairns?"

"Back to Ardelve," she lied.

"What's for you there; yon drover?"

"I belong there more than I do here, Coll."

"I'll not be shaken off so easy, Gaddy. I thought you loved me?"

"Too much to see you taken down an' humiliated."

"Is that the bee buzzin' in your bonnet?" said Coll. "Well, I can tell you now I'll give up my place in their presbyterian heaven, aye an' risk a spell in their presbyterian hell, before I'll let you go anywhere without me."

"I thought . . . I thought you'd tired of me."

"I'll never tire of you. It's those long-nebbit villagers I'm tired of, Gaddy; that, an' my own inability to make you my wife."

"I told you before, Coll, I do not need t' be your wife."

"What is it? What's really brought you here?"

"Go before the kirk. Tell them what they want t' hear."

"No," said Coll.

Five or six small flakes of snow drifted down out of a sky that appeared unchanged. The farmer removed his bonnet and looked at the flakes adhering to the material. He turned and surveyed the hill of Drumglass against which were bands of dark cloud ruled straight as pen lines on vellum.

"For me," said Gaddy. "Do it for me, Coll."

"Are you testin' me, woman?"

"Aye, I suppose I am."

"For what reason?"

"I need to be sure, Coll."

"Of my love, is that it?"

"Of my place."

"Place?"

She put her hands on his forearms and drew him to her. The little weightless flakes of snow beaded his silver hair and the air around was suddenly whirled with whiteness and the shadows of whiteness. Coll responded, uncertainly at first but then with passion, wrapping his arms around her as if to protect her from the long slough of wind that ran cold before the cloud.

"I don't understand what you want from me, Gaddy."

"Tell them. Face them. You see, I've only one foot in Eden yet, but the other's firm enough on the ground."

Hugging her against his chest, Coll laughed.

"Defy them; that's it?"

She did not answer. He pushed her a little away from him so that he could see her face, see the tears that swam in her eyes.

"An' if I don't, you'll leave Balnesmoor?"

Weeping, she nodded.

It was no empty threat; Gaddy Patterson was not that sort of person. She had delivered him a solution to his own confusion. He must make a stand or he must step back into the life that he had suffered before the stranger came to Balnesmoor and the drover smacked his herd of garrons up on to the Nettleburn.

It was snowing thick and fine now. Flakes melted on her cheeks with the tears.

"It's not for me I ask it, Coll. It's for . . ."

"Anna. Aye."

"Elspeth too."

"But what of Etta, what of my wife?"

Gaddy had no hesitation in putting it to him.

"Give her the farm, Coll."

"The farm? Dyers' Dyke? But, God in Heaven, what would she –"

"Pay for the man to run it. Let her have your old life. Come with me down t' the Nettleburn."

"We'd all starve."

"We'd sell cattle. We'd live well enough, just you an' me, for all we'll need."

"Gaddy, do you know what you're askin' of me? To give away the Dyke, my father's –"

Coll cut off his protest. His father had lived plump on credit. He had put silver in the kirk plate and drunk ale in the inn – all on the credit that a good name had brought him. No thought for tomorrow. No thought or care for the value of inheritance. It was a tenant property in any case, held in the palm of the laird. He owned nothing, now that he thought of it, except the stock that *his* back-breaking labour had saved. He cared for nothing housed at the farm, not even Etta. He was attached to it only by the habits that the community had imposed upon him. His future was short. His past dragged at him like chains. What *did* he need? Not Dyers' Dyke, those millstone acres. Not Etta.

184

Though it seemed that Gaddy was asking him to give up everything, everything did not amount to a peck of peas.

"There's another way out of it, Gaddy."

"What way is that?"

"Payment. It's no longer as it was when I was a laddie. No, I can *pay* the kirk to let me go."

"Will you do it, Coll?"

He took her hand and led her across the hem of the field, following the thorn hedge which had already turned from black to near-white. Together the couple looked down upon the roofs which were visible from the ridge, on smoke from chimney holes and pots bending before the sweep of the blizzard.

"I'll come part of the way with you, dear," Coll said.

"Coll, answer me: will you do it?"

"By God, I will," Coll Cochran said.

"Ten guineas?" said James Moodie. "Ten guineas for what?"

"To take my name out of the Black Book."

Peeling them from a roll in his hands, the farmer put the banknotes in a line upon the table. The four elders, and Mr Leggat too, inched back from the notes as if from something contaminated.

"Ten guineas," said Parry. "Dod, but that's a king's ransom. The laird his-self would not be asked for such a fine."

"Is that bribery?" said Ian Dewar.

"Bribery it is," said Moodie.

"Minister, what do you have to say to it?" asked Coll.

It was Friday evening and the meeting of the kirk-session had been hurriedly convened at Coll Cochran's instigation. James Moodie and his mother had speculated on what Cochran could want. They had come up with the solution; he wanted to beg for clemency. But Mr Moodie had confided in his mother that he would not yield to any tearful plea and would remain adamant.

"It's punishment money," said Coll. "So, Minister, is it legitimate for the kirk to accept it in place of public rebuke?"

185

"It is," said Mr Leggat, with a pained expression. "There are countless precedents."

"Among noble folk an' landed gentry there's precedent, not for the likes of him," James Moodie snapped.

"So it's one set o' rules for the rich an' another for humble tenants as far as the kirk's concerned, is it?" said Coll.

"Not at all," said Mr Leggat. "Indeed, ten guineas is a most extravagant sum for a farmer to put out. It has, like the widow's mite, more value than, say, a larger sum extracted from Sir Gilbert."

"Sir Gilbert would never get himself in such a position," said Symington.

"There's no argument with the size of the payment," put in Ian Dewar, shrewdly. "But I'd like to know what Cochran thinks he's buyin' with it."

Mr Leggat took it upon himself to explain. "It's an offering made in lieu of public rebuke. Certainly it's a more sensible form of settlement than a dressing-down in front of the congregation. Such a sum would contribute greatly towards the fund for the raising of a school in the parish, for instance." The minister glanced round his elders but found no enthusiasm for this project. "It is well within the ambit of parochial session to accept a monetary token as penance for sin of this calibre."

"Just money?" said Parry.

"Ten guineas is hardly 'just' money," said Ian Dewar.

"It wouldn't matter a jot if it was a hundred guineas," said James Moodie. "It's a bribe, that's what it is."

"It's not a bribe," said Coll. "I wish to make restitution."

"An' receive pardon?" said Mr Parry.

"I'm not bothered about the pardon."

"You mean, you're not here to repent?" said James Moodie.

"Indeed I'm not," said Coll.

"You mean, you intend to continue with your filthy fornication?" James Moodie cried.

"I intend to continue a relationship with Gaddy, aye."

"In that case," said James Moodie, "keep your black money, Cochran."

"Hold on now," said Ian Dewar. "Hold on a shade."

James Moodie was on his feet, pointing a finger of accusation at the farmer. "We are not t' be lured into the snares of Mammon. It's our duty to this community, to say nothin' of God, to cry your shame to the four corners of this parish, aye, an' any other parish you an' your damned whore might scuttle to."

One step took Coll to the table. Leaning across Symington's shoulder he caught the collar of James Moodie's coat in both fists and jerked the man on to the table.

Banknotes fluttered. Mr Parry clutched at them while Dewar, quick to realise what Cochran intended, flung his chair backwards and scrambled to his feet. He made no move to protect his fellow elder who, dragged like a stott across a slaughterman's block, skidded on the polished wood with arms folded over his head. But that was not enough for Coll.

Shouting, "What did you call her, you ha'penny toss?" he lifted Moodie, no lightweight, on to his knees on the table and, setting him first with a grazing blow from the left hand, pumped his right fist into the middle of the weaver's face.

Blood started at once, flecking from Moodie's nostrils. He clasped his hands to his broken nose like a crier. To give Moodie his due he would have carried the fight to Coll if Dewar had not snared his coat-tails and restrained him.

It was a side of Coll Cochran that nobody had seen before; and a side of Moodie too. Tearing his coat from Dewar's grasp weaver lunged at farmer and carried him to the floor, thumping and punching like a delinquent byre-lad. For several minutes not even Mr Leggat could separate the men and was obliged to stand back, protected by Mr Symington, while skin and hair flew.

It was comic; it was also pathetic and, while it lasted, it was unspeakably violent. It breathed of another age, of another less civilised climate, with chairs tumbled and notes and papers flying about, the men shouting and grunting as their fists found marks.

If Coll had gained the upper hand, if Coll had triumphed, then James Moodie's life might have taken a different course altogether. But the weaver was young and strong and wounded, and all his rage at life's frustrations flowed into his fists. He had Coll down, pinned full-length in a corner, a knee in the older man's chest. It was the moment to stop, the venomous exchange over. But Mr James Moodie did not stop. He pummelled and pounded on Cochran's exposed face until the farmer twitched and screamed and blood smeared his features in a pulp. And the elder was screaming too, spewing out filth, curses and oaths that would have caused any tink or drover to blush scarlet, a rain of obscene and blasphemous accusations that, when recollected, showed what really simmered in Moodie's brain, the guilt, the lust and the jealousy that nobody had previously uncovered.

It took the combined efforts of Dewar and Symington, one to each shoulder, to haul James Moodie from the insensible body of the farmer, and the whole weight of Mr Parry dumped upon his legs to subdue him. All three elders and the minister would never forget that blackness, that contused and bloody visage, and the hatred in the weaver's pious eyes.

It was all hushed up, of course. The fall from grace of a fellow elder was not the sort of thing you prattled about in the inn. Even wives, mouthpieces to the community, party to most secrets, were kept in the dark about the reason for Jamie Moodie's decline as a power in the kirk. Even Mr Parry, clay in his spouse's hand, would only mutter in response to her pressing, "Wouldn't have thought it of him. Wouldn't have thought it of him at all."

There was, however, a darker and more serious matter to serve as a rood-screen between Moodie's murderous outburst – none of the session believed that it was self-defence – and his eventual resignation from offices and committees.

It was touched off by the fact of the elders' silence on the happenings that Friday night.

It was still generally believed in the village that Coll Cochran would catch it from the pulpit on the following Sunday. The church, therefore, was packed with an expectant congregation. James Moodie was not in attendance. He was crouched like a wounded fox in the back room of the cottage with a great billed arrangement over his face to protect the broken bones in his nose. In fact James Moodie did not even know that, at a special meeting between elders and minister, it had been agreed that the best thing to do was to accept Cochran's "donation" in lieu of outcry and let it go at that.

Though Mr Leggat was not entirely satisfied with the outcome of the chain of events he too, being a man of moderate temperament as well as conviction, thought prudence was the better part of process and informed Cochran by messenger that he was no longer wriggling on the hook.

The messenger found Coll seated on a bench at the gable-end of the barn, though the Saturday was cold and there had been a light fall of snow. His face was as chopped and contused as a mouldy turnip, swollen purple and yellow with the right eye closed and a hack the size of your thumb on the middle upper lip where a tooth had broken through. The messenger, a young lad from Harlwood who did occasional errands for the manse, delivered the letter which Coll Cochran read.

"Will there be a reply?"

"Bloh."

"Beggin' pardon?"

Coll shook his head. "No. No rapplah."

Coll gave the lad tuppence and he went away. Coll folded the letter into his pocket and said not a word about it.

Docherty was curious. He had not entirely accepted the old man's explanation that he had ridden into an oak bough and been slashed off his pony; mainly because Coll had not ridden out on either pony for weeks. The explanation, made at the dinner-time table, was really not for Docherty's benefit but Etta's. She did not deign to spear for the truth for fear of showing her delight at this first sign of punishment for the ill that her husband had inflicted upon her. Not Docherty and not Coll could have guessed that the woman half-believed that it was the hand of God that had reached out of the gloamin' and smote her evil sinning man in the face.

Come the Sabbath, though, while Coll was still stiff as a three-day corpse and doing little but guddle about the byre,

189

Etta did have occasion to address herself to him about three-quarters of an hour before bells were rung for morning service.

"I've put out your black an' your gloves," she told him, coming in the door of the byre without preliminary.

"What for?"

"Kirk."

"I'm no' goin' to kirk."

"Aye, but you'll have to."

"I don't have to."

For a moment she appeared stricken, then, striking her head and shoulders forward, eyes luminous, she shouted, "GOD CAN STRIKE YE WHEREVER YE HIDE. GOD CAN FIND YOU."

Mania of this hue had not been part of Etta's visible eccentricities. The regular imbibing of ether, however, has curious effects upon the human brain and there was no doubt that Etta Cochran's reasoning had become as tangled as a bramble bush over the past months. Harry Rankellor would have spotted the signs and might even have given accurate diagnosis of their cause. But Rankellor was in Edinburgh and nobody else cared enough for Etta Cochran's health to pay close heed.

"No doubt He can," said Coll and went away into a stall to hide behind a heifer.

"NEXT TIME GOD'LL SHRIVE YOU WITH A LIGHTNING BOLT."

Coll snorted painfully and put another dab of grease on his split lip.

He had not deemed it wise to appear before Gaddy in his present state. He did not completely comprehend what Etta was bawling about. He guessed she thought he was due for a crying from the pulpit and he did not enlighten her to the contrary.

It might then have been Coll's fault, might have been James Moodie's fault there at the last. Neither of the men were blameless, any more than Gaddy was blameless. But, come that Sabbath day, any straw would have snapped poor Etta Cochran, and a wheen of folk, Mr Leggat included, were to wish they had warned her that her patient awaiting of public vindication would not come to pass.

Knowledge, even a whisper of it, would have tapped the pressure that built in Etta during the progress of the service, a mounting expectation detectable, so her pew-neighbours claimed, not only to eyes and ears but even to the nostrils. They said later that you could smell the desire on her, dry and sulphurous like gunpowder in the pan of a musket.

She was dressed in black bombazine stuff, a hat of clenching black straw and black mittens. She had no colour, except on her cheeks which showed two glowing spots like fever fire. She sang no psalm, for her lips did not move. She offered no prayer, for she did not close her eyes. If she took in any word of the sermon or the readings it made no impression upon her and might have been Hebrew or Greek. But when it came to that time, after the reading after the sermon, when it was the duty of the Reverend Leggat to pull together the threads of the morning's preaching and, mounting again into the high pulpit, deliver his oration against sin and sinners, Etta pulled herself upright. She was poised with hideous expectation, a smile like a rictus spreading across her teeth.

When Mr Leggat indicated the various meetings which would take place during the coming week, Etta did not lose patience. When Mr Leggat informed the kirk that Mr Moodie was indisposed and offered prayers for a rapid restoration of health, Etta did not despair. It was only when Mr Leggat turned and began to step down from the pulpit, down the six-step staircase, that it dawned on Etta Cochran that her husband had slipped through the net and had once more escaped not her wrath but God's.

It was too much for someone in her condition.

She rose slowly, like something long submerged, and with a waterlogged breath screamed aloud.

They were all there that day, Sir Gilbert, his wife, two of his sons and all his daughters, servants from the house, grooms and cattle-keepers. Even his grieve, Sinclair, and Sinclair's wife were there. They all sat stunned, in high pews and low. It was shocking. There was no leniency for laughter, though only a few could make out Etta's garbled invocations, cries for vengeance, repugnant in their intensity. For one minute, two minutes, Etta Cochran craned and screamed while Mr Leggat and his elders remained frozen in horror and the folk in the pew with Etta quailed away from her.

It was Sinclair who put an end to it, to the hysteria and fury. He got up from his seat, crossed the aisle and walked to her. People scrambled out of the pew to let him in. He caught her firmly by the shoulder. She wheeled and raked him with both fists. But Lachlan was ready for that. He snared her wrists and pulled her against him – still screaming she was – and held her so tight that she could not draw breath. In ten seconds she crumpled into sore, sore weeping.

Sinclair led her from the kirk, his arms about her.

Shaken, Mr Leggat hastily concluded worship and, by the side door, went out to see what comfort he might offer the poor deranged woman, only to find that she had gone, taken home by horse-gig by the grieve.

Sinclair spoke quietly to Coll. He informed him of what had occurred in the kirk. By now Etta was like a woman in trance. Her eyes were staring and unblinking. Her mouth champed like that of a nanny-goat working cud. There was a bizarre jut to the lower jaw that knotted the muscles and tendons of her throat like briar roots. She had not lost her high colour, though, nor had the burning faded from her cheekbones. Rankellor would have been summoned if he had been in residence. But the nearest person with experience of medicines was an old witch-woman, a herbalist, who lived out by the mills of Balfron. She was harmless enough but not, Sinclair declared, the sort of person he'd want to examine his wife.

"What should I do, Lachlan?"

"Put her into her bed and keep her warm."

"Should I find somethin' to give her? She's got more bottles than an apothecary."

"God, never!" said Sinclair. "It's poisons out of those very bottles that's brought her to this state."

Coll nodded. He had never had to nurse Etta before, not properly. During her many bouts of "illness" he had always been sure that she would not suffer decline while he was out about the duties of the farm. He had given her then attention of a sort, but had never worried about her.

Guilt nagged him again. He was more genuinely solicitous of his wife than he had been in years, putting his arm about her, leading her into the kitchen and through it to – here he hesitated – to the bedroom ben the house. He sat her on the end of the bed, their bed. Fumblingly he unbuttoned her bodice and took it off. He could go no further, though, with the unfamiliar task and left her in her shift, black skirt and stockings. Meanwhile she watched him out of unnerving eyes with a smile that did not relax its rigidity.

Coll put his hands under her knees, hoisted her on to the bed, pulled down the blanket and got her, somehow, beneath the covers. Arms bent up across her breasts, she lay on her back, silent and motionless, staring up at the rafters.

She whispered, lips cudding over the words.

"What was that, Etta?" Coll stooped to put his ear close to her mouth.

"Coll. Coll."

"Aye, Etta. I'm here."

"Coll, Coll, Coll."

"Wheesh now, dear. Wheesh. Don't fash yourself."

"Coll, Coll, Coll."

"Etta, are you in pain?"

"COLL. COLL. COLL. COLL."

The belling of his name was followed by peals of laughter that shook her like demons and bounced her body upon the mattress. Coll tried to calm her, pressing his hands against her stomach. But she reached out and clung to his arms and hoisted herself upon them so that he could feel not only her inhuman strength but even, he imagined, the madness boiling in her.

He wrenched himself away.

Docherty came into the bedroom. He still wore his sack, for he had been shifting potatoes, and had muddy clogs. Sinclair had routed him from the barn and sent him into the house to assist. Sinclair, it seemed, had had enough. Etta disturbed him. Her irrationality was difficult to explain as anything other than an affliction of excessive passion. Hysteric affections were not unknown. Sinclair had heard of their lunatic irregularities, though he had never before seen anyone thus possessed. The grieve rode off with the horse-gig before he could become further enmeshed in Cochran's quagmire.

In this matter at least, Docherty was more humane than the grieve. He had witnessed such a fit before. It was a womanly disorder to do with the bleeding and its sudden suppression, so he had heard. But a Fintry wifie who had succumbed to it had been the victim of grief and fear, a new young widow threatened with eviction, and her with four young mouths to feed. She had behaved like this, though the onset was more rapid and the fit more violent, with frothing and slashing. He had been working on day-labour at the landlord's farm when she had fallen into the state and had been present when, convulsed, she had died right there on the cobbles outside the back door.

Docherty moved past Coll and took a look at Etta whose great torn peals of laughter had changed into tragic wails and floods of tears.

"What, in God's name, can I do?" Coll was beside himself with helplessness.

"She needs a sedatin' draught," said Docherty. "She'll swell her brain otherwise or burst the fibres o' her heart."

"But what . . .?"

"Has she got any opium, or laudanum?"

"I canna abide to feed her those foul things."

"It'll have t' be somethin' strong," said Docherty.

"God, Docherty, I don't even know what medicines are there."

"I'll take a wee look, with your permission, Mr Cochran."

"Aye. You do it."

Etta had sunk back upon the pillow, hands like rat's paws scratching and scraping the air in front of her eyes. It seemed to Coll that she was tearing at some invisible material, at an apparition that only she could see, a skin which was enveloping her. He tried again to communicate, to offer the comfort of his presence. He had not forgotten that it was his name that she had called out. But Etta was, once more, unreachable.

Docherty returned with a blue-glass bottle, shaking it in

his hand like a dice-cup. "I'll need a spoon."

Coll fetched one from the drawer in the kitchen dresser. He took it back with a cup of water from the bucket and stood by Docherty while the labourer uncorked the bottle and sniffed.

"What the devil is that stuff?"

"Chloral."

"Chloral's for the tooth-ache, is it not?"

"Aye, boss, an' for a wheen o' other things besides."

"What ails her; do you know?"

"Hystericals."

The word resonated vague meaning in Coll's memory. It sounded correct. He had little option but to trust Docherty not to take his wife's life, though that too might be a mercy.

"Are you sure it is chloral?"

"Look, it's on the wee label. It's syrup. Dipper's Chloral Antondyne. I can read, see. See. Dipper – he'll be a doctor – Ch-lo-ral . . ."

"All right. Dose her a spoonful. It might make her sleep."

Etta was still wailing, but more softly now, still tearing at the air, though with less dreadful determination. Her throat had not relaxed and there was spittle about her lips. It seemed as if she was choking on some great bolus of emotion.

"I'll give it to her."

Coll took the bottle, poured syrup into the spoon. The bottle now was almost empty. Whatever effect the patent medicine had, Etta must have used it liberally for he had a vague recollection that she had purchased it from a particular packman in the early autumn. Ether and Chloral. Small wonder her brain was swollen and distempers and humours had taken over her intelligence. Gripping her neck firmly with one hand he advanced the spoon.

To his surprise he did not have to fight her. She was eager for it. Reaching greedily, she took the spoon into her mouth and sucked it clean.

She engaged with her husband briefly. Blinking, she peered up into his concerned face.

"More," she demanded.

Coll glanced round at Docherty.

The young labourer shrugged.

Clawing at his arm, Etta shouted, "More, damn you. I want more. I *need* more."

Hastily Coll gave her the last eight or ten drops from the bottle. For all he knew he had poisoned her. But Docherty was present and Docherty would vouch for his honesty and the fact that Etta had asked for a second measure of the medicine. After all, if packmen sold the filthy stuff it could not be lethal.

She was scrabbling to reach the spoon, like a calf to a milksop.

He yielded, watched her suck the sticky substance and swallow.

She smacked her lips outlandishly.

"Etta?"

She laughed, quite humanly, broke wind and stretched her arms above her head, curling her fingers around the spar of the bed-head. She stretched again, yawned, and frittered away more wind; then, as if that had been all that had troubled her, wallowed on to her side and cowled the blankets over her head.

"Etta?"

Cautiously the men drew closer, Docherty at Coll's shoulder. Together they looked down at the tiny piece of the woman's visage that could be seen, peering at them from the swaddle. Her eyes were not starey now, but heavy. Her mouth was slack.

The men looked at each other, questioningly.

"It's . . . it's supposed t' make a person sleep," said Docherty.

"She needed it."

"Aye."

They stepped back then halted, riveted by a strange sound that emerged from the woman's pursed lips.

"What's she sayin', boss?"

Coll did not answer at first though he could just discern the lilt and form slurred into groaning melody.

"*Ma loolie, loolie, loolie-lo, loolie, loolie-loo-lie. Ma loolie babby's gaed tae Heav'n, ana'r Daddy's for the grave-oh. Loolie, loolie, loolie.*" Etta sighed. "*Loooooo-lie-loooooow.*"

"She . . . she used to sing it to our bairns when they were

just wee things," said Coll quietly. "Long, long ago."

"I see," said Docherty. "Aye, well. Aye, well. Come away, boss, an' let her sleep."

Coll allowed the labourer to draw him from the bed and into the kitchen. There was wetness in the corner of his eye but it was not, as Docherty believed, a tear for the memory of the bitter-sweet days when he and his wife were young and all the world's time unrolled its promises before them. Coll was not thinking of Etta at all. He was thinking of Gaddy and his little baby daughter. Something in the mingling of events and the resurrection of the sad and sinister lullaby made the farmer's blood run cold.

"Leave her bye, Mr Cochran. Maybe she'll come right again in the mornin'."

"Aye, maybe she will," said Coll.

But he did not, for one moment, believe it.

That very forenoon Gaddy had finally summoned up courage to dismiss the auld wife and send her back to her lamented cottage in Blanefield. They had not met on the best of terms, nor did they part so.

Mrs Boyle's bite was just as sharp as her bark and she left with a sniff and no offer to return the weekly portion that Coll had paid her on the previous Thursday. It wasn't the money that made Gaddy so glad to see the back of her but the fact that she did not care one jot about the children. She had attended to their welfare but betrayed not one ounce of affection or pleasure; no sham of severity or sternness, either, but a genuine, mercenary selfishness, brushed into a crest by snobbery.

"I'll bid goodbye tae ye then, leddy, but tak' a warnin' from my lips, if ye drop more brats dinna come lookin' for me tae do nursin' work. I'd rather starve than suffer here again."

Standing, Anna in her arms, Gaddy saw Mrs Boyle off the premises without a word of farewell.

It was high time she gathered herself together, put the strain of the pregnancy and birth behind her and sorted things out before early planting.

In a month, Anna should be of a normal weight and,

Gaddy hoped, a wee bit less demanding; then she would be able to get back to the lazy-beds and planting potatoes and to the breaking of new rigs. She would, perhaps, have to do it without Coll's aid. She hadn't seen him for four days and was changed enough in character not to harbour any great trust in him to return. She was curious, though, as to what had transpired at the Friday night session meeting and whether or not Coll's name had been thundered in shame from the pulpit that Sabbath morn.

More to appease a desire for news than to have him roll up his sleeves for spading, Gaddy longed for Coll to come again to the Nettleburn.

Still, that Sunday Gaddy was happy enough to be rid of the auld wife and to have the place to herself once more.

She fed Anna, played a wee while with Elspeth, broke long branches with an axe for a good bright fire, and made a batch of potato pies, adding an egg yolk and a gill of milk to thicken the scraps of boiled mutton. Elspeth ate one while it was almost too hot to juggle, and one more at supper time, while Gaddy, whetted by the afternoon's exercise, did justice to two. The rest of the batch was put away cold inside an iron pot, safe from the mice, in case Coll came.

It was about eight when Gaddy bedded down with her bairns.

Anna would waken squirming and pewling about the hour of midnight. The baby had set her own times, frequent little suckings. She would be awake before daylight, which did not come into the hut until eight or thereabouts. Tomorrow Gaddy would try other things, chores that she had to re-learn with a baby on her hip or shawled to her breast. At least the weather was holding and the threatened long fall of snow had come to naught, though you could feel it pressed behind Drumglass.

It was after the midnight feed. Anna lay sound and Elspeth, thumb in mouth, was buried in the short bed, snoring gently. Heavy and languorous, Gaddy was floating on the straw when the sound came to her.

She stirred herself a little.

Instinct told her it was neither of the girls. She thought it must be deer come down off the moor and that perhaps sleet was falling fast across the high tops, driving the hinds before it. Perhaps it was a hare; or a fox. Thought of a fox made her open her eyes. But the fowls were silent and there was only a faint, unhurried *eh-heh-eh* from one of the she-goats, a noise as unremarkable as the rumbling of the burn.

Gaddy tried to stay awake but could not.

She did not hear the scrape of the door or see the crow-winged flapping of the bombazine skirt as it crossed the line of the hearth.

Gaddy heard nothing at all to rouse her to save her infant from Etta Cochran's "Divine" revenge.

"Boss. Boss. Waken yourself."

Coll groaned and opened his eyes. He had been lying like a man in a coffin on the narrow, boarded bed in the tiny closet-like room, with ill-fitting blankets sliding off him and the January cold making his face ache.

"Docherty?"

"Aye."

The labourer had a dirty brown blanket draped over his shirt. He was bare-legged and his feet were naked.

"What's up? Is it yon cow wi' . . ." Coll put his feet to the floor.

"I think the missus has gone, Mr Cochran."

"Gone? Gone where, man?"

"I canna say. But I have the dog in wi' me these cold nights, and the dog scented . . . well, sniffed somethin'. I looked out the bothy window and saw, well, I think it was your wife, boss."

Coll was out of bed immediately. He flung open doors and looked down on the twisted blankets in the larger bedroom, at the pillow with its vacant indent.

"God in Heaven, she's gone."

"She'll be wanderin' in her sleep. I feared as much. Yon chloral . . ."

Coll had already lit a paper taper at the fire and touched it to the wick of the candle on the shelf above the hearth.

He pulled the candle down and covered its flame with cupped palm as he whisked it to the array of bottles, vials and jars along the shelves of the dresser.

Shivering, Docherty watched. "The syrup, was it not finished?"

"Damn the syrup," Coll hissed.

Both men conversed in strained and urgent whispers as if Etta was still asleep or listening through the open door while they conspired.

With a sudden sweep of his arm Coll dashed the bottles to the flagstone where they smashed and bounced. Disregarding the broken shards he got down among the debris and pawed over it, holding the candle forward, hot wax melting on to his fingers and thumb.

"It's the ether. It's that filthy devil's stuff. She's taken the ether. I should have flung it out. Damn me for a soft old fool. I should have burned it out there in the yard; aye, an' all of these poisons."

"But . . . but . . ."

"Quick, Peter," Coll hissed again. "Get on your breeks an' boots."

"But . . ."

"Damn it; hurry."

"But why's she run off with a bottle o' ether?"

"She's taken it to the Nettleburn."

"To the . . . What in God's name for, boss?"

"To kill somebody," Coll said.

The men went on foot, running as fast as they could by the track. Docherty, being young and foolhardy, would have risked the moor's skirts but Coll knew that the moor could be dangerous in the darkness and had no wish to risk falling into one of the many little ravines that scarred its border with the grazings. On the track, by the faint pearly light of a new moon in a clear sky, he could go as fast as his legs would carry him. He urged Docherty on, though, and the young labourer took off between the oak trees at a sprinting pace.

It was Docherty then who reached the Nettleburn hut first.

He burst in through the wicket door in time to see Etta

lift the infant girl from her cot and crush a great wad of sharp-reeking rags down into her tiny face.

The odour alone should have wakened Gaddy.

Elspeth was immediately out of sleep, screaming as at a nightmare. It was dark within the hut; the fire had burned near to embers. But there was enough light to define the dark shape of the woman by the cradle; silent now, silent as a ghost, with only the stink of the sodden pad to tell her purpose.

She held the baby away from her and swung as Docherty crashed in. She let out a devilish shriek and flung the ether bottle into the fire, where, like fine-grained powder, it exploded in a flash. She flung the baby too, casting it away from her with such callous indifference that Docherty, for a split second, supposed that it must already be murdered.

Plunging forward, he caught the frail, skinned-rabbit bundle just before it dashed on to the hearthstones. Action and screams were woven into one. He rolled, hugging the baby to his chest while Etta danced like a fiend upon him, her shoes sharp as hoofs. She was, Docherty now knew, possessed by demons. Mad, he would say, without any qualification or embellishment which might diminish the finality of her condition.

Gaddy was on her knees, wailing and reaching out her arms. Sitting bolt upright in the little bed, Elspeth howled inconsolably. Docherty had no notion of where Etta Cochran had gone to. One moment she was trampling upon him, next, she was gone, gone as if she had dissolved into black smoke and been sucked up through the hole in the thatch.

Docherty sat up.

He heard the baby choke and gag, so he pushed her out towards Gaddy then, without hesitation, rolled on to his feet and thrust himself out into the night.

He did not know why he pursued Etta Cochran. In his confusion, he truly believed that she had dematerialised and that he would find no trace of her. Perhaps it was to confirm that supernatural event that he rushed once more out of doors, swung this way and that in search of her, without expecting to see her. She was there, though, arms raised and skirts billowing around her, a stain on the smooth curve of the pasture where it dropped down by the route of the burn towards the birches.

Coll had come through the gate into the field, hirpling and hobbling towards the hut, stitched and badly winded.

He shouted, "There. There, Docherty."

Docherty shouted, "I see her."

He ran after the flying figure in great leaps down the steepening hillside. Then, with a final hollow cry, Etta vanished into thin air.

Docherty stopped, amazed and afraid until Coll limped up to him.

"She . . . she . . . *did she*?" Coll gasped.

There was a little splash of light behind them in the hut doorway, a lantern or candle or brushwood tossed on the fire.

"I think," Peter Docherty said, "she would've smothered the bairn."

"Did she do it?"

"I don't think she had the time."

"Where is she then? We'll have to find her."

"Mr Cochran – she just disappeared."

Coll's hand on his shoulder took away some of the young man's foolish fears.

"She'll have fallen into the Nettleburn," Coll said.

They went forward together, tentatively, though the shoulder of the burn was not steep and the drop down into the rock-strewn basin was no more than five or six feet.

It was enough, though, quite enough to kill Coll Cochran's wife.

They found her lying in the burn, clear water filling her skirts and winding out her hair like cress, bubbling down over the boulders and over her upturned face. If there had been daylight they would have seen that her eyes were wide open and her mouth gaping with the slow weight of the water making, in the end, pretty distortions of her features. But they were spared that, Coll and his helper.

They pulled her from the water and up the bank on to the grass before they could be sure that she was dead.

Crouching, Coll let out a roaring sigh.

He wiped his hands on his thighs and stood up.

"Stay with her, Peter. Just for a minute or two."

"Right, Mr Cochran."

No harm, however, had come to the infant. Scarlet-cheeked and tousled, Gaddy had her in her arms. The ether had not affected her greatly and, apart from a little sickness which had discharged the fumes from her gullet, Anna appeared to be none the worse. Not so Elspeth who, hanging like a monkey to her mother, howled still in memory of that horrid awakening, and could not be pacified.

Quickly Coll explained to Gaddy what had occurred.

It still had not sunk into the farmer's intelligence what the death of his wife might lead to, and how it might, in the circumstances, be construed. To Coll, she had died by her own hand, not as a result of any injurious act that he, or Peter Docherty, had performed.

Gaddy was more astute.

"She must be moved, Coll."

"What? Aye, brought here."

"No, no. What's taken hold of you? She canna be found in this vicinity."

"But the sheriff's man – damn, Rankellor's not here – the laird then must attest that the body –"

"*Not here*," Gaddy insisted.

"But . . .?"

"Or they'll say we did it."

"Did what, Gaddy?"

"Murdered her."

"But she was the one intent on –"

"How can we prove that? It would be our oath against all yon suspicions."

"Peter Docherty, he saw what happened."

"Aye, an' they would say Peter Docherty had been bought."

"Och, Gaddy! You're haverin'. It canna be done aught but legal, an' that means leavin' the body, Etta, where she is until an authority can see how it happened."

Gaddy was on her feet, Elspeth clinging to her shift. For a minute or so she ignored the little one's cries.

She faced Coll squarely, eyes blazing. "Who'll trust us, Coll? If it's whispered that we conspired to do your wife to death, we'll hang. God, Coll Cochran, can you not *see*?"

Coll swallowed, rubbed the stubble on his chin then, mutely, nodded.

"Take her back to the Dyke," said Gaddy.

"But there's Docherty . . ."

"Get him to help you."

"He'll tell everybody what –"

"Not him, Coll. If you keep him in work an' pay him, he'll not open his mouth. He's no' very old but he's old enough to have knocked about. Peter Docherty knows the right time o' day. Besides, when he's done it, when he tells his first lie, then he'll be an accomplice."

"Gaddy, it doesn't seem right."

"It isn't *right*, Coll. But it is *necessary*."

"Aye," the man said. "Aye, I can see sense in it. But she – Etta – she's soakin' wet."

"Stop findin' reasons for hangin' us, Coll Cochran. Go an' do what I've told you. Put her by the pond behind the farmhouse. She was – what? – drunk, I suppose you'd have to say, steerin' mad with whatever she'd supped." Gaddy lowered her voice. "Besides, Coll, she came here with a purpose; to kill your daughter. Aye, an' the rest of us too, maybe. She's dead, Coll, and we didn't kill her. The three of us who saw her here tonight know that full well. Do you want your wife to take *us* to the grave with her? That's what it could come to, if tongues tattle."

"This mornin' in the kirk –"

"Never mind this mornin'. I'm concerned about tonight. Take her back to Dyers' Dyke. Where she's found matters not to the poor bewildered woman."

"You're right, Gaddy. Aye, you're right."

Coll put up no further argument. He returned to the embankment above the Nettleburn where Peter Docherty, shivering in his loose shirt, stood back ten or twelve yards from the dark shape on the grass.

"Listen," Coll murmured, standing close to the labourer.

Docherty said, "She shouldn't be found here, Mr Cochran."

Coll let out a wry grunt.

"Will you help me, Peter? Will you put in with us? If

you're in need of inducement, I'll see that you have work as long as I've the let o' land."

"It'll be bad for her, what they'll say about her." Docherty jerked his head in the direction of the corpse. "It wasn't really her fault. It was yon damned bottles, an' the devils inside them got to her brain. But if folk found out what she'd tried to do here this night – poisonin' a helpless wee creature – they would curse her name in the grave."

It hadn't occurred to Coll, in his state of shock and emotional exhaustion, that even dead he had to protect Etta from the effects of her actions, that she, his wife, still had one thing to lose. It was typical of the charitable Docherty to have thought of that reason before the other one.

Coll clapped him on the shoulder.

"Can we manage her, Peter? It's a damned long haul back to the Dyke."

"We can cradle her on a hurdle, boss."

"Grand idea," said Coll. "I'll away an' cut one down."

So Coll Cochran bore his wife home secretly to Dyers' Dyke laid out on a length of hazel weave and placed her gently by the pond at the tail of the cattle-grazings, half in and half out of the water.

It was to this spot that Sir Gilbert Bontine and his grieve came to inspect the remains of the poor demented woman in the first cold glimmer of daylight. Having related all visible evidence to the account that Cochran and his man gave of the fit that had driven her out to be lost in the darkness, and having discovered no mark of violence upon her, the laird made due report, without jot of malice or blame, to Sheriff Wilson of Kilsyth who accepted it without inquiry or scrutiny and duly pronounced the death to be but a hapless accident.

Gaddy Patterson and her children, the hut on the Nettleburn and Etta's murderous mission went unrecorded. The wife's good name was saved. She was pitied for what she had suffered and for the melancholy humours which had finally ruptured her brain. Etta had tenfold more mourners at her funeral than she ever had friends in life. But Gaddy was not present to draw attention to the state of things and cause more stinging whispers round the pump.

In the eyes of the kirk, as well as the law, Gaddy had no part in the final act of the tragedy that set Coll Cochran free which was why, after a decent interval of a year, Mr Leggat saw fit to marry the couple in the sight of God and to baptise their daughter, Anna.

PART TWO

Elspeth

ONE

Questions in the Wood

In the spring of the year of 1808 a great gale had scythed from the Baltic and struck the east coast of Scotland like a fist. It had punched through Stirling and along the Carse with force enough left to tear thatch and level hedges in the land of the Lennox.

The big white willow that had marked a boundary of marsh ground in the elbow of the Lightwater from the time beyond memory had also fallen victim to the violent air. It lay tumbled now in a flux of alder, birch and briar in what was known in the parish as Fumarts' Wood since it had once been the home of a slink of polecats. The willow had been howked out by the roots. Tangled branches spread about the trunk in a green cavern which, come harvest month, was so festooned with growths that it made a fine flit for pigeons and a hide for deer and foxes.

When the Cochran girls came down to the wood that August evening, however, there were no large animals to fright and the pigeons *croo-crooned* and sailed off without alarm or the din that might have given the game away.

Anna Cochran was a skilful stalker. She held her sister by the hand, leading her through the velvet grasses and wild flowers that grew sweet and profuse on the floor of the wood. Though less practised than Anna, and much less eager, Elspeth was used to treading soft, for she had learned that stray animals were more often caught by gentleness than domination.

The girls were of a height, both tall, both slender and, though busked by the summer sun and unfashionably brown, as beautifully different a pair as could be found for a hundred miles around. Their beauty was uncommon, so much so that it brought yet another waft of suspicion down on the family, the silly suggestion that there had been a pact with the devil to buy such startling looks for a couple of hill-wild lassies.

It was known that Gaddy would sell her very soul – and maybe she had, aye – to give her daughters any morsel of advantage. She had even *paid* for schooling, had seen them walk to Harlwood, all four miles – had walked with them when the weather was hard – when the master of Balnesmoor had indicated he would have no truck with educating girl-children after the age of nine.

Anna had grown as dark as Elspeth was fair and, in spite of her sickly infancy, had caught up with her sister in all ways and outstripped her in many. She was bold and saucy to the point of annoyance and as full of herself as Elspeth was retiring. But the wives in the village, who still had no good word to say about any of that mongrel stock, did not rest their slanders with Anna but chose to call Elspeth sly instead of shy. Some of the older women would spit three times when she went past in case there was truth in the tales about her origins.

The community had made sure that Elspeth Cochran was not kept ignorant of the fact that she was a foundling. Gaddy, though, had foreseen the hurts that such information would cause and had prepared Elspeth for it, with a tale related piece by piece. But Elspeth, secure with Mammy and Daddy and not at all clear what a bastard really was, not at the age of five, adjusted well enough. She never felt herself to be different within the bosom of the family, different from her sister Anna. She did not even consider that they were no blood kin at all. When jibes grew too sore, however, in the hovel-like schoolroom by the Head o' the Brae, Anna would flay about her both physically and with her tongue to protect her elder sister. But as they grew older Anna seemed less keen to engage in battling like a champion, particularly if boys were doing the taunting.

"Teasin'," Anna would say. "They're just teasin' you."

By the time she turned fourteen Anna had an instinctive awareness of the power that her beauty gave her. When her bleeding began – almost at the same time as Elspeth's – and her breasts burgeoned, she used that power mercilessly to turn steadfast admirers and moonstruck lads into oafs who would flush like poppies and stumble over their own feet from the effect of a single, sliding, sidelong glance from the dark-lashed eyes.

For three years or so Elspeth suffered liftings and lowerings of the spirit, restlessness and blank depressions, even occasional bouts of fatigue which had nothing to do with the pile of work that she, like every other child, was expected to do in the hours of daylight. There never seemed to be any confusion in Anna. Perhaps there was, though, and she just never spoke of it, not even to Elspeth. Anna was always sure, always certain – and often very wrong.

It was no mystery to Gaddy what ailed her daughters in these seasons. In the strictest of societies the blood ran hottest. Even in Balnesmoor in which, it being a Lowland parish, there was a degree of general enlightenment, there was enough suffering to bury the memory of what it was like to be young and spunky. High-born or low, ill-reared or strapped into submission, there was a time in every female when her body did her thinking for her, and not all the brain- or book-learning or a daily dose of the Scriptures would gainsay it.

Unlike the majority of mothers, though, Gaddy was not forgetful of her own stormy passage into womanhood. She could remember still the torments of that feckless spell when, no matter how she tried to occupy her thoughts, they centred on things she had been told were wicked. To Gaddy had come Donald McIver. The drover's uncouth assumption that she was ripe for plucking had been half-way right. But that was on Cruachan and over forty years ago, not in Balnesmoor in the nineteenth century.

"Anna," Elspeth murmured, "are you sure we should?"

"Ssshhh!" The younger girl pressed her sister down on to one knee. "Listen. Can you not hear them?"

"Anna, I'm not interested in –"

"Big fibber. You are so. You wouldn't have come if y'hadn't been."

"If they see us . . . if they should catch us . . ."

"Aye, that would be fun, an' them the way they are," Anna whispered. "No, no, I tell you, if they see us keekin', they'll turn red all over an' run cryin' to their mammys."

"It'll soon be dark, Anna."

"Not for an hour yet. There's light enough. Come on."

She gripped Elspeth by the wrist and dragged her on hands and knees under the trunk of the toppled willow and along the green tunnel towards the roots.

There, through a gap in the lush August growths, a stretch of the Lightwater was visible up to the old Mill of Kennart and the lumpy stone bridge that arched over the leap.

It was to the Loup o' Kennart that the boys came in the cool evenings after a day's toil; village lads, smiths' apprentices, cobblers' sons and the burly heirs of farmers, who looked, naked as well as clad, like men though they had only the wit of bairns, most of them.

Elspeth knew that Anna had made this "keeking" visit frequently on hot summer evenings when the river was low and the pool below the rock-pots had dust on it and dandelion down and the dapp of many flies. Shelves jutted over it and the current coiled down through runnels carved out of the rock. There were no dwellings near since the mill had been gutted by fire and burned near to a shell. If any of the gentle sex required to cross the Lightwater on such evenings they would go round below the Loup and over the new brig at Wrassles' farm. The young men and would-be men had possession of the bridge and the pool and made full use of the privilege. It was strange that none of the older males bathed in the stretch, but it was not considered dignified, and dignity was all after a lad reached a certain age.

Anna parted the leaves further. Her eyes were round and her lips pursed. In spite of herself, Elspeth was drawn to watch, attracted as much by the sounds of laughter as by a desire to see men naked.

"That's Robbie McTear," said Anna.

"Where?"

"On the bridge."

"What's he doing?"

"He's going t' dive."

"On to the rocks?"

"Over the rocks. He's good at divin'."

"How do you know so much about it?"

"I've seen him before."

Totally unaware that he was being admired by members of the opposite sex, Robbie McTear displayed his prowess to impress his brethren in the pool below. Toes gripping the rough stone parapet, he raised his arms and with a spring plunged outward and down. He split the water perfectly and emerged on the end of a chain of bubbles, to the cheers and jeers of friends on the bank. Hair sleeked across his skull and his body white in the dark brown water, he paddled to the rock shelves and climbed up upon them.

"Look how he's sittin'," said Anna.

"I see."

In a flail of limbs two youngsters pitched into the pool, wrestling in mid-air, parting only when they struck the surface.

The boys were untrained swimmers, born to it like otters. Even in the height of summer the water was cold, for it ran through granite for a good part of its course and gained no warmth from the final half-mile of sandstone. It was not only to the swimmers in the pool, though, that Anna gave attention. She also admired the groups that lounged upon the grass and on the west-facing pinkish slabs, catching the last rays of the westering sun upon their flesh.

Face scarlet, though there was nobody to see the blush but her sister, Elspeth protested in a breathless whisper that she found nothing to interest her.

Never before had she seen an unclothed adult male. She was well aware of sexual differences and as well versed in the ways of reproduction as any country lass, for modesty was a false virtue, preached but not seriously practised. What Anna had persuaded her to do, though, was more than daring; it was dangerous. Few other girls, however tweaked by curiosity, would have had the gall to admit such an interest and dare to spy on the boys.

It did not arouse Elspeth to see them thus. She envied them their ease and naturalness but did not, as she had imagined she might, find their maleness frightening. It was impossible to relate what she saw to herself. It was like catching sight of an osprey or a kingfisher, a sight she

213

would not forget, something rare and mysterious, but not frightening.

"There's Sinclair," said Anna, nudging her.

Elspeth had already picked out the Sinclairs, nineteen-year-old Matthew and his fifteen-year-old brother Alexander.

She had shared a school bench at Harlwood with Matt, a circumstance that Anna had envied since she was stuck next to wee Sandy, who was unprepossessing in the extreme. Matt Sinclair had inherited his father's authority, though not his complexion. His hair was flaxen, not swart. He had sensual brown eyes and a magnificently strong physique, broad in the shoulder and chest, tapered at the waist.

In the raw – to Anna's eyes at least – Lachlan's oldest was even more handsome, more desirable. She emitted an affected sigh and fanned her face with her palm.

"Would y' not like to be down there with him?" she said.

"Never," said Elspeth.

"I mean just you an' him."

"Anna!"

"I'll wager you wouldn't do much bathin'. He'd sweep you up in his arms an' carry you off into the bushes."

Elspeth felt betrayed by her sister's word-picture; the romantic thing-of-the-heart dream of Matt Sinclair as husband curdled into coupling. That was the difference between Anna and she. Her youth notwithstanding, Anna already cast boys as lovers, as creatures to crush her in their arms and give her unimaginable pleasure. Elspeth's dreams were softer and more modest, of hands touching, affectionate whisperings, swift stolen kisses. She had to struggle to hold tender longings against Anna's realities.

Elspeth was no giggler, no exchanger of invented intimacies, nor was she coy. She had inherited, by example if not blood, much of Gaddy's pragmatism. A stranger making the acquaintance of the Cochran girls might have supposed Anna to be the cuckoo in the nest and Elspeth the natural child. Elspeth cherished the possibility of a wooing, a court-ship, a marriage and a life with Matt Sinclair who was not only handsome and polite but had prospects on Ottershaw and would provide more enduring joys than Anna envisaged. The "possibility" had, in recent months, become quite fixed in Elspeth's mind for Matt had spoken to her at the kirk gate on several occasions and again at Murphy's provision store where, so Elspeth chose to believe, he had loitered in the hope of meeting with her.

He had "tone" had Lachlan Sinclair's boy, and the benefit of an education. Some of the manners of the nobility had rubbed off on him since he was in contact, through his father, with the Bontine heirs. There was about him an air of assurance that, in itself, was glamorous to all the girls of the parish, though to none so much as Elspeth Cochran, or so Elspeth thought in maidenly conceit.

She did not stare long at Matthew. It embarrassed her to think that she had diminished him by having a secret over him. When Anna made another comment, of considerable lewdness, Elspeth snapped at her and dragged away, backing through the willow tunnel.

Anna was after her in a flash.

"What's blazed you up then?"

"It isn't proper."

"Proper! Huh, you're gettin' to be a right prig."

"But it isn't."

"Please yourself. At least your precious Matt'll have no surprises when it comes to the bridal night – unless somebody better catches him first." Anna knew exactly how to wound. "I'm goin' back."

"Why?" said Elspeth. "There's nothin' . . ."

"I like to watch them. For two pins I'd shed my skirts and join them."

"You wouldn't!"

Anna hesitated, weighing challenge and the glory of such an escapade against its inevitable aftermath. Shrewdly she did not take it further.

"Wait for me," she said.

"I want t' go home. I've pleatin' to finish."

"You canna go home without me. Mammy'll wonder where I am."

Elspeth put on a scowl which even Anna recognised as meaningful. Elspeth would not now compromise nor be swayed. "I'm waitin' five minutes, that's all."

"I hear you."

"Five minutes."

As Anna rustled back into the brush, Elspeth crawled out and stood with her back against the trunk of a little birch tree that had been pressed out of the soil by the willow's fall. She could still hear shouts and laughter from the river, like an intrusion from the sky, empty and shell-hollow. Closer was the individual chirrup of a blackbird and from the stand of elms by the Blane bank, the ugly quarrelling of rooks. Dappled grass, thick with a hatch of gnats, and bars of shadows projected by the slanting sun made the horseman almost invisible.

The animal was grey and the man, in fawn leggings, brown calfskin boots and a loose skirt of cream linen, took on the pattern of the landscape. Mount and rider were both so totally motionless that Elspeth first saw them without recognising what her eye had picked out or being startled by its significance. When she looked again, though, the horse had raised its head. She caught the tiny silver tinkle of the martingales. The man too moved, though only a fraction. His face, which had been screened by a leafy bough, became visible.

Breath clung in Elspeth's throat. She pressed herself against the birch, praying that he had not noticed her, but knowing that Anna and she too had been spied upon as they had spied on the boys in the Lightwater. She kept still for what seemed an unendurable time before the rider moved again. She sensed that he was coming for her almost before he completed the small, masterful fondle of the rein that caused the mount to turn half on and walk towards her across the clearing. Rooted, Elspeth did not know what to do. Should she scurry like a rabbit back under the willow or call out to Anna, risk alerting the bathers? Should she do as Anna would, advance to meet the man?

If it had been any other man but Randall Bontine perhaps she would have found the nerve. But Bontine frightened her as he frightened all those folk in Ottershaw and Balnesmoor who did not detest him. There was no middle ground of tolerance among the parishioners for Sir Gilbert's oldest son, the renegade heir who preferred war to sheep-rearing and the burning sands of Egypt to the parklands of Otter-shaw and who, on those very few occasions when he deigned to take leave in his father's domain, flaunted himself as a King's officer before men whose overwhelming fear was that they would be pressed into service for the Crown.

Randall Bontine smiled. It was the knowingness in that smile, its possessive arrogance that made Elspeth cry out.

"Anna. Anna."

She cared not who heard. She would have welcomed the swarm of village lads. On his towering stallion the young laird seemed to threaten her with more than passing shame.

"Call her, yes, call her." Bontine had halted the stallion with the touch of a gloved finger on the rein and a clap of spurless heel upon its flank. "Two pretty girls are better than one for a gentleman to admire."

Elspeth flexed her knees, prepared to dart into the tangle.

"Stay where you are, girl."

She could not take her gaze from him. He had high cheekbones, a thin upper lip and the hawk-nose of all the Bontines. But the crimped half-healed scar that hitched the corner of his mouth was unique, the brand of a warrior. She had heard, from whom she could not remember, that he had fought a duel with a Frenchie in the shadow of the Pyramids and had been slashed with a sabre; the sort of nonsense the lads invented over the fire or up in the misty hills in the lambing month. But now that she saw Randall Bontine up close, Elspeth could believe that the tale was true.

The stallion drifted closer, barring her angle of escape.

"Anna," she said again, hardly above a whisper.

Anna could not have failed to hear her. Elspeth risked glancing down at the fronds that screened the exit from the tree-cave. There was no sign at all of her sister.

Bontine dismounted. He swept his right leg across the saddle horn, released from the stirrup and landed lightly, his fingers still pinching the rein. The horse was caparisoned like no other mount that Elspeth had ever seen; a soldier's horse, the sort of charger that a Light Dragoon would have in the stable for his own use, even if he rode it only once every three or four years. In Bontine's left hand was a crop of soft plaited leather. He rested it lightly across her breasts as if it was a sword and she a Frenchie he had just made captive.

"Talk with me?" he said. "Tell me your name?"

"I . . . I'm . . ."

Everything he did was light, so light. It was as if he too was made of plaited leather with a thin stiff core of India rubber.

"Speak out, girl. I'm not the owner of this tract of palsied waste. Am I? No, the Wrassle fellow has it, I'm sure. In any case, your name?"

"Co . . . Cochran, sir."

"Never heard of you. From our parish, are you?"

"From . . . from up on Drumglass."

The crop stirred, stroking her like a caress, then flicked away. Bontine tilted his head back and looked down his nose at her. Through the collar of the unlaced shirt she could see hair on his body and a medallion of pinkish skin, another scar.

"Hah, yes! You're the child of that drover my father took pity on, are you?"

"I . . . I . . . I am, sir."

"Damned pretty. Do you know that? Are you aware of being damned pretty?"

"No, sir."

"And damned desirable."

"I've got to away home, sir."

"I take it you know who I am?"

"Laird Bontine."

"I'm not the laird yet, thank God. My father's the laird. In time I may be saddled with this blighted place. I daresay it will have its compensations, if the tenantry are breedin' beauties like you."

Elspeth bent her knees. Again he was too swift for her. The crop brushed her breasts once more.

"From Drumglass, you say. Kennart's a fair step from the hill. Oglin' the boys, were you? Ah, yes. You see, I know how little girls behave when they have a mind to be naughty. That's it, isn't it? You were spying on those rustic Adams."

Elspeth felt a flush spread like fire across her face and

218

throat. But she had lost her first fear and was angry at his supercilious insolence, the fact that he had caught her in a deceitful pursuit.

"Yes, Laird Bontine."

"What would you say to being driven down to the Loup on the point of my riding-crop and forced to confess, hm?"

"I would be ashamed, sir."

"I'll wager you would. What if the boys spied on *you* in a state of nature? How would you take to that? How would you like *your* pretty secrets revealed?"

"I would hate it."

"In that case, perhaps I shall choose another punishment."

"Punishment?"

"Nothing too severe, I assure you. What shall it be? A kiss? Yes, a simple kiss from your ruby lips and I would be prepared to forget the whole affair."

"I . . . I don't kiss gentlemen."

"Don't you, indeed? Have you ever had an opportunity to kiss a gentleman?"

"Let me go home, I beg you."

"Not until I have my forfeit."

"I canna give it, sir."

"Give it you must, Miss Cochran."

She darted suddenly to her left, away from the birch, hands thrust down upon her skirts to prevent them snagging on briar and bramble. For a split second she thought she had eluded him. But there was no escape from this man. He shot out a hand and caught her by the wrist, yielding so that he did not hurt her, then he drew her back. She came, it seemed, pliantly.

"Wait, just wait."

It was Anna who spoke. She had slipped unnoticed out of the willow thicket and had hidden herself safe in a clump of alder. Elspeth could never be sure whether her sister had stayed to give her protection or from devilment and love of risk.

Anna, hands on her hips, flounced across the carpet of flowers and grasses, skirts swishing about her, her head held high as any lady's. She had the arrogance of a lady too; it did not sit ill on her or seem exaggerated and foolish as it did when Elspeth or other village girls played the game of being grand.

Bontine did not release Elspeth. He drew back and spurred the horse's crupper with the handle of the crop to make the stallion dawdle away on paid-rein so that he could see the intruder.

"Two beauties; I was right," he said.

"Let my sister go, Laird Bontine," Anna said.

"Not yet. We are in process of striking an interesting bargain."

"If it's a kiss you're wantin' will a kiss from me not do as well?"

Bontine laughed, then, with a wag of his head, stuck his tongue in his cheek and inspected Anna with candid insolence.

"Better, I'd say."

Anna had come close to him. She showed not the slightest trace of apprehension. There was no flush on her cheek, no quaver in her voice, only an unladylike dew of perspiration upon her upper lip.

"Let Elspeth go, sir, an' you'll have your forfeit."

"Am I to be ordered about by a trespasser?"

"Please," murmured Elspeth. "Please."

He released her as if he had forgotten why he was restraining her. It was almost as if she had ceased to exist for him. He had eyes only for Anna.

"I'll need your promise," said Anna.

"My promise? My God! What a conceited little vixen you are." Bontine was not angry. "What promise is this?"

"To say nothin'. An' to be happy with one kiss."

"Hoh! Are you equipped to bargain with me, girl?"

"Promise."

"For a brat from off the hillside you are certainly versed in flirtation. Very well. I give you my word. As an officer of the Eighteenth Hussars. Is that to *mademoiselle's* satisfaction or do you wish my seal on it?"

In consternation Elspeth watched her sister sidle close to the man and, taking the untied ribbons of his shirt between fingers and thumbs, draw him close. She kissed him full upon the mouth, upon the scarred corner of the mouth, roving her lips against his for three or four unendurable seconds. It was the gesture of the ribbons that Elspeth would recall.

Kiss complete, Anna did not at once release her hold upon the laird's son.

"Is it paid now?"

The smile he gave her was almost, though not quite, tender.

"Ah, yes, my lady. It's paid."

He stepped back.

The girls ran, Anna first and Elspeth following.

They ran and ran until there seemed to be nothing in their lungs but sand, their legs whipped by vetches and tall thistles and jarred by the heat-baked ruts of the marsh.

Out of the wood, Anna headed straight for the distant slopes of Drumglass. Only the thick thorn hedge that shored the side of the new Stirling to Glasgow turnpike halted her. Together, gasping, the sisters fell to their knees. Elspeth canted her head and stared behind her in fear of seeing the snorting grey stallion in their wake. But there was only the flimsy line of the wood and the empty ridge of green pasture beyond, not even the laughter of the lads in the pool to remind them of the beginning of the escapade. Everything, even shame, had been blotted out by the encounter with Randall Bontine.

"Oh, och, oh!" said Anna. "I'm sore, I'm sore."

"Did . . . did . . . he . . . hurt . . .?"

"He was . . ." Anna rolled on to her back on the slope by the thorn hedge. She spread her legs and arms, forming a cross upon which the last rays of the August sun fell like blood.

In concern Elspeth knelt beside her sister.

"Anna?"

"He was . . . *wonderful.*"

Memory of that profane moment caused the younger girl to give a strange, delicate shiver; then, abruptly, she sat up.

"Elspeth, where are you goin'?"

Marching furiously towards the hedge gap, Elspeth cried, "Home," in such a tone that Anna had no option but to scramble to her feet and follow.

Though convinced that she was a heroine, wild in love with the romantic, sword-scarred dragoon, all that presently concerned Anna was whether or not she would be found out.

"Don't tell Mammy. Promise you won't tell Mammy."

But Elspeth, who had wriggled through the hedge, crossed the turnpike and was running up the side of a stubble field towards the safety of the Nettleburn in the solemn, snuggling shadow of Drumglass, gave no answer and no promise.

The nursing chair was warped and its seat had been re-thatched a dozen times or more. But it served the aging woman just as well as it had done when she was in her prime. She had corked the forelegs, which gave the chair a comfortable tilt, and had wrapped sacking round the spar to rest against the wall by the hut door. From this position, rocking slightly, Gaddy could survey her little estate and, though her eyesight was not at all what it had been, look out to the hills of Dumbarton and the mountains of Argyll.

The French wars and the predations of Napoleon Bonaparte upon trade in Europe had been an ill wind that had blown good for certain agriculturalists and craftsmen who thrived on scarcity of imports. High rents and swingeing increases in living costs had gnawed away much of the benefit that derived from top market price on wheat and beef, wool and woven goods. The strath showed the pattern of change quite clearly. Small patchwork rigs had gone now; Nettleburn was almost the last of them. Fences replaced traditional short hedges and sheep grazed over pasturage that had once pranced with black cattle. Acre upon acre of bronze stubble showed how much of the bottom had been turned to cereal crops. In the wake of harvest, fortresses of straw and regiments of stook guarded the dusky fields, as if the French Emperor had commanded a new invasion upon inland Scotland and these were the country's lines of defence.

By Gaddy's side was a little tray with a jug of cold weak tea upon it, a loaf of sugar and a painted cup. In warm months this was her usual refreshment and, so her daughters teased, it was by dint of addiction to tea that she had acquired the complexion of a Hindostan.

Gaddy's sallowness had increased, her skin freckled with small brown moles. She had developed creases in profusion. For the rest, there was an ample quilting of fat, so much so that she could not labour long without resting to catch breath. But Gaddy did not care a fig about her appearance. After all, she was no doyenne of society. She did not venture into Balnesmoor these days, preferring the company of her hens and goats. She received news of the world, near and far, through the chatter of her daughters.

Coll had died without warning. He had collapsed while chopping wood on a brisk March morning and had been gone before Gaddy could reach him. Since that day, Gaddy had become withdrawn. The girls agreed that the shock of Daddy's death had shaken her faculties and disengaged her from all but the immediate, habitual concerns of the steading. It was not that she neglected them. On the contrary, she was more loving, and more strict, than she had been when Coll was alive. But something in Mammy had burned out. There were times when the girls, with all the sagacity of youth, suspected that she had turned a wee bit fey.

The girls themselves had come in for a few shocks following Coll's funeral. It had never been clear to them from whence came their meat and drink, from what source income was derived. They knew, of course, that they were not prosperous like Doctor Rankellor or nearly as well coined as, say, James Moodie. But they were aware, if not altogether appreciative, of the fact that a potato crop hit by frost would not ruin them or bring hunger as it did to the children of other tenants in the neighbourhood.

Throughout childhood and adolescence, for Anna and Elspeth there was always enough; extras too, little luxuries that set them apart from most of their schoolmates, gew-gaws brought back from markets at Balfron, Falkirk, Doune or Glasgow; tea and glassware, ribbons and rings, shoe-buckles and books. Indeed, there were more books in the box below Elspeth's bed than in the length of Main Street. Lovingly handled, the books were read aloud by lamplight or pored over in the daylight neuk into which Coll had fitted a window. Not until after Coll's death in the spring of 1805, however, did it dawn upon his daughters that most of the family money was earned at Dyers' Dyke and not by selling produce from the Nettleburn.

It also came as a great surprise to learn that Peter Docherty was an employee and not, as they had always supposed, the rightful tenant of the Dyke. The arrangement had been forged when the girls were tiny and no fuss made of it. Unwilling to stay at the farm, to move Gaddy and his children into a fusty kitchen haunted by memories of Etta, Coll had persuaded Lachlan Sinclair to allow him to appoint Peter Docherty as a "manager".

It was a unique contract, though it did not involve subleasing, something to which Sinclair would never have agreed. Docherty worked the Dyke single-handed. He was paid an annual wage for his sweat and received a portion of the profits which remained after deduction of "improvement" money. In seven years out of ten, cattle and crops raised on the Dyke flushed Coll with credit. He had even leased an extra four acres on the Nettleburn and kept, with Sir Gilbert's approval, a parcel of Blackface Cheviot sheep to see how they would fare on the hill pasture.

Peter Docherty did not reside in the farmhouse. He continued to make his home in the bothy. The grieve was insistent that the house be kept in a good state of repair, which was done. But its kitchen and bedrooms remained dank in spite of regular firing and had a nasty smell which daunted even Anna from prying within.

"Why doesn't Peter live in the house?" Elspeth had asked when she was eight or nine years old.

"Because he has no wife," Gaddy had told her.

The explanation was accepted without further enquiry. After all, the bothy was hardly much smaller than their own "house" which held four people not just one.

Peter Docherty revealed the truth to the girls a few weeks after Coll's burial. He did so at Gaddy's request. It was Peter who had dealt with matters of law entailed in deciphering the will which Coll had left in the keeping of Lachlan Sinclair and which had been drafted by the selfsame lawyer who drafted the immeasurably more complicated documents of Sir Gilbert himself.

It said much for Sinclair that he granted Coll favours. There was no commercial truck between the estate and the farmer, apart from prompt payments of rents. Coll did his own selling of cattle, wool and such crops as he took off his properties. For all that, Sinclair did not shun the eccentric family on the hill or speak against them in public or in private. Perhaps he admired the spirit of adventure and elementary signs of rebellion against systems which bred guilt and fear and manacled men and women to the treadmill for all their born days. But if he did, he breathed no word of that sentiment either.

In any case, Lachlan Sinclair had a family of his own to catch all the attention he could spare from the affairs of the estate. He had his children to educate – he was a staunch believer in education – and to incorporate into the busy world of Ottershaw as soon as they reached an age to work for their keep.

Matthew, his oldest, was currently employed as a horseman in the rough-and-ready company of the stable-hands. In due course he would be apprenticed to the cattle, then to the foresters, until, in time, Lachlan would propose to the laird that Matt be articled as an assistant grieve. Matthew would not be as young into the job as Lachlan had been; Lachlan did not believe in youth being spoiled by an excess of opportunity. Even so, Matthew was a handy young fellow who had had dinned into him the ineffable politeness to his superiors which was the hallmark of a manager.

Work for the girls of the Nettleburn was of a different hue; work without advancement or prospect; work for the day's shilling or the reap of the crop; work added to a round of tasks which, while not unduly taxing, accumulated into a monotonous burden.

Anna was full of chafing resentment, Elspeth more stoical. Each accepted that marriage was the only viable route out of Nettleburn and offered their only prospect of lasting security. They were keen for it, keen and mildly ambitious, full of under-the-blanket whisperings about handsome young men who would provide them with silks and laces, with servants to do the drudge work, leaving them only such onerous chores as selecting menus and entertaining genteel friends to tea at half past four o'clock. There would be a carriage and pair for their use. They would go to town every fortnight and reside in an inn with a maid and a coachman to keep them safe from ruffians. Anna believed in the fantasy but Elspeth saw herself as Matthew Sinclair's wife, living in a house like Mr Sinclair's in the pleasant parks of Ottershaw, as secure and respectable and as sure of her identity as a Balnesmoor lass could be.

It would have amazed the girls to discover that marriage was also on Mammy's mind.

Gaddy was less fey than her daughters imagined her to be. She snipped a finer cut of daydreams than the pair of them put together. Gaddy was cunning, however. She kept her ears open for what passed between Anna and Elspeth, for whisperings, protestations, sudden bursts of laughter, for sly glances to see if she was really dozing on the nursing chair; then Gaddy would listen that little bit more attentively, without a flicker of her lids and never an intrusion.

What Gaddy heard by eavesdropping both disturbed and pleased her. She was disturbed by Anna's tempestuousness, pleased that Elspeth had her heart set on Matthew Sinclair. Gaddy could think of no better young man for her foundling bairn to marry than the grieve's son. There were other Sinclair lads but they were too young to catch Anna's eye. Not for Anna the stoory Sinclairs. She would strike her own fish when the time came, would reel it and gaff it and Gaddy would have no say in the matter.

Gaddy was in sound health apart from breathless spasms. But she was no longer young by the lights of the day. She was anxious lest she die as Coll had done, without a moment to bid farewell. If she snuffed out before the girls were wed, one or other might wind up as she had done, prey to a bully like Donald McIver. It would be better if she settled each with a husband and a bairn or two to bind them, even if that binding marred their happiness until they grew used to it. She could have told them how she had wasted her youth in bondage to necessity. She could have told them how the dozen years she had shared with Coll had been

226

recompense for earlier sufferings. She could have told them what the love of a man meant, how the kiss and the clasp changed as the years went by, how the blood cooled and the heart grew ever warmer if there was love in the home. She desired for her daughters a marriage no less loving than her own had been. But of such matters Gaddy said nothing to her daughters who would find her advice tedious at best.

When, in the brazen dusk of evening, the girls came panting crossly up the hill, Gaddy did not stir from her chair. She rocked with a flexing of her calves, let the amplitude of stomach and thighs create a steady rhythm. She had not been asleep. She had noted the direction from which Elspeth came – across the turnpike – and how Anna ran after her until the steepness of the hill took its toll and Elspeth, stronger and more active, carried away.

She had heard Anna's distant cry – *Promise you won't. Oh, promise you won't* – and it intrigued her. She was tempted to probe into the source of the latest quarrel between them for it was abundantly clear that they had been arguing and that tempers had been lost.

Elspeth, however, had the wit to pause. Screened by the trees of the old track, she gathered breath, smoothed her skirts and patted down her hair before she came up, walking now, across the sheep-graze east of the burn. She even managed a smile and stooped to give her Mammy a kiss before she went indoors.

Anna was only sixty or seventy yards behind her sister. She had not paused to calm and collect herself in the trees. Hardly glancing at Gaddy, she ran on into the hut.

Gaddy rested her head against the rough stone wall.

"Promise you won't;" a loud whisper. "If you promise, I'll give you the brooch, Daddy's brooch."

Gaddy's brow creased.

It must be serious if Anna was bartering her precious brooch. Coll had brought it from Glasgow only weeks before his death and it was the only one of Anna's possessions that Elspeth had ever coveted. It was a meek enough trinket. It gained value in Anna's eyes only because her sister was so attracted to it. Now the brooch had been tossed into the bargaining ring. Why? Gaddy wondered.

"Keep your old brooch."

Elspeth was hurt, frightened and angry.

"I'll give you it, give you it right now," said Anna.

"I don't want it."

"Don't tell. Please, 'Pet."

"Ssshhh, she'll hear us."

Then Anna spoke low and soft and urgent. Even Gaddy's ears, attuned to her daughters' secretive timbre, could not catch the gist of it. She could not make out what Elspeth had by way of a secret that Anna desperately wanted kept from her mother.

That it had to do with the evening's expedition, Gaddy did not doubt. That it had to do with lads, or a lad, Gaddy did not doubt either. She knew that the boys of the village – Matt Sinclair would be one of them – came up from the river to loiter at the crossroad on the turnpike, where Balnesmoor and Kennart were split by the new metalled surface. Her daughters would not have been the only lassies who "happened" to be picking wild flowers or searching for herbs along the hedgerows. But what had Anna done or said? What could be so outrageous that she had fallen to begging for her sister's silence?

"Keep your brooch, Anna."

"But . . ."

"How *could* I tell?"

"You . . ."

"I was there, too, lest you've forgotten."

Anna chuckled. "Aye, so you were. You're frightened Matt finds out."

"Yes. So how *can* I tell? But it'll not happen again, Anna, I'll promise you that."

"No," said Anna, "No, it won't. Not here, at any rate."

Gaddy let out a soundless sigh. Her concern was not lightened by the little she had heard. It had to do with Matthew Sinclair and with shame; Elspeth's shame, not Anna's.

She lowered the nursing-chair to the ground. The corks gave a little squeak as she settled her weight.

Instantly there was dumb silence within the hut.

A moment later Elspeth appeared at the door.

"Mammy?"

"Aye, dearest?"

"Come inside, Mammy. It's gettin' cold."

"Where's Anna?"

"Gone to bed."

"The nannies'll need a chew of green stuff."

"I'll give it them. Come in."

Gaddy pushed herself to her feet. She lifted the little chair by its spar and padded towards the door of the hut. Elspeth had already come out to seek a rind of kail or some other gnawing bits for the goats in their enclosure up the hill.

Gaddy paused.

"Is it over, then?" she asked.

Elspeth's face showed apprehension.

"What?"

"Have the pair of you settled your quarrel?"

"What quarrel?" said Elspeth, then, with just a drop of guile, managed a wry smile. "Och, aye, Mammy. It's settled. All done an' put away."

"Till tomorrow, I suppose."

"No, Mammy, for good an' all," said Elspeth emphatically before she strode away to the goat pen to hide her embarrassment.

In spite of his peculiar style of going at things, nobody ever accused Coll Cochran of being "an afternoon farmer". He had put his back into the multitude of jobs that came round month by month like ropes on a maypole. Those that he was unable to undertake himself, because of his age or a division of interest between the Dyke and the Nettleburn, he worked to cost with the utmost meticulousness, using Gaddy and the girls as labour.

Schooled by old Coll, Peter Docherty had matured into as sound a farmer as one could find in the Lennox. With Coll gone to his rest, however, it seemed that the miasmas of Dyers' Dyke were creeping forth again.

Docherty, for all his skill and sweat, was finding it hard to make ends meet. He had mown that August, taking his luck with the warm spell, and had saved by it, since the process was cheaper than a reaping. He had made barn room for the long-strawed haul and had used Anna and Elspeth as gatherers and Gaddy, puffing, as binder. There would be time lost when it came to thrashing the grain which had weeds in plenty in it, but the straw itself was valuable and he would account for the quantity when he held back kye for winter fattening. Besides, he would not have to thrash the daily quota unaided; the girls would take turn about to flail and they – Elspeth at least – were good, careful workers. Now he had to eke out until the spring sales, hope that the three-year increase in beef would continue so that he might take a maximum profit from the well-wintered herd when he parcelled it out to the butchers and fleshers in March or early April. Docherty, like Coll, sold in that manner and made better money for it, just as Gaddy had taught Coll to do. But the spring, so it seemed to Peter Docherty, was a long trail away and he, like Coll before him, felt a foreboding sense of the Dyke closing in on him.

There were times when Docherty would stop on a glowering afternoon and lift himself and stare from the hill at the forlorn house, imagine he saw a wisp of smoke stealing from the chimney, though he had lighted no fire that day in the empty hearth. It was not welcoming smoke nor cheerful, but more of a fume, like something evaporating from an uncorked bottle. It made him shiver and glance away quick, back to the ploughshare or shears or the dung-barrow. There were times when he was crossing the empty yard in the gloaming when he would swear he could hear thin laughter within the dwelling and the echoes of it rippling out and out across the Dyke's original acres like a curse.

Peter Docherty had his wage. Gaddy paid his settlement from the annual budgeting, but there was more work and less extra year by year for the thirty-eight-year-old bachelor, and little to spare for the improvements that were needed just, as it were, to stand still. He had a rig of turnips which seemed to demand constant hand-hoeing, more than he could ask of Anna and Elspeth. He found himself gloomily obsessed with the little patch, drawn there before daylight with the handle near frozen to his fingers and dew clubbing his boots with mud. Thistles screwed up through the bound sod of fallows even where no thistles had grown before. He hadn't the hours to spend on their elimination, nor the immediate cash to dung all the acres that required it. With September's toe in the door, he would need to plan for sowing the summer fallows, those that Coll had set into rotation, and for seeding the clover-lays as soon as rain ended the modest August drought.

It was all so lush, dusty and benign. The barn was whiskered with grain-straws. The beasts were fat as burgesses. But small things nagged at Peter Docherty, the inescapable feeling that the Dyke was slipping stealthily out of his control.

What really nibbled at Peter was the fact that he was single. What Peter Docherty needed was a wife to share his house, his bed and the thousand-and-one minor concerns that buzzed in his bonnet.

As a young man, Peter had been considered a decent catch by the daughters of humble tenants. He had taken advantage of his attractiveness to "sample the wares". Later, though, when it became clear that Peter would not be lured to the altar, the lassies became extremely wary. He was forced then to turn to the women that drifted with the hirelings or the girls that lurked behind the taverns on market days. Later still, when he had lost his gullet for paid couplings, he would take the gypsy girls if they gave him encouragement. But as he passed into his middle thirties, the lack of a wife seemed more and more to toll the knell of his youth. Peter also wanted to be sole tenant of Dyers' Dyke. It was not that he would ever see Gaddy homeless or hungry. But he resented the fact that she was lease-holder of the farm and that he worked for a woman. His ranklement increased as the years rolled past.

Peter Docherty was keen to own the lease of the Dyke: Peter Docherty was in love with Gaddy's daughter – yet it did not occur to him, in his innocence, that the fulfilment of one need might bring fulfilment of the other. If he married Coll's daughter might he not come into possession of the farm into which he had poured his youth? It was obvious, too obvious for Docherty, that Elspeth might bring him, as dowry, a contracted share in the farm. But Peter kept his longings and anxieties separate. Instead he brooded about the future.

She came skitting up the track by the field from the farm about three o'clock in the afternoon. Peter was out with pony and coulter scarifying a couple of acres of tired grassland, for the grazings were knit tight above the Dyke and airing the mat was good for the grass. With the coulter set high he could rip through it quickly enough to make it worthwhile.

When he caught sight of Elspeth, however, he wound the rope, halted the pony and leaned on the shafts with his bonnet tipped back from his sweat-sleeked brow. The breeze that came up from the strath tousled his hair. He felt happy to see her, nervous too. He greeted her with less affability than he intended, thick-tongued.

"What d'you want?" he asked.

She had a broad-bladed sickle over her shoulder.

"I've been sent to cut bracken for your byre."

"Did y' have to be sent?"

"What's bitin' you today, Peter Docherty?"

The Cochran girls had taken to using his given name only a year or so ago; until then he had been Mr Docherty. Peter enjoyed the informality.

"Nothin', nothin'," he said, more affably. "Aye, I could do with a good strew of bracken. It's still sappy enough to make good dung but it should slash down easy if you've a mind to work the elbow."

"Will I bind an' carry it down?"

"No. I'll bring the cart up the morn."

"What if it rains?"

"It'll not rain, not with the wind from the east."

"What if the wind changes?"

Only the tip of her tongue peeping between her lips and the twinkle in her eye told Peter that Elspeth had not been daunted by his gruffness. She was teasing him. By God, though, but she looked pretty, brown-armed in the pared bodice with skirts hitched up and her apron wrapped to the shape of her hips. He would be hard put to concentrate on the coulter with her working only a few yards away at the edge of the field.

"The wind'll not change 'til I tell it," Peter said. "An'

232

I'll give it no order 'til the bracken's in the back o' the byre."

"How much will I cut?"

Now she was serious and it was Peter's turn to joke. He inspected the fern-line then let his head cant towards the slopes of Drumglass and the gash of the burn-head.

He pointed. "See the sheep, yonder?"

"Aye."

"Stop cuttin' just before you fleece them."

She laughed.

All Docherty's cares fled, leaving an ache that he could not identify, did not dare identify.

Common sense told him that Elspeth Cochran was not for the likes of him.

While Elspeth was at Dyers' Dyke, Anna had gone down to Ottershaw with a couple of pails to purchase milk for butter-making. Buying milk was necessary since none of the nannies was yielding at that season. Though the return journey would be a struggle, the pails heavy and unwieldy, Anna had volunteered for the task. She adored visiting the big house and its vicinity and seized every excuse to go there, to gossip with the servants in the yards and have the chance of catching a glimpse of one or other of the Bontines. On that particular afternoon, in the aftermath of her encounter with Randall Bontine, she was even more agog than usual. Having slipped the pails into the cool of the dairy she had gone prying into the stables in the hope of discovering the stallion and, perhaps, its owner.

The horse was there, unmistakable in its breeding. There were few blood-horses of that quality in the county, though Anna was no great judge of horse-flesh. The stallion was being "walked" round and round a strawed track by none other than Matthew Sinclair.

Anna loitered by the stable arch until she was sure that none of the horsemen was about. They were ill-tempered chaps and jealous of their domain. She saw only Matthew and a couple of young striplings who were digging manure from one of the stalls into a heap. The air was heavy with the smell of the dung. Flies droned about the place, adding to the hot, lazy atmosphere of the afternoon. Matt wore a shirt which had worked loose from his breeks. He was sticky with sweat and he gave all his attention to the towering grey which, like most high-bred animals, was nervous and apt to be unruly.

It would be more than Matt's life was worth to have the horse pull loose, rampage about the yard and damage itself. Even Anna could see that the young man was cannily shy of this job. If he had not been the grieve's son, had not proved himself trustworthy, he would not have been granted the privilege of exercising the best beast in the stables.

In a crescent of shade she waited by the arches until Matt came past her, trotting.

"Matt? Matt, it's me."

"Who?" He did not take his eyes from the stallion's head.

"Me. Anna."

"Go away."

"Is he comin' this afternoon?"

"Is who comin'?"

She slid around the breast of the column that supported the arch but Matt had broken into a trot, running barefoot within the horse-track, keeping the animal to the outside of him.

Anna waited until he came round again. He could see her now without having to glance away from his charge.

She called out, "Mr Randall. Is he comin' to ride?"

"Would I be knockin' the strut out of this devil if he was booked t' be ridden?" Matt answered.

The stallion surged into the halter and near yanked the young man off his pins. Matthew did not resist. He had developed a style for handling the brute, had reached rapport with it, as much as a man could ever reach with a horse.

Anna sidled along the inside wall.

The stable boys scraped their dung-shovels and toiled as if oblivious to her presence which, of course, was far from the case.

She saw Matt ease the stallion, lightly imposing will on it. It was difficult to realise that not quite one day ago she had watched Randall Bontine not only ride the selfsame

234

beast but have it stand meek as a lamb on slack rein.

Matt came round again, a little more slowly. He gave Anna about half his attention now.

"He's awa'. Went off this very mornin'."

"Went where?"

"T' join his bloody regiment, I expect. He'll be fightin' the Frenchies again now the war's started up in Spain."

"Did he . . .?"

Anna watched Matt trot away from her. It was just as well that he had moved out of earshot. The question that had hovered on her tongue had been silly. She had been about to ask if Mr Randall had said anything about her. As if the laird would converse with a common horse-boy about an affair of the heart. She felt, however, quite reduced and forlorn. She sagged against the wall, disinterested now in Matt and the spirited stallion.

To her surprise Matt halted close to her and, breathing heavily, held the stallion still. It was so close in the yard that the horse too was lathered and snorting. It gave the small female intruder an inspection from its lofty liquid eye.

Matt said, "What're you askin' about Mr Randall for?"

"I've no particular reason. I saw him last night, that's all."

"Saw him? Where?"

"Down by the turnpike."

"I never saw you at the turnpike."

"Why should you see me, Matt Sinclair?"

"We cam' past about eight, from the Loup o' Kennart."

"I've more t' do with my time than peer about for the likes o' you," said Anna haughtily.

"I never said –"

She interrupted. "What were you doin' down there?"

"Bathin'."

Anna curled her lips and made an unladylike retching sound in her throat. "Lads bathin'. How common. I never thought o' you as one o' that vulgar herd, Matt Sinclair."

He shrugged, not appearing to be wounded by her insult.

"Bloody hot yesterday, so it was."

"Is the pump not good enough for you?"

"Where was Bontine?"

"Goin' over the hedges into the marsh, over towards Wrassle's."

"Over the bloody hedges. God! the bloody dog'll do this beauty in if he takes the turnpike hedges oft enough. He isn't scraped, though, so he must've flung him high. Did you see it?"

"Elspeth was with me. She was lookin' for you."

Matt appeared not to have heard. "Aye, Randall can damned ride, I'll say for him, one of Georgie's bloody officers though he is. Damned army."

"You've got a right ill tongue in your head, Matt Sinclair."

"I'm sorry. It's workin' here. The horsemen . . ."

"Aye, it'll be the right place for the likes o' you," said Anna. "Elspeth was with me, did you not hear me?"

He lowered his head, making no sudden movement, and rubbed his brow on his shoulder. He looked, for an instant, vulnerable and beleaguered. Anna felt a pang of regret for her sharpness. But she was taken aback when Matt said, "I'd have come up sooner from the brig if I'd kenned you'd be there."

"Me?"

"Aye."

He was older than Anna by almost three years. Perhaps it was his maturity that made her flirtatiousness less effective. He showed no reluctance, no hesitation. He came out with it with the sort of candour that turned Anna's jibes aside like feather darts.

"I'd have come just t' see you," he declared.

"Elspeth . . ."

"Not Elspeth." He shrugged. "You."

"What makes you think *I'd* want to see *you*?"

"If y' don't, you won't."

"What's that?"

The horse grew impatient and swaggered, picked up its forelegs and hoofed, strong and dainty, at the straw path.

"Will you be there t'night?" Matthew asked.

"I certainly will not."

"I'll be there. No' wi' the lads, either."

"But . . . but what for?"

"I' see you."

"I . . . I'll . . . be too busy."

"Half an hour past seven o'clock – if you're not 'too busy'."

He met Anna's eye and smiled. There was no arrogance or undue assurance in his expression but the smile made him appear almost raffish. Then he clicked his tongue and led the stallion into a soft padding walk and, on the bend, into a trot again.

Anna waited but when Matt came round once more, he ignored her. He did not take his gaze from the horse. It was not discourtesy, Anna realised, though she was displeased. It was Matt's manner of telling her that he had work to do and that pleasure must wait.

Pleasure? Would it be pleasure to walk down the lanes with Matthew Sinclair? After the mouth-kiss with Randall Bontine . . . But Mr Randall had gone and it might be many months, many years before he returned.

Sensible resignation stole over Anna as she went out of the yard and returned to the dairy to find a cow-maid to dispense the milk. Though she remembered that kiss, that feverish few minutes by the fallen willow just as vividly as before, some of the lustre had gone out of the memory. She remembered too Matthew Sinclair stripped to swim in the river but that image did not attract her as much as the dip of his head to his shoulder, his smile and his directness.

Anna paused by the dairy gate where the shadows were deep and cool and redolent of milk. She touched her fingers to her cheeks, lightly, so lightly, then giggled.

Of course she would "happen" to be at the crossroad tonight at half past seven o'clock. She would scamper through her chores and be off before Elspeth returned from cutting bracken at the Dyke.

It was as if she had been given a nice new brooch. She saw how Elspeth would covet it and that made it invaluable to her. No trinket, Matthew Sinclair; if questions were asked, she would answer without hesitation and, for once, honestly.

Elspeth would hate her for it.

Poor Elspeth!

TWO

The Scarlet Cloak

What love there was between Lachlan Sinclair's oldest lad and Gaddy Cochran's younger girl blossomed with considerable swiftness, not a fragile thing like a dogrose but rough and rampant like a great weed which found accommodation in rich, moist soil. Its strength protected it from choking and thrust aside more tender shoots so that it sprouted fast, all leaf and, as it transpired, no root.

Elspeth learned of the relationship before it was a week old, Gaddy a day later when she discovered her elder daughter shaken by tears which, for once, she was unable or unwilling to hide from her mother.

"Who told you of this?" Gaddy asked, an arm about Elspeth's shoulder.

"She . . . she did. Anna did."

"It might not be the truth, 'Pet."

"It is. I . . . I saw them t'gether."

"Together? Where?"

"Away down by Elmfoot."

"What were they doin' there?"

"Walkin'. Hands about each other."

"Were you spyin', Elspeth?"

"No, I was not."

"Was it before or after you saw them that Anna told you?"

"Before. I went t'see if it was true."

"And it was, aye, aye," said Gaddy, with soft sympathy.

"When she went for the milk for the butter, that's when he asked her to go walkin' out with him."

"Anna told you nothin' at the time?"

"Not 'til later, Mammy. Not 'til he'd . . ."

"Until he'd what?"

"Told her he loved her."

"There, there, dear. Lads'll say funny things sometimes. Things they don't mean."

A huge yellow moon had been anchored over the Campsie Hills these past few nights and the air was pungent with the perfumes of the earth and the nocturnal musk of dew upon hedgerow and stubble. If Gaddy had been young and protected from hunger and here, in this sheltered corner of the Lennox, she too might have been carried away by it. She could not, however, steel herself against the hurt in Elspeth's heart or find the words to console her for the loss of something which had existed only as a promise in the imagination, not in reality.

There was no wickedness in Matt Sinclair, of that Gaddy was certain. She had known the family too long. She had spoken with the young man often enough to wager that he was as honest as was his father. But the season and its mellowness – and Anna's capriciousness – made Gaddy more fearful than she let on to Elspeth.

"Perhaps it'll wither when the cold nights come," she said. "They'll see little of each other then an' when the winter's gone Matthew might have gained sense again an' see that you're more his sort than Anna."

"I don't know that I am. *She's* the one they all like."

"Only those lads who have no patience."

"I thought Matt had patience."

"There's no accountin' for it," said Gaddy, more to herself than to Elspeth.

"For what?" said Elspeth.

"On what draws a young man to a particular lass."

"He was *mine*. She *knew* he was mine. I told her so a *thousand* times. I'll never tell her *anythin'* again, not *anythin'*. I'll not exchange a word with her *ever again*."

It was on the tip of Gaddy's tongue to tell Elspeth to fight for her young man but she thought better of it.

There was no evidence in Elspeth of that seeking, self-drawing quality which Anna evinced. But the news had given Gaddy pause. Anna was her child, Coll's child. She was of their making; yet, times, Gaddy wondered at the traits the young girl showed, if they were reflections of her attitudes or Coll's sides of nature that she had never noticed in her husband and did not care to remark in herself.

There was less mystery to Elspeth, though she had been born with a secret. No solution to her heritage was possible now, no glorious revelation of her parentage. All that remained was the weathered stone in the kirkyard without so much as a name upon it. Yet Gaddy felt more comfortable with Elspeth than with her own flesh-and-blood daughter. It was as if she had birthed one sort of child and raised another.

Gaddy did not cajole Elspeth into giving up her antagonism. The lass was entitled to resent Anna at this period, to be angry with her.

Elspeth's pride had taken a sore bruise and it was to the healing of that injury that Gaddy addressed herself.

"Even if Matt, if he finds somebody else . . ." Gaddy said.

"So long at it's not *her*."

"Even if it is Anna, dear, it may just mean that he wasn't the man you supposed him to be, not the right one for you."

"He was. I *know* he was."

"You're young . . ."

Gaddy regretted having spoken the words as soon as they left her lips. It seemed that she was doing her daughter down as if she was a blethering child. Child she might be still in her Mammy's eyes but Elspeth thought of herself as a woman grown. She was entitled to suffer passionately as a woman would. The fact that a hurt of the heart was novel did not make it less severe. On the contrary, it made it all the worse.

"Many a lad'll go daft about you yet," said Gaddy. "You'll have your choice, 'Pet. An' a fine range of choice it'll be."

"It's Matt I want. Just Matt."

More tears, a deluge of them; with Elspeth emotions were always real and unfettered, without that edge of self-awareness that marked Anna's every word and deed.

"For the time bein'," said Gaddy cautiously, "you'll have to let Matt make *his* choice; even if he chooses your sister."

"*She* knew."

"But," said Gaddy, "I don't think Matt knew you liked him. Did he?"

"He could've guessed."

"Lads aren't much good at guessin'."

"*She* could have told him."

"What would you have done if you'd gone walkin' with Matt just to discover he only wanted to talk about Anna?"

Elspeth was not hypocritical enough to invent a lie.

Gaddy stroked her daughter's hair.

"Maybe you'll find there's a better fish in the sea," she said.

"Oh, who'll have *me*? I'm nothin' in this world but Anna Cochran's glaikit big sister. That's all I am."

"Blethers, girl! Pure blethers!"

"It's only men like . . . like Mr Docherty that'd have somebody like me."

Gaddy's hand continued its soothing caress but her eyes opened quite wide, unseen by the girl.

Surprised by the statement which had unwittingly popped out, Gaddy said, "There's worse about these parts than Peter."

"Peter!"

Gaddy did not press the point. She was shrewd enough not to sing Peter Docherty's virtues there and then. But she felt lightened by the innocuous slip on Elspeth's part. Had Peter Docherty spoken to Elspeth about his feelings for her? If Peter meant nothing to Elspeth why had she raised his name at all and not that of Johnny McSherry whose father was head quarryman, or young Walter McGowan who was considered, according to Anna, to be a dashing young rake, though he was really only a coach boy and a bit on the short side at that? It was not *their* names that had dropped from Elspeth's lips but the name of Peter Docherty. Mr Docherty. "Their" Peter.

Gaddy had considered Matt a good catch for Elspeth. Might he not be an even better catch for Anna, if that's how the young man's sentiments were already shaped? How much more settling for her bold and tempestuous daughter might Matt be as a husband? She doubted if Matt Sinclair would buckle to Anna's moods or put up for long with her airs and graces. If he was half the sort of man that his father was then he would knead her to the shape of a wife. He would also keep her safe not only from the hardships of life but from herself and her nature.

Aye, Matt for Anna, Gaddy thought. For Elspeth, perhaps, hard-working, lonely Peter Docherty. Dyers' Dyke would be kept in the family as Coll had dearly wished.

"Mammy?" Elspeth said.

"Hm?"

"I want Matthew, *nobody else.*"

"We'll have to see, then," said Gaddy placatingly. "We'll just have to see what changes the winter brings."

But winter came uncommon early, riding close on the Indian summer's heels. And the changes that fell about the Nettleburn thick and fast as snowflakes, pleased nobody, not even Anna.

Whatever their age, sex or station, the children of honest, God-fearing folk found the long winters difficult to bear. Their freedom was circumscribed by the shine of the sun. With dark drawing in earlier with every passing week the lads' work was compressed into a daylight span, while the girls, those refined enough to spin or stitch or sew, were expected to be slaves to the candlestick, seated by the hearth soon after supper and busy at some piece of industry.

Candles of tallow, candles of wax, oil for lamps for those that could afford it, all had to be costed against the savings made. But the lassies themselves had little thought for pennies scrimped and shillings earned by their nimble fingers. Each prick upon a thumb, each cut from a thread, each drop of blood might have come from the heart as they remembered summer nights' passions and conjured up romances that might come with the spring.

Socialising and courting did not suddenly cease; rather they dwindled away, waning like the swollen moons of August and September. When the Harvest Home was passed – in Balnesmoor, early in October – only Hallowe'en stood between the young people and New Year.

The old clandestine festivals had paled, though late fairs were chance enough for a lucky few to jaunt and young men in full-fledged craft or trade could, if they wished, trudge out in any weather to seek companionship in the Ramshead or the Black Bull or, if they were not of a reekin' disposition, to visit friends or relatives. It was much rarer, though, for women to be seen in the lanes and on the highways. They needed, it was thought, a firm and moral purpose to venture from the shelter of the home and any excuse, except kirk meetings, was frowned upon.

High on the slopes of Drumglass, in the tiny house there, Anna Cochran was a prisoner of her sister's vigilance. All loyalties had been rubbed out by Anna's enticement of Matt Sinclair. Elspeth made it clear that she would not hesitate to "clipe" if Anna sneaked out after Mammy was asleep. Anna did not doubt that Elspeth meant what she said. Her pliant elder sister had suddenly become inflexible.

There was still some sport about, football scrimmages on the green, boys capering, girls loitering about the fringes of the field. A weekly group met at Mr Leggat's manse to advance their knowledge of the Bible.

Anna persuaded Mammy to let her attend Mr Leggat's lessons, though her piety was all pretend.

"I'm pleased you're takin' an interest in the kirk," said Gaddy. "Would I be far out in my guess, though, that Mr Matthew Sinclair has also developed a sudden need to comprehend the Word o' God?"

"I really couldn't say."

"He'll be there," put in Elspeth, "with his tongue hangin' out."

"How about yourself, 'Pet?" Gaddy asked. "Would you not like to go along too?"

"I'll rot first."

"Aye, rot's what you'll do, like as not," said Anna.

It irked Anna that Mammy did not appear to take Matthew very seriously. If Elspeth and Mammy had had an inkling of what was really going on between Matt and her, they would have been a lot more fiery in their reactions. But Anna was not foolish enough to blurt out details that had better remain secret. She was caught in a web of her own making. She did not now know how to unravel it. She did not know how to escape from Matthew Sinclair who, fanned by her boldness, could no longer be refused the ultimate experience of love.

Anna, therefore, was not entirely pleased when Elspeth refused to accompany her to Mr Leggat's house on Tuesday evenings. Gaddy insisted that "somebody" must undertake to meet her at the field gate and "somebody" must agree to return her thither by twenty past eight o'clock; and yet Anna could not confess that it was Matt she was afraid of, afraid to be alone with Matt.

In many ways, Matt was just the same lad she had always known, solid, quite slow, with a dour sort of dignity that reminded her of Mr Sinclair and the awe in which she had held the grieve when she was younger. But there was another side to Matthew Sinclair now, a devilish, insistent, rough-handed rogue who appeared only when they were alone. He did not have the patience to be persuasive nor the imagination to realise that she needed flattery and soft compliment. Instead he gave her touch, the power of his presence, made her conscious of his need of her as if that was compliment enough. It did not take Anna long to lose assurance. The trouble was that she *did* respond to his need of her. But she did so grudgingly, thwarted by his directness, robbed of manipulation.

When Matt touched her, when he crushed his mouth upon hers, when he fondled her breasts, Anna was aroused. Each additional liberty was taken on the basis of its predecessor. To placate him, to find the limit of inhibition, Anna did not struggle to protest. At every encounter she let him take one step closer to the act that would hoist her from girlhood, would make her a woman.

It had many names. She had heard most of them. She was eager for experience. But she wanted it on her own terms, terms that were inexplicable to Matt Sinclair. What was more, she could not draw away into coyness, pretend that she had been insulted. She still thought of herself as bold but she found no support in the courtship for that image of herself. She was passive. Yielding. Silly. Yet there was nothing silly in what they did together, how his tongue made her breasts stiffen, how his hands made her moist. Nothing silly in the ardour he displayed when she touched him as he touched her in the September twilight.

Gaddy seemed eager to foster the courtship.

It was known now that Matt Sinclair and Anna Cochran were "paired", that it would only be a matter of time until they were betrothed. The speed with which she had become committed to a young man whom she hardly knew dismayed Anna. Willingly she would have palmed him off on Elspeth just to be free again.

She talked of her sister, sang her praises; Matt would have none of it. He wasn't interested in the blue-eyed Cochran. He was interested only in Anna, his desire centred so fiercely that other girls had ceased to exist for him. To appease that desire, to be shot of it – and, perhaps, of Matt too – Anna finally gave in to his will.

He took her crudely against an oak tree five or ten yards from the track. There was no pleasure in it for Anna, and precious little, she suspected, for Matt. It was quick, painful, dirty and unsatisfactory. When he pulled away from her and she sank to her knees he showed solicitude and, oddly, a degree of awe. He got down beside her, careless of stains from the damp ground, took her hands in his and looked into her face.

"God, but you're beautiful," he said, as if he had been blind to that fact before.

Anna leaned into him, her thighs pressed together. She needed him more at that moment than ever before. But there was no time. Gaddy or Elspeth would be at the field-gate at any minute, holding the lantern, watching for them.

"You are, you're beautiful."

"I'll need to go, Matt."

"Was it sore?"

"I'm fine."

"You'll not . . . not tell anyone?"

"Aye, I'll be puttin' on the scarlet cloak an' paradin' up and down the Main Street first thing tomorrow."

"What?"

Matt did not understand sarcasm. Perhaps he had never

heard the lassies' euphemism for loss of virginity, that fancy, pretty phrase whispered wherever girls met. The "scarlet cloak" of womanhood. The words were trash. But she could not recant, could not become as she had been. The grand event had been marred by haste and stealth. Anna felt deceived, as much by the loss of belief in its importance as by the fact that it had given her no pleasure at all.

She asked Matt to step away while she tidied herself. This he did with a moodiness that gave Anna hope. Perhaps, having had his will, Matt had also found it disappointing, would tire of her, fall out of love just as rapidly as he had fallen in.

Elspeth was the lantern-bearer, sent by Gaddy to guide her sister home. Elspeth said not a word as Matt and Anna came towards her, though she was surprised to notice that Anna walked a little in front and that Matt did not touch her.

When they reached the gate Matt said, in a thick, embarrassed voice, "Here she is, then."

"Thank you," said Elspeth, stiffly.

Matt Sinclair had never been aware that Anna's big sister had been in love with him. He had too many other things on his mind. He grunted and went off without even bidding Anna a good night. On the ill-defined line of the track, he broke into a jog.

Elspeth stepped back. Anna unlatched the gate and let herself into the field. Usually she would have hitched her skirt and climbed the spar to save fussing with the rope. But Elspeth did not appear to notice. She had gone on into the field, lantern in hand. She paused only at the fences, where potato beds and goat-pen made a maze into which it was easy to blunder in the dark.

She let Anna sidle past her towards the house.

Inside, Gaddy was waiting.

She smiled at her daughter and, without guile, asked, "An' what did you learn tonight, then, dear?"

Anna burst into tears.

Anna was never able to forgive her mother for what happened next. It was, the girl thought, almost as if Mammy had been waiting to pounce.

Certainly, Gaddy's reaction was not as either of her daughters would have predicted. Gone was the apparent feyness, the half-asleep quality. Mammy seemed, Anna thought, to grow larger.

"Right," she said. "Right," when Anna had blurted out the reason for her distress.

"He didn't . . . he didn't . . . I let him, Mammy."

"Right," said Gaddy again, already preening her hair and fastening it up with small pins. "Right."

"What . . . what are you doin', Mammy?"

"Goin' to pay a visit."

"*No*," said Anna, wailing. *"No."*

"An' you're comin' with me."

"I won't go."

"Aye, but you will. It's not for your sayin' now, m'lass."

"A visit?" said Elspeth, stunned by what she had heard and, less astute than Anna, unable to deduce her mother's intention.

"Right. Mr Sinclair should be at home."

"Oh, no! Mammy, *don't* go there."

"An' where else are we to go?"

Gaddy flung the heavy shawl about her shoulders and plucked from a shelf a lacquered black straw bonnet that had graced her head only a dozen times in half a dozen years.

The girls gaped at her as if she had been transformed before their eyes, changed into a witch.

"Come you with me."

Gaddy clasped Anna's trembling hand and dragged her towards the door.

"What about me?" said Elspeth. "Will I come?"

"It's none o' your concern. Stay right here."

"Mammy," said Elspeth, "take the lantern."

The candle within the glass had not been extinguished and Gaddy swung the lantern towards Anna.

"You carry it," she commanded. "An' no nonsense."

"What *good* will it do?" Anna shouted. "Goin' *there*?"

"It'll get you a husband."

"*A husband?* Matt? I don't *want* Matt for a husband."

247

"Aye, you should have thought o' that before."

"I don't want *him*."

"You'll want him quick enough if you've a bairn inside you."

"*I haven't.*"

"Anna, get out that door."

"*I won't.*"

They had been spanked before. Once or twice Coll had taken a willow switch and snapped it across their calves and Gaddy had given them an occasional roasting on the behind, more for carelessness than wickedness. But never before had she raised her hand. When she slapped Anna across the face, Elspeth winced too.

Anna did not react; that was the oddity of it. She hesitated, the weal white, then reddening, upon her pretty cheek, then said, "*Won't.*"

It was a pitiful, crumbling defiance. She was a product of discipline and, at seventeen, had no moral backbone, no knowledge of how to stand up for herself.

Gaddy's hand on her shoulders made her collapse. She was led out of the Nettleburn and down the path by the burn meekly enough.

From the hut doorway, Elspeth watched the candle-glass bob and diminish, like a last ray of hope. She was aghast at the impact of the last quarter of an hour, at the over-whelming changes which Anna's foolishness had incurred, at the manner in which her sister's life had been suddenly, drastically altered.

She threw herself down on Anna's bed and stared into the flickering fire. She tried to imagine what it would be like to have a man touch her intimately, to squeeze open her body, what it would be like to wear the scarlet cloak. She felt shut out from that knowledge but, curiously, not weakened now by her innocence. She could discern that it was not necessarily a favoured state and that she was better for having her choices still to make, untainted by punishment and humiliation. Loss of volition was the price Anna would have to pay for knowledge.

Thumb in mouth, Elspeth blinked at the flames in the

hearth. She could envisage the scene, Mammy and Anna's arrival at the Sinclair house, that neat abode of brick and plaster guarded by an orderly arrangement of evergreens and a scarf of lawn. She could see Mr Sinclair, standing on decency and dignity, siding with Mammy. Most vividly, she could imagine Matt, sullenly hidden in a corner. The image reduced him in her eyes. Though she wanted Matt still, in Elspeth's heart was a faint, cool sense of detachment from the trouble her sister had courted, relief that it had not come to her in that manner.

Still with the tip of her thumb in her mouth, Elspeth soon fell asleep. She did not waken until, like mourners from a funeral, Mammy and Anna returned.

There was never any question of Anna and Matthew wriggling through the net of convention.

Father was the grieve, and the grieve abided by a code so inflexible that Gaddy could not have found a better champion for her purpose if she had managed to resurrect one of the old Scottish knights. Organisation was Sinclair's strong suit. He took refuge in detail from the hurt and disappointment that he felt in his son. It was typical of the man that he did not accuse Anna of having lured his lad into fornication. Sinclair believed that the male of the species was bound to protect and respect the female and that a man should be less harried by emotions. Lust was a wild emotion and, like flitting seed, had to be hemmed and harnessed.

Aileen, Sinclair's dumpy wife, might have gone at Gaddy and defended her son with more spite and venom if Lachlan had given her an opportunity. But the grieve knew his wife too well. He understood the irrationality of motherhood. He wanted no truck that night with anything that smacked of the irrational.

The decision was made within minutes of Gaddy's arrival with the tearful, terrified girl.

The whole transaction – for that's what it was – was conducted in the kitchen, with Matt's brothers and even his young sister, in her night-clothes, gathered around. As Elspeth had envisaged, Matt stood in a corner in the shadow of the Dutch dresser with a face like a sunset, glowering, saying no word unless his father demanded it.

After the situation had been made plain, the grieve did not rant and roar; he drove straight to the core of the matter.

"Matthew, is this true?"

"Aye, father."

"It was you who made the advances?"

"Aye."

"Very well," said Lachlan Sinclair. "I take it, Mistress Cochran, that you're not unwilling to accept my lad as husband to your daughter?"

"I'm not enamoured o' the circumstances, Mr Sinclair."

"None of us is that. However, what cannot be mended had best be endured."

"Since they were . . . courtin'," said Gaddy, "it seems to me that there's enough between them in the way of affection for a marriage bond to be no punishment."

"Has the lass any objection?" Sinclair asked.

Gaddy answered, "She has none."

Sinclair turned to his son. "You, Matt, have you objection to doin' your duty and makin' this lass your wife?"

Matthew glowered.

"Well, speak out; have you?"

"No."

"If there was no possibility of Anna becomin' . . ." said Gaddy.

"That possibility is in the forefront of my mind too, Mistress Cochran," Sinclair said. "It had best be soon done, I'm thinking."

"There's no need for a half-mark marriage, though."

"Indeed not," said Sinclair. "I will approach the elder and arrange for the banns to be posted and suitably declared within the month."

"An' the weddin' itself?" said Gaddy.

"November, shall we say, the last Saturday in the month?"

"November will be fine," said Gaddy.

It came as no great surprise to the Reverend William Leggat to receive announcement of a betrothal between Matthew Sinclair and Anna Cochran. Being unacquainted with the background to the intention of marriage, the minister experienced a small glow of satisfaction at this continuing of "tradition". Of course, he knew full well that it wasn't a tradition in precise terms but, in the fullness of his years, he regarded the life of the folk of Balnesmoor and Ottershaw as a tapestry into whose weaving he had thrown a thread or two.

Long ago, William Leggat had defined the boundary of vanity and pride. He could condone in himself a fair scatter of the latter and pull out like weeds as many instances of the former as he could trace in his character. Pride, though, in what Gaddy Patterson had made of the chance that he, with Rankellor, had given her was warranted. She had raised the foundling and her own daughter as fitly as a mother could. She had given old Cochran, in his twilight years, as happy a home as a man could ask for. Now the Patterson woman's daughter to Cochran would marry into the Sinclair family and a new strain would be formed. If the issue of the marriage inherited the girl's looks and the boy's strength, they would be bonnie additions to the parish and mainstays of its future.

The minister's voice was warm as he read the announcement of intention and, as had become his habit, added a brief personal commendation of it, as if he had been the matchmaker.

The congregation had grown used to Mr Leggat's sentimentality. The majority would have preferred to take their religion with less sugar and a mite more vinegar. But they were stuck with the minister, as he was stuck with them. He was harmless enough to have in the manse in a period when, in general, there was prosperity and increase round about and the clamp of presbyterianism had slackened.

If the minister had been privy to certain intense *tête à tête* conversations that were taking place in the grieve's realm and up on the Nettleburn then he might have had cause to think again and to allow a degree of cynicism to tint his rosy view of youth and love.

The cottage lay in pine woods and a good half-mile from the grieve's house, up a narrow, winding hard-pad that, when rain fell, became a burn. It had been empty, the cottage, for seven or eight years, since the crew of foresters had been reduced after a decade of felling and rib planting. Sinclair, though, had kept the dwelling in repair, dry-roofed and sound. Even so, it was a dour sort of place, there in a clearing among the trees; like a hermit's cell. He took Matthew up to it on foot in the middle of a drizzling afternoon, the boy with a sack over his head like a Catholic penitent.

"This is your cottage. You may have half a day every other day to work on it," said Sinclair, standing in the centre of the tiny kitchen, his head just beneath the beams. "Next week an' the week after. Tell Mr Lithgow I gave you release. Tell him too that from the first day of December you will not be workin' in the stables."

"Where'll I be then?"

"With the foresters."

"I like the horses."

"Aye, then you must learn to like trees as much."

"How long'll I be with the foresters?"

"Until I decide you've enough experience of the work."

"How long'll that be?"

"A year, two years."

"Bloody –"

"Guard your tongue, Matthew."

The young man slung the sacking from him. "Is this you gettin' rid of me?"

"I'm not vindictive, though I've every –"

"Aye, aye, you'll be tellin' me, I suppose, you'd have done it anyway, even if she hadn't –"

"*She*, as you call the lass who'll soon be your wife, she didn't do anything."

"Did she not?"

"Did she? Did she drag you against the tree?"

"She needed no coaxin'."

"More fool you for leading her."

"Ach, she's all right, I suppose."

"She'll keep you warm, there's no denyin'," said Sinclair; a surprisingly candid comment.

"She's bonnie, right enough," said Matt.

"No prettier lass in these parts, Matt."

"D' you like her?"

"She'll keep you on your toes."

Matt managed a grudging lopsided grin, which did not survive long against his prevailing depression. "They all say I'm bloody lucky."

"Is that what they say?" said Sinclair.

"Aye, the horse-men are cabbage-green wi' envy. They say —"

"I've no need to hear you repeat their talk. God knows, I've listened to their chatter for years. They know no more about attending to a wife, about building a solid foundation for marriage, than they know about the pyramids of Egypt. They are ignorant men, Matt. Oh, I don't tell you this to make you despise them or cock your snoot at them. But you're not like them, nor do you need to emulate them, nor share their habits. I hope you've had a better example to follow than stable-hands."

Matt kept silent; he had heard his father's solemn lectures before. They were not without wisdom, a little of which rubbed through the boy's bristling conceits. Those who thought him quiet and well-mannered and stolid were wrong. Damn them, had he not shown them how wrong? He had cocked his leg over the prettiest lass in the Lennox and would marry her. There was no disgrace in doing what half the lads in the shire would have done, or wanted to do. He had beaten them. She had chosen him, Matt Sinclair, and not because his bloody father was the bloody laird's anointed, either.

"You'll learn a lot from the foresters," Lachlan Sinclair went on, "concerning the benefits of industry. They are intelligent chaps and care much for what they do. In all immediate matters you will answer to Mr McDonald and you will apply yourself to learning from him all that you can about the management of woodlands."

The estate presently employed four foresters. They lived in their own mysterious community in cottages grafted on to the border of the dense woods that clung to the eastern slopes of Drumglass. Matt knew them — just — by sight and by name, but had no acquaintance with any of them. His father did not hire nursery-men to fill the gaps left by

253

felling. He gave careful instructions to Kenneth McDonald and left the execution to him. McDonald had come to Ottershaw from a position as gardener at Pearshill Castle on Tayside. He was a giant of a man who spoke no friendly word to anyone. The prospect of spending a year or two in the daily company of such "industrious, intelligent chaps" did not cheer Matt in the least.

Matt was too young and too gauche to tunnel his imagination, pin the future with clarity. He could not see himself as grieve, bowing and scraping to Mister Gilbert or, worse, to Mister Randall for the rest of his life, nesting in the bloody forest like a bloody squirrel; nor, when he considered it, could he see Anna being happy with that sort of existence, though she would be delighted if, by a miracle, he could be promoted to grieve right there and then.

"The sack," said Lachlan Sinclair.

"Uh?"

"Pick up the sack," said Sinclair. "This is your dwellin' now, Matt, and you must see that it's put in a state of order and kept so. There's a piece of ground, to provide you with vegetables, which I'll expect to see broken and ready for seed come the spring."

Matt picked up the sack, folded it and draped it over his head again. He looked bleakly round the cramped interior of the cottage. He had no need to open the room's back door, to peer into the closet-like room there, where a bed and a cupboard would fill all the space. He had no desire to crawl over the boards, searching for cracks and weaknesses, to catty-creep across the roof. No desire at all to feather this nest – as his father would have done. He could not see it with a fire flying up the lum, a pot of stew bubbling on the stone, could not imagine Anna laying a table for him, or on her knees chalking the flagstone. He could not even imagine how they would occupy themselves in the long winter nights, here in total privacy.

When his father placed a hand on his shoulder, Matt started guiltily.

"Take comfort, son," said the grieve. "You'll not be the first lad to fall into marriage in this awkward manner, nor will you be the last."

Matt Sinclair was not, however, comforted by his father's generalisation. The few minutes of anticipation that he had enjoyed at the prospect of his bridal night shrivelled as he was steered out into the clearing, into the rain once more.

At the Nettleburn, things were no more cheerful. Anna's incredulity at the coming nuptials had numbed her into such a state that her mother feared she was "coming down with a distemper".

Elspeth knew better. She was so overcome with pity for her sister that she had put her hurt and anger aside and had offered a flag of truce.

Suspecting her motives, Anna had not rushed into Elspeth's arms to pour out her heart. The quarrelsome intimacy of their relationship had changed, like so many other things, in the period of a month. Never again would the sisters be honest with each other, nor would they exchange confidences as of old, nor vie one with the other in a competition so ancient that it had no name and no fixed rules. Anna believed that she had won. Elspeth thought that she was the victor; even if Anna had caught herself a handsome husband, *she* still had the liberty to make a reasoned choice.

Marriage was much on Elspeth's mind in that rainy prelude to the winter. The quick, silly fevers had been poulticed out of her by Anna's betrayal. Mulling it over, she realised that Matthew Sinclair had never been the man for her. Any lad who would let his common sense be stirred like eggs in a jug by a girl as obvious as Anna was not the stuff that husbands are made of; so Elspeth told herself.

On the immediate horizon, however, there were no suitors, no queue of calf-eyed chaps waiting at her door with posies. Without Anna's company she would be limited in making contact with aught but the labouring kind, unless she joined in the kirk fellowships where there were rebels as well as stuffy conformists. But the kirk ponds would not yield her what she sought, for the parish had extracted from the personality of its minister a kind of laxness, a softness that made no appeal to the kind of man Elspeth fancied.

What her ideal male would be made of, Elspeth had no clear idea. When she counted over the young and the not quite so young men with whom she was acquainted, none attracted her unduly.

She kept a weather eye on Anna, however, noted the sullen mood, the dark circles under her eyes and the frown printed in the centre of her brow. Such direct information as Anna delivered on her state of mind and the flux of her emotions could not be trusted.

For instance, the girls were feeding the nannies one day in the rain when Anna, without preamble, caught at her sister's elbow.

"In spite of what you think, I love him."

"I never doubted it, Anna."

"I'll make him a right good wife."

"Once you learn to cook properly."

"That's not the only thing I'll have t' learn t' do properly."

Taken aback, Elspeth was about to ask her sister exactly what she meant but Anna had retreated, stumping off across the muddy field with the empty feed bucket, the shawl held over her head. Elspeth did not pursue her.

Later, only three days before the wedding, late at night when Mammy was snoring in deep sleep and Elspeth had been on the edge of dropping off, she was awakened by Anna's sudden impulsive bound on to her legs.

"What is it? What's happened?"

"He kissed me today. He told me he would love me 'til his dyin' day. He told me there was no other woman in the world as pretty as me."

That afternoon there had been a "family visit" to view the cottage in the pine woods. Mr and Mrs Sinclair had been there, and Matt. It was one of only four occasions since "the night" on which bride and bridegroom had met. Surrounded by parents, they were permitted a few moments of privacy in the cottage's barren kitchen.

Outside, Mrs Sinclair had simpered and made appropriately hypocritical remarks to Mammy, while Mr Sinclair had engaged Elspeth in conversation about news she might have acquired on the British Expedition to Portugal, whence Master Randall Bontine had gone, so it was believed. Elspeth had read very few up-to-date journals since Coll had died, though Peter Docherty would occasionally bring her reading matter from the cattle fairs.

Conversation on that subject ended when Sinclair consulted his fob-watch and shouted, "Matt."

Anna and Matt emerged at once from the cottage door, almost on the run it seemed to Elspeth. They were coo-ed at by Aileen Sinclair and Mammy before they all walked back, the afternoon being dry, to the Sinclairs' house for a dish of tea.

Elspeth groped about in the darkened hut, found Anna's hand and gave it a squeeze. "I'm glad."

"Are you *really* glad?"

"I swear."

"He *does* love me."

"Yes," said Elspeth.

It was then that she recognised a quality in Anna that she had not detected before; desperation.

"It'll be a grand wee cottage when it's sorted," Anna said.

"Aye."

"Will you miss me, Elspeth?"

"I'll come down t' see you."

"Will you miss me?"

"Yes, I'll miss you, silly."

Involuntarily she reached for Anna to draw her down, to hug her. But her sister slid from her arms, fearful of how sympathy might trap her into revealing the truth. She was back in her own bed, in the lower shelf, before Elspeth could say another word.

Elspeth hesitated, then leaned over the board. The faint red glow from the hearth showed nothing. Anna was huddled against the wall.

"Anna?"

"Ssshhh! You'll wake Mammy."

"Anna, are you –"

"Go t' bloody sleep."

Three days later, at noon, Miss Anna Cochran and Mister Matthew Sinclair were married by the Reverend Leggat in the sight of God and forty assorted relatives and friends that Lachlan had drummed out for the service and for the prolonged, but unusually staid, celebration that followed.

It had been Elspeth's intention, as maid of the bride, to see her sister away, out of the long room in the Ramshead that Gaddy had insisted on hiring, and along the road in the lighted chaise that Sinclair had supplied, to be child-like again with the children of the Ottershaw tenants and the Sinclair family. But she, and the children, had no opportunity for noisy revels in the dark street, for Anna and her big, rubicund husband slipped away quiet and were gone before they were missed.

In any case, Elspeth had something else to occupy her attention – Mr Peter Docherty.

In the early hours of the morning a sudden sharp frost had turned the mud to crackling and laved the undergrowth not with pretty hoar whiteness but with sheaths of wet ice. The puddles on the track had grown icy teeth and Elspeth picked her way carefully between them on her way to the Dyke. With no breath of wind, cloud hung motionless over the tops of the Campsies and layered the mountains beyond the loch. It grew colder with each passing hour, though all the signs were wrong for frost and surely it was far too early for snow?

Peter was stumbling about the yard. He had put on his flannel vest backwards and his scarf was coiled about his face like a man with toothache. His complexion was the colour of slag, his eyes swagged heavy. He hadn't, it seemed, the strength to lift a straw bale and was dragging one along untidily, intent upon reaching the field. A trail of straw indicated that he had made the arduous journey several times already.

When he caught sight of Elspeth, Peter instantly dropped the bale.

Raising his hand he ran clumsily towards her, while she tried to suppress her amusement at the state the poor man was in.

"I was the worse for drink, Elspeth," he shouted, wincing at the clamour in his skull. "I was reekin' an' ill-tongued. I beg your pardon, lass."

She had been thinking of poor old Peter Docherty since

she rose, wondering how he would treat her and if he would mention his astonishing behaviour at the wedding celebration. It might be, Elspeth told herself, that he'll not remember anything at all in the stone-cold sober light of day.

Coughing, Peter supported himself with a hand against the bothy wall. He wheezed and shook his head.

"It . . . it was the barley brew, lass. The drink, I swear. I don't know what came over me t' say such things t' you." He squinted. "What . . . eh . . . what exactly *did* I say?"

"All sorts o' things, Mr Docherty."

"What . . . what sort o' things?"

"Modesty forbids me from relatin' them, Mr Docherty."

"Barley fever's a terrible thing," Peter groaned.

"Have you not lit the fire?"

"I . . . Nah, nah."

"What're you doin'?"

"It'll snow afore dark. So I'm luggin' feed."

"Finish wi' that bale. I'll see to the breakfast."

"Maybe it was the whisky," Peter said. "Whisky on top o' ale never agrees wi' me."

"I know fine you didn't mean any of it," said Elspeth, stepping into the bothy and leaving the bewildered Docherty to fathom out what it was that he didn't mean.

She was seldom within Docherty's house. It had the smoke-blackened, unhomely atmosphere of a smugglers' cave. Though he was an orderly farmer, Peter gave no attention to his own comfort.

Elspeth raked out cinders from the fire and, using kindling from the basket and a few rolls of peat, soon had a blaze going. An old pair of leather bellows helped fan heat into coals. She sluiced and refilled the black kettle from the cistern in the yard and hung it on a low chain. Soon steam wisped from the spout. Elspeth had a rummage in the larder and, ignoring a mouse crushed in a trap on the floor, found all that she needed to make the farmer a hearty breakfast.

Not much better for the slap of cold wind in his face, Peter returned from the field.

"Wash, please, Mr Docherty."

He nodded, took a towel from a peg behind the door and

made his way, with an outward show of enthusiasm, to the trough. As Elspeth finished preparing the meal, she heard him blowing like a grampus and pretending that he was enjoying his ablutions. He came back. His shirt was damp around the collar and his hair was slicked down. He sat at the table as instructed. Elspeth put a freshly brewed bowl of tea before him. He steamed his nose above it as if it was balsam then, glancing at Elspeth, sipped the scalding liquid.

"God! That's grand! What is it?"

"Mammy's tonic. She thought you might need it. That's why I came."

"Aye, but what?"

"Brandy. Thomas Mixem's Real. Mammy says it has the wonderful virtue of puttin' all things right."

"It's puttin' all things right wi' me, I can vouch."

"You'll be ready for your breakfast, Peter?"

"Feed away, lass."

She had cut bread from a round loaf and had basted slices in a mixture of egg, butter and flour in the skillet pan, adding two slices of fat ham late in the cooking. The ham was taken from a quarter side that hung in a net in the larder and that provided Peter with a staple by way of meat. She sat by him when serving was done and drank tea, without the benefit of a dash of Thomas Mixem's Real from the little bottle in her skirt pocket.

As far as she could recall, it was the first time she had cooked for a man, apart from her father. It gave her pleasure to watch Peter eat. It also caused her to wonder how Matt had been fed that morning, for Anna was a careless hand at the pots. She wondered too, before she rejected speculation, if her sister would have been wearied by Matt's passionate embraces, for she thought of male appetite as being voracious and insatiable.

Looking at Peter Docherty, remembering how he had poured out his heart in a garbled fashion, she brought image upon image and saw herself joined with the aging, untidy farmer. Would he be as agile and vigorous as Matt?

Peter pushed away his plate. His hair had begun to dry in the warmth from the fire at his back. It sprung up in unruly curls, each tipped with grey, like hoar frost.

"By God, that did me the world o' good."

"It was Mammy's idea that I come."

"To save me from the torments o' the damned. It was kind of her, Elspeth. Give her my profound thanks." He sat back in the chair, holding the tea-bowl in both hands. After a pause, he asked, "Was it very offensive? What I said t' you last night?"

"No. Not very."

"Just what did I say, lass? It's worse not bein' able to recall."

"Just havers, Peter. Barley fever."

"Och, go on. Tell me."

He *did* remember. He remembered the gist of it. She felt sure he was using drunkenness as an excuse to take up the subject again, albeit obliquely.

"You said I was prettier than my sister. But you said you envied Matt Sinclair for gettin' one of the Cochran girls, since you had no hope of gettin' either."

Peter Docherty reddened and swallowed.

"What else?"

"You said you'd rather . . ."

"I think it's comin' back to me."

". . . rather have me for a wife than ten Annas or a hundred other lassies."

"I recall now. Say no more about it."

"You said if you'd any sense you'd go down on your knees an' walk through fire –"

"Did I say that?"

"You did, I swear: walk through fire from here to Killearn an' back again to ask me to be your wife."

"I *was* drunk."

"So it was just the whisky doin' the talkin', was it?"

"It must've been."

"They say there's truth comes out o' the grape. I wonder if the same holds for whisky," said Elspeth.

She sensed what was coming next and retreated, reaching for his plate. He pinched the edge of the plate between finger and thumb and prevented her whisking it away. Anxiously, he peered up at her.

"What if it was the truth, Elspeth?"

She spoke quietly. What she said was rebuff sufficient to the occasion. She had no need to salt it with snappishness.

"I would tell you what I told you last night, Peter."

"An' what was that?"

"I'm o'er young for you."

"Twenty years is the difference. I'm a settled chap, as you know. Aye, you know me as well as anybody since I've watched you grow up," he said. "Grow beautiful as a rose in bloom."

"I think it's the weddin' got you started."

She shook the plate. He released it, giving her reason to walk out of sight of his eyes which contained confirmation of his extravagant, inebriate declarations of love.

She had noticed occasionally how Peter looked at her but had thought that it was no more than a fatherly sort of affection, for she equated him, in a manner, with her father since the two were paired by profession. When she was a child, she had thought that they were paired in age too. Twenty years separated them. Many a young lass was married off to a man old enough to be her father, even in society finer than that found in Balnesmoor. In some folks' scheme of things Peter Docherty would be the perfect age to be shaped as a spouse to a modest young girl of nineteen.

The chair scraped. Peter turned. She was close to him, her skirt brushing his shoulder in the confines of the bothy room.

"I'd open the farmhouse again. I'd scrub it an' paint it an' buy new furniture in Falkirk. We could have a table, crocks, a Dutch dresser, a clock even, if that's what you wanted, Elspeth."

"Peter."

"Aye?"

"Not yet."

"Is that a refusal? I'll not be hurtit, lass, if it is."

"It means 'not yet'."

"Have I a chance?"

"I canna say."

"Who else but you *can* say?"

"It's too quick, too unexpected."

He nodded, quite wisely, as if the paternal streak in him

262

condoned her common sense at not rushing into promises to frowzled bachelors.

"Listen." He got up suddenly. He took one of her hands, still with the plate held in it. She looked at the plate, not at Peter. "Listen, lass, we'll not speak of this again. You have my word on it, Elspeth. I say this because I've no wish to give you cause to desert me. It'll be just as it was before yesterday. I'll say nor do nothin' to give you offence."

"Peter, I'll come to lend a hand."

"Work apart. It's your companionship I need."

"I'll be here tomorrow, as usual."

"You've no cause to fear me."

"I know that."

When he left the bothy, Elspeth gathered the dishes and pans and put them in the wooden tub filled with warm water from the kettle and set to scrubbing them with a little canvas pouch of moss that Peter had handy for the purpose. She could hear him moving about in the byre across the yard and was not unduly surprised when, just as she was wiping the dishes dry, he stuck his head round the door again.

"Eh, lass, did you happen to mention . . . you know, to your Mam?"

"No, Peter. Nor will I."

"Thank God for that," said Peter Docherty and with a smile was gone again.

If only Peter had known, Elspeth thought, that her mother might be his staunchest ally. She could no longer be sure how Mammy would react. But she had the strong suspicion that a man like Peter Docherty might, in Gaddy's eyes, be just the ticket to provide a husband and a son-in-law.

There was no doubt that Peter wanted her. Drunk and sober he had made that plain. She had been blind not to notice it before he did, before he blurted it out.

No, she would breathe no hint of Peter's proposal to Mammy – just in case. She was not ready yet to wear the scarlet cloak, in or out of wedlock, nor was she ready to settle for being a humble farmer's wife. She would marry when it suited her, not before. And not, she suspected, to poor Peter Docherty, however much he loved her.

THREE

Weaver's Wooing

Anyone from out of the parish who caught sight of James Simpson Moodie driving his brand-new horse-chaise, which he referred to by the brand-new Frenchified name of Cabriolet, down Balnesmoor's Main Street on his way to call on Sir Gilbert Bontine, might have been forgiven for supposing that he had been born a gentleman and had inherited not only his wealth but his style. Behind the graceful shell of walnut wood, however, lay a history of savage, untrammelled commercialism.

With strife, riots, plummeting wages, corruption, heavy taxation and the encroachment of mechanisation, weaving was not what it had been twenty years ago. Day and daily, hand-loom weavers were going to the wall, to prison, and to the grave. Only the fittest survived. James Simpson Moodie had proved himself fit through many trials of acumen and industry. The Cabriolet, his strong, chestnut horses, the little lad on the step trigged up in buttoned tweed amply confirmed it. James Simpson Moodie not only believed himself to be superior to his brethren, he had proved it a hundredfold.

It was difficult, if not impossible, to associate the gentleman with the elder. Moodie was no longer as pompous as he had been when he and his sisters resided in the cottage opposite the manse. The sisters were long gone, married to men of enterprise, living far from the Lennox. Old Mistress Moodie still reigned over the household, though, running a ratchet of servants, cooks, gardeners and grooms. But not, emphatically not, running her son.

How it had happened was a mystery. Where the capital had come from was a matter for much speculation. In reality there was no mystery at all. Initially the money had come from the sweat of Moodie's brow and the burning of quarts of midnight oil back in the mid-90s. The energy that once he had pumped into the kirk, into making himself a damned laughing-stock – Moodie saw his young manhood in perspective now – had been rechannelled into the worship of Mammon, into the getting of gold.

For five long, exhausting years, Moodie had plied his loom in the parlour of the rented cottage. For five long years he had sent his sisters out to address the finding of markets for the sundry cloths that came from his back-breaking labours. Then, with every penny saved, he had taken work out to other hand-loom weavers who, many of them, were feeling the pinch. He had paid them by the piece, not generously. He was careful, however, never to apply too much screw for he needed the best workers for best work. A year later – his sisters both married the twelvemonth – James Moodie was at last able to fulfil the shining ambition which had kept him stooped over the yarn for sixteen hours out of every twenty-four, seven days in the week. He left his loom for ever. To other hands now would fall the task of weaving woollen cloth. Let other backs break, other fingers stiffen, other eyes weaken. He was free of the clacking device and other men would make his money for him. That was Moodie's secret. Demonic industry. It had lifted Jamie out of slavery and set him on the path to becoming rich.

But the career was not so simple when regarded in its details. Deals were woven with even more care than the cloths. Wheels were greased with small bribes, later with large bribes. More and better outlets for his plaids, kilt-stuffs, blankets and fine woollens thus came Jamie's way. Mr Moodie was crafty. He delivered quality up to the mark, in the exact quantity prescribed, on the hour of the agreement. He backed his "wee gifts" to persons of influence with undeniable service. But if one of his sprawling gang of cottage-weavers was one thread out in a pattern, one garment short, a half-hour late when the wagon called for the lot, then that man was damned never to work for Moodie again, though he pleaded and grovelled and cut his piece-rate to the bare bone.

Moodie was as adamant in commerce as he had once

been in matters religious. Black was black and white, white.

It was the beginning of an age of opportunity and many an opportunist failed through over-reaching himself. Not James Simpson Moodie. He bought his market first, his labour second, his raw materials last of all. He owned sheep in other men's pastures, fleeces in other men's warehouses, yarn that looped off the spinners' wheels faster than the eye could see. He had a stake in a dye-works. In 1806 he employed a shock-haired young genius, whom he met during a tour of the Yorkshire mill weavings, not only to design new patterns but to see to the development of proper dye-stuffs. Mr Moodie read only technical reports. Mr Moodie spoke only with experts. Mr Moodie journeyed to centres of the woollen trade in the Scottish Borders and far down into England to "see how different folk do things differently", really to scout for advantages that might serve his future.

Patiently he waited for the day when Napoleon Bonaparte would meet his inevitable fate, not that Europe might be free of oppression but so that he might invade Paris with his agents and bolts of fine tweed. In a decade the quality of Scotch cloth had soared. In many a foreign market it was more sought after, for its density, than English products; Mr Moodie played no small part in that progress.

There was, however, no "empire" that anyone in Balnesmoor could detect. James Simpson Moodie's "interests" were not conglomerated in any one place. They sprawled across four shires, were "lost" in a hundred villages, five hundred cottages. The extent of his holdings could be tallied only from records of income and outgoings which were penned, by Mr Moodie and no other, in two tall ledgers that never left a locked chest in Moss House.

Only two men in all the world had a notion of the sort of power in the woollen textile trade that Mr Moodie had earned for himself and might hazard, as an exercise, a decent guess at the extent of his fortune. But they knew better than to speak of it, not even to each other.

Robert Rudge and John Scarf were Mr Moodie's principal agents, his left hand and his right. They dealt through lesser agents and managers who knew James Simpson Moodie only by reputation and not by sight. Rudge and Scarf, like Moodie, were men fired by ambition to rise high in the world. Their employer trusted them not at all. He used them, gave them responsibility, shed many minor chores on to their shoulders. But he lay in wait for them, out of sight like a fox in the hay, with his eyes always on them, just waiting for the occasion when one or other would pocket a pound he had not earned; then he would see Rudge, or it might be Scarf, swing for it, by God he would – and the other would be a saint ever after.

On arrival at Ottershaw Mr Moodie left the handling of the Cabriolet to the boy, who had as assured an air about him as his master, though in pint-size.

Moodie went around the front of the big house to enter by the front door. He gave his greatcoat and hat to Hunter and went upstairs to the library. Moodie was dressed in the height of quiet Edinburgh fashion in double-breasted coat, high stock, pale buff kerseymere breeches and half-boots polished black as bitumen. He exuded virility. He had a breadth to his chest and a strength that a professional wrestler would have envied, the result of years of pulling the lever of the loom and of deliberate exercising with two flat-irons to take the crook out of his spine. Brown-eyed, dark-haired, Moodie was a strikingly authoritative figure in contrast to the elderly laird.

Gout and gallstones had diminished Sir Gilbert's goodly humour. To all but his grandchildren he was a miserable, irascible old man. He huddled in a quilted gown, a stocking-cap stuck on his bald pate, his swollen feet and legs encased in dirty wrappings of lamb's-wool smeared with an unguent that Hunter had made up for him by an apothecary in Balfron. He left the sanctuary of the library only on the warmest summer forenoons or at the end of lambing to have the flock run before him while he sat in blankets on the terrace below. To Moodie, Sir Gilbert Bontine was no grand lord of the manor. He was a professional sheep-breeder, with the knowledge and wherewithal to experiment. The relationship between the ex-hand-loom weaver and the decaying gentleman could be summed up in one word – Cheviots.

In a part of the country given over to the grazing of the hardy Black-face, which could thrive on coarse, exposed mountainsides, the Cheviot was a rare sight indeed. But Cheviots had a close fleece of straight wool and, properly sheared, provided the quality that Moodie required for fashionable products of the looms. Moodie paid Sir Gilbert top price for white — unsalved – fleeces; forty-five shillings per stone of 24 lbs of wool. With the closing of trade with the Baltic, it had become difficult to acquire tar for smearing at any reasonable cost. This suited Moodie very well. Naturally, Sir Gilbert had tried tobacco-juice dips, which were cheaper but tainted the wool. On Moodie's advice, he had abandoned this practice. Sir Gilbert had also introduced. for a brief period, new Leicesters. But their wool, though abundant, was inferior to that of the original flock of Cheviots and, under Moodie's influence, the old laird was content now to build upon what he had.

Cheviot sheep were becoming more common, though some die-hards complained that they lost their teeth too early. Other farmers were trying out Black-face ewes on Cheviot rams for hardy crossbreeds. Sir Gilbert held to pure-bred stock. He had learned too how to divide the flock and partition ground for ewes, weaned lambs and dinmonts, how to save lush grass for certain feeding seasons. He made his profits in several ways. Fattened wethers would fetch eighty shillings on killing day, and second-best rams could be hired out for the season to farmers in the Ochils and the Grampians for as much as a hundred-and-fifty guineas.

It was about such matters that the conversations of Sir Gilbert and James Simpson Moodie were composed. There was little or no small talk. Sheep were their meeting ground, the field of their obsession.

That particular morning, however, Moodie had another piece of business to discuss with Laird Bontine, not entirely divorced from the care and feeding of Cheviot sheep, of course, but not quite what Sir Gilbert expected.

Moodie was given coffee, a refreshment he favoured over wine or spirits. When the servant had departed through the door of the long room, the weaver plunged at once into business.

He explained what he wanted, and why.

Sir Gilbert, head tucked into the collar of the robe like a mouldy old owl, scowled and squinted at his guest. Facial distaste did not signify displeasure, however, but merely indicated that his feet were throbbing.

"Dyers' Dyke?" Sir Gilbert said. "It is not mine to give, my good chap. At least, it is not mine at the moment."

"How long does the lease have to run?"

"Nineteen years, less eleven since renewal. That is – eight years."

"I'm reluctant to wait eight years, Gilbert."

"I've no reason to reclaim. I mean, Docherty has the acres in good fettle. Cochran saw to that. He grass feeds. Sinclair provided him with the base compounds but Cochran paid for them."

"Does Docherty continue the improvements?"

"I have heard nothing to the contrary, although, to be candid, I leave it much to Sinclair since the sheep went off and Cochran, before his demise, restored cattle."

"But the sheep – the Cheviots – they did thrive, did they not?"

"Throve and prospered."

"What sort of wool weight did they provide, do you recall?"

"Much as my own. They were salved, though. I could not dissuade Cochran from it. He was intent on smearing."

"Too many fleas an' tics on the ground after cattle," said Moodie. "He was being cautious."

"Perhaps, perhaps. He would have gone for white wool, I'm sure, if he had been given time."

"Time," said Moodie. "Eight years is too long to wait for expiry of the lease."

"In which case you have my apology, James. There's little I can do to speed the process. She has it sealed on paper. Uncommon the arrangement may be, but it was composed by my own legal gentleman, Mr O'Hara, who is regarded as an expert in contractual matters and in the laws of heritable property."

"Heritable property?" said Moodie.

"Cochran wished to ensure that the tenancy would pass down."

"To the Patterson woman, his wife?"

"To the daughters too," said Sir Gilbert. "Damned peculiar thing for a man to do."

"I was under the impression," said Moodie, "that tenancy of leased property reverted to the disposition of the land-owner on the death of the assignee."

"Invariably, invariably," said Sir Gilbert. "But Cochran was a damned persuasive fellow as you may recall, having had dealings with him yourself."

Moodie grunted. He had had few direct commercial dealings with Coll Cochran. Rolling and punching on the floor of the manse in one's hot-headed youth was hardly the basis for a relationship of material value. He had, however, spied on Cochran, particularly on the Cheviot flock which Cochran had bought and raised on the coarse acres of Dyers' Dyke. If it had been mere Black-faces, Moodie would have expressed no whit of interest. Cheviots were another matter. The thrive of the flock intrigued him. He had scrounged what information he could at the time from Sir Gilbert, also from Sinclair. It was, of course, Sir Gilbert who had persuaded Cochran to experiment with the breed.

"May I enquire, Gilbert, as to who persuaded whom to do what?"

"Pardon?" Sir Gilbert cupped a hand round his ear.

Moodie explained in simpler terms.

"Ah-hah! Ah-hah!" said Sir Gilbert. "Aye, yes, yes. The fact of it, James, is that I heard from Sinclair that Cochran was keen to extend his tenancy through legal acquittal, a document, to ensure that his lawful wife and female heirs reaped for a period the benefits of his not inconsiderable labours upon the larger and the smaller portion."

"Did – may I enquire – Sinclair press you into a decision?"

'Sinclair felt it was nothing we would lose by."

"Sinclair's always been keen on the Patterson woman. Now he has her incorporated into the bosom of his family," said Moodie. "Be that as it may – let's return to the Cheviots."

"I would not at once agree to put the tenancy into the hands of a woman and two girls. But there was the 'manager' – you know that story, of Docherty – and when the matter of the Cheviots arose . . ."

"Did Cochran come to you with the suggestion that he raise a select flock of Cheviots on his acres?" asked Moodie, fishing.

"He did. First through Sinclair, then upon his own asking."

"I see," said Moodie. "He sought your advice?"

"Who other would he call upon for advice on Cheviots?"

"Very shrewd of the chap, though."

Sir Gilbert showed his rotted teeth and winked. "I was not entirely oblivious to the ruse. It was done to fascinate me, to curry favour towards his extraordinary proposal regarding the tenancy."

"In short, Gilbert, you capitulated."

"There was no loss of gain," said Sir Gilbert. "I took no risk with the possibility that all the damned sheep would die of bloat or turn bald with nibbling laurel. I had no hand in the purchase of the flock – which was hardly more than a dozen head at first – though Sinclair inspected them on arrival to make sure they were healthy."

"Cochran obtained his unusual lease, did he not?"

"I'm no prophet, James. I didn't imagine that Cochran would fall over in a seizure with eight years standing on the tenancy."

"Two plots of ground, too," said Moodie, with the faint implication that he might have been less generous than the laird if he had had the ownership of such farmlands.

"The Nettleburn is nothing; a patch, no more. It should be planted with trees, perhaps, for it's far off the road."

"Yet the grass is excellent, I'm told," said Moodie.

More brown teeth, more winking and twitching; Sir Gilbert eased his swollen legs carefully until he was half-turned to Moodie, close enough to stretch out his old hand and place it on the younger man's shoulder.

"Aye, yes, aye. That's what Cochran proved. The grass *is* excellent."

Moodie said, "I take it – you must excuse my temerity

271

in putting this to you, Sir Gilbert – I take it that you would not consider a sale of Bontine land?"

Sir Gilbert was not shocked. He might be senile in appearance, rattled now and again in speech, but his brain was perceptive enough and he still relished the machinations of petty dealing. It had come to him what Moodie was about with this request.

Sir Gilbert gave a straight and unequivocal reply.

"I would not, James."

"That's as I expected."

"Not even to you. Not even if you tempt me with your gold. Not even if you promise to buy pure-bred stock from Linburn, each ewe with a pedigree as long as an arm, each ram sired by Standish. Bontines do not cut off their body."

"I would take a thirty-year lease."

"On Dyers' Dyke?"

"On the Nettleburn too."

"Why?"

"I intend to become a progressive wool grower."

"You? In plaid and boots, tramping the hillside with a wedge of cheese in your sack and a dog at your heels? I can't see it, James."

Moodie smiled. "I wouldn't tend the flock personally."

"It would be all Cheviots?"

"Certainly."

"But the ground?"

"I would invest in improvements. I would run the pastures from the edge of the moss all along the ground above the track, that whole length from the quarry to the steep of Drumglass."

Sir Gilbert's eyes grew luminous. A dozen years seemed to fall from him. In an almost sprightly manner he hoisted himself from the chair and, using his stick, picked his way to the tall windows. He braced himself and peered out at the marginal view of the half-high hillside above the trees.

Moodie rose too and joined the laird at the window.

"It can be done, Gilbert. It can be cleared. The grazings can be brought to good growth by diligent preparation and planned protection. Not too many sheep."

"How many?"

"Three hundred."

"Three hundred, do ye say?" Sir Gilbert was impressed. "How many acres do you wish to lease from me?"

"Three hundred," said Moodie. "The long strip."

"It would be a sight, would it not?" said the laird. "Aye, James, though I might not survive to see the pastures white with God's creatures, it would be a fine thing for my sons."

"I cannot wait eight years. I need the leases turned to me within a year."

Sir Gilbert turned, staggered; Moodie supported him with an arm about the waist.

"I can find no means, short of outrageous tyranny, for evicting the Patterson woman. I'll not do it, James, not even for you and a thousand white-fleece sheep. After all, man, *she* is one of my flock. It would be a grave thing for the family's reputation if I failed to attend her interests too."

"Few men would be so generous," said Moodie, grimly.

Sir Gilbert leaned his shoulder against the glass, dabbed a forefinger on the pane. "I can recall the sight of her sprachlin' across the park, as if it was yesterday. She was a handsome creature when she was in her prime."

Moodie made no comment.

He said, "The younger girl is recently married, is she not?"

"To my grieve's son," the laird replied.

"Leaving the elder child – unwed – with her mother?"

"So I believe," said Sir Gilbert, still gazing out over his rain-dabbled parklands to the trees.

"Cochran's legacy," said Moodie, thoughtfully, "must surely contain instruction as to the redisposition of the leases in the event of marriage."

Sir Gilbert had lost concentration, lost interest in this twist of conversation. He had heard Mr Moodie's request and, in all conscience, had been unable to grant it. Yet the weaver's scheme to run the long rolling strips of the foothills into one renovated pasture had caught the laird's fancy.

"Gilbert?"

The old man rolled against the window and lowered himself to the wooden seat. It was cold so far from the fire.

He shivered and plucked the collar of the robe about his chest.

"Hm?"

James Moodie was again standing by the fire, hands clasped behind his back. He seemed so possessive in that posture that Sir Gilbert had a faint, sad qualm, wishing that his soldier son could be more like him, or that "Wee Gibbie" might show some of Jamie's determined vigour.

"I can't do it, James. I can't fork the women out," said the laird.

"Indeed you can't," said Moodie. "However, it would be highly advantageous if I might see a copy of Cochran's will to ascertain what provision he made in the event of marriage of the legatees; the daughters. In addition, with your permission, might I inspect the leases?"

"That's a simple enough thing to arrange, James."

"I would be obliged to you," said Moodie.

The laird bent to knead his kneecaps with his fists. The ache had gripped him afresh, creeping upwards with the chill in his limbs.

He said, "What will the documents show, however, that might benefit your intention?"

"Perhaps they will indicate that the descent of the leases goes with the daughter."

"What's that you're saying?" Sir Gilbert shook his head.

"I want possession of all half-hill grazings from the quarry to the Nettleburn on a thirty-year renegotiation. You see, Gilbert, I'm weary of joggin' about from post to pillar like a damned drover. I'm anxious to bring my business close to the place of my birth, to Balnesmoor."

"Business?"

"I have offered for Kennart."

"Kennart? But why?"

"To build a blanket-mill there."

"But you don't require fine wool for blanket-making."

"The blanket-mill would be the hub of it, only the hub."

Sir Gilbert Bontine shook his head at the audacity of the man. Out of shifty wee elders came such giants of commerce; a sympton of the age they lived in, he supposed. For all that, he was startled by the scope of James's vision. Moodie had indicated that it would not stop with a blanket-mill, which meant he had in mind one of the new-fangled manufactories.

Sir Gilbert did not disapprove. On the contrary.

"But what, pray, does this programme have to do with the Cochran woman and the clauses in the farmer's will?" said the laird.

"I agree that evicting sittin' tenants without just cause would be unpardonable," said Moodie. "But in settlin' this matter, I am – in confidence – not prepared to be patient."

"It seems to me there's no means of settling it, James."

"I believe there might be."

"How?"

"By marriage."

"Marriage? Whose marriage?"

"My marriage."

"And who would you choose to marry, may I ask?"

"Elspeth Cochran, of course," James Moodie said.

It was the nineteenth day of her marriage, hardly more than a week before Christmas, though there was no trace of seasonal cheer in the cottage, particularly at the unholy hour of a quarter past five in the morning.

At first Anna thought he was romping. Matt's high spirits, however ungentle, amused her and made her feel close, especially as they usually led to romping of another kind in the pine-framed bed in the back room. But it was not playfulness that caused Matt to snap the blankets from her body and leave her, shift twined about her legs, crying in the bitter half-dark, "What are you doin', Matt?"

"Time you were up."

"God, what time *is* it?"

"You've to make me a peck."

"You're not due 'til seven."

"I'm due when I say I'm due, Anna."

She leapt from the bed, reaching for her undergarments, as Matt banged into the kitchen. Quivering with cold and anger, Anna followed her husband. She had been warned, by no less a person than Mr Sinclair, that Matt was moody and truculent but she had dismissed the opinion as biased.

275

She had learned quickly enough that Matt was no model of Lachlan. Of a different stamp, his quietness and apparent politeness had been signs of repression, fear of and respect for the iron hand of the grieve. But the grieve was a mile away, in his own home; this was Matt's domain and she was Matt's wife, for better or worse. It would be well for her to bear in mind that the son was not, emphatically not, fair and firm like the father.

But Anna was resentful, without judiciousness. She had much to learn; and Matt to teach her.

"When *are* you due?" she shouted.

"Six," Matt told her. "Seven yesterday. Six o'clock from now on."

"But, but why?"

"Because I do what I'm told wi'out askin' stupid questions," Matt snapped. "Now get that bloody fire kindled."

"You said you'd see t' the fire."

"I said nothin' o' the bloody sort. I lit the fire for you because I had the extra hour. Now it's time for you t' start behavin' like a decent wife." He spoke less viciously. "You shouldn't have to be told that, Anna."

He seated himself by the dead embers and pulled on his thick stockings and half-boots, stiff, greasy things with nailed soles necessary to grip the slippery walks of the forest.

Every night he fussed with the boots, laving suet-fat into the leather, tapping the nails tight with a tiny black hammer. He sharpened the axe too, rasping it on a whetstone, dripping oil on it, buffing and polishing the head of the tool endlessly, endlessly, until Anna felt she might scream at his sheer monotonous concentration. The axe was a mark of his low station. It seemed quite wrong to Anna that he should give it more than casual attention. She had married a stranger, a handsome boy; he was not at all what she had expected him to be.

If anything, the kitchen was colder than the bedroom. Flagstones were set into earth foundations, the hearth sunk slightly below the level of the floor. The overmantel was a pine log, stripped and varnished. Matt had lit the candle in its holder and set it there. At that hour the wan yellow light served only to accentuate the bleakness of the room.

Matt stamped the boots on to his feet. Scratching on the stone, the nails set Anna's teeth on edge. She bit off protest and bent to the hearth. She knew perfectly well how to set a fire but Gaddy had spoiled her and she had never been required to be efficient and thorough, not when she was clever enough to evade the more unpleasant chores most of the time. The same held true for cooking. Gaddy, even Elspeth, had let her off with so much that incompetence had become ingrained. Now, even when she tried, she found it difficult to do the simplest chores. It was an anomaly that not many – and certainly not Matt Sinclair – would understand, how a girl who had been reared in a hut could have remained ignorant of the rudiments of housekeeping.

"What the devil're you doin'?" Matt shouted.

"Puttin' on twigs."

"God an' Jesus!" He pulled her back. "Clean the hearth first. Scoop out the ashes."

"What with, Matt?"

Tears, heavy and cold, gathered under Anna's lids. She snuffled. But Matt had already grown wise to that particular ploy and was not taken in by it.

"*This*." He kicked the heart-shaped shovel across the hearth.

Perfectly well she knew what the shovel was for. She employed it when Matt was at work, though mostly as a griddle for roasting chestnuts. But she felt thick and dull-witted at this hour with the strap of the rain on the roof and icy wind sneaking under the door to nip her bare legs and feet.

Matt sat down again, solidly, hands on thighs. Anna did not dare defy him long enough to find her woollen bodice and shoes. For eighteen mornings she had wakened to the crackle of the fire and tadpoles of warm light darting on the floor and the smell of simmering oatmeal. She had snuggled into the straw mattress listening to the weather, listening to Matt, waiting for him to come and say, "Up now, sweetheart," to come again in five minutes and say again, "Up, or it'll be the worse for you." She would refuse to rise from the bed until he roved his hands under the blankets and tickled her and made her laugh.

She had known in her heart that such carryings-on would not last long but the phase had ended so abruptly that she was hurt by it. It was not until many years had passed that Anna could ask herself if she, not Matt, had been responsible for transforming her husband into a bully and a lout, if it had all gone wrong for her in those first weeks of wedlock.

She plied the little iron spade, unused to being observed while she worked. Tears rolled, unforced, down her cheeks but she pursed her lips and turned her back to her husband so that he would not see them. She lifted the spade, piled with white ash, then rose and ran across the kitchen with it. When she opened the door the ash blew back on her and spread in a grey, gritty blizzard across the kitchen.

Matt shook his head in disgust. "Use the bloody box, Anna, that's what it's for."

Anna had often watched Mammy dumping fire ash into a wicker creel, but the difference in shape, the sophistication of the special rectangular box with its sleeve of iron, had scattered her sense as the draught had scattered the ashes. Matt was right to chide her, though she would not admit it to herself there and then.

"Sweep it up," he said.

She closed the door, put down the spade, went for a broom and scratched frantically at the litter on the flagstones.

"Matt, I canna help it. I'm not used t' lookin' after –"

"Better get used t' it then. I didn't marry a whore. I married a wife."

So that was it; he had been as spoiled, in a way, as she had been. What he expected was a perfect duplicate of his mother, fledged in all the housecrafts and dedicated to his welfare. Rage suppurated in Anna. She whirled on him.

"Aye, an' what did I marry, I wonder," she cried. "You're not your damned father yet, Matt Sinclair, that can bellow out orders an' have everybody jump. Even your mam."

Temper bred temper and Matt exploded at this apparent insult to his family. He gave Anna a shove that sent her sprawling into the hearth. "Next time I'll leather you 'til you canna stand up."

For an instant Anna was contrite, afraid, realising that Matt too was lost in the unfamiliarity of this shared intimacy, that he had no more wish to be stuck with her than she had with him, that change rankled bitterly within her husband too. She switched again, pleading for understanding. "Matt, I'm sorry. I'll . . . I'll do my best."

Matt, however, had no sympathy to spare. Her terms weren't good enough for the grieve's son. He snorted, hooked his jacket and muffler from the peg and, without a word of consolation or farewell, stalked out of the cottage into the darkness.

For several minutes Anna sat where she had fallen.

Hugging herself, she gazed upon the half-open door which creaked mournfully on its hinges. She could hear the pine boughs thrashing in the fretful wind, could smell the dank odour of the undergrowth. She sniffed back her tears. What would Matt do, she wondered, if she threw on her shawl and ran home to Mammy on the Nettleburn, refused to return to the prison the Sinclairs had built for her in the forest, refused to return to Matt's bed, ever again? Mammy would send her back, of course. Matt was her lawful husband and she belonged, in everybody's eyes, not only with him but to him.

Anna got to her feet. She was shaking, sick with shock at the incident and what it had revealed of the true state of her marriage and the bitterness that twisted within Matt Sinclair. She could not equate her husband with the boy who had run the thoroughbred round and round the stableyard at Ottershaw only a handful of months ago. What depths were there in Matt still to be uncovered? She shivered violently.

Hurriedly she scraped a hollow in the ashes in the hearth, those that she had neglected to remove. She searched in the basket for twigs, made a little cone of them, lit it from the candle and squatted before the flames, though there was no heat yet. Soon, however, she was able to add stick then splits of cordwood and to hang the kettle upon its hook with some hope that it would boil.

She took the candle and, shielding it with her hand, went to the door.

"Matt," she called. "Matt, are ye there?"

She expected no answer. Her husband would be half-way up the path to the hut in the clearing a thousand feet into

279

the forest, stumbling through the darkness and the rain. She experienced a twitch of pity for him but her own misery soon extinguished it. She closed and latched the door then went into the back room.

She secured the candle in a water-dish and, without undressing, rolled into the bed and pulled the blankets about her. Her feet were like pieces of ice. She rubbed them together, with vigour at first then more languorously. She wiped her nose on her wrist and burrowed deeper into the folds of clothing.

Matt would not return to stir her out now. She would have no callers; the day was far too wet for Mammy or Elspeth to trail down from the Nettleburn and Mrs Sinclair, as Matt constantly bragged, was far too conscientious to curtail her own housekeeping to visit a daughter-in-law of whom she thoroughly disapproved.

Damn the Sinclairs. She cared not a jot for their good opinion. In any case, when March came and the new calves were born, work would be found for her in the dairy at Ottershaw. She would be expected to cook, clean, sew for Matt Sinclair – and to toil for six or seven hours every morning in the milking parlour for an extra few shillings a week. Only having babies would bring respite from out-work.

Anna slid her hand over her stomach. Had Matt already put a bairn in her? She prayed to God that he had not, not even for the freedom it would grant her to stay home all day. She didn't want a child, especially *his* child. A child would mean more work, more mess and less of Matt's attention.

Anger mulled into pleasurable resentment, an emotion which warmed and soothed Anna, such was her selfish nature. She would sleep for most of the morning, by which time the filled kettle would be simmering and the fire would have warmed up the kitchen and she would take pleasure in her breakfast, lingering over it.

Drowsily the young wife stared at the guttering candle. Smiling like a child she let herself drift into sleep, dreaming of summer. Summer gone, however, and not summers yet to come; dreaming of Randall Bontine.

* * *

280

The tale that James Moodie told the laird was more than half true. He had deceived the old man, however, in the matter of his motives and the inspirational nature of his notion that marriage to Elspeth Cochran might bring him the tracts of land upon which he had set his heart. In certain aspects of character Mr Moodie was still the wee kirk elder. That role had been played with such conviction for so many years that it had shaped the man for ever.

Unlike Peter Docherty, Moodie did not want the young woman as a helpmate and companion. He saw her in a different and more complex light, as something so valuable that she could not be bought and as something – what? pagan? – that tempted him by the legacy of blood. Etched into his memory was the face of the dead girl, the stranger. Her lineaments, her pathetic anonymity were more vividly retained than any other image. For James Simpson Moodie she had personified an ultimate degradation. She had died not only without dignity but without identity. For the kirk elder, for the prosperous weaver, she embodied a destiny which he feared more than he feared the eternal fires of hell.

Moodie had not consorted with whores and gypsy lassies as had Peter Docherty. He had known but three women. The comparatively brief liaisons had been entered into with caution and abandoned without regret.

The first genuine affair had been with the wife of an Edinburgh feed merchant. It had been furtive enough to stir Moodie's fondness for plot and contrivance. Mrs Matilda Dobie had not been particularly passionate or instructive, though.

The second *affaire de coeur* had been more satisfactory in all respects, ornamented with all the trappings of romantic tragedy. Deirdre Garstang was the only daughter of a well-to-do wool grower who lived in a great gaunt house in the middle of a Perthshire moor. Deirdre was of the Roman Church and, to boot, was reputedly dying of the consumption. She was not expected to marry. She could not, in any case, have taken a Presbyterian for a husband. At thirty years of age, Deirdre had the dark, hawk-handsome features of a prophetess. Scholarly, in-turned, mystical, she had lured James Moodie to her bed during one of his infrequent visits to Garstang House. She had practically broken his spine with her enthusiasm for love-making.

For three years the weaver and the "dying" woman had been lovers, although they had, in fact, shared a bed only eight times. The affair was mainly conducted in a series of scalding letters from Deirdre to James and, at the rate of one to five, rather dry responses from James to Deirdre, missives which were carefully composed to give nothing away. In the end the correspondence had died a sudden death; not that Deirdre succumbed to fretting of the lungs. She went on a visit to cousins in Norwich and there met and swiftly married an Assize judge. Deirdre was, to Moodie's knowledge, living still, quite happily, with her widower husband in Yarmouth.

In many ways James Simpson Moodie was a man riddled with conceits, yet he did not assume that he need only snap his fingers to have women running at his beck and call. He was by no means ugly and took care by grooming to hide the scars that thirty years of manual labour had inflicted upon his frame. He could, of course, have "purchased" a wife, and a very good wife at that. Stirling society, not to stray as far afield as Edinburgh, offered a fair stock of well-brought-up young women who would be only too delighted to marry into money.

But James Moodie would have no bargain wife. Indeed he wanted no wife at all. He wanted only Elspeth.

He thought of Elspeth obsessively. Gaddy Patterson's daughter. It was not the girl he would have to woo but the mother. The girl could have no knowledge of him, really, bear no animosity towards him. She had never known him as Jamie Moodie, the minister's lickspittle, Jamie Moodie, the cottage weaver. If she was aware of him at all, it would be as a wealthy and influential gentleman. Age had no part in the reckoning.

Any other mother of any other daughter in the parish would have rolled on his doorstoop like a mare to have him encourage thoughts of betrothal in her daughter's breast, particularly if the woman was a widow. Gaddy Patterson, Moodie believed, was different. He had created a little legend about the highland woman. For all his guile, he felt a shade daunted by the task he had set himself, at least by the beginning of it – making the first move.

For six or seven years, since the girl had begun to advance towards womanhood, James Moodie had taken every opportunity to study her. He did not lower himself, or degrade her, by spying upon her but would, from time to time, put himself in a position to observe her closely. Though he was no longer a member of the Balnesmoor kirk – he had transferred to Harlwood soon after retirement as Mr Leggat's elder – he occasionally took Communion there. He made a point of turning out for every festival at which the Patterson woman might attend. The girls, both of them, were remarkably pretty, though there was in the younger a stridency that did not suit Moodie's picture of a wife. As Elspeth grew to maturity, however, James Moodie's qualms vanished. He must marry her. There was no other solution.

Gaddy had no inkling of the weaver's intention. No thought was further from her mind. Elspeth, when she thought of Mr Moodie at all, regarded him in approximately the same category as the laird himself, as a "social presence" and hardly as a real person. Mr Moodie was distinctive because of his carriage and his mode of dress, not because of his personality which he made no effort now to impose upon the community.

James Simpson Moodie spent a great deal of time pondering a method of approach to his wooing of Elspeth Cochran. He decided that he had best make a start to the business very soon and that he had best be brave and straight about it. He had been patient long enough.

It was, though Moodie had no means of knowing it, upon the selfsame day, eighteen years before, that Coll Cochran had first declared himself to Gaddy Patterson. Christmas fell upon the Sabbath. Mr Leggat celebrated it thoroughly, though there were Scottish parishes, not a hundred miles away, where Christmas was hardly recognised at all.

The morning brought intermittent squalls of freezing rain. The weather had not been clement for almost a three-month, though snow had been kept at bay by wet, west winds. Tattered as an old shawl, cloud dragged across the hills and obscured the loch and mountains. It was a dull, somewhat thin assemblage at the kirk. Mr Leggat's increasing feyness and the state of the weather did not encourage Christians to turn out since the discipline of the kirk habit had waned in Balnesmoor.

Mr Moodie cantered up in a smart little gig with a hood to it. His mother came, like a duchess, in the Cabriolet with the tweedy wee lad riding behind and the Moodies' groom at the reins. Nobody who noticed the arrival of the procession thought much about it, assuming, perhaps, that the Cabriolet would be used after the service to convey guests back to the house for a bite to eat or a glass of Madeira.

After Mr Leggat had wended through the service, hemming and hawing and smiling fondly, Mother Moodie was escorted by her son to the Cabriolet and the groom and the lad whisked her off along the Harlwood road, while Mr Moodie returned to pass words with Sir Gilbert's wife and Young Gilbert in the lee of the kirkside gable.

Mr Moodie, Young Gilbert later remarked, must have been early at the sherry decanter, for his eyes were much distracted and he stammered now and again which was *most* unlike the weaver chap, who was notoriously abstemious.

What distracted James Simpson Moodie was the sight of Gaddy and Elspeth Cochran gathered with the Sinclairs.

It had not occurred to Moodie that Lachlan Sinclair might provide transportation for the whole family, including his newly acquired relatives from the Nettleburn. But Sinclair had certain duties to attend to for Sir Gilbert's wife in the getting of a carriage from the yard of the Ramshead and, to Moodie's relief, Gaddy and her daughters and the stalwart son-in-law set off on foot down the Main Street.

Minutes later, just as the first fortuitous slashes of a fresh squall romped over the rooftops, Mr Moodie brought the hooded gig round from the inn yard and, clipping briskly, drew it up adjacent to the Widow Cochran and her daughters.

The four stopped.

The four stared.

Moodie mustered a friendly smile.

Now, his decision made, the weaver permitted himself to meet the girl's eye. She looked less surprised than her mother or sister, almost – Moodie could not but indulge the hope – as if she had already remarked his interest in her.

"Not much of a Yule," he said, leaning from under the canopy. "In the matter of climate, I mean."

"Indeed, it is not, Mr Moodie."

It was the younger girl who answered him. She spoke out boldly. He did not take his eye from Elspeth, however. She wore a becoming, plain-ribbed pelisse of fair quality kerseymere; lined, Moodie noticed. It had not been bought at Balfron market with a shilling and sixpence. Her slipper-shoes were fashionable rather than practical and had rounded toes, not the nebs that marked them as the model of yesteryear. The Cottage hat was held in place with a thin scarf of Kashmir-patterned wool. What was more, the girl wore the clothes well, without that swaggering dash which distracted from their proper line.

"Did you find enjoyment in the service, ladies?"

Elspeth could be in no doubt that the question was asked of her.

She hesitated, gave him a glance from her blue, blue eyes.

"It had the merit of not bein' over long, sir."

Moodie laughed. Damn it, if he had to play the gladsome gallant he might as well do it thoroughly. He was famed for his sobriety; let her find novelty in his gaiety.

Rain skated down the slope of the roof and was flung from the shaven eaves.

"If," said James Moodie, quickly, "you are returning home to the Nettleburn, Mistress Patt . . . Cochran, or, indeed, are journeying t' spend the day with your wedded daughter at Ottershaw, may I offer you a ride under the hood?"

Gaddy breathed high in her chest, as if the wind had robbed her of enough breath to reply.

"If you're makin' an offer open to –" Anna began.

Gaddy intervened. "We're goin' home, Mr Moodie, in company."

"It's a verra long way in this rain," Moodie said.

It was an amazing thing to behold, James Moodie thought, how recognition of his intention seemed to come at once upon the girl. She might have been raised at Bath

or Tunbridge Wells or in the drawing-room of Lady Mac-
linden in Edinburgh's George Street and not by a drover's
drab and a coarse hill farmer, so polite and modest was her
response.

"We'd be thanked if you would, sir," Elspeth replied. "If
it's no inconvenience. My mother finds the road heavy in
the wet season."

"It's not inconvenient in the slightest," said James
Moodie, getting down from the gig.

He held the rein with his left hand and offered Gaddy his
right. He noticed how the younger one, the married one,
dug her sister's ribs with her elbow and whispered to her,
though he could not catch the words because of the tune
the rain was playing. Unformulated plans for Gaddy and
Elspeth to return to the gloomy cottage in the pine woods
at the hind end of the Ottershaw parks were abandoned on
the spot. Perhaps it was out of peevishness that the younger
one tried to persuade her Mam to stick to her guns.

Gaddy hesitated.

Elspeth gave her a gentle prod with the flat of her hand.

"Go on, Mammy."

Gaddy glanced at the man's outstretched hand then
looked up into his face, into his eyes, in search of transform-
ation and some sign of contrition. All the old enmity was
still in her, left lie from days of long ago. She could not
easily put aside the ranklements that Moodie's hostility had
engendered. But the hill was long, the going heavy and the
wind did suck her breath away. Besides, it would be wrong
of her to wish upon Elspeth the petty spite that had lingered
through half a generation. For Elspeth's sake, she would at
least be civil.

"Thank you, Mr Moodie," Gaddy said.

She allowed him to hoist her up by the slung-step into
the conveyance which, not being large, dipped under her
weight.

"Miss?" said Moodie.

Elspeth's hand touched his. He closed his fingers on her
fingers. The weaver would not have negotiated for mere
touch but, having achieved it in the unspectacular demon-
stration of politeness, found that it thrilled him. She went

up lightly, settled without fussing, hard against her mother's massive flank.

Moodie gave the younger girl and her dummy of a husband a curt bow. "I'm sorry I haven't the big carriage with me but you must use your young legs to be away home quickly out of the rain."

"Never mind us," said Anna, sharply. "We'll be all right." Possessively she snaked her elbow through her husband's arm. "Matt an' me'll be home in two shakes of a lamb's tail, won't we, sweetheart?" She tossed her head, for her sister's benefit. "We've a big rib of fresh beef waitin' in the roastin' box, haven't we, Matt?"

Matt Sinclair made no contribution to the conversation. He watched sullenly as Mr Moodie climbed to his seat, gave the shiny canopy a jerk with his hand to tip it well forward, clicked the reins and was off with Gaddy and Elspeth as if he had captured them for ransom.

Gaddy watched closely to see what she might expect of him.

Peter said, "It was the decent thing t' do, I suppose, Mistress Cochran."

"To ask himself in?"

"I thought you said you did the askin'?"

"He tied the horse t' the gate an' 'escorted' us across the field. We could hardly leave him standin' outside, what with the rain lowerin' in again."

"I don't understand why you're so hot an' bothered," said Peter Docherty. "By the bye, where's Elspeth?"

"At home. She's got work t' do for me today."

Peter nodded.

They were seated in the shelter of the barn, Gaddy on a broken straw, Peter on a milking stool. He was smoking a thin clay tobacco pipe which he held between crooked fingers. The acrid haze made Gaddy cough but she could not object. Coll had taught him the habit. Besides, she liked to see a man enjoy tobacco. But the smoke did catch her down the line of the breastbone. She had found the plod up the track, with mud like melted lard, very hard going.

Peter said, "What did he say, Moodie, when he came in?"

"Precious little worth hearin'."

"Did he take liquor?"

"He asked for a dish of tea."

Docherty laughed. "Aye, that'd be a strange sight, Weaver Moodie sittin' in yon hut jugglin' a cup like a lady."

"There's nothin' wrong with the hut, Peter. It's been a fine, dry house for me an' mine these eighteen years."

"I intendit no offence, missus."

She couldn't imagine why she was waspish with Docherty. He had done her no harm. Neither, when she thought of it, had James Moodie. But old scars ached in Moodie's company, though she could find little enough trace of "the elder" in the man now.

Peter said, "Moodie must've said somethin'."

"He talked with Elspeth about sheep."

"Sheep? Since when did Elspeth become expert in that subject?"

"Since she herded the Cheviots Coll bought."

"Aye, Moodie would talk about Cheviots all day."

"What d'you mean, Peter?"

"He was for after buyin' the Cheviot wool clip from Coll when he had them, but the master wouldn't sell."

"I've heard naught about this," Gaddy said.

She was puzzled, and slightly annoyed; Coll had usually confided in her, sought her advice, especially where livestock was concerned.

"It was done here at the Dyke."

"How long ago?"

"I canna remember. When he had the Cheviots on the grass. Six years, would it be?" Peter said.

"Coll breathed not a word about it."

"He maybe felt there was no need. He turned Moodie down flat."

"Was it Moodie himself?"

"Aye, the second time. The first time it was his agent. Rudge was his name, I recall."

"Coll refused t' have truck with him?"

"Refused outright."

"You heard the talk, Peter, I suppose?"

"Nah, nah, Mistress Cochran. I just caught the gist o' it."

"Then Jamie Moodie came?"

"I was surprised. So was the master. I mean, what's a puckle o' sheep, just the twenty-four head, t' a man like James Moodie? Him that owns so much."

Gaddy said, "Much is made up of little, Peter. Besides, Moodie needs all the fine clip he can buy to feed his spinners and dyers."

"Aye, that's true enough."

"Did Coll raise his voice?"

"Not that I can recall. They talked in the yard for ten minutes, then – aye, I remember now – then they shook hands."

"And?"

"I asked the master, after Mr Moodie'd gone away, if he'd sold his fleeces before shearin'. Mr Cochran said he'd burn them in quicklime first."

"How did he say it?"

"I thought at the time," said Peter Docherty, "that he never really meant it. I thought he was pleased 'cause Moodie had come t' him, 'cause Moodie thought the Cheviots were worth buyin'."

"Moodie only wanted wool, not mutton?"

"Aye, only the wool."

Gaddy sat forward, resting her arms on her stomach.

"We keep no sheep now, Peter, so what could he be wantin'?"

"It'll be nothin'."

"It was somethin'," said Gaddy.

She was more perplexed than she had been before she had arrived at Dyers' Dyke. Peter was being anything but helpful. She wondered if his vagueness was a trait that had come lately, because of his age, perhaps.

She had had a burrow round the Dyke, too. She had not been pleased by what she had seen. The yard was no longer spick and span as it had been on her last visit. She had trusted Elspeth to report if anything was amiss at the property. But Elspeth had said not a word. Perhaps the deterioration had happened gradually. There was nothing that Gaddy could precisely put her finger on. But for a farm tarpaulined for the winter months the Dyke did not seem tight enough. Was Peter letting go?

This past year or so she had been too occupied with other matters to pay much heed to Dyers' Dyke. From now on, however, she would make regular calls upon Mr Docherty, under some pretext or other, to ensure that he did not allow the well-tended acres to slip into sourness and disrepair.

She got to her feet, earlier than she had planned.

It had been – in some ways, at least – a wasted journey from the Nettleburn. Peter had given her information but no opinion and no interpretation. Maybe she had been wrong to expect it of him. Coll had been the policy-maker, the director and manager. Peter had never been called upon to take real responsibility.

"Are all the cattle out yet?" she asked.

"Aye, they are, Mistress Cochran."

"Cows in calf, too?"

"Aye, it's dry enough in the big field. They'll not suffer much strain yet."

"It's thick, Peter. It's thick everywhere," said Gaddy. "I can tell you without seein' it. Bring the beasts in today or tomorrow."

"But –"

"The barn's stapped wi' feed. Here it's the end o' December, an' only the hardiest should be left on the grass."

"There's grass on, Mistress Cochran. I swear it."

"Would you have them fallin' ill? Damp's the forerunner o' disease, Peter."

"It was t' save the muckin'."

"Can you not cope, Peter?"

He turned his head away and spat tobacco juice into the hay. He closed his fist on the bowl of the clay pipe, intending only to smother the plug, but the anger in him was betrayed by the snapping of the stem. He cast down the crushed fragments to the floor and rubbed them with his boot.

"Aye, I can cope. I just thought a few days' extra grass, since there's been so little snow . . ."

"I'll go out an' see them, Peter."

He seemed about to argue with her but sense got the better of him.

"Will I harness a pony cart for you?" he asked.

"I'll walk. Can I see them from the west gates?"

"Aye, most o' them. Would you prefer them herded, Mistress Cochran?"

"Not today, Peter."

Peter did not seem as easy with her as when Coll was alive.

She would compliment him on the condition of the beasts even if they were lying on their sides with their tongues poking out. She would butter him up today. But tomorrow she would see to it that Elspeth carried orders and that Docherty obeyed them to the letter. Fattening stock must be byred before the snow came. What had possessed Docherty to be so tardy and neglectful? She must ask Elspeth if she'd noticed a change in the man. If, in the lassie's opinion, it reflected or was a reflection of the change in the state of the farm itself.

Peter put on his bonnet and wrapped his muffler around his neck. He hunched his shoulders, though it was less damp and raw than it had been, and walked by Gaddy's side, slow-stepped, across the yard. They walked without exchanging a word as far as the west gates, where three fields joined in awkward corners and the hedges were ramped.

Gaddy went up to the gates and leaned on them, first one and then the other, taking a prospect of the cattle that cropped the scant grass. Docherty stood beside her, not following the rove of her gaze at all, not concerned, apparently, with the cattle.

"I . . . I . . . eh, Mistress Cochran?"

"What is it, Peter?"

"Moodie. Mr Moodie."

"What about him?"

"Is he after the lease o' the Dyke for sheep?"

"Makin' sweet with me to persuade me to change?" said Gaddy. "Aye, I've been struck with the same thought, Peter."

"Or . . . or . . . or . . ."

"Or what?"

"Or is he after Elspeth?" Peter Docherty said.

"Elspeth?" Gaddy swivelled to look into Docherty's eyes, to see if he had gone lunatic. "What would a man like Jamie Moodie want with my Elspeth?"

"What any man would want," said Docherty.

"But Moodie's a . . . a . . . He's wealthy."

"An' she's bonnie."

"Aye, she's that," said Gaddy.

"Any man would want her. Just to see her is t' want her," said Peter Docherty, ingenuously. "God, I'd want her m'self, I tell you, if I had his coffers."

"Want her? How?"

"The way a man wants a woman, missus. In bed. In wedlock or out of it."

"That'll be enough, Peter."

His face was shot crimson. Tobacco had stained the corners of his mouth so that he appeared appallingly mournful.

"I . . . I . . . had t' say it, missus."

"Moodie," said Gaddy Patterson Cochran. "I'd see her wed to the de'il first."

But Gaddy's denunciation did not comfort Peter Docherty. He had heard that sort of statement before, made in exactly the same sort of tone. Like Coll with the Cheviots, Gaddy was flattered that her daughter had caught James Moodie's eye, that the weaver might consider Elspeth good enough to be his wife.

Defeat and despair came over Peter Docherty at that moment.

Gaddy was already turning away from the gates, already setting her feet towards home.

"Mistress Cochran?" He spoke woodenly. "What about the cattle?"

"Hm?" Gaddy did not even glance round.

"What about the beasts?"

"Bring them in, Peter. Just bring them in."

He let her go alone. She had lost interest in him, in the cattle, in Dyers' Dyke. She was thinking, no doubt, of Elspeth.

Peter watched her hurry down the straggled path that would carry her wide of the farmhouse down on to the moor

292

track, saving a quarter of a mile. She could not wait to be home now, to discuss with Elspeth how she felt about the damned weaver, the damned "gentleman", the damned kirk elder who had had the luck to change his life around. If Elspeth did not feel like giving *him* an answer, her Mam would coax, cajole and wheedle until she did. And Docherty knew what, in the end, that answer would be.

There would be no waiting for James Simpson Moodie.

Only for poor Peter Docherty.

He glowered across the gates at the cattle, picking and cropping the thin winter grasses, then he turned away and trudged downhill towards the yard.

Damn her, he would bring them in when *he* felt like it, not on some woman's casual command.

It was too strange and exciting a piece of news to keep. Elspeth was in no doubt that her mother's prediction would in due course come to pass. She was woman enough to realise what Mr Moodie's glances signified, not so maidenly-modest that she did not respond to them, flirting with her eyes.

Jamie Moodie: James Simpson Moodie. It was hard to realise that the strong, handsome man who rode in a Cabriolet and wore fine clothes was the same person that had once tried to ruin her father. She had not, of course, heard all of the story, only scraps of it, acquired in the course of conversations and by eavesdropping. Neither Anna nor she had thought much of Moodie at all, had found insufficient interest in his history to press Mammy for details.

Gaddy was outspoken on her return from her visit to Dyers' Dyke. She went on for a while about Peter Docherty and how insolent he had become, how she was displeased with the manner in which he was attending the farm. It would be a lean crop that would come off the Dyke that year, Gaddy declared. Elspeth was surprised by her mother's accusations; a novel development, this spite at Peter. Elspeth wondered if it had anything to do with her. Four or five minutes later, however, the truth was revealed.

Without preamble, Gaddy said, "Docherty says James Moodie's lookin' for a wife."

"Oh, an' who's he lookin' at?" said Elspeth. "One of the Bontine lassies, is it?"

"No. You."

"Peter's rantin', Mammy."

"Why did Moodie come here?"

Lamely, Elspeth explained that it was a kindly gesture. Gaddy, now, would have none of it.

For ten or fifteen minutes mother and daughter discussed Mr Moodie's possible intentions, with Elspeth denying the suggesting that such a wealthy and well-positioned gentleman could have the slightest interest in her, and Gaddy, in the course of the debate, becoming more and more emphatic.

It was the following forenoon before Elspeth could get away from the Nettleburn and down to Ottershaw to visit Anna.

She had been hurt by her sister's "stealing" of Matt. She would probably never get over it as long as she lived. But – time being what it was to young folk – most of the anger and pain had receded. She hoped that she would find in Anna a suitable audience for her news. She needed, as girls will, a confidante.

To Elspeth's surprise, Anna was on her hands and knees on the floor of the cottage kitchen, slopping about in water and scouring the flagstones with a cake of pipeclay. She was unused to the stuff and it had gone soft and slimy in her grasp. It would not make the nice fan pattern on the stones that housewives like Mrs Sinclair could achieve.

Anna's hair hung in rats'-tails over her face. Her skirts were sodden, her bodice unlaced so that her breasts showed, speckled with dirt from the clay block. The door of the cottage was ajar and, though there was no welcoming flicker of light within, Elspeth entered without the formality of knocking on the latch.

"Anna?"

The young wife started with excessive violence, guiltily spinning from her knees into a sitting position and, in the process, upsetting the wooden bucket of lukewarm water so that it rattled over and spread a tide of greyish liquid across the flagstones.

"Och, it's you, is it? Don't you know enough to knock?"

"I'm . . . I'm sorry."

Anna scowled at her sister then flung the soggy clay block into the empty bucket and got to her feet. She wiped her hands carelessly across her breast, leaving a chalky stain.

"What do *you* want?"

The bruise was too obvious to ignore. It had turned a turnip shade of yellowish purple and remained swollen, giving Anna's brow and eyelid a quizzical upward cock.

Elspeth, who had no reason to suspect the truth, asked, "Did you knock it on somethin'?"

"Aye."

Sympathetically the elder girl reached out as if to touch the injury.

Anna flinched away.

"Is it sore?"

"Aye, it's bloody sore," Anna said. "I was on a chair – cleanin' the mantelshelvin' – chair couped – I hit my head on the shelf."

"It must've been bad. When was this?"

"Three – three days ago."

Anna's lips were tightly compressed. She looked older, much older than her years. It was not, as Elspeth might have believed, the tiredness of bedroom activity that marked her sister but the sort of weariness that she had remarked in field women. Anna's mannerisms were unaltered, the quick impetuous gestures, but their meaning was different, indicating a kind of anger that had to be constantly controlled.

"Did Matt not bathe it?"

Anna laughed curtly. "Matt? Oh, aye. Matt saw to it for me."

She looked down at her shoes; shoes, not boots, the silly little slippers in which she had been married, already relegated to daily use and far too dainty to be serviceable.

The water had formed a scummy puddle in a hollow of the floor. In the hearth the fire, such as it was, was surly and smoky. On the table were crocks and a cog, the latter rimed with congealing gruel. There was a stale air in the cottage, imprisoned by the motionless dampness of the clustered pines, with no wind about and the cold growing as the day approached noon.

"Mammy has an unguent for bruises," said Elspeth. "I could've brought it, if I'd known."

Anna snorted, stooped, picked up the bucket and righted it. She dropped the cake of pipeclay into it, then, to Elspeth's amazement, unkirtled her skirt and, in her underclothing, knelt and mopped up the water with the garment.

"Needs washed, anyhow," said Anna. "It'll not dry, not in this weather."

"You need a good fire an' a string."

"Aye."

Elspeth did not offer to assist Anna. She was unsure. She did not feel welcome. She had forgotten the purpose of her visit. It was not until the younger girl completed her chores with the cloth and had put it and the bucket outside by the door that Elspeth remembered. It had not slipped far from her mind, of course, but it seemed trivial, almost cruel to chatter about her "prospects" to a girl, a woman, so thoroughly settled into domesticity.

"Is Matt with the foresters?"

"Aye."

"Does he like it?"

"I suppose he does."

"Hasn't he told you?"

"He tells me precious little," said Anna, adding, "like all men."

Elspeth pretended to share the wifely secret. "That's true."

Abruptly Anna asked, "What brings you down here?"

She was spread-kneed before the fire, feeding fir cones and twigs into the smoky mass in an endeavour to coax heat from it. The kettle, its lid lost, was on the hearth along with a gruel pot and a greasy griddle. On a platter on a stool lay a small lump of brown beef, the remains of the Yuletide feast, dry and unappetising. Perhaps Anna intended to flake it for a potato pie or a pease pudding or as stock for a good thick soup. The beef too, Elspeth noticed, had acquired a coating of dust and ashes.

Flame suddenly licked from one of the fir cones, caught a vapour from the coals and bent a wand of golden light up the chimney's throat.

"God, that's better! It's a damnable hole, this," said Anna.

But the appearance of the fire flame seemed to relax her a little. Seated on the hearthstone, she tugged her skirts over her knees. Circling her shins with her arms, she hugged herself, like a bedraggled pixie.

"Sit yourself down, 'Pet," Anna said. "Give me your chat." She forced a smile. "Even a busy wifie can surely spare ten minutes to gossip wi' her sister."

After a certain hesitation, Elspeth informed Anna of James Moodie's visit to the hut and the graciousness with which he had treated her. Prompted by Anna's immediate interest she told of Gaddy's belief that the weaver was moving towards a courtship.

Anna did not laugh out loud. On the contrary, her brows knit and her lips pursed and she clasped Elspeth's hand, questioning her very seriously indeed. Anna did not think it a foolish or premature conclusion; nor did she doubt that Mr Moodie's deliberate manoeuvre might have a romantic purpose.

The sisters discussed other motives, found none that seemed logical by their lights and returned swiftly to strategy as if the gentleman had already declared himself.

"Do you think he's too old for me?" Elspeth asked.

"He's not all worn away, like Docherty, is he? I mean, he's supple still."

"It's his own hair too."

"I liked his wee whiskers," said Anna. "Very dandi-fied."

"It's the fashion in England."

"How would you know?"

"I read it in the *Journal*," Elspeth replied.

Anna said, "Him an' his two carriages. I've no doubt he'll get you one all for yourself. Remember how we used t' talk about being wed to a man who'd do that?"

"It doesn't seem possible," said Elspeth. "I think I'm dreamin' it."

"You're not, you're not." Anna was anxious to share vicariously in her sister's good fortune and, at this stage, showed no trace of envy. "It was you he wanted in that gig of his. I was there. I saw how he looked at you. He – he *caressed* you with his gaze, eh?"

For the first time in many months the sisters giggled together. Anna put her arm about Elspeth's shoulder. The fire toasted their backs and bottoms and chased skittering little draughts back across the floor like mice.

"Mammy must be mad," said Anna.

"I don't know what she's thinkin'," said Elspeth.

"She never guessed?"

"Peter Docherty put the idea into her head. Mammy thought Mr Moodie wanted the patch."

"The Nettleburn?"

"The Dyke."

"Maybe he does," said Anna. "Maybe he wants that too."

"For his sheep?"

"He hasn't got any sheep of his own, has he?" said Anna.

"I don't know," said Elspeth.

"If he hasn't, perhaps he wants some. Matt heard how he was sniffin' round the old mill down at the Loup o' Kennart."

"The mill at Kennart? What could Mr Moodie –"

"Away an' don't be daft, 'Pet. For a manufactory. Kilt cloth or blanket looms. There's plenty folk round here to fill the benches at cheap rates."

"See if Matt knows any more. Mr Sinclair's bound to have all the news that's going," said Elspeth.

Anna winked. "Leave it t' me."

Elspeth said, "Be sure Mr Moodie doesn't find out."

"He's too wealthy to care," said Anna. "Think on it, 'Pet. Livin' in yon grand mansion, wi' servants at your beck an' call."

Abruptly Elspeth felt herself withdrawing from fantasy in a kind of panic. Anna had made it seem too real, too close. She got to her feet.

"What would happen to Mammy if I – if I married? Not him; anyone."

"If it's James Moodie, he'll build a parlour just for her. His Mammy lives at Moss House. They'd get on fine."

Elspeth was uncertain. She could not imagine Gaddy separated from the Nettleburn, could not envisage her mother tending the patch on her own. She was no longer strong enough. Age had robbed her of her independence. Besides, she had never been alone in the hut in the shadow of Drumglass. She had always had somebody to care for, to care for her.

The notion of Mammy being left at the Nettleburn filled Elspeth with guilt and apprehension. But the tug of adventure was not to be denied. The prospect of becoming the wife of a wealthy man excited her, regardless of its risks and its problems.

Anna had learned the first lesson in the hard school of reality. She, however, issued no worldly warning to her sister.

There was nothing subtle in the girls' planning.

Marriage and the making of a wife were the only advancements that life would ever offer them. They could not climb out of the furrow of their own accord, as Jamie Moodie had done. No goal would be set for them as it had been for Matt Sinclair. They had but one chance, a chance that Anna had already squandered.

On that dreary day at the end of the year, Anna might have drawn Elspeth's attention to the yellowing bruise on her face and the drab, depressed state into which, in a few brief weeks, wedlock had sucked her. She would not, could not, bring herself to talk frankly to Elspeth. Instead she involved herself in madcap speculations about the course of Mr Moodie's advance to the altar and just how best Elspeth might exploit the man's infatuation.

Chatter kept the sisters happy for most of the afternoon.

If James Simpson Moodie had known how the Cochran girls talked and talked and talked of him, he would have been more amused than flattered, for he had already charted the progress of a courtship which, to the weaver, was not merely business but a demand of the heart.

Mother Moodie's wits, like the blades of ticking-scissors,

might have been blunted by over-use. Even so, she so worshipped her son and was so familiar – she believed – with his moods that she was the first to realise his true intention in respect of the Cochran girl. The fact that Mother Moodie would not have known a thing about it if Jamie had not elected to plant the matter in front of her spy-glass did not diminish her credence in maternal acuity.

Mary Jean Moodie had always been a dominating and demonstrative woman, though it had availed her very little in the course of her marriage. She used the material trappings with which her son had surrounded her in the evening of her life to enhance her regal opinion of herself. Though she had complete control of her limbs she preferred to be lugged about the mansion by a couple of the younger servants – those not fast enough to evade delegation – under the supervision of her maid, Betty, and the house-steward, Tolland.

Tolland was a true gentleman. He had been reared in big-house service and had studied the manners of the gentry in Edinburgh and Dunblane. It was Tolland's quiet, dry voice that corrected the master's occasional lapses in social niceties. Putting up with vulgar old dames was nothing untoward for Tom Tolland. But Mr Moodie was raw enough to imagine that the added burden required an added emolument and Tolland was sufficiently courteous not to correct his master on this minor point of behaviour.

Mother Moodie was transported, then, like the Queen of Sheba, servants grunting on either side of her chair, Betty fussing around with footstool, cushions and cordial decanter, and Tolland grandly opening doors and clearing the way from room to room, as the old wife wished. Few things in life gave Mother Moodie so much pleasure as these attentions, few things ever had. When she prayed in her bed at night it was to offer thanks to the Almighty for having given her a son who had given her this.

The chair was her pride and joy. In fact it was a Charles II armchair with spiral members and a carved front stretcher which any amateur antiquarian could have identified from fifty feet away. But James had had the chair upholstered in an ornate brocade, seat, back and padded arms, and had informed his mother that it had once belonged to Queen Mary of Scotland. Tom Tolland was in on the secret and, when slyly asked by the old woman if her son had exaggerated the chair's pedigree, staunchly perpetrated the lie with a few wee curlicues òf his own devising.

It was in the chair then, accompanied by her retinue of four, that Mother Moodie was brought out of the rear ground-floor parlour, carried down the corridor, across the hall and into the drawing-room at the front, where her son awaited her. It had been at James's specific request that she had been brought hither.

Carefully she was set down, the chair balanced on a small Moroccan carpet that protected the polished floorboards between the long settle and the fireplace.

The room was uncluttered but nevertheless managed to convey a certain individuality. A beautiful little rosewood spinning-wheel occupied one corner, so dainty that it might have been awaiting the advent of a fairy princess to lightly tap its treadle. On one wall a framed tapestry depicted a romanticised scene of highland life, while facing it was a huge, gloomy canvas in an ornate gilt frame which showed a shepherd idly leading his flock down a leafy English lane.

Jamie had been standing by the tall windows which overlooked an odd arrangement of four privet hedges designed to protect the occupiers of the drawing-room from the stares of indigent natives who might be passing on a hay cart or riding on the roof of the Harlwood Flyer. It was not a day to take in the panoramic view, for boiling black cloud lowered over the mountains and rain fell in shrouds upon the strath.

Jamie had not been admiring the rain, however. He had been engrossed in a recently published pamphlet on the tenancy of land in the grazing districts of Great Britain, intrigued by a listing of patrons which included several dukes and even more earls. Jamie read with a spy-glass, not a spidery little object like his mother's gilt-wired lens but a big, round, convex glass set in horn. He did not cease his study during his mother's entrance and waited until her peppery voice had delivered its last command and the servants, including Tolland, were ranked behind the chair facing him.

"Ah, Mother," he said, glancing up as if she had stolen into the room on tiptoe. "Thank you, Tolland. You may leave us now."

"Me an' all, sir?" said Betty.

"You an' . . . You too, Betty."

The entourage departed speedily. The doors closed behind them.

It was many a long month since mother and son had been contained together in total privacy; even in the small dining-room there was usually a waiting-girl present during supper.

"My cordial. She forgot t' leave my cordial," said Mother Moodie, stirring herself round about. "I telt her t' bring it."

"I shan't keep you," said Jamie. "You'll be back in your own room in a brace of shakes, Mother, I promise."

Mother Moodie was slow but not yet in absolute dotage. She sensed that something important was in the wind. She wondered if some tremendous financial calamity had befallen her son, if he had brought her here to tell her that they must return to the cottage in the village, that she must rouse herself to go out again in the cold rain to scratch for orders and to deliver parcels of finished cloth. She felt exceedingly stoical about the prospect, probably because she realised it was as remote as the chance of the moon falling out of the sky and into Loch Lomond.

She squidged about on the cushion, put the glass to her eye and squinted at Jamie.

He put down his pamphlet and reading lens and seated himself on the end of the settle. He studied her for a moment or two before he spoke.

"I have it in mind t' give a tea-party," he said.

"A what?"

"A *tea*-party, Mother."

"You?"

"No, not me. You. I want you to tender a few invitations to tea."

"What time?"

"Since it's winter an' dark early, shall we say three of the clock?"

302

"What day?"

"One week from today, Mother. That's next Wednesday."

"A *tea*-party?"

"It's the done thing for people of our standing, Mother. You've been to tea at Ottershaw, don't you remember?"

"Poor fare it was too."

"I shall see to it that it will not be poor fare at my tea-table."

Mother Moodie did not argue that point. She squinted once more through the glass. She was puzzled by her son's announcement. She could think of no reason why he would sacrifice the meat of a work day to entertain. He had, from time to time, given small dinner parties, usually for business acquaintances; all-male affairs. She was packed off to her room with a tray and forbidden to make any sort of appearance at all. But a *tea*-party. She began to inch towards the truth — from a reverse direction.

"What'll I say t' them?"

"Say anythin' you like, Mother."

"Anythin' about what?"

"Talk about the weather, the servants. How do I know? You must be able to talk about somethin'. I tell you what to do – let them talk to you."

"I'll be obligated t' answer, shan't I, though?"

"Mother, for God's sake . . .!"

"*My* tea-party, *my* tea-party."

Jamie's lids drooped and his voice became muted, almost a croon.

The old woman glowed inwardly. Once more she had tried him to the limit of his patience but he dared not show his temper to her. It cheered her to see how her son bent to her will even now. Aye, he might fancy himself to be a big man but, as far as she was concerned, a wee shirt still fitted him.

Jamie said, "Aye, Mother, your party. But it'll be my list of guests. I have had invitations printed. I'll see to it that Tolland fills in the day and the time."

It was Jamie's respectful way of saying that Tolland would sign her name since she could not guarantee legible penmanship.

303

"What guests?" the woman demanded.

"Leggat."

"Him?"

"It would be no proper tea-party without the minister," said Jamie.

"Gibbie's wife?"

"No, not Alicia."

"Who then?" She was on to it now.

Jamie said, "Doctor an' Mistress Rankellor."

"Him!"

"Mistress Cochran an' her daughter."

"Hah? Hah!"

"It'll be pleasant for them to meet again. Under my roof."

"Daughter," said Mother Moodie. "*Her* daughter?"

"Yes."

"In the gig at Yuletide. Her?"

"Who told you . . .? Yes, Mother."

"Why?"

"It's time to make peace with auld enemies. I've no mind to let these ancient feuds continue. I wish to show magnanimity."

"What's that? Magginominy?"

"Never mind." Jamie got up, a smile on his face, the fake boyish smile that he used to charm her. "Will we have our tea-party, Mother?"

"Is that her name – Maggie?"

"Mother, her name is Elspeth."

"It's her, isn't it? She's who the *tea*-party's for."

Jamie made a round, round eye and looked abashed and sheepish. He came to the old woman and put his hands upon her bony shoulders and peered at her through the lens of the spying-glass.

"Yes," he said. "I canna keep secrets from you, can I? Aye, you're far o'er quick for a laddie t' fool for long."

"I'll no' live for ever, right enough."

"Och, you might."

"You'll be needin' a woman to look after you."

"But I'll no' find one as douce as ma auld mither. Never, never in a thousand years o' searchin'."

"But do you think she'll do?"

Jamie stood up. The chill charm of the lad was gone out of him. She saw him nakedly, unfamiliarly. She felt the queer ache that she had not felt before, not even when his father died. She had known that she would some day lose her only son. She had stiffened herself to accept it, not to show hurt. But the years had rolled past and she had forgotten her resolution and had begun to believe that Jamie would be faithful to her until her dying day.

Now she was old and feeble she needed his unshared affection more than ever; yet she had served her three score years and ten, and could ask no more from the Lord, nor from her son.

She would cry later in her bedroom when the candles were out.

Now she must show him only a brave face.

"Will she?" the old woman asked.

"Yes, I truly think she'll do."

"Send out the invitations then," Mother Moodie said.

The tea-party, as it turned out, was more of a success than James Moodie could have anticipated. Before the guests arrived on the Wednesday after New Year, however, the event had been in danger of foundering on the reef of Moodie's reputation.

Gaddy to Elspeth: "First he comes here, an' now we've to go there. I'm inclined t' send him a refusal."

Elspeth to Gaddy: "The invitation's from his mother, not him. He might not even be there."

"He'll be there. She canna write properly."

"He's buyin' the old mill buildings down at the Kennart."

"How d' you know so much about a rich man's business?"

"Anna told me."

"Who told her?"

"Mr Sinclair."

"Will Sinclair be at this *soirée*?" said Gaddy.

"Mammy, it'll be for ladies."

"Ladies; well, don't think I'm goin' to pretend I'm a lady. It might be the thing for the likes o' Mary Jean Moodie, but I'm no' givin' myself airs an' graces because of a printit letter."

305

"I'll write the reply."

"An' deliver it, I suppose."

"No, I'll have it delivered by wee Tam Short. He'll do it for tuppence."

"See, it'll cost us a pretty penny before we're done."

"I've the white dress I got from Daddy."

"It's too tight for you now. An' too light for January."

"I can wear my —"

"Why are you so eager to go to this function?"

"I've never been to a real tea-party."

"I've lived *my* life wi'out such fripperies."

"Indian and China; think on it," said Elspeth, teasingly.

Gaddy turned the card in her hand and studied the back as if the true reason for the unusual invitation might appear there.

"Say we can go, Mammy, please."

"He's in league wi' the de'il, that man Moodie. Always has been, always will. I want you to have nothin' to do with him, 'Pet."

"Unless you're there, I won't," said Elspeth. "Am I not good enough, is that it, Mammy?"

"Good enough? God, aye, you're good enough. You're good enough for the King's own tea-party, never mind Jamie Moodie's."

The girl could sense now the conflict in her mother, though she did not fully understand its sources. There was a strange trace of fear in her Mam which warred with native pride. There was also, perhaps, that quite natural anxiety about what is best in any given circumstance for one's child to do. It took a woman of considerable strength to set aside her prejudices, even one at a time, and to capitulate with opportunity, and with the plain surface common sense of the thing.

Elspeth to Gaddy: "In that case, I take it we'll be attendin'."

Gaddy to Elspeth: "Fetch your white dress out o' the kist 'til I take a look at it."

Gaddy also took counsel with Mr Leggat. She was pleasantly surprised to learn that the minister was included in the guest list, together with Mr Rankellor. At least she and

306

Elspeth would not be without allies in the weaver's lair.

Mr Leggat to Gaddy: "I have not been to visit in Moodie's home before; have you, Mistress Cochran?"

Gaddy to Mr Leggat: "I wouldn't be visitin' there now if it wasn't for Elspeth bein' so eager."

"Ah, well! Ah, well! It will do the child no harm to broaden her outlook."

"Elspeth's no child now, Minister."

"No, I suppose she's not. To me, these days, everyone seems much younger than they were. The Moodie house is very fine, I've heard."

"I canna understand why he would ask the likes of us."

"Ministers are always victims of the tea-taking set."

"I meant us, me an' my daughter."

"To add ballast to the assembly, perhaps."

"Ballast?"

"Beauty," said Mr Leggat, hastily. "Beauty and . . . ah, and ready good humour. After all, I don't believe Moodie is quite of our generation. No, no, indeed, not by a score of years."

Gaddy had no interest in mathematical accuracy. She did not feel herself to be as old as William Leggat or Harry Rankellor, though she equated them with "her generation" since they had been her supporters and patrons since the first hour of her arrival in Balnesmoor. On the other hand, it was true what the minister had pointed out; Jamie Moodie was a deal short of her weight of years.

It was on the tip of her tongue to confide her fears to Mr Leggat. Five or ten years ago she would not have hesitated. But of late the minister's grasp of inferments had slackened. He would, perhaps, be injudicious enough to talk of the match outside the walls of the manse and its garden; and, after all, there was no "match" yet, except in Gaddy's imagination.

"Mr Moodie and I have hardly exchanged a civil word in eighteen years, though he's generous to the kirk here in addition to the kirk in Harlwood. I've always found his mother, however, to be a woman of character," said William Leggat.

"Mary Jean? Aye, she's all that."

"I expect that, having settled thoroughly and domestically in our small parish, James Moodie wishes to offer the olive branch. *Pax*, to make peace."

Gaddy to Mr Leggatt: "It may be that he intends t' marry."

Mr Leggat to Gaddy: "No, on that score I must disagree. James Moodie is not, in my books, at all the marrying kind."

Marriage between Anna and Matt had not brought, after all, a mingling of the Cochrans and Sinclairs. Gaddy saw no more of Aileen and Lachlan Sinclair than she had done before the wedding in November. She was, in truth, rather relieved. She found Sinclair daunting still and Aileen too severe for her taste. She saw precious little of Anna either, and had not cast an eye on Matt at all, except on Christmas Day at the kirk. Communication between the Nettleburn and the Ottershaw forest cottage was left to Elspeth.

Anna to Elspeth: "A card! God, but it's a nice thing t' send out invites on a printed card. What did Mammy have t' say about it?"

Elspeth to Anna: "Didn't want to go, so she didn't."

"But you persuaded her?"

"Indeed I did. I hinted we might not be 'good' enough."

"That'd do it."

"Aye, it did."

"Who'll be there? Will the Bontines be out in force?"

"I think not," said Elspeth. "The minister an' the doctor."

"Fuddy, fuddy, fuddy!" said Anna, in a *tra-lah* sort of voice.

"I know not who else. Dull bein' the rage, ain't it?"

"Still, *we* can guess what it's all for."

"Mr Leggat says Mr Moodie wants t' make peace."

"Wants to make sheep's eyes at you, more like."

"Anna!"

"That's what it's for, you'll see. To show you off in front of his old Mam. Make sure she approves. Jamie'd never court a lassie his Mammy didn't give the wink to."

"Blethers!"

"Think on it, 'Pet. Do a wee reflection. Christmas. Now this tea-party."

"You'd think I was bein' prized like a heifer."

"Not so far wrong, that," said Anna. "Fine folk are verra concerned wi' breedin'."

"Anna!"

"Spare me your red neck, 'Pet. That's why Moodie's takin' a light to you. Because you're young and sturdy enough to bear him eight or ten children."

"If I can."

"You're not of Mammy's family, so he has no pedigree for you. Maybe he thinks he knows who you sprang from, your 'blood'."

For Elspeth this suggestion was too far-fetched.

She had been impressed, however, by her sister's sharpness. It was true that a man in James Moodie's position, an owner of property and businesses, would require sons who would, when he grew too old, take on their father's mantle. She felt strange even thinking of Mr Moodie's touch, his caress, let alone the intimacy that he would expect from her and which, as his spouse, she must endure. In contemplation, it seemed quite different from the fancies she had entertained about Matt or – and this was a secret she had not shared even with Anna – about Peter Docherty.

In spite of gossip about his behaviour in the past, Elspeth could not imagine Mr Moodie being cruel; yet she found it hard to imagine him enjoying the pleasures that came with wedlock. Love her? He might! But as *what* would he love her? She could expect no answer to that question until she got to know him better. The chaste rituals of courtship would prevent friendship in advance of ceremony.

Elspeth to Anna: "Mammy's let out my white dress."

Anna to Elspeth: "If that doesn't captivate the weaver-man, he'd be better marryin' a ewe."

None of the three Cochran women had ever quite been able to decide what had possessed Daddy to buy a pair of white muslin day dresses. Perhaps Coll had, for an instant, looked on his daughters with a less than paternal gaze and had objectively realised that they were finer creatures than were usually set down on rough hill land. Perhaps he had foreseen the day when society would take note of them. For whatever reason, he had returned from a sale at Bridge of Allan one summer's evening with two identical parcels which contained the wonderful, but totally impractical, dresses.

Each consisted of a trained underfrock and tunic, had long sleeves and square *décolletage*. One was in plain Grecian white, the other – which Elspeth had claimed – with a patterning of forget-me-nots. The girls had spent many hours "dressing up" in the wonderful frocks but had never had an opportunity to wear them in public.

Gaddy was correct; the dress *was* too light for a bright, biting January day. But Elspeth was willing to suffer for the sake of vanity and Gaddy, who had gone more readily along the road with her daughter than she pretended, capitulated.

The dress was altered. The hem was re-hung over an underskirt, the wrist-bands let down an inch so that the spider-net lace would fall gently over the hands. There were slippers of blue leather – to be carried across the field in a basket – and a refurbished pelisse which did not, alas, quite match the dress but would be essential if Elspeth was to survive the rigours of the walk to the Moodie residence. One last touch was added by the stockings. Gaddy tinted them a pretty carnation-pink, using a dolly-bag of Empson's Dye Crystals. The colour did not exactly match the slippers. Anna would have protested vehemently at this tiny blemish in an otherwise perfect scheme but Elspeth did not mind. Sense told her that Mr Moodie would hardly be scrutinising her ankles.

On the morning of the day of the tea-party the weather was anxiously studied for sign that it would break before a quarter past two o'clock, at which time final decisions would have to be reached about apparel.

The afternoon was as crisp as the morning had been.

Elspeth dressed in the chosen finery and Gaddy in her Sabbath best. The woman had no thought for herself, only for her daughter. Hair up, bonnet on, fine white dress clinging to her figure, Elspeth was breathtaking. Not only was she beautiful but she had an assurance that her mother had never possessed. It was not that Gaddy has been shy, far from it, but Elspeth, though excited, was confident of herself. The prospect of drinking tea with gentlemen and ladies who, Bontines apart, constituted the parish's nobility, at least the rural equivalent of the *bon ton*, including its "new" money, did not distress her at all.

Although it had not been arranged, mother and daughter found the Cabriolet at the field gate where it had been waiting for a half-hour. Macgregor, the coachman, and the boy in tweeds solemnly saw the ladies aboard.

The big carriage was coaxed back along the track, bare, winter oak boughs lightly scraping the folded hood. Peter Docherty was half-way down the lane from Dyers' Dyke. He saw them very well – after all, he had been on the lookout for them since the carriage had gone past – but he did not return Elspeth's cheerful wave. He stood stock-still, hands on his hips, looking what he was – a farmer's labourer soured by suspicion.

"Pay no heed," said Gaddy, when Elspeth turned enquiringly to her.

"But he saw me. I know he saw me."

"Docherty doesn't know where he is." Gaddy patted her daughter's arm consolingly. "He doesn't know his proper place, 'Pet, that's all that's bitin' the man. Now, sit back an' let the folk see us."

It being winter there was no seasonal work for the village women. They came to their house doors and out on to the road to gawp at the sight of the highland woman and her witch of a daughter as they sailed grandly past in Mr Moodie's chariot. The tongues were struck dumb by the unexpectedness of it. Gaddy cared not. She revelled in the ride, remembering that rain-driven afternoon when the bitches had stoned her, and her with a sick and ailing child in her lap too; had stoned and jeered and chased her away up on to the fringe of the moor.

James to his mother: "I think it went well enough."

Mother Moodie to James: "Aye, they ate enough bread an' butter an' drank enough tea."

"Everybody seemed in good fettle. I haven't heard laughter like it in this house before."

"I'm sorry I'm not a wag like Harry Rankellor, if that's what you're implyin'."

"Mother, for Heaven's sake! I implied nothing of the kind. Even you laughed at Rankellor's tales of surgical practice in Edinburgh."

"Lies, I expect."

"Possibly!" said James Moodie. "But hilarious, nonetheless."

"*She* laughed, I noticed. *She* laughed loud enough for all of us."

"Nonsense! She behaved fine. She's not like you, Mother. She's not used to this form of existence."

"She's bonnie."

"Oh, you did notice that much."

"I canna say otherwise."

"She'll not shame us, will she?"

"Are ye askin' my opinion?"

"Of course."

"I thought you'd already decided."

"I have. But I would value your opinion, even so."

"When," said Mother Moodie, "will you make her a proposal?"

"In March."

"Can ye bide so long in your desire, Jamie?"

"I'll ask her in March, Mother, because it'll be the most convenient month in which to have her answer."

"She'd never dare refuse," said Mother Moodie to her son.

"I hope not," said James to his mother. "No. She'll not refuse, I'm sure."

On the twelfth day of January winter breathed on Scotland. It snowed for eighteen hours. Gusting winds carried the flakes and laid them in fluted drifts, burying the gables and backs in the village and making a long chute out of the roof of the hut at the Nettleburn.

Instructed by her mother, Elspeth climbed the glacial slope and raked the weight of stuff from the thatch lest it break the beams beneath.

It froze that night, and snowed again at twilight on the

following evening, in a series of granular spirals which danced like spectres across the moor. The drifts grew deeper, constantly changing shape to accommodate shifts in the wind. Soon they were carved in whalebacks and crests and draped like swathes of muslin over houses, hedges and head-high shrubs. It was never really cold, however, and in the following weeks the snow thawed slowly without ever becoming hard.

And that was the winter of that year.

Six weeks of lying snow finally washed away in the last week in February to uncover snowdrops, crocuses and other welcome portents of an early spring.

Riding on a garron, Moodie's boy, whose name was Luke McWilliams, arrived at the Nettleburn one forenoon. The pony was as fat and shaggy as the wee lad was lean and smooth. In the breast pocket of his jacket he carried a letter for Elspeth. With the long rake, she had been cleaning out potato beds for the planting. She was daubed with mud and her hair, under an old shawl, was in disarray. The lad gave her a disdainful inspection as he handed over the letter. She opened it and, leaning on the rake, read it. It was another invitation, written in James Moodie's hand this time, not on a printed card.

She was requested to accompany Mr Moodie, along with her mother, to ride in his carriage to view his new property at Kennart. Any afternoon within the next two weeks would be agreeable. Reply might be given verbally to the "little Mercury" who, Mr Moodie assured her, was perfectly reliable and the soul of discretion.

"Wait," Elspeth said. "Would you like a drink of milk?"

The boy's lip curled. "Milk? Nah, but I'll tak' a sup o' ale, if it's offered."

Elspeth shook her head and, without apology, crossed to the hut.

Blanket drawn across her legs, Mammy was lying down. She had recently acquired the habit of taking an afternoon nap and had not shaken off winter's lethargy. She slept on her back, hands raised by her head as if to press back a smothering pillow.

Elspeth knelt by the bed.

"Mam?"

Gaddy wakened with a start. She rolled over, reaching for her daughter's hand. At that moment, Elspeth thought, she looked frightened, as if she doubted that she would wake at all.

She showed Mammy the letter, patiently read it aloud. The highland woman struggled into a sitting position, bolstered on her elbows.

"Can the man no' speak?" she said, when Elspeth finished. "Him an' his letters."

"It's the style, Mammy. Shall we accept a ride in his coach, as he asks?"

"Tell him we're busy."

"He offers any day at all. I'd like to go."

Gaddy regarded her daughter sullenly.

"After what Mr Sinclair told you?"

"It's for that reason I wish to talk with Mr Moodie."

"Are you hopin' he'll go down on his knees an' make a proposal of marriage?"

Six months ago Elspeth would have denied it. Now she was bold, though not quite as forward as Anna. Was it Jamie Moodie's interest that had kindled confidence? She had acquitted herself well at the tea-party. Gaddy had been complimented by Mr Leggat, even by Mary Jean Moodie, on her daughter's manners. Since then, however, Gaddy had come to view Moodie's courtship, if that's what it was, in a different light. She trusted Elspeth's common sense not to encourage the man further. But perhaps the girl was too honest to string the weaver along with a series of trivial rejections.

Elspeth said, "Aye, I am hopin' Mr Moodie will propose marriage."

"I guessed as much."

"What day, Mammy?"

"Tomorrow," said Gaddy. "The sooner it's done with, the better."

So Elspeth gave an answer to Luke McWilliams. Luke McWilliams conveyed it back to Mr Moodie who received it with veiled delight.

*

314

James Moodie did not come in the Cabriolet. He drove the gig, hood folded down. It was furnished with rugs for the ladies' comfort and brocade cushions for Gaddy.

There were narrow lanes to travel, including the Nettle-burn track; James Moodie did not wish to score the panels of the big coach and have to foot an exorbitant bill from the French polisher. He was proud of the handsome coach. Besides, the gig was more companionable. He managed to squeeze Gaddy into the horseshoe compartment behind the board, propped with cushions and swaddled with rugs, like an effigy displaying Moodie's wares.

On the seat, however, there was room in plenty for the weaver and his lass. Elspeth was just as attractive in a shawl wrapper as she'd been in a dress. Shawls were not considered vulgar since the Princess of Wales had taken to wearing one to the theatre. James was pleased to note that it was made of quality wool and in Indian design, probably a product of Dalgety's manufactory in Glasgow. He was gratified that he was being taken seriously.

The afternoon was dry. The brisk east wind saw to that. The sun did not manage to press through streaked grey cloud but it was by no means unpleasant. Mr Moodie did not hurtle the gig along like Wattie McGowan's Flyer. He maintained an easy pace. Once the turnpike was reached, the horse's hoofs beat out a leisurely rhythm on the metalled surface.

From the bottom road it was possible to look back at the range of the hills, to see – if not the hut – at least the prominent gash of the burn against threadbare slopes, to see, too, cameos of activities which spring engendered. Shepherds were stirring their flocks to separate ewes from tups, parcelling out the best pastures for lambing. Elsewhere were chains of cattle, speckled pure white flocks of gulls in the wake of ploughs, and shapes of smoke from burning bracken or the tidy-fires of foresters. It was a scene of quiet industry. Distance hid the line of poverty and its monotony.

Moodie drew the horse left at the crossroads, steered the gig down the narrow road towards the bridge that crossed the Lightwater above the Loup o' Kennart. If the location reminded Elspeth of the shadows of summer, she gave no sign. There were other sights to distract her. Visible, as the gig approached down the gentle hill to the bridge, were smoke columns, dark and acrid, that rose from a builders' encampment pitched on the rise of the field above the mill.

There were a dozen men, four or five ponies and a huge draught-horse attached by light chains to a sled. On the sled, ready for removal, was a massive timber beam, charred like ebony.

Moodie stopped the gig on the south side of the bridge.

Behind the weaver, Gaddy leaned forward.

It was obvious that the men were stripping the shell of the old mill. Work had not long commenced upon the task. What was not obvious was Mr Moodie's purpose in bringing them here.

The weaver wore a little smile as he watched the labourers. They were well aware who he was. Even the draught-horse seemed to find extra muscle. The sled creaked as it tipped and dragged up a ramp of wetted earth to a dump behind the canvas tents.

Elspeth said, "So it's true then, Mr Moodie. You are rebuildin' the old mill."

"Indeed I am."

"They're not from these parts, the men," said Gaddy.

"I brought them in from Dumbarton," said Moodie. "They hire out as a gang an' have experience in the constructions of buildings. The materials'll be brought from Drymen, mainly."

"Is it a manufactory you're buildin'?" said Elspeth.

"After a fashion," said James Moodie, cautiously.

"I thought they only had them in the towns," said Gaddy.

"There's labour enough round Balnesmoor to meet my requirement," said Moodie.

"It'll take workers from the fields an' the farms," said Gaddy.

"Only weavers," said Moodie. "Besides, it's my intention to provide dwellings." He glanced at Elspeth. "It will be, in effect, a little village of weavers; do you see?"

"All slaves t' your looms," said Gaddy.

"Slaves? No, they'll be paid well enough," said Moodie. "It'll be a place to be proud of when it's established."

316

"What will you produce?"

"Blankets at first," said Moodie. "At a commercial price. I intend to install the newest innovations in machinery. The looms themselves an' wool-thread spinning devices will be operated by the thrust of the water, through a wheel."

"Like a grinding wheel?"

"On the same principle."

"How long will the work take t' complete?" Elspeth asked.

"To have the mill producing cloth, about a year."

The draught-horse was being held at the head by two young lads. Though the air was cold, the majority of the men had removed their coats and worked in shirts and waistcoats. They appeared quick and eager, as if infected by James Moodie's desire to outstrip progress, to see his vision made manifest. With stout iron bars and sickle-like drags they hooked into the enormous beam which, unroped from the bed, inched backwards. Suddenly the lads urged the horse into motion. The sled jerked. The beam rumbled from it. Shouting, the labourers leapt back as the beam tumbled downhill and jammed, half-ended, in a trench. The men fell upon it, hacking the timber with their hooked blades as if it was the carcass of an animal.

Elspeth noticed how noisily the Dumbarton gang went about their tasks, strident as crows, unlike farm workers who, though talkative, spoke softly as if the land and its crops and flocks might be startled by intrusion. The young woman found a strange fascination in the sight of the raddled building beset by the demolishers. She felt a pang of regret for the changes that would be rung here, a first slight murmur of her own inevitable decline.

James Moodie said, "Shall we step down an' take a turn by the river, Elspeth?"

"Yes. I could do to stretch my legs."

"Mistress Cochran?" said Moodie, adding, before Gaddy could accept his invitation, "Perhaps you'd prefer to stay where you are, in comfort?"

Gaddy paused, then said, "Aye, I'll keep an eye on you from here."

The gig-horse was made fast to the post by the bridge-end where it fell to cropping scant dry grasses from the verge.

Moodie helped Elspeth down and led her across the bridge. Below, the Lightwater ran clear brown from snow-melt up by its source in the Fintry hills. The current gurgled ineluctably through the carved pots and channels in the bedrock, oblivious to Moodie or the clamour of his hirelings from Dumbarton.

Elspeth's heart beat a little more rapidly when James offered her his arm. She had an impulse to turn her head, seek her mammy's approval even for that gesture of courtesy. She put her hand in the crook of his elbow, stiffly and formally. They strolled over the bridge and turned, not towards the workings, but along the river-bank, still, however, in view of the woman in the gig.

"Elspeth, I brought you here for a reason," James Moodie began. "I was keen for you to see that I've plans and what those plans entail. I'll tell you, Elspeth, though it will not be common knowledge, that I'm acting alone in this venture. Unlike the Border clothiers I've no institutional finance or co-operative funds at my back. I'm told the Lennox isn't the right place for a mill. I'm told there's insufficient wool in the area. I'm warned I'll need to import the stuff at the devil's own cost, since wool is half the composite cost of producing cloth. I'm told all sorts of things, given all sorts of advice, mostly by men who know little or nothin' about my business, who haven't a tenth of my experience of cloth-weaving."

"Why are you takin' me into your confidence, Mr Moodie?"

"Can you not guess the reason?"

"No, I canna."

"Because you, Elspeth, are included in my plan."

"I am, am I?"

If the weaver caught the edge in her tone he chose to ignore it. More probably he was oblivious to it, lost in the excitement of laying out his scheme. Never before had he put his ambitious project into plain words. Even to James Moodie, it sounded grand. He took her hand. They had ceased their stroll, stopped on a sward above a crumbling cliff of red earth, above the pool of Kennart.

"Elspeth, I wish you to become my wife."

Plain, direct, unequivocal; he searched her face with anxious brown eyes. It seemed that the great, determined, ambitious James Simpson Moodie was uncertain.

"I see," Elspeth said.

She glanced across the span of the bridge at the gig. She could see her mother, like one of the big, lichen-patterned stones that the Dunbartonshire labourers had uprooted, the rugs disguising her.

"Give me an answer, Elspeth, I beg of you. Consent to be my wife."

She slid her hand from his grasp. She rubbed her fingers across her hips as if to smooth the creaseless garment.

"My answer is no, Mr Moodie. No. I'll not marry you."

His mouth closed into a small round orifice through which he uttered a hollow little cry of dismay.

"Think awhile, Elspeth. Don't be hasty."

"I've thought about it, Mr Moodie. I'd be less than truthful if I claimed it hadn't crossed my mind that I'd won your attention."

He caught her wrist. "It's her, is it not? It's your mother, the highlander. She forbade it, did she not?"

"It's *my* answer, Mr Moodie, not my mother's answer."

Elspeth turned, tugging at her arm. James released her instantly. He followed as she walked back along the riverbank to the gap in the hedge by which they had entered the pasture.

In a low, demanding tone, he asked, "Why, in God's name? Elspeth, why do you turn me down? Don't you believe you could bring yourself to love me, given time?"

She rounded on him, looked straight at him, quite unflinching.

"No, James. I wonder if you will ever really love me."

James Moodie closed his eyelids and lowered his head, a gesture of defeat. It was as if he was ashamed of the hurt that she had caused by giving him the only explanation which he must accept as the truth.

He murmured, "I will Elspeth. I do. I love you now."

But the girl had passed on through the hedge-gap and did not hear him. She reached the side of the gig and stopped, head tilted.

"Did he ask you?" said Gaddy.

"Aye, he did."

"An' what did you answer?"

"I answered as we decided. I told him I wouldn't marry him."

The highland woman frowned. If malice stirred in her breast she gave not the least sign of it.

In Elspeth's eyes were tears.

"It's over, lass. Have no fear. Jamie Moodie'll not ask you a second time."

Minutes later the weaver returned from his reflection by the bridge.

Without a word he climbed on to the board and snapped the reins free of the post, clicking the horse into motion.

He did not speak to either of the Cochran women until he dropped them at the field gate just below the Nettleburn; then all he said was, "Good day to you both."

The weaver's wooing was over.

FOUR

The Long Dark Day

It was Lachlan Sinclair who had scotched Moodie's chances with the Cochran lass. He had not acted with evil intent or as a means of reducing the weaver. But the grieve was leery of connivance. He felt, quite wrongly, that somehow he had been made party to a deception which would mitigate against the best interests of the laird, not to mention the Cochrans.

In digging to the root of the "arrangement" between Sir Gilbert and James Moodie, the grieve had given no thought to feelings and emotions. He did not understand women. Never had. His ideal image of womanhood was Aileen, his wife. He admired, respected, perhaps even loved Aileen because she had shaped her life to suit him. She served and obeyed him without whine or whimper, would put his convenience high above her own, ever and always. She was sure, she was steadfast, a perfect model of convention, not subject to fretting or weeping, to the usual vagaries of the female sex. Quite naturally, it did not occur to Sinclair that Elspeth Cochran might be better off with the weaver, a man of complex desires, than with a lad of her own age and station.

It was Moodie's present circumstances, not his past, that Sinclair resented. It had not been difficult for the grieve to discover "what the weaver was about" in seeking to inspect the signed leases for Dyers' Dyke and the Nettleburn. Sinclair had been the laird's instrument in drafting these leases in the first place, and felt he carried a weight of responsibility in respect of the tenants as well as the laird.

The old man was no match for his grieve. A few gentle questions coaxed all the answers from Sir Gilbert, answers which did not please Mr Sinclair. He could see how a chap like the weaver, self-made, hungry and with a fabled amount of gold in his possession, could infiltrate the stronghold of the Bontines, pick off piece by piece little parcels of land, buy himself into the upper bracket, all ill-bred and ill-prepared. The radical in Sinclair deplored entrepreneurs like James Simpson Moodie who would exploit the working man, the honest cottar, far more ruthlessly than any laird would do. Though short-sighted in some respects, Sinclair was equipped to take the long view when it came to power and inheritance. He would do all that he could to stifle the schemes of men like Moodie before they could seed and flower and proliferate.

If Sinclair had known what was happening up at the Dyke, however, he might not have intervened. If he had been less deductive and more intuitive, the tragedies of that summer might have been avoided. As it was, Sinclair did what he thought was right. Nobody held him to blame for what followed.

He had gone to Gaddy with the leases in his wallet. He had shown her the precise wording of the terms. He had told her precisely what Coll's will entailed, how the disposition of the lease of the Dyke would go with Elspeth in marriage. He had explained how Anna, after her mother's death, would "assume" the lease of the Nettleburn. It was beyond Gaddy's comprehension. She could not fathom why Coll had stitched up such a patchwork. Sinclair could throw no light on it. What was obvious, when the grieve explained it, was that James Simpson Moodie wished to acquire both the Dyke and the Nettleburn. Since the laird had refused to renounce the leases without good cause, Moodie had determined to acquire one at least, if not both, by marrying Elspeth.

At Gaddy's request, Sinclair met with Elspeth and patiently framed his explanation of Moodie's courtship. It was not up to Sinclair, however, to advise Elspeth how to respond in the light of this new knowledge: that part was up to Gaddy. Elspeth needed little enough persuasion. She saw her position with great clarity and, though she had lingering doubts, made no silly arguments in Mr Moodie's favour.

"Have no more to do with him, 'Pet."

"No, Mammy. I must put a stop to it."

"A stop?"

"Wait 'til I'm asked."

"An' then?"

"Give him a refusal."

Gaddy hadn't the heart to deny her daughter the right to receive a first proposal of marriage. But she was dreadfully concerned lest some seam of deceit had been opened in Elspeth and the girl intended to betray not Moodie but her Mam.

Gaddy's relief and gratitude to her daughter was considerable. She would have picked over the afternoon's conversation like a cat with a pigeon's bones if Elspeth had allowed it. But something in what she had been forced, by sheer common sense, to do had hurt the girl. She refused, quite snappishly, to discuss the matter further. It was over, done, the opportunity denied. No more need be said about it.

Gaddy nodded, too happy with the outcome to press Elspeth to explain.

James Simpson Moodie would just have to find another tract of land to accommodate his flocks. Dyers' Dyke was cattle graze and would remain so for as long as she breathed. The Nettleburn, though by comparison small, was her Eden, her home. Nothing could alter that. Nothing but disease and disaster, acts of an unfathomable destiny.

It had been eight days since Elspeth had called to work at the Dyke.

Lately, through the winter months, Docherty had claimed that he had nothing for a girl to do. He had been taciturn, almost brutish in his behaviour towards her since he had learned of Moodie's courtship. She had been, of course, to pitch her hour's labour with the flail or to parcel out feed for stalled beasts. But not for eight days.

On her last visit she had addressed no word to Peter Docherty nor he to her. He had been out with the plough – late with the plough – turning for spring wheat. He had ridged the turnip field in preparation but, as so often happened these past months, had missed the appropriate period and had traded wheat for barley. The loam was in good heart, however, and Docherty had hoped to get away without reploughing, using only the grubber to raise twin furrows, a deep bed for the barley seed. He said nothing of his intention to Gaddy, gave no reason for his change of procedure, had gone on with it on his own initiative.

Elspeth had expected to find the field ribbed and ready for sowing. Indeed, she had come for that purpose, with wooden pattens on her feet and twine to bind up her skirts. But the plough stood in mid-field, canted. The textured lines stopped at it. The large waxy clods of the earlier turning, heavy and dark even after a week's east wind had given them a firing, filled the bulk of the field.

Never before had Elspeth seen such a thing, not without reason of weather. It disturbed her. It brought again the depression which the prospect of hard labour had partly lifted. She had hoped to lose herself in fatigue, for padding a soft barley patch was exhausting and a sower could not grasp but small handfuls of the plump, slippery barley, making progress slow. But she wanted to delve into monotony, to wear the incidents of the past weeks out of her, to find her spirit again upon the fields of the farm her father had owned. Most of all she hoped that she might cheer Peter by telling him, in her own way, that Jamie Moodie was not the man for her.

She climbed the ramp to the hedge and stared in bewilderment at the abandoned field.

What had Peter been up to? Was he sick, or was he lying drunk in the bothy? Such a conclusion would not have occurred to her a year ago. But Peter had changed. It was almost as if the Dyke, benign though it appeared on that calm March morning, was sucking him down into indifference, inch by unprotesting inch.

Pattens clacking on the dry surface, Elspeth ran the last few yards up the lane to the farm.

If there had been a wind from the hill she would have smelled it earlier. But it was not until she rounded the gable of the bothy that the nauseous stench assailed her nostrils. It was not one stink but several, all of them corrupt.

"Peter? Peter, where are you?"

324

The bothy door hung open. From the bed trailed a tangle of blankets. The fireplace was a pyre of dead wood ash. On the table two mangy tom-cats pawed among the greasy crocks and pans.

"*Peter?*"

There were bottles too; the oval green flagons of coarse glass which were common in Balnesmoor and which contained whisky from Aberfoyle's illicit stills.

Elspeth backed into the yard. She turned and stared at the farmhouse. Shuttered windows. Door stoutly closed. Rising above its rooftop, though, was a haze of smoke, rancid smoke which bore the stink along. For a fanciful moment she imagined that it was the sealed house which was oozing that sickening effluvia.

She cut wide of the dwelling, away from barn and byre, down the narrow vennel that took her out above the dung heap. Hens pecked, clucking, about its base and the rooster topped it. In the home field a dray-horse and two ponies grazed. The beasts raised their heads and stared at her as she put her hands to her mouth and bawled, "PETER. PETER DOCHERTY."

There was no answer but a muffled echo from the vennel.

She skirted the dung heap, went through the hedge by a hole at its base and ran across the home field towards the ploughing.

She still feared that she might find him lying dead in the furrows, smitten, as Daddy had been, by a sudden seizure of the heart. Then she stopped in her tracks. Shading her eyes, she peered at the east neuk where barley field and hill grazings linked in a line of thorn and briar topped by a pair of young beech trees.

Smoke purled upwards, stemming and branching in the air from several sources which she could not identify.

Walking, nervous and alert, she crossed the grassland and climbed the stone dyke which gave the farm its name. Perched on it, she peered intently at the smoking stuff. It reeked so badly that she gagged and buried her nose in her sleeve as she crept the last two hundred yards along the base of the wall.

A dozen grey-beaked hoodies squabbled over the feeding.

Overhead – she should have noticed them before – two buzzards wheeled, crying with that high *key-key-key* sound. A dog-fox, slinking off with carrion in its mouth, scowled back at her before trotting into the ditch that angled from the trees.

Elspeth could see now. See charred flesh, pale raw bones protruding from it like shoots of new growth. But there was no spring of life here, only the carcasses of eight or nine bullocks. Cows too for all she could tell from the remains.

Fists clenched to her mouth, she forced herself to study the mounds. She had seen dead beasts before but never anything like this.

God! she thought. *He hasn't even done this properly. Hasn't even managed to dispose of them properly.*

How many? Eight or nine? Ten or a dozen?

Impossible to tell.

Suddenly she shouted and flung her arms wide. The hoodies squawked angrily and waddled away. She shouted again, roaring so harshly that her throat hurt. She dragged stones from the wall and pelted the regiment of crows until they all took wing and flapped into the tree branches.

She scrambled back over the wall and started for the farmhouse to find Peter. Failing that, she would run down the track to find Mr Sinclair who would summon help to save the black cattle upon which their livelihood depended.

But it was too late.

More bloated carcasses lay by the back wall of the byre. Docherty had left the ropes on their forelegs. She could see the scores in the earth where he had dragged the bodies. She could imagine the massive muscular effort it must have taken to shift so many so far. Why hadn't he used the horse or the ponies? She could not understand it. He had manhandled the stotts out of the byre, as well as skinny little calves and two fine cows.

It was as if, in eight short days, the sky over Dyers' Dyke had rained death and Peter had drowned in it.

He had drowned in another substance too.

She found him in the byre.

He was sprawled on a heap of foul straw, dung-splattered, half-naked, in a drunken stupor. In their stalls survivors champed and bellowed to be set free from pain, given freedom to kick into the open air where space and sweet breath might cure them still.

She knew at a glance that the herd was finished.

Only three aged cows seemed to be normal. All the fattening beasts lay swollen-limbed, roaring wetly. Some of them were streaked with blood from incisions about the hocks. She could smell fever off them, the sour pungency of dribble and droppings and steam from their wretched coats.

Bending, she shook Docherty by the leg.

One green-glass flagon, empty, was buried in the straw under his head. Another was clasped to his chest. Like the beasts, the labourer dribbled at the mouth and was enveloped in a rotten aura. Ill or sick-drunk? Still Elspeth could not tell, any more than she could identify the swift and fatal disease that had consumed the herd.

"*Damn you, Docherty, waken up,*" she screamed.

Lips champing thickly, he stirred. His lids flickered. She glimpsed the dull, metallic sliver of his pupils.

"Peter. It's me. It's Elspeth."

He managed a grin, mumbled, "Ach, it's yersel', lassie. Ach, lassie. Here an' snuggle doon wi' auld Peter, eh? C'mon, c'mon. I'll tak' it afore the weaver gets his bloody share, eh?"

She kicked him hard on the buttocks but he did not seem to notice the blow, to feel its painful jarring. Still grinning, he hugged the bottle tighter and burrowed into the dirty straw. Before Elspeth could kick him again, he snored fatly. Dead damned drunk.

There was no more that the girl could do, either for Docherty or the suffering cattle. She was stricken by helplessness. She backed away, turned and rushed out of the byre into the air. Skirts pinched into her thighs, she ran frantically down the lane, through a hedge into the moor field, a route that would shorten the time to Nettleburn, the time it would take to summon Sinclair from Ottershaw.

Mr Sinclair would know what to do.

She stumbled once and fell.

On her knees, she swivelled to look back at the farm.

The haze of burning hung over the house. Buzzards still

327

swirled in the sky, omens, if Elspeth had but known it, of worse things to come.

They pulled Docherty out by his ankles. They dragged him mercilessly along the slimy floor into the yard. Hearn, one of the Ottershaw cattlemen, doused him with water. Docherty gasped and twitched. He was kicked by a boot much harder than Elspeth's and given a second bucket of water in the face. He sat up, yelling, as if he had been wakened not from fuddled stupor but from nightmare. Hearn yanked the labourer to his feet. With a hand behind his neck, he steered him towards the bothy. Mr Sinclair's instructions had been specific; sober him up as quickly as possible.

Gaddy had been fetched on the light cart from the field gate. Nothing could be done until Mr Sinclair and his cattlemen got there. Fortunately Lachlan Sinclair had been in the yard behind the home farm and the grieve had whipped up a team within minutes of Elspeth's arrival. He had broken out a mare and had ridden off two-up with an old man named Bob McClorty behind him. McClorty was versed in veterinary medicine. In sixty years of service to the Bontines he had doctored thousands of ailing beasts. A wisp of a man, with a pointed face and tufts of white hair above his ears, he wore a seaman's stocking-cap and had with him, in two canvas sacks, certain implements and chemicals. He rode behind Sinclair, hanging on like a bairn.

Before the cart brought Gaddy and the others to the high farm, McClorty was well into his work.

Hearn went into the byre. He came out again almost at once.

"Will ye come in, missus?" Hearn said.

Gaddy clambered down from the cart.

When Elspeth made to accompany her mother, however, Hearn put out a hand to prevent it.

He said, "Nah, nah. Nobody but the leddy. It might be catchin', ye see."

Hearn was a tall, whey-faced man who reminded Elspeth of her father, though he was ten or twelve years younger than Coll. She did not question him but stood aimlessly by the cart with the other helpers from Ottershaw while Gaddy entered the foetid gloom of the cattle-shed.

Gaddy was not inside for long; five or six minutes at most. When she came out again she was ashen beneath her tan. There were tears in her eyes. She staggered to the doorpost and leaned against it, hand to her breast.

Elspeth ran to her.

"Mammy, what is it? What's wrong with you?"

"It – it – it –" Gaddy averted her head and retched. Chest heaving, she retched again, drily. "It's like to be Black Quarter. He, McClorty, he bled them. Black. Like treacle. Only the oldest cows'll survive it."

"An' the others?"

"He'll see them slaughtered."

"All of them?"

"Aye, every one," said Gaddy.

By nightfall the grazings of Dyers' Dyke, its byre, barn, yard, vennels and lanes stood silent, scoured of all cattle.

There were no familiar sounds, only the sinister hiss of the quicklime which had been spread upon the dung heap to cauterise infection, and the cooling snap of timbers within the byre itself. That building now was nothing but a shell, the interior having been fired with coal-oil once all the carcasses had been hauled out. Diligently Bob McClorty had slaughtered the surviving beasts. Hearn had supervised the removal of the bodies to the moor's edge where they were burned upon pyres and the reeking remains raked into pits. Ottershaw men carried out the tasks with distaste but without complaint. They knew only too well how infection might carry in the air and had a vision of their own sleek, pampered charges slumping into a similar state. It was "the new way" of dealing with cattle blights. Sinclair's ruthlessness in issuing the slaughter order reflected enlightenment.

Gaddy had been taken home by Elspeth. Even at Nettle-burn, though, the stench was thick and the glow of the fires from the moor two miles away patched the underbelly of the cloud when dusk came down. There was no escaping it, not that night nor all the following day. It was not until the rain came, steep and heavy on a brisk west wind, that the hill slopes and the village were freed of the taint of Docherty's carelessness, for, as an enquiry soon discovered, Gaddy Cochran's cattle had been poisoned.

There was no cart or fine carriage for the Cochran women now, just the pair of them, mother and daughter, Gaddy and Elspeth. Anna had expressed an interest but, through Matt, Sinclair had discouraged her. Marriage had removed her from the circle of concern, at least as far as Dyers' Dyke was concerned. So the women walked that old track between the oaks in a brief lull in the rain that had ushered March out and April in. No gentle showers, a steady downpour had lasted for almost a week without pause or let. It had turned the fields to quagmires, the paths to streams and had caused lambs to die of chill in a way that frost would not.

Sinclair had sent the message via Hearn. It was not so much a request as a command.

There would be a meeting between owner and tenant at Dyers' Dyke at one of the clock. Neither Gaddy nor Elspeth had ventured near the farm since that hideous day a week ago. Gaddy was full of tearful dread at the prospect of a return.

Lachlan Sinclair was waiting for them in the yard, though they arrived punctually. He was not alone. Two strangers were with him, gentlemen by the cut of their clothes, serious fellows of an age with the grieve. Three horses were tethered in the barn and Hearn was visible in the doorway of the bothy. Of Peter Docherty there was no immediate sign, though Anna had told them that Docherty was being kept under lock and key in the loft of the stables at Ottershaw.

Gaddy and Elspeth were dressed in their sombre Sabbath best, but the hems of their skirts had collected mud on the track and their feet were wet.

"This way." Sinclair gestured towards the door of the farmhouse which had been unlocked and stood ajar.

Gaddy hesitated, her hand tightening on Elspeth's arm.

"What is it, Mammy?" the girl whispered.

"I canna."

"Canna go in there?"

"Come along, please, Mistress Cochran," said Sinclair.

He gathered the women with his arm and, in spite of her reluctance, Gaddy found herself being coaxed into Etta Cochran's parlour.

A fire had been lighted, shutters taken from the windows. She could not be sure, but it seemed that the place had been scrubbed and broomed. Even so, she could detect in the atmosphere an ineradicable mustiness, aura of a woman long, long dead.

The kitchen table had been draped with a linen cloth. There was a decanter of wine and stemmed glasses upon it and, laid neatly before the chairs, wallets of papers and documents. A horn ink-stand and a quiver of pens stood there too, like a weird charm left over from pagan times.

"Sit yourselves down, please," said the grieve.

He drew out a chair for Gaddy.

Elspeth sat to her right hand, facing one of the strangers, who, a moment later, was introduced as Mr Royle, a gentleman of the law. The other man was given a name, Mr Peart, but no definition. Neither of them smiled. Both seemed fussy, anxious to be on with business.

Sinclair took the chair at the head of the table, back to the window. He opened his kidskin wallet and peered at the script on the top leaf.

"It is," he began, "a matter of considerable ill that's brought us here today." He glanced at Gaddy. "I represent the interest of Sir Gilbert and the Ottershaw estates, by the bye." He pointed his nose to the paper again. "It would seem, by dint of enquiry, that a calumny has been committed by the appointed manager of this property, the farmstead and grazin' acres known as Dyers' Dyke, which is, by due arrangement with the former tenant, now deceased, held by the widow, Mistress Gaddy Cochran."

"Substantially correct, Mr Sinclair," said Royle.

"Within the will, in codicil, however, an extension of the lease falls to this young lady, Miss Elspeth Cochran, upon the death of her mother," said Sinclair.

"Against which procedure I advised, may I remind you," put in Royle.

Sinclair drew in a breath and released it. Clearly he was not inclined to be interrupted again.

Royle, not in the least chastened, said, "Go on, Mr Sinclair. Go on, if you please."

Sinclair said, "It's to settle the matter of the forfeiture of claim to the lease that I've called you here today."

Gaddy stiffened.

Sinclair went on, "I wish to make it plain that Sir Gilbert has sympathy with the tenant, Mistress Cochran, but that the unusual circumstances surroundin' the lease have created a pitfall."

"Pitfall?" said Gaddy.

"Capital," put in Mr Royle. "Capital in the form of ready cash, or labour against a loan."

"I dinna understand," said Gaddy.

"If Mr Royle'll permit me to continue," said Lachlan Sinclair, "without inter – without comment for a minute or two, I'll make it all plain to you, Gaddy."

Elspeth held up her hand, as if taking an oath.

Sinclair said, "Aye, what is it, lass?"

"I think I understand," Elspeth said. "It's your concern that with no stock on the grazings an' no crop yet in the ground there will be no income from the farm this season."

"Late plantin' will bring you something," said the man called Peart. "But, you see, you haven't the labour."

"There's Peter," said Elspeth, ingenuously.

"Ah, yes! Docherty," said Sinclair. "We'll talk about Docherty presently."

Mr Peart, who was not so thrusting as the lawyer and who seemed to have more facts at his fingertips, leaned across the table and put his hand upon Gaddy's. It was an amiable gesture, indicating that he bore no personal grudge and had no selfish stake in the proceedings. Facts were facts, however, and could not be denied.

Peart said, "How much cash *can* you raise, Mistress Cochran?"

"A wee bit."

"How much? Six hundred pounds?"

"I . . . No. Not as much as that."

"Am I right in supposin' that your main income came from the Dyke?"

"Aye, from the sellin' of the cattle, three or four times in the year."

"That's your main source of income?"

"We sell potatoes."

"Is there much to be had from that?"

"It pays for its own labour, sir," said Elspeth. "Not much more."

"So – cattle provided you not only with livings but with workin' capital?" Peart asked.

"They do," said Gaddy.

The man's hand left her fingers. He pressed his palms together in front of his mouth, as if he had a leaf of grass and was about to blow upon it to make a rude little tune.

"Your cattle are gone. Fatstock for spring sale an' beasts for summer. Cows and calves. All gone. You have fields which you have to pay for, an' not a stott or heifer to graze them. It'll cost you a fortune to put kye back on the grazings."

"I can start wi' just a few head. I'll buy wisely. Ask Mr Sinclair. I might not look much like a drover t' you, sir, but I've still got a drover's eye for beef cattle."

"There are too many acres," said Mr Peart quietly.

"And the rent's high," said Elspeth. "Could we not put to barley or some other late crop?"

"How would you plough? How would you harrow and sow, weed and reap?"

"As we've always done."

"Hire labour?" said Mr Peart. "It's impossible. You haven't money to pay the term's rent, to buy seed, to hire all the labour you'd need. Besides, there isn't enough arable ground on the acreage to be profitable."

Elspeth understood now that it was Mr Peart they had to fear. He was an expert in agriculture, one of the "improvement" brigade, perhaps. Sinclair had brought him along to cloud the issue with facts and figures. Did they not understand, none of them, that there was more to scratching a living than bushels per acre and kye by the stone weight? Her mammy had started with a hut and a handful of ground and had made a life out of it.

Elspeth opened her mouth to defend her Mammy's will and determination. Then her eye was drawn to Gaddy, to the heavy features and the heaving chest and, with horror, the girl realised that what had been possible only a few short years ago was beyond the woman now. Determination could not shake off the weight of the seasons, the burdens of age.

I will do it, Elspeth thought, grandly. *Mammy can instruct me. I'll do what she did.*

And at once, like an answer from her brain, came the realisation that she could *not* do what Mammy had done. She did not have the strength, nor the experience of hardship that would be essential if she was to drag the Dyke back from ruin and into profit.

What had been possible ten years ago, or fifteen, could not now be brought about. Rents had soared. The prices of seed, stock and labour had increased tenfold. Mr Peart, Mr Sinclair and Royle, the lawyer, were not gathered in the farmhouse that day to make sport; nor were they exploiters. They had assembled to bring the light of truth to Gaddy, like missionaries preaching conversion to the new materialism.

Elspeth said, "If the laird would give us a year –"

Sinclair said, "Ten years would not be enough, lass."

Gaddy said, "What are our choices, Lachlan?"

Sinclair answered, "Resign the lease here an' now."

"Give up Dyers' Dyke?"

"Aye."

Royle opened his mouth but Lachlan Sinclair silenced him with a wag of the finger.

Gaddy's head had slumped upon her chest. She appeared, for an instant, to have dropped off to sleep. She breathed with a steady rhythm and, as Elspeth could see, she wore a little quirking smile.

"Mistress Cochran?" said Sinclair, at length. "Gaddy?"

The highland woman looked up.

"Will there be money, improvement payment?" she asked.

Sentiment, it seemed, had been set aside. The pragmatical part of her had surfaced, had faced up to the inevitable loss of the Dyke's income and the legacy that Coll had left them.

Sinclair gave a little grunt that might have been amusement.

Again Royle opened his mouth. Again Sinclair silenced him.

"I might manage fifty guineas," Sinclair said. "Dependin' on Mr Peart's evaluation."

"Fifty guineas," said Peart, "from what I've seen, would be fair."

"Lachlan?" said Gaddy.

"Take it, Gaddy."

"Elspeth?"

"Aye, Mammy. Be rid of it. We can scrape by on the Nettleburn."

"That," said Gaddy, "will have t' do us, 'Pet. Give me your pen, Lachlan. I'll sign the paper."

From the wallet before him the grieve extracted a simple document. He studied it for a moment then slid it across the table to the woman. Peart dipped and shook the pen and put it into Gaddy's fingers. She stuck her tongue into her cheek and laboriously shaped the letters of her name as her daughters had taught her to do.

The men, and Elspeth, watched.

Gaddy sat back. Peart took the pen and returned it to the ink-horn and all of them waited in silence while the ink dried upon the document.

Sinclair retrieved it, replaced it in the kidskin wallet.

"I'm sorry, Gaddy," he said.

Gaddy nodded and made as if to rise.

It was Royle who stayed her.

He said, "Madam, I'm afraid that's not quite all. There's another matter we must bring before you."

Elspeth said, "About Peter Docherty?"

"Alas, yes."

"Is he sick of the ailment?"

"No," said Sinclair. "He's sick of bad conscience. There's more to it than there seems. If you'll grant permission I'd like to send for Docherty – who's outside – so you may hear from his lips the cause of this ill thing."

"Whisky, d'you mean?" said Gaddy.

335

"Will I send for the man?"

"Yes," Elspeth said.

Docherty was clean-shaven and dressed in his best clothes. His hair was slicked down with water and, save for the sag of despair to his shoulders, he appeared as respectable as Elspeth had ever seen him.

He entered hesitantly. Hearn gave him a nudge into the kitchen.

Nobody stood to greet him, nor was he offered a chair. He found his own spot, standing by the side of the fire.

During the minutes that it took for Peter to be summoned, Mr Royle helped himself to a glass of wine. To Elspeth there was something in the gesture of wine-drinking that was close to obscene. Peter's pathetic isolation seemed to be increased by it.

Docherty gave no greeting to anyone in the room, not even Elspeth.

"I would be obliged, Docherty, if you'd tell Mistress Cochran how the animals fell sick," said Peart.

"It happened quick," Docherty said. "They were in grand fettle. Never better. Bloomin' wi' health, missus. Then I noticed how one or two o' them were showin' lame. Fetlock. Hock. Nothin' verra serious, though I keppit an eye on them. Then it was bloodshot eyes an' the dribble. They went down like fits, missus. Fell down in the stalls, an' in the back field where I had some out for the air."

"Peter, Peter. You should've sent for me," said Gaddy.

"You were – busy."

"Continue," said Sinclair.

"Two days an' a single night an' the whole damned lot o' them were sick. Dyin'. Dyin' faster than I could destroy them. I thought it might burn itself out. But it never."

"Did you not have an opinion," said Peart, "as to what the cause might be?"

"I thought it was the fever."

"For God's sake, man, *why* didn't you seek aid?"

"I told you, sir. I hoped it would —"

"How did you dose them?" Peart asked.

"I tried the knife here an' there. The blood was black an'

336

thick. But there was so damned many, sir. It was on them afore I could think."

"So you dragged them out an' tried to burn them?"

"Aye. I did."

"An' dulled your conscience with spirits?" said Mr Royle, sipping wine. "Negligence deserves hanging, if you ask my opinion."

"I was weary, so weary," said Docherty. "Honest t' God, Mistress Cochran. It happened like a lightnin' bolt out of clear sky. They were so healthy, puttin' on weight at a fine rate."

"It was just an act o' God, Peter," said Gaddy, with a negative wave of the hand as if to dismiss not only Docherty's suffering but the whole affair. "You couldn't have done more than you did."

"But," put in Mr Peart, "it *wasn't* an act of God. Was it, Docherty?"

"It was – I know now – it was the feed."

"What feed?" said Gaddy, sitting up.

"You had an inklin' it might be the mash, Docherty, did you not?" said Mr Peart. "Is that not the reason you hid the cauldron an' the oil-jars under the hay in the back of the barn? It crossed your mind you'd made a damned foolish error in the feed of the poor brutes."

"Fullness of the blood," said Gaddy, bolt upright now. "God! Over-thrivin' caused the illness. It's like the Black Quarter in its effects. I saw it two or three times."

"I did it for the best," said Docherty. "We've been slidin' down here, slippin' down an' down. The Dyke. I was afeared it would go back like it used t' be when she was here. I mean, when the first Mistress Cochran was alive. I thought they were puny."

"You kept them out too long," Gaddy cried. "They'd have put on beef wi' care."

Elspeth said, "Were they not diseased, then?"

Mr Peart answered her question. "It was not, at first, a contagion at all. I was puzzled too, until we – Mr Sinclair – uncovered the linseed oil."

Gaddy pushed back her chair and rose. She was angry and made no attempt to hide it. "I told you many a time,

337

Peter. Never rush the feed. Never give live mash. Is that what you thought you'd do? God, Peter. *You* killed them."

Sinclair rose too and came to Gaddy to calm her. He put his arm awkwardly about her shoulders and tried to press her back into the chair. She resisted, then yielded, still glaring furiously at Docherty.

"Damn it, missus, I never *tried* t' kill them. I was hopin' for a fine fat herd. They looked it too, before –"

"It's a common sign," said Mr Peart. "I might have been deluded into supposin' it was contagious Black Quarter if it had been me who'd examined them."

"The oil would be rancid," said Gaddy.

"Yes. We found the mash pot, as I've told you," said Sinclair. "But it was the jars of linseed told the true story."

"Why did you hide the jars, Peter?" said Gaddy.

"I was – I was – ashamed, Mistress Cochran."

"Too damned man-proud to admit your error to a woman?"

"If the oil was bad, can we not make a claim against the persons who sold it?" said Elspeth.

Peart and Royle glanced sharply at her, surprised by her astuteness.

Sinclair shook his head. "The seller of the oil's not known to us."

"Where did Peter get it, then?" said Elspeth. "Peter, tell us who you bought it from?"

Flushed, Docherty did not meet her eye. He said, "I never knew his name. He came wi' it on a cart. Offered it cheap."

"You paid him good money? Without testin' the oil?" said Gaddy.

"I tested it. I tested it. It smelt and tasted fresh."

"He gave you the sample jar, did he not?" said Peart.

Docherty grunted. Obviously he had been led through the entire interrogation in advance by Lachlan Sinclair.

"It's of small matter now," said Gaddy, "but what price did this packman charge an' how much did he deliver you?"

"I thought I'd feed at a gallon a week, in the mash, a gallon per head. For eight weeks. I bought a hundred an' sixty gallons. He had it on two carts. He said he'd be back wi' more."

"A hundred an' sixty. What charge?"

"Cheap, missus. Cheap. Eighteen shillin' the hundred-weight. It's sellin' at twenty-six in the marts," said Docherty, as if he could still justify his misjudgements and errors, the compound of which had been to bring the woman and her daughter to the brink of ruin. "I was feedin' a shillin' an' sixpence each the week. An' they were thrivin', I tell you. Thrivin' like roses."

"Except they were poisoned," said Gaddy, curtly.

"Missus, I never meant harm."

"No, maybe you did not, Peter. But harm came of it."

"It's this place. It's the Dyke. Damned be it. It's *her*. It'd blight anybody in time, this bloody parcel o' tainted ground. I swear there's nights I can hear her laughin' at me. Aye, her. I can see her standin' there in the doorway or out by the pond where we –"

"Enough, Docherty," Sinclair rapped. "I need no super-stitious nonsense out of you. Any 'apparitions' you fancy you've seen came out of a whisky flagon."

Quietly, Docherty said, "It's the truth, Mistress Cochran."

"Maybe it is," said Gaddy. "Maybe I'm well shot o' the place, Peter. But since I am, I've no billet for you."

"I know it. An' I'm sorry."

"Stay," said Gaddy, "'til the term's out. It's a week or two yet. Have you objection, Mr Sinclair?"

Sinclair hesitated. If he had located even a trace of spite in Docherty, he would not have agreed. But it was in his mind that the labourer would not want to linger, that he would be off on his travels, in search of another bothy in which to lay his blanket, and another field to turn, before the week's end.

"None," said Sinclair. "Would you leave us now, Docherty?"

Unescorted, the labourer slouched out of the kitchen.

Sinclair said, "I felt it right for you to hear the whole sorry story, Gaddy."

"It's not the whole story," said Elspeth. "I'd like to know where the tainted oil came from."

"We've seen the last of the packman in these parts," said Peart.

339

"He may, of course, not have realised that the oil was sullied," said Royle, over the rim of a second glass of wine. "I think one would have difficulty in proving in a court of judgement that the seller of the oil acted other than in good faith. He might reasonably claim that the oil was ill-stored after purchase, or that –"

"Thank you, Mr Royle, sir," said Sinclair. "If you would be good enough, with Mr Peart, to take a breath of air outside. I'll join you presently."

The lawyer and farm valuator left the kitchen.

Sinclair lifted a wine glass and held it out towards the highland woman. "Will you?"

"No," Gaddy said. "But, if you find this work thirsty, take a touch yourself."

Sinclair poured a half-thumb of the ruby liquid and drank it in a swallow. He dabbed his lips, not, Elspeth noticed, with his handkerchief but with the back of his wrist.

Behind the grieve, rain spotted the window. She listened for the drum of it on the roof, but heard nothing, as if the farmhouse was absorbent and consumed such sounds.

"Mistress Cochran: Gaddy," Lachlan Sinclair said. "I'm sorry it has come to this. Truly, I am. Coll had a difficult time here, Lord knows, but with your help and support he defeated the – God, I'm beginnin' to sound like Docherty, with his wraithes and evil spells. Hard work will lay any ghost. But it *is* beyond your powers."

"Aye," said Gaddy, wistfully. "It is now."

"Will the Nettleburn sustain you both?"

"It's sustained us both before now," Gaddy said.

"I may be able to assist."

"I'll take no charity," said Gaddy, adding, "not even from you, Lachlan Sinclair, long as I've known you."

"You took it once."

"Kindnesses; not charity."

"Is there a difference?"

"To me there was – an' still is."

"You'll never be without shelter an' food, I promise."

"Again, my thanks. But the Nettleburn will do us fine."

340

"Your special shelter, hm?"

"It's that, an' more," Gaddy said.

Sinclair got to his feet and lifted the kidskin wallet. He tucked it under his arm. "Do you feel that you are well rid of this place?"

"It meant grazin', cattle, an' that meant a livin'; a good one at that," said Gaddy, struggling to her feet too. "But I care not for the place, as I care for my own hut. It was never mine, this farm, except on paper. I didn't share its memories."

"Perhaps Coll would have been a mite relieved, too?"

"Perhaps he would," Gaddy agreed.

The grieve ushered her out, Elspeth following.

The rain was light, wind-driven before a billow of dark clouds from Fintry way. It would be a half-hour before lashing rain reached Balnesmoor. Sinclair only had a horse for each of the men and Gaddy was no longer the shape to ride behind.

"Don't tarry, Elspeth. Hasten home as quick as you can," Sinclair said.

He waited, politely, to see the girl and the woman around the corner of the bothy gable before he swung into the saddle. But he passed them only a step or two down the lane, preceded by Royle and Peart. Where Hearn and Docherty had got to, Gaddy did not care. She walked sedately after the horsemen, Elspeth holding her arm, giving her support.

The girl had not fully understood Peter Docherty's references. He had always seemed like a chap who had his feet in boots and his boots firmly planted on the ground. But Mammy had taken meaning from his ramblings, and the temper in her, and the bitterness, had gone at that minute. Now, however, the stiff set to Mammy's chin was back, and her eyes were quite hard, like mica.

When the riders had passed out of sight down the village road, Gaddy stopped to catch her breath. She stood motionless for a long minute looking back at the lineaments of the farmhouse and its deserted outbuildings pasted like canvas against the sodden sky.

"He can have it an' welcome," she murmured.

"Who can have it?"

"Moodie."

"James?" said Elspeth. "Do you suppose the laird'll lease it to him straight away?"

"'Course he will. Moodie always gets what he wants."

"He didn't get me, Mam," said Elspeth.

Though the girl made the statement simply and without irony, Gaddy chuckled, "That's true."

Tucking Elspeth's arm in hers she turned from sight of the Dyke and stepped out towards the oaks again.

Elspeth said, "Mammy, *is* Dyers' Dyke haunted?"

"Not yet, lass," Gaddy answered. "Not yet."

He came to her in the wee small hours of the morning. It was still dark outside and the embers of the fire in the hearth gave little illumination. Wakening with a start, sitting up in bed, she sensed rather than saw him.

"Elspeth," the voice whispered again. "Elspeth."

Slipping from the bed she groped for, found and hefted up the kindling axe from the hearth.

"Who's there?"

"Peter Docherty."

Holding the axe in her fist, Elspeth drew a blanket from the bed and wrapped it about her.

Mammy snored, not stirring at all. Four or five years ago Mammy would have wakened at the slightest sound. Things changed. Things changed. Elspeth tiptoed to the half-open door.

"It's me right enough," Docherty said. "Can ye come outside for a word or two, lass, eh?"

Against the salty pre-dawn light that coated the moor, she made out his silhouette. Cloud rolled ragged and cold across the summit of Drumglass. She shivered, drew the blanket tighter around her and, dropping the axe by the post, went out of the hut. She was not puzzled by Docherty's arrival at such an ungodly hour of the morning. He had come to say goodbye.

She moved away from the hut to the sweep of the burn where a fold gave protection from the wind. Peter preceded

342

her. He carried a pack-roll in his arms like a swaddled bairn, a bulky poacher's creel slung over one shoulder. He wore his best boots and thick breeks, vest and coat and, on his head, a hat she had never seen him wear before, a round-crowned, wide-brimmed, jaunty monstrosity that must have lain hidden in a chest for twenty years; since last he had been on the tramp, perhaps.

"So, Peter, you're leavin'," she said.

The grass was wet on her feet and ankles. But the air smelled so fresh and sweet that she did not object to the discomfort. It was, after all, only a half-hour before her rising time. Down in the woods a rook croaked sleepily and a moist burble of song from a mavis started the early chorus.

"Aye. I've nothin' to keep me here. It's better if I make m'self scarce without delay."

"I'll . . . I'll miss you," Elspeth said.

It was not quite the truth. Now it had come to it, she had only the faintest pang of regret that Peter Docherty was passing out of her life.

"You wouldn't like t' come wi' me?" He made a joke of it, with a snort of laughter at the question's end.

"I canna leave Mammy."

"No. You're a grand lass, Elspeth. I think it's me that'll do the missin' more than you."

"Where'll you go?"

"God knows!"

"Fintry?"

"Nah, nah. I've had enough o' closet villages. I'm for the city. I hear there's dairies in the big towns now, so they'll be in need o' cowmen. Failin' that, I can throw in my lot wi' a labourin' gang. Diggin' out the new docks, maybe."

Elspeth did not know what to say to him. She sought for appropriate phrases, words that would not sound too false. Perhaps she would miss him when he had gone as she might miss an uncle or a cousin, an absence of someone familiar in the habitual round of the days.

Peter surprised her, however.

Outright, he asked, "What did ye tell the weaver?"

"I told him I wouldn't marry him."

Peter said, "He'd take it bad."

343

"Aye, he did."

"Did he shout?"

"He sulked."

"Was it her, was it Gaddy persuaded you?"

Elspeth shook her head. "There's too much hidden about Jamie Moodie for my likin'."

Peter Docherty paused. "Listen, lass. I've nothin' t' give you as a keepsake. Nothin' you'd want, anyway. But I can give you advice. Steer a track well wide o' Moodie. You'll never be mine now, more's the pity. But I hope to God you'll never be the weaver's."

"I'm safe enough, Peter. He'll not humiliate himself by askin' again."

"Will he not? I wouldn't wager a bawbee on it."

Elspeth gave a soft, embarrassed laugh. But Docherty was deadly serious.

He said, "I didn't tell Sinclair everythin'. The grieve would've laughed me to scorn, accused me o' jealousy if I'd told him what I think."

"Peter, what are you sayin'?"

"The packman who sold me the stinkin' oil," said Docherty.

"What about him?"

"I think he was sent by Jamie bloody Moodie."

"Och, Peter! No."

She spoke as if she was humouring him, as if he was half drunk and amorous or maudlin, as if he was the youth and she the adult grown with experience of the world.

"Don't pamper me, lass. I've no proof. But I've no gain t' make from lyin' to you, have I?" Docherty said. "It's what I bring you, Elspeth. The packman's name was Fitter."

"How do you know? I thought –"

"There was a laddie wi' him. The laddie did the luggin' o' the jars. An' the laddie let it slip. Called him 'Mister Fitter'."

"Why didn't you tell?"

"If it *was* Moodie – an' I'll swear the weaver was at the back o' it – then this Fitter mannie'll be harder t' trace than a flea in a forest. But bear that name in mind, Elspeth. Dinna forget it. Fitter."

"James wouldn't kill cattle deliberately."

"He gets what he wants," said Docherty.

With a sudden shiver, Elspeth recalled how she had answered her Mam just yesterday afternoon. She said nothing now, though. She was troubled by the information that Peter Docherty had imparted. What he said was honest. She did not for an instant doubt his good faith in telling her. But she doubted his reasoning. He had no evidence that James had anything to do with the cartloads of rancid oil, that the packman had been Mr Moodie's agent. It was too vague, too ill-defined. She could not – entirely – accept Peter's avowals that his guess was close to truth. She would, however, obey him. She would not forget the name: Fitter.

Darts of buttery light showed among the clouds to the east and there was a strong toss of wind that shook through the trees, silencing the birdsong, causing the labourer and the girl to turn their backs to it and hunch their shoulders. Docherty's hat flapped on its thong. He slapped his hand to the crown to hold it on, lest it proceed before him, bowling away down the fields to the turnpike, and reach Glasgow before he did.

When he spoke it was strongly, like the freshening air. "Well, lass, I'll be on m' way. Ye know, I tarried here too long. It was never meant for Peter Docherty t' squat in the one place for such a while." He snapped down the hat brim and tightened the knot in the thong. Hands free, he turned and hugged her. He kissed her mouth. "At least I'll have a tale t' tell in the public houses, eh? How I kissed the bonniest lassie in all the land. An' if any lout dare argue he'll taste m' knuckles."

The strange thing was that he meant it. His cheerful optimism had returned, battered and uneven like the wheel of an old cart but capable still of trundling Docherty along happily enough. If there had been more of that quality in him, less of the self-pity and defeatism that Elspeth had come to regard as ingrained weaknesses, perhaps she might have come to love the ageing labourer more. But it was too late, too late to change her destiny.

She hugged him in return and impulsively kissed him on the mouth.

"There," she said. "Safe travel t' you, Peter Docherty, an' a secure harbour at the end o' it."

"Goodbye t' ye, lass."

"Goodbye, Peter."

He turned and strode away, spring-stepped in spite of the pack and the poacher's bag, more lively than she had ever seen him.

On her lips he had left the faint taste of whisky.

And in her heart, doubt.

August ushered in a spell of pleasant weather to atone for a squally and uncertain summer. Much rain fell in May, June and throughout July. The good folk of Balnesmoor and Ottershaw were heartily sick of clod and clump, of wading in fields that had the consistency of gruel. Weaver Moodie's fine new flock of Cheviots, driven up from the Borders after the spring sales, had their hardiness well tested in the wet, and the would-be wool-grower had to be content to check his plan of expansion for a year since new-sown grasses did not root well on Dyers' Dyke. The Macfarlanes, a shepherd family James employed to dwell in the farmhouse once occupied by Coll and Etta Cochran, found their yard awash and kitchen plots floating away on seepage from the pond, though the house itself was tight enough. Work on the mill at Kennart continued intermittently among days of heavy rain when levelled foundations quaked and walls, bare high as a knee, slumped without warning. Great mackerel sunsets delighted all for a day or two. An odd afternoon of calm sea-blue above the hills coaxed sudden crops upward. But the climate mirrored Elspeth Cochran's mood and made earning extra difficult in a year that had been damned enough, one way and another.

Anna was no happier at Ottershaw. She found, though, that she preferred the company of dairymaids and cowmen at the home farm to the solitude of her pine-wood cottage and staring at Matt's sour face when he was at home. She saw very little of her sister and only occasionally, out of a sense of duty, toiled up the hill to visit Mammy, to take her a press of cheese or a pat of butter and enquire about her health. It was a matter of no importance to Anna that the

346

Dyke was gone. If, like Elspeth, she had been unwed, she might have made a fuss about "her rights". But there was nothing in the lease to save her from a sentence of marriage, nothing to be lost, as far as she could see, in turning over the putrid acres to Jamie Moodie. From Matt she learned that Mr Sinclair had finally come down on the side of amalgamated farms and declared his belief that patch steadings and rig systems had had their day. Capital investment was crucial to the successful establishment of big-yield estate and, Matt said with a bit of a sneer, his father had the notion of making Ottershaw into a model for every land-owner to follow.

Elspeth was much away from the Nettleburn. It was her first taste of field-labour as a hireling. Though she had mingled with casuals at the Dyke in appropriate seasons, she had never gone out with hand open to ask any man, even Mr Sinclair, for payment. It cut against the grain of independence in her. She felt that somehow Mammy and she had slipped in the scale of things.

It was not that Elspeth had ever given herself airs and graces or played the lady to the daughters of other tenants as Anna had tended to do. But she was different from them in some mysterious manner and, throughout girlhood, had been made aware of it as she had been made aware of her own good looks.

She had applied herself, had taken all the opportunities offered, in schooling, for instance, but each catch at bettering herself had been construed as an eccentricity or, worse, as an arrogance that ill fitted a female person. She had toiled with hoe and flail, churned butter, sickled bracken, fed goats and plucked fowls, washed blankets in freezing burn water, axed deadfall daily for the fire, and had done more than her share of back-breaking field-labour; nobody would deny that she was industrious. But she had also dared to ride in James Moodie's carriage and had walked in her finery with the wealthy weaver on the river-bank and had taken tea at his house. The elephantine memory of the village at large had many a slight stored against her. When she was obliged, by the ruin of the Dyke, to seek the sort of servants' work that was the lot of most of Balnesmoor's women, they revelled in 'Pet Cochran's "downfall" and pricked her with insults while she crouched in the rows among them.

It was not the slanders and slights that worried Elspeth so much as her reaction to them. She agreed with the villagers; she did not belong among them. She might be, as they were, a product of byre and barn, stackyard and cornrig, but a different tune was touched from her strings. During that uncertain summer, Elspeth at last admitted it. She kept tight rein on anger and hurt and took her shillings with a fierce sense of pride. In time, she believed she would settle to it. But August brought warm weather and, as the month progressed, heat and an unrelenting dryness that, by first harvest, had burned into drought. For Elspeth there would be no settling and no solution, only an end which nobody, not even James Moodie, could have foreseen.

Heat wavered over the moor. At the height of noon and in the short cooling hours of the night the great quilt of heather and broom seemed to breathe as shallowly as Gaddy, with a suspiration of quite desperate quality, its shag crackling. At other times it was so silent, so abnormally still, that the girl imagined all the beasts lay stunned or dead and that the birds had gone north in search of a breeze. Only buzzards, eagles and hawks thrived, pinned against enamel, drifting on whorls that tricked the eyes into believing that the whole hillside was melting like coloured clay.

Elspeth worked in grain fields so dusty that they seemed to be enshrouded in fog. Raw throat, itching thighs, the scald of sweat on the body's secret surfaces made labour a torment. A sturdy young horse, ironically hauling a water-cart, expired suddenly in the shafts. One strapping young lad from Wrassles' went stone-mad, foaming and gibbering as if demon-possessed. He had to be chased and roped and led away for a soaking and a spell in a darkened loft. At least three babies were dropped prematurely in a swelter of pain, lost in the deep, dry, rattling sea of corn. Fist fights were ten for a penny among the men; in the ranks of the women cat-shrieks and scratchings, brief exhausting fits of temper that marked as ugly the long days under a thudding sun.

Yield was heavy, a bounty for tenants and owners, a fat

haul stripped fast off the crumbling earth. But those who had planted late or shoddily found little to reap at all. Shallow-rooted cereals and tuber crops shrivelled for lack of moisture. Some cattle died, swarmed with thirsty black flies. Streams dried up. With the Nettleburn down to rock and baked earth, Elspeth was obliged to add to her days' toil by lugging water three miles from a cistern on Short's farm, paying for it by the bucketful. Blane, Lightwater and Endrick stepped down inch by inch, shrinking almost visibly in the latter days of the month, until there appeared to be no flow at all in them, only scum-coated stagnant ponds with fish floating dead on the yeasty surfaces.

Night brought no relief for aching, blear-eyed labourers. Magnificent twilights, dusted with rose and powder-blue shadow, went unappreciated by a populace who scanned the heavens only for congealing cloud and signs of rain. Many villagers slept, like drovers, in the open air. The heat indoors was suffocating. Houses were wrapped for snugness and could not be rendered light and airy to suit the freakish climate. Indeed, there had been longer spells without rain but none in living memory during which the sun beat down with such hellish hot intensity.

On the Sabbath, to a half-empty kirk, Mr Leggat offered intercession for precipitation, prayers that went on near as long as the damned drought. At Ottershaw, Mr Sinclair fell back on contingency plans for transporting water to gasping stock. He even bought water, as precious as whisky, from Montrose, carting it in a train of wagons from Loch Lomond, half the work-force on any given day being employed on liquid duties.

Anna found the cottage in the pines a wee thing cooler than other spots but enjoyed the stone-floored, stone-walled dairy best of all. Like the other maids, she loitered long in the sluiced chambers where cream pans and churns were stored. In the woods, Matt and his fellow foresters watched for spontaneous fires, and did not a jot of hard labour lest a spark start the whole hillside alight. Up at the hut on the dusty ravine that had once been the Nettleburn, Gaddy dragged herself about, tended her poor goats and chickens and dolefully sprinkled water drops from a rag on to the dying potato beds.

The end of the hot spell came slowly. Gradually darkening skies hung over mountains and hills, flat as parchment. For a day, a night and a morning the accumulation continued and, even with the sun gone, heat increased oppressively. It became difficult to draw breath. Every movement engendered sticky sweat. Temples thumped and eyeballs ached as the low, unemphatic cloud pressed down upon the Lennox.

By noon of the second day the beasts were roaring in misery. Moodie's sheep, many of them, had flopped on to their sides. In the stubble fields the cart-garrons were totally intractable and draught horses kicked viciously as if man had become their enemy. In the library of the house of Ottershaw Sir Gilbert let the fire go out and sat by the window basking in the oven-like heat. But only the laird was content. Most other folk in the Lennox felt sickly, waiting for the first ripple of wind that would presage rain, for the welcome rumble across the loch in the cauldron of the glens that would announce the end of discomfort and of drought.

The morning of that day was dark as doom. Gaddy was unsettled, uneasy. She shivered, sweating. She felt the leaden weight in her breast grow heavier. She started at each and every little sound; the flutter of a hen, the sudden scream of a gull, the cry of a child somewhere on the turnpike, thin and shrill enough to penetrate the heavy stillness. The goats were restless. They would not settle to crop, would not lie down. Drumglass turned from grey to black in the course of a couple of hours and, yes, away across Loch Lomond she glimpsed a flash of lightning and heard the faint, skin-tingling mutter of first thunder.

Over on Dyers' Dyke, the Macfarlanes prudently drove the Cheviots out of fields bounded by trees. On the parklands of Ottershaw, Lachlan Sinclair's lieutenants were hard at work, shifting flocks and herds away from the Lightwater on to higher ground. Sir Gilbert's prize rams were rounded up and steered from a tree-circled pasture into pens at the home farm. The dairy was double-drenched to protect the day's yield from turning in the pans. Anna was nervous and, though she could not imagine why, afraid for Matt up there in the cathedral of pine, oak and beech.

For Elspeth on that particular day there was no hire work. She had been to Short's farm to buy water. Saddled with yoke and wooden buckets, she plodded back along the track. She felt horribly exposed and darted glances at the coal-black cloud which filled the horizon and had by now blotted out Ben Lomond and the mountains of Argyll. Against that sombre, unwrinkled screen gulls flocked, stark white like bone shards. Chittering, a wheel of swallows arced over the thorn hedge and, shifting axis, tilted off through the motionless boughs. Down through the trees, enlarged by the steep fall, Elspeth saw rooks abandoning their twig-nests. Vulgar, rude-voiced and loud in the gathering gloom, the birds quarrelled about the wisdom of obeying instinct, then, even as she watched, massed, rose and winged away beneath her line of sight, leaving the rookery deserted.

Elspeth began to run. Water slopped from the buckets, soaking her skirts. She clutched at the yoke, crushing it against her shoulders. She fled as if the hounds of hell might spring from the mouth of the cloud, as if the flicker of lightning, quite distant still, might shape into a spear that would rive her as she ran. Shaken and confused, her mind sought reason: Mammy will be frightened, Mammy will want me safe home, Mammy should not be alone, Mammy had always hated the thunder. Mammy!

Nervousness had swelled into fear. Now fear exploded into terror as deer burst without warning from the underbrush. Not roe but rough-coated, antlered reds, a stag followed by a parcel of hinds. For an instant, they seemed to be aimed at her. Elspeth shrieked and flung herself free of yoke and buckets. She threw herself into the roots of the hedge on the track's high shoulder.

Mouths open, laved with spittle, eyes rolled red, the deer stampeded past her, kicking up a choking dust and, led by the stag, attacked the slope, breaking through or leaping over the hedge. Elspeth watched, awestruck, as one hind tore her belly on the thorns, struggled, braying, and ripped loose, leaving strips of hide, russet hair and a splash of fresh blood upon the spikes. Then the animals were gone, galloping across the corner of the fields towards the open reaches of the moor, there to brave whatever broke from the iron sky.

On the track the earth had already absorbed the spill-water from the toppled buckets. Elspeth left them where they lay. Possessed by fear now, she ran as the deer had done, with turbid determination, through a hedge gap and across the field towards the sprig of woodsmoke that marked the location of the hut, the protection of her mother's arms.

Behind her, as a deafening peal of thunder split the sky, blobs of rain scattered like sown seed, solid and stinging on the parched ground. Just as Elspeth reached the lazy-beds, rain began. In the same instant, thunder bellowed across Drumglass. Sickles of lightning cut the sky loose from the hem of the moor. A sulphurous band of light showed, temporarily outlining the hill as the rain increased and the wind came.

Gaddy stood by the corner of the hut waving anxiously, summoning her bairn. In tears, Elspeth wrapped herself in Mammy's strong arms and was led into the hut. Gaddy barred and roped the door then sat with her arms around Elspeth who cowered, trembling, in a corner of the hearth.

Cracks of thunder shook the hut's foundations as the storm gripped Balnesmoor in earnest.

"It'll soon blow over, 'Pet," said Gaddy, with more courage than she felt. "It'll not last o'er long."

But the storm did not dwindle. It went on and on, bellowing loud, throughout the afternoon and far into the night.

The air turned chill. Rain sizzled on the thatch and plopped in spots upon the room beneath. The wind flung droplets down the hole to explode with puffs of steam among the pots. All afternoon the highland woman stayed safe behind the door. But, with night not far off, she dared draw it ajar on its rope-hinge and peered outside. Slate-coloured trees flung back images of the gale. Sheet lightning down the strath made the crests of water brilliant as silk. Fighting the tug of the wind, Gaddy drew indoors again and knotted the rope fast.

Rain struck the thatch like lead shot. Thunder reverberated in the stone corries of Dumgoyne where the red deer had sought sanctuary.

Gaddy shook her head. "It's beyond anythin' I've ever seen. Still, by mornin' it'll all be gone."

"There will be damage, Mammy," said Elspeth.

"Aye. Much of it," said Gaddy.

"Come, an' I'll lie in your bed," said Elspeth.

Together, mother and daughter spent the night snuggled close for the comfort it gave against the unremitting fury of the elements outside, against forces that had no reason and no rule.

Morning did not bring respite.

As dawn seeped reluctant light across the breast of the moor, jowls of rock behind which the Nettleburn had its origins collapsed and blew outwards in a waterspout. Within minutes the burn had broadened to a torrent. Rock and slurry, the sediment of the moor, vomited down its course and wiped everything before it as far as the woods of Ottershaw.

Elspeth had not been properly asleep when she heard the boom. Even amid the cacophony of sounds that beat about the hut, making her ears ache and her brain reel with its volume and variety, there was something so alien in that particular noise that she shook Mammy's shoulder, crying, "What's that? D'you hear it? What is it?"

Gaddy sat upright. She had not removed her shawl. It draped her body like a shroud. She had heard such a noise before, long ago, coming from Ben Cruachan. It had terrified her then, when she was younger than 'Pet was now, and she had never quite put from her mind the sight of the river of rock and mud which sprayed down from the mountain. Slip of the land, the crofters had called it, and had run from the steadings, though the fall had not come close enough to the tiny community to do damage. There had been cattle killed, however, overtaken where they stood. Gaddy could recall the sight of bodies mashed in the receded tide of scree and mud.

She had no time to do anything, no breath to explain.

She pushed Elspeth, sending the girl to the floor. She

stepped over her and dragged her to her feet. Elspeth had taken off her skirt and top but wore a bodice and undergarment. Modesty must go by the board. The moment seemed to mount to a pinnacle of panic as Gaddy scrambled to the door and tore at the bar and the rope. The wind sucked the door from her grasp. Now they could hear the thunder that came from the hill, not from the sky.

In the dim light of dawn the Nettleburn stood high above its banks. The sward was awash, the patch already swirled with water as high as the ankles. Many, many sounds accumulated; a bleat of goats, the clash of trees, the voices of the wind. But they were swiftly consumed by the mammoth chuckling roar of the waterspout which had forced a cascade out over the rim of the burn and, trailed by rocks, sent a huge, streaming wave over the cradles of the burn.

Gaddy wasted not a second. She pushed Elspeth before her, shouting, "*Run away. Run away. Run for the gate. The gate.*"

To go downward, down the line of the path towards Ottershaw would hold them to a quarter of the field which would, at any moment, be swamped.

Elspeth, however, would not leave Mammy behind.

She snared Gaddy's wrist with her arms and bodily dragged the big woman away from the door, dragged her through the broth of water that had come down already, dragged her along by the hut gable and across the border of the lazy-beds. The dark-brown soup through which the women waded was all that was left of carefully nurtured plots. The flood had been steady and the hillside was already a gigantic waterfall as overloaded, half-choked drainages spewed out excess. Gaddy was shouting about the goats. The poor beasts, on their tethers, huddled in the lee of the roof. But Elspeth had taken her mother's warning and knew that they dared not tarry to release the nannies, however cruel it seemed to leave them there in the path of the floodwater.

It had never occurred to the girl before that the burn could be transformed into a raging, destructive force. She had seen it swollen many a time. But even then the force of it was mild. Now there was no burn-line visible. It was all brown tumble and foam. It gave out a hideous gobbling

354

noise as if it was greedy to suck. But it was the tide that leapt downhill before the spout that really frightened Elspeth. She had the sense to keep dragging Gaddy towards the ribbon of heather, angled towards the back of the village, towards Dyers' Dyke, not downhill.

Thirty yards, forty yards, sixty yards from the site of the hut – the tide struck them. Knee-deep, waist-deep, up to the ribs. Elspeth thought that it would whip them from their feet and drown them. Drowned, there on the moor. Drowned by rain. It seemed so daft, so mad. Elspeth struggled to keep balance. Mammy had gone down. The shawl floated from her shoulders. Grabbing the garment, with every ounce of strength in her body, Elspeth pulled Gaddy from the water. Upward, climbing, she struck out for the cluster of big boulders that marked the end of the patch. Gaddy floundered then half rose and, taking the dead weight from Elspeth's arms, clawed upward too, up to the safety of the high ground where she flopped on to her back and closed her eyes.

Rain fell upon the woman's face. But Elspeth, though locking her mother tightly with her arms, for three or four minutes gave her no attention at all.

Her gaze was drawn downward to the hut.

The wall of slurry, stones, mud and water mixed, surged over the rim of the moor and belched into the dwelling. It skated over the thatched roof, swallowed it and, by its tonnage, flattened the gables beneath it. The nannies had no hope of survival. But three or four of the hens, driven mad by fear, found wing. In shaking bundles they swooped and hopped ahead of the flood until, one by one, it sucked them down.

Elspeth could hear the hut disintegrating; not loud, not resistant. It went with no more fuss than a dung-ball dissolving in a puddle. Beams stuck up, then swooped away after the thatch. The stand of the stone chimney remained only a split-second longer then, with a little weak wimple, ducked underwater too. That was all there was to see. The hut which had stood for a century or more, which had given her mother refuge and whose walls had contained her infant life, whose plantings had nourished her, whose thatch had kept her snug in all seasons for almost twenty years vanished like a brown leaf. She could hardly believe the evidence of her eyes. Thorn hedge, track, alders, underbrush, then the hefty trees; only their bulk dispersed the flood and dissipated its awful energy. She could hear it still, though, diverted into a dozen lesser falls, crashing and snarling downward to the turnpike, to join the huge, stained-silver floods that covered the floor of the strath.

"Mammy," she murmured. "Mammy, oh, look."

But Gaddy did not answer her.

"I wish she would die," said Anna. "Really, I do. I mean, what sort of a life can it be for a woman like her, stuck in a bed in our back room? She's never goin' to get well. You can see that for yourself, 'Pet. It'd be better for all concerned if she just passed away t' her rest."

"Be quiet," said Elspeth.

"She canna hear me."

"No. But I can."

Young Mistress Sinclair was silent for a moment. She held a dish of tea in both hands and, knees apart, toasted her thighs at the crackling fire, skirts hitched into her lap. She stared into the flames while Elspeth, behind her, laid platters on the wooden table in preparation for supper.

The kitchen was new-pin clean; yet it seemed cluttered and, oddly, impermanent. A long-straw mattress was stuffed into the chimney corner and a bundle of blankets and bolsters occupied more precious space. Two large baskets contained such items as Elspeth had been able to redeem from the mud trash that the flood had left in its wake; clothing, a few sodden, buckled boots and, ironically, the brooch that Coll had given Anna in what seemed like another age.

"Rankellor's given us fair warnin'," Anna went on, after a tactful pause. "It's only a matter o' time. I'm just sayin' I wish, for her sake, it could be sooner."

"She's comfortable enough," said Elspeth.

"Och, she's not in pain, an' I'm bloody glad o' that," said Anna, her back still to her sister. "But it's no life, is it?"

356

Elspeth rattled the soup cogs, clacking them down.

"Who am I hearin'?" she demanded. "Is it you, or is it Matt Sinclair?"

"Don't you start on Matt." Anna turned. "He took you both in, did he not? I mean, where would you have been if it hadn't been for Matt? Oh, you'd not have gone without a roof over your heads but it'd have been a loft above the stables. She wouldn't have lasted a night there, would she? So don't you give Matt the edge of your tongue."

"I wouldn't have asked for his charity," said Elspeth, evenly, "if Mammy hadn't been quite so ill or if there had been somethin' left on the Nettleburn, even a dry bit of ground."

"All I'm sayin' is, what're you goin' to do if she lives for another year?"

"Don't you understand?" Elspeth snapped. "She's *mortal* sick. Her heart is so swelled up it might burst at any minute. You saw the worry on Rankellor's face when he put the listening trumpet to her breast. Never heed the doctor; look at her."

"That's what I'm sayin'. That's all I'm sayin'. I wisht she'd –"

"Do you want us t' leave?"

"Where would ye go?"

"Never mind that. Does Matt want us to leave?"

Anna sucked her nether lip. She put the tea-dish on the hearth and folded her hands into her lap, staring once more into the fire as if she hoped to find there an inspired lie.

There was no hiding the truth. Her husband had been giving her whacks because of the changed circumstances. She couldn't blame Matt. The small, cramped cottage was his domain. He came home tired after a day's labour and he needed proper rest. All they had had, really, in this remote, dank little house had been privacy. It was one thing to live crowded with sisters and brothers, quite another to lodge strangers in your own home. She had much sympathy for Elspeth. She *was* concerned for Mammy's welfare. But she had Matt to think of too. It was unfair to ask him to endure the "arrangement" for long.

It was Mr Sinclair who had resettled 'Pet and Mammy

357

here, brooking no opposition. She – so Anna told herself – didn't much care one way or the other. In fact, there were certain advantages in having Mam and 'Pet here. Company for one thing, the housekeeping that Elspeth undertook as a matter of course, and the extra bit of money that her sister contributed to the purse from her work in the Ottershaw fields. But it hurt Anna to know that her Mammy was just through the door, in the cramped and gloomy room, and that she could give her nothing or, sadly, seek from the big woman comfort for her own predicament.

"Well, does he?" said Elspeth. "'Cause if he does, he'll have to come right out an' ask us."

"He wouldn't be so cruel," said Anna, without conviction.

"You mean, he's scared of his father."

"I'll not have that. I'll not have you wiggin' on my man."

Anna got to her feet, ready to begin a quarrel. Argument was quite in tune with her ire and frustration. A good old sisterly fight would cheer her up and clear the air.

But Elspeth had held up her hand, as if to signal peace. "Listen."

"What is it?"

"Mammy."

"Oh, God!" Anxiety nipped Anna's heart.

She quailed before the implications of the sound from the back room, from every sound that emanated from there. She was unfamiliar with the woman who lay still and uncomplaining beneath the blankets, alienated by her fragility.

"Oh, God, 'Pet. What's happened?"

It was nothing; a cough, wheezy as a torn bellows.

"She's all right," said Elspeth.

"Go an' see," Anna, in agitation, urged.

Though she, not Elspeth, was Gaddy's true-born daughter, Anna could not bear to nurse her mother, could not endure the infirmity, the loss of attention, the corporeality of illness. Steeling herself as for an ordeal, she would enter the back room once each day. With a tense smile on her lips and loving phrases dying on her tongue, she would stoop over the ruined body to plant a hasty kiss upon the brow. It was Mammy's eyes that chilled her, eyes in which not only love but even recognition had been almost extinguished.

Gaddy coughed again. If Anna had been alone in the cottage with the woman, which she never was, she would have flown to the door in distress, sure that the ordinary sound signified death. Elspeth, however, though more caring, seemed in some respects casual to the point of callousness.

"Better go, better go, 'Pet," Anna insisted.

"It's just a tickle in her throat."

Nonetheless, Elspeth went to the closed door and opened it quietly. She passed into unlighted gloom. Anna took a step closer, head cocked to listen, to hear if any words were exchanged.

She felt, too, excluded.

Two or three minutes later Elspeth returned.

"She's thirsty," she said. "I'll take her some tea."

"Will it . . .?"

"No, it'll not do her harm."

There was medicine in a tall fluted bottle, a syrup which Doctor Rankellor had left after his visit, a day after the flood.

The old doctor had been roused from retirement. Many souls were in need of his attentions in the aftermath of the storm. Two bairns had been trapped in a cottage in Killearn by a smitten ash tree, and one had died of head wounds. In Balnesmoor there had also been a death. Old Mistress Meldrum, near ninety years of age, had been blown off her feet by the squall and had drowned ten yards from the back of her cottage, drowned in a puddle two feet deep. These, and many fractures and abrasions had been treated by Rankellor and by a young layman named Carswell who had studied as a bone-setter and now lived in Drymen.

A heavier toll had been taken from stock, however. Many herds had been decimated by flooding along the confluence of the Blane and Endrick and on low grazings by the Lightwater. Hundreds of beasts had been drowned, four oxen and a horse poled by lightning bolts. Damage to properties was extensive, from minor tearing of thatch and slates to chimney-stacks crashing and cots crushed by trees.

On Wrassles' farm the buildings had near vanished underwater and Tam Tait's place, like Gaddy's, had been swept
away on a torrent from the hill. The inundation of the strath
had ruined the later harvests and had tugged away much
stooked grain, washing it down into the loch or piling it
about the bridges. James's new mill building at Kennart
had half collapsed. Only the brig's high arch had saved it
from crumbling under the force of the spate. If the brig had
gone, the mill would have gone too and Moodie would have
been out enough silver to make even his pocket pinch.

But to Anna and to Elspeth the tales of hardship and
misery paled beside their lot. Of the Nettleburn's acres
naught was left but slurs of mud and small rock that had
hardened like candle-grease and stretched nine hundred feet
from the spout to the turnpike. In a year or two, Rankellor
said, nature would freshen the scar with new growth. But,
said Mr Sinclair, the hardy stuff of fern, bracken and thistles
would root first and the moor would loop closer to the road
than it had done for a century.

The goats were drowned, together with the rooster and
most of the hens. Stored crops and planted beds were lost
in the rubble that had once been a dwelling. Picking over
the scar, three days later, when it had begun to dry a little,
Elspeth had retrieved clothes for washing and the object
that had drawn her to search at all, the wooden chest in
which Gaddy kept her silver. It stuck forth from the mud
on the slant of the thorn hedge, close to the carcass of one
of the nannies. The family savings – forty-eight pounds –
were intact in the linen pouch in which Gaddy kept them
wrapped, old-fashioned guineas for the most part and one
wet banknote.

It appalled Anna to discover that there was so little. Had
there never been more? she asked her sister. Had there never
been more between the Cochrans and poverty?

Elspeth shook her head. She could not answer. In matters
of economy Mammy had not taken her into her confidence.
It seemed so inconsequential: money. It also seemed that
she – they – had been raised in a cloud of illusion. How
close, indeed, had been the edge of penury. How aware
Gaddy must have been of it in spite of Coll's strange

"arrangement" with lawyers and lairds. In a snap of the fingers both Dyers' Dyke and the Nettleburn had gone.

All the other losses were blotted out by Mammy's seizure of the heart. Said Rankellor, offering ambiguous comfort, she should by rights have died there and then. And though she kept it deep buried in her heart, Elspeth wished sometimes that Mammy *had* died on that wild morning in that wild place, for the fitting end it would have made to a life thus lived.

Elspeth poured tea into a bowl. She added sugar from a caddy on the shelf, stirred the brew and blew on it to cool it. She carried the bowl and a round spoon ben the house while Anna, suspicious of even this simple act, skulked in the kitchen.

The faintest whiff of smoke from a candle made Mammy choke; she was therefore committed to live in gloaming, motionless, if she was to survive at all.

It had been five weeks since she had been lugged down from the hill like a gralloched hind on a frame carried by six strong lads off Ottershaw, though they could ill be spared that particular day. Since then Gaddy had spoken hardly a word. It was not that she had lost the power of voice but that she had suffered a distemper of the brain, brought on by shock and an irregular heartbeat.

Elspeth fed her, washed her, changed her linen, lived with a silence which was neither approving nor disapproving but seemed so indifferent that it changed her Mammy completely, made her almost a stranger. Never had Elspeth loved the woman more. Never had she guarded that love against intrusions of pity for herself or fear for her future. What she feared most was that Mammy would endure in incontinence, in helplessness, until a wee wriggling worm of loathing entered her, Elspeth's, heart and ate away the memories that she cherished. This, for Anna, was a lump of flesh; not Mammy. Elspeth – yet – would have none of that.

She settled herself on a wooden chair drawn close to the side of the bed.

"Mammy?" she murmured. "Mammy, I've brought tea."

Gaddy fed in weak wee swallows; bread-and-milk, a whisked egg, a spoonful of broth or brose, hardly enough to keep a mouse alive. She appeared to derive most enjoyment from tea, from its lukewarm sweetness and pleasant astringency.

Elspeth raised her three or four inches on the pillow. Gaddy could not bear to sit up – or to lie flat. The groaning squeeze of air in inactive lungs told of pain. Spasms of the constricted heart would touch her features like a taste of vinegar, making her lips purse and eyes crinkle. Holding Mammy's head with her arm, Elspeth nestled the bowl into a fold of the blanket. She dipped the spoon and brought it to the woman's lips. Gaddy sipped dutifully, her unfocused gaze on the spoon. Did she not recognise the hand that held it, the face close to hers?

Again Elspeth brought the spoon for supping. With her knuckle she gently wiped the drip from Mam's chin.

As she did so, Gaddy's fingers closed on hers.

"Ho – home?" Gaddy whispered. "We'll – go – home."

"Soon, Mam."

"Net'burn?"

"Aye, to the Nettleburn."

Gaddy frowned slightly.

"Dark here."

"I'll bring a light when I come t' bed."

"Go – go – home now, 'Pet."

The woman's agitation disturbed Elspeth. Emotion meant danger. Excitement might cause another seizure. Harry Rankellor had explained it in some detail.

"See sky," Gaddy said.

"Everythin's fine, Mam."

"Plantin' time. Milkin' the kye," Gaddy said.

At what point in the scale of her life had memory alighted? It was unimportant. What was important was that she was showing interest, asking questions. Perhaps, after all, Mammy would return.

Elspeth put the spoon into the bowl.

"We'll be goin' home soon," she said. "I promise. Soon you'll see the sky again, Mammy, see the moor an' the hill."

Gaddy's chin slumped on to her breast. A smile played

at the corners of her mouth. There was, Elspeth thought, a trace of contentment in the sad, opaque eyes. The mood was destroyed by the sudden crash of the cottage door.

Matt Sinclair's voice rang out, "Is she still in the land o' the livin'?"

"Shut your big mouth, Matt," Anna shouted.

The outside door slammed shut. The young man's shadow encroached into the bedroom. He had been drinking. He usually had when he came in this late. Anna was by his side, tugging him. He jabbed her with his elbow.

"Ach, it's your dear sister, is it? Pleased t' see me home, are ye, 'Pet?"

"Matt, come away. Come away. I've got soup for ye," said Anna, deftly parrying his casual blows. "Leave Mammy in peace."

That was all there was to it.

Matt slammed the door of the tiny room, enclosing the dying woman and the girl in darkness.

Elspeth – Mammy too, perhaps – could hear his laughter, Anna's protests, then her squeals.

Tonight, Elspeth knew, she would be wakened by the sounds of rough love-making. Tensely she would lie listening to the gasps and grunts that the thin inner wall could not keep out. Mammy would hear too. That was the untenable thing, the ugly thing. There was something appallingly selfish in Matt's parade of lust. If she had been Anna, and Matt's wife, how would she respond? She was not Anna, though, not even of the same stock. Now, at last, she was glad.

She brought the teaspoon to her mother's lips, trying to pretend that she could not hear the big, raucous, male voice booming in the other room. "God, if it's peace she's needin', I can gi'e her peace. A bloody bolster o'er her mouth'll gi'e her peace in two minutes."

In darkness Elspeth brushed her mother's cheek, felt tears. It shocked her to realise that Mam had heard and understood it all.

Awkwardly she put an arm about Gaddy's shoulder and, choking back her own sobs, hugged her.

363

"There, Mammy, there. Never heed him."

They were Matt Sinclair's prisoners, jailed by circumstances and infirmity.

But Elspeth was not without will and, at that humiliating moment, felt her resolve stiffen into decision.

Late that night, crouched in the back room by a penny dip stuck in a bottle, Elspeth composed a letter which she delivered next morning, just after daylight, long before the village was awake.

One day later a lad from Moss House brought a reply.

It was not so easily arranged. James Simpson Moodie was enmeshed in sundry business ventures and was obliged to cancel and postpone several important appointments. He gave no indication of harassment, however, at the hour of two o'clock on the following day, when Elspeth Cochran, trim and tidy in her Sabbath best, was shown into his drawing-room.

Circumstances had changed dramatically in his favour. But James Moodie did not preen in front of her. He gave little hint in his manner or his speech that things had fallen much against her. He was a touch less effusive, a little bit dry, perhaps, but just as courteous as he had been half a year ago.

Dyers' Dyke was his, the Nettleburn too if he wanted it, mud-fouled though it might be. The young woman came without "dowry", without advantage. Yet he respected the fact that she presented herself without haughtiness or servility, with a pragmatism that, on the surface, reflected James Moodie's own character.

He gave her a glass of sweet Spanish wine and enquired after her mother's health. His sympathy was formal but genuine.

The girl waited politely for his invitation to speak.

He gave it, saying, "And what is it you wish of me, Elspeth?"

She put the wine glass on to the table and, sitting upright, hands folded in her lap, met his gaze.

"Do you still wish to marry me, Mr Moodie?"

"A change in fortunes," James said, "has occasioned a change of heart; is that so?"

"Aye, that's the substance of it."

"Elspeth, what I have to gain from takin' you as my wife is not what it was six months ago."

"I've nothin' to bring, I admit," the young woman said. "Except a lot of conditions."

James Moodie was surprised. "Conditions?"

"Perhaps it would be fair t' tell you my conditions before you give me an answer," said Elspeth.

James Moodie said, "That wouldn't be fair at all. No, Elspeth, you can have my answer first. I do still wish t' marry you."

She sighed.

James Moodie said, "Contrary to what you may have thought – or may have been told – my proposal had nothin' whatsoever to do with the obtaining of land."

"Is that true, James?"

"I swear it."

"What other reason –"

"Don't be daft, girl. Have you never looked in a mirror?"

If any man other than the weaver had given her such a reply she would have blushed with pleasure at the compliment. Though there was no trace of unctuousness or insincerity in James Moodie's tone she would have preferred a response that smacked of practical benefit.

"I expect, though," James went on, "you've less romantic inclination in you than I have. Put forward your conditions, Elspeth, and we'll negotiate upon them, since you seem to regard me as little else than a manipulator. I'm no fool, though, and I'm quite sure you don't wish to marry me for myself. No matter. I've more in my heart than a cash-box an' a rack for ledgers. Much more."

It was almost as if James had heard of the accusation that Peter Docherty had levelled against him. It was on the tip of Elspeth's tongue to challenge him, to hear him deny it. At that warm moment, she would have believed his denial implicitly. She would have put the slander out of her mind for ever. Caution, however, stayed her.

She said, "My mother'll die soon. She has severe constriction of the heart. According to Doctor Rankellor, she'll last no more than a month or two."

On Moodie's face, strangely, there was an expression of sorrow, not mere courteous response, not gravity, but a kind of hurt. Elspeth did not understand it. Her mother had always been his enemy.

James Moodie said, "I hadn't heard that it was mortal, this illness."

"She may pass away in her sleep this very night," Elspeth said. "That's how 'mortal' it is."

"God in Heaven!" Moodie exclaimed.

"It's imperative that you understand there's no hope of recovery of her strength. She's not even an invalid who'll respond t' medicine and good nursin'."

James nodded. "I see, I see."

"If you want, you can talk with Harry Rankellor."

"I don't doubt your word, Elspeth," said James. "Are the conditions you speak of t' do with your mother?"

"We're lodged with my sister an' her husband. We're not welcome there. It's too small, too cramped a cottage for any sort of comfort or harmony. You have rooms here."

"She won't come. Gaddy – your mother – she won't allow you to bring her under my roof."

"She has no strength to resist," said Elspeth. "Besides, if I ask it, she'll do it."

"In that case," said James, "we'll bring her here at once. This must, however, be a separate issue from that of our marriage contract. I'm not so dark a villain as to take advantage of mortal illness."

"No," said Elspeth. "I'll marry you freely, James."

"I'll have no martyr, you understand?"

She managed to laugh. "I'm too pretty t' be a martyr, am I not?"

But there was no humour in the weaver. He said, "Elspeth, it's not 'an arrangement' I'm after. I want you for a companion as much as anything else."

"If you wish, James, you may announce our betrothal. Mam an' I will be guests in your house for an unspecified period. I'll require a clean, light an' airy bedroom for my mother. At the top o' the house, if possible."

366

"Lookin' out to the hill?" said James.

"Yes."

"She shall have it."

"After my Mam . . . passes on, after a short period of mourning, three months, say, then we'll be wed."

"Those are your conditions?"

"They are."

"I would have done — I will, indeed, do – all that you ask without holdin' you to an engagement to marry."

"I'm ill enough thought of in Balnesmoor," said Elspeth, "in bein' courted by the weaver. To live in his house an' not marry would damn me for ever."

James gave a snort of laughter.

"Damned here if you do; damned there if you don't, hm?" he said.

"It is agreed between us, James?"

James Moodie rose and came forward. He took her hands and coaxed her gingerly to her feet. He kissed her awkwardly on the cheek, as a father might kiss a daughter.

"It's agreed," he said. "I'll send a carriage down to Ottershaw first thing tomorrow."

"Not good enough for you, I suppose," said Anna. "Can't get enough attention here t' suit you. Well! Take her then, and go."

"Aye, an' don't come whinin' back," Matt Sinclair added.

The young forester had sent word to his superior that he would be late in arriving at the clearing camp that morning. He claimed – and who was to deny it, since, whatever his faults, he was still the grieve's son? – he claimed that he was required to assist in the transportation of his wife's mother to a place where she could be nursed. He did not mention Moodie or the fact that his sister-in-law would also be residing under the weaver's roof. Such confession stuck, for the time being, in Matt Sinclair's throat.

To Anna, Matt gave little thought, though she'd wept against his chest for a good hour the previous night, crying like a damned bairn because her Mammy was going away.

But something else rankled in Matt's gut, the view he had had of Elspeth, the comparisons he had been forced to draw between the sisters, between the one he had married and the one who had escaped him. Elspeth was everything that Anna was not; an obedient servant, dutiful in her attentions, guarded with her tongue. How she would have served him in bed was something that Matt would muse upon in the years ahead, though not with any great depth of interest since he was stupid enough to believe that one woman was no better than another when it came to pleasing a man in that way.

But Matt was delighted to see the back of the highland woman. Sick, enfeebled, she was nothing but a burden and a distraction to Anna when he needed all Anna's attention for himself. He had no idea of how Gaddy Cochran would be removed from the cottage to Moodie's mansion without seriously endangering her life. It was more out of curiosity than concern that Matt Sinclair loitered for half the morning about the cottage doorway.

Anna had been hurt by Gaddy's acquiescence. Mammy had made it known, even through her exhaustion, that she was willing to do what 'Pet suggested. None of them could be certain that the woman knew what her destination would be and Anna had lost her temper and shouted at her mother from the doorway of the bedroom, "Moodie's house! You'd stay wi' Moodie rather'n your own flesh and blood?"

Mammy had managed to nod, though her eyes were slitted and she seemed puffed up, all mouth and cheeks. She had struggled for breath for two or three minutes before she found expression.

"As . . . as 'Pet says. Aye," she'd whispered.

Now Mammy was going, not to live in Moodie's house but to die there.

Elspeth had finally managed to steal her away.

When the Cabriolet rumbled up the narrow path through the pines, its fine paintwork was scratched by the needles. The blinkered horse was guided under the splayed boughs only by the expertise of the coachman.

In a fit of near-hysteria, Anna cried out, "You canna take her. You canna take my Mammy," as if the coach was a funeral cart and the bed – the entire bed – was a coffin.

Elspeth's eyes were wide, her mouth set. She had not

expected this of James Moodie. It was a sign of his complexity.

The interior of the handsome, expensive Cabriolet had been stripped of upholstery, pared almost to the shell. It had been fitted with a cradle of wooden blocks and a series of leather straps. The work had been done overnight, thoroughly designed and executed. Behind the Cabriolet, walking in line, came Moodie's gardeners and two of the Macfarlane boys; six men in all. But of all the gestures that the weaver could have made to convince Elspeth that he had a soul, the most telling was his presence.

In tweeds, workmanlike, James Moodie was seated on the coach-board by the driver.

It was James who stepped down, who moved to the place by the door where Elspeth waited, who took her hand and kissed it, tenderly.

"Is Gaddy inside?"

"She is, James."

Matt Sinclair edged forward. "It's my house, ye know."

James Moodie swung his head and looked the young forester up and down.

"Have I your permission to enter, then?"

Sir Gilbert, even the Duke, could not have forbidden the weaver at that moment.

"Come, Elspeth," James Moodie said.

Followed by the young woman, James went into the cottage, into the back room.

Gaddy had no awareness of times. She lay in a half-raised position, her gaze fixed on the ceiling beams, her mouth slack, chest rising and falling laboriously. Elspeth had washed her and combed her hair, had changed her gown and put on the lace-hemmed cap, a woollen shawl about her shoulders. But for what purpose, it seemed that Gaddy could not deduce. She could not connect the shouted arguments of the previous evening with the events that were occurring now.

James Moodie took off his hat.

"I'm sorry indeed to be seeing you reduced to this, Mistress Cochran. I'll inconvenience you as little as possible."

Four men crowded into the bedroom; Matt Sinclair was not one of them.

It had the smoothness, the efficiency of a well-rehearsed ceremony. It had been practised in advance, Elspeth reckoned. The mattress was lifted from the frame with Gaddy snugly upon it. Elspeth stood by her all the while, holding her hand, while Moodie's four servants kept the mattress level. The bed was quickly dismantled, taken through the doorways and assembled again by the side of the Cabriolet. Gaddy, slung in the mattress, was eased out through the doorways too and put with great care back upon the bed. There were no women servants – all men – but they were as modest and gentle as any woman could have been, what with the master there to have their ears at the least guffaw or snicker.

"Go to it, lads," Moodie ordered.

The bed was elevated, again to a plan, taken up into the shell of the Cabriolet and set fast within the six wooden blocks, strapped firm about its frame.

The men stepped down, all save one who stood at Gaddy's feet, watching the bed for any sign of sway.

"Elspeth, do you have baggage?" said James Moodie.

"There are two chests an' my dower-bag."

"Marshall," said James Moodie. "Fetch them."

The servant of that name stepped lively, hoisted up the two little chests one by one and tucked them under the bed, put the soft-cloth bag there too.

"Are you ready, Elspeth?"

"I'm ready."

"On to the coach-board with you, then," said James, handing her up.

"Mam! Mam!" Anna shouted. She rushed from Matt's side towards the coach but James Moodie caught her, held her.

"You may call to see your mother at any time, lass," he said.

"I'll never see her again," Anna wailed.

"You." James beckoned Matt. "Attend your wife, please. We mustn't keep the patient in the chill air one moment longer than's necessary."

"Bloody –"

"*What?*"

Matt Sinclair's ruddy features contorted with suppressed anger. But he did not dare defy the power of the weaver mannie. That's what it was, though. That's what Matt saw in all the show. Not love, not respect, not even Christian charity. It was naught but a display of power, subtle and efficient but ruthless nonetheless.

"Drive," James Moodie ordered.

The weaver did not mount on the board. He walked ahead of the coach, as if leading a procession. Behind him came four servants in a column, while one more brought up the rear.

Turned upon the seat, Elspeth did not glance back at the little cottage, at her sister and her sister's man. Her eyes never left her mother's face which, as the pines dropped away, changed and smoothed and became tranquil. It was as if the smell of the autumn morning and the pure autumnal sky had lifted the great weight from Gaddy's breast and brought her final relief.

She died somewhere along the turnpike.

Elspeth liked to believe that it happened at the turn to the track to the hill, where Drumglass peered down through a gap in the oak trees and the bracken glowed like bronze. But she could not tell properly, for Mammy, smiling, had just fallen fast asleep.

Gaddy Patterson Cochran was laid to rest in the kirkyard of Balnesmoor old church on Thursday afternoon. It was a calm, mild sort of day, though no sun shone and pale mists gathered early over the stubbles on the strath, and the mountains of Argyll had a far, flat look as if they had receded out of respect for the drover's woman, the cattle-grazer's wife.

William Leggatt, not himself in the best of health, presided emotionally over the interment and read at length from the Book of Ecclesiastes and delivered by way of eulogy, which was a form not much in fashion for women, an odd, rambling lecture on the changing times and virtues that had been lost.

The service was well enough attended by menfolk of the parish, some who had known Gaddy hardly at all but had been drummed out by the grieve and by James Moodie, gentlemen who took the order of kin to the deceased, though, strictly speaking, her only male relative was Matthew Sinclair.

Matt, out of duty, presented a solemn enough figure in the front rank of the mourners, by his father's side. Harry Rankellor, bent and very shrivelled, flanked the young forester and surprised the son-in-law by shedding a tear or two at the lowering and by blowing his nose loudly into a spotted handkerchief. More surprising still was the fact that James Simpson Moodie wept as well, with dignity and restraint into his spread right palm, though some claimed he was hiding his foxy grin and others that he was laughing up his sleeve since at last he'd got rid of the highland woman, even if he hadn't ousted her, quite, from the parish.

But Elspeth knew better.

Anna and she watched from the road beyond the wall, adhering to the ancient tradition that debarred women from the graveside.

Elspeth saw how James wept. She was taken aback by it, never doubting that it was genuine grief that brought tears to the weaver's eyes. After all, Moodie had been the first one in Balnesmoor to see her Mammy, along with Mr Leggat and Doctor Rankellor. She had heard, in various versions, of that dramatic night near twenty years ago when she was found and revived and bargained for. She had heard too how Jamie Moodie had done aught in his power to "protect" the foundling bairn from falling into the hands of a drover wifie; but she had an original view of James's behaviour now, saw it as an excess of concern, an allegiance to duty. She was sure, absolutely sure, that James would behave differently if he had his term again. Even so, the tears were unexpected, like so many things about James Simpson Moodie, part of the great puzzle of the man.

Anna wept sorely. Elspeth hugged and consoled her sister until Matt emerged from the gate to take over the duty as best he knew how.

Elspeth felt less shaken than she had imagined she would.

She did not, in the open air, spill one drop from her eyelids. She did not have to fight against sorrow; she did not feel it.

In a sense she was relieved that it was over, that Mammy had not suffered unendurably. It lightened her to realise that Mam had died where she would have wished to be, travelling the open road under a broad sky, not far from the Nettleburn where she had grasped at happiness. It was not a fantasy. Elspeth did not practise deception nor proclaim herself in clichés as Anna tended to do, re-knitting the history of the past years as if nobody at all could recall their reality.

Elspeth had stayed with James Moodie and his mother, their guest in Moss House. Gaddy had been laid out, as if she was a blood relative, in the long room, laid out with all ceremony in a lined casket, padded with sachets of linen fat with dried lavender. Now she would return to James's house, with James – and Gaddy would not be there. Gaddy had never lived there. Memories of her Mammy lay only on the high hill. She felt that Gaddy would never be far out of mind if she could look out at the breast of the sunlit moor or at Drumglass dusted with early snow.

The sisters parted at the gate. Mr Sinclair led away most of the men for a draught of ale and a nip of whisky at the Ramshead, having ensured that Matt would see his wife home and would wait with her at the Sinclairs' house.

James, however, gave his attention to Elspeth and walked with her in broad sight along the top of the Bonnywell, past the cottage where once he'd laboured with such ferocity.

"Are you very distressed, Elspeth?" he asked.

"Strangely, I'm not."

"I'll take care of you, you know."

"Yes," she said, distantly.

But those who peered from the wee windows which had once framed the faces of Moodie and his kin did not believe that a mere twenty years could have changed the elder into a gentleman and wondered at the pattern that had woven Jamie Moodie and Gaddy Patterson's foundling into the same patch of cloth. They had no answer, no solution; nor, indeed, had Moodie himself. There *was* no simple answer. Simple answers were for simple folk and Moodie, a mature man of business, was far from that. He had a depth and complexity which did not show on the surface. He was not being deceitful when he claimed affection for the girl, nor did he intend to harm her. For all that, Gaddy Patterson's daughter had no guard against the things of the past, things that she did not comprehend, which had belonged to a style of life that seemed to have gone out of fashion like black twist pantaloons and hessian boots, rough and ill-shaped but comfortable.

On Moodie's instruction, Gaddy had been buried close to the resting place of the unknown girl who had been Elspeth's natural mother. Perhaps it was only coincidence, for the kirkyard kept no special location for the poor and deprived; all were – or had been – the same in the eyes of God and the kirk session in Jamie Moodie's day, though the elder had not, at that time, approved of such democracy. Coll Cochran was buried in the same quarter. On the other side Moodie had already paid fee to reserve three plots for himself, his mother and his wife. Nobody, not even shrewd Lachlan Sinclair, had remarked upon it at the time and there was no chain of demarcation to show who owned the plots or who would eventually lie in them.

It was as if, though, James Simpson Moodie had ordained Elspeth's life for her, had already brought her so much into his power that he could prescribe the very place of her death.

Early that evening James dismissed his mother to her parlour. He wanted to dine alone with Elspeth in the hand-some, panelled room. It was warm, for a coal fire had been lighted, and the candles were new, slender and clear. Heeding James's suggestion, Elspeth did not wear mourning but put on her best dress; tomorrow would be time enough to show sombre weeds and grieve sore for Gaddy.

Towards the end of the dinner, after the servants had gone out, James said, "I regret that your mother never lived here."

"Why, James?"

"I don't know. It would have seemed . . ." He left the sentence unfinished.

"It was better that she died as she did, in the open air."

"She could have talked with my mother about old times, times past, an' we could have listened and learned."

The girl glanced up at him. "Mammy's dying as she did – it changes nothing between us."

Moodie hesitated. It cost him effort to speak the words.

He said, "I'll not hold you to your promise."

Elspeth said, "Don't you wish me to stay?"

"Yes, of course."

"To be your wife, still?"

"As soon as discretion allows."

"How long is that?"

"Five or six months, I would say."

She tried to read his expression but he revealed none of his feelings to her. She was obliged to accept his word on it. But there was in him a faint trace of agitation which surprised her almost as much as his tears at the graveside earlier that day.

"At my august age," he said, striving to make a joke of it, "I daren't tarry too long. In the meantime, you will stay here."

"It's hardly seemly."

"Where else would you go?"

"My sister . . ."

"To that pig-wallow on Ottershaw? Good God, lass, I'll have no bride of mine comin' to the kirk out of yon squalid place."

"It was in such a place I was raised, James."

"You'll stay here. Damn the tongues. My mother will be a fine chaperon. You can be *her* guest, if it distresses you to be mine."

"You never liked my mother, did you?" Elspeth asked, without preliminary.

Moodie's eyebrows lifted in surprise. He hesitated again, shrugged. "I never understood her."

"So you resented her."

"Perhaps I did."

"Were you jealous of my father?"

Elspeth's acuity was disturbing but James did not evade the question.

"Perhaps." He shook his head. "No, not jealous. I

375

thought that he, Cochran, had something I wanted. It turned out to be otherwise. She seemed so, so damned free, your mother. She gave him that. You won't understand."

"Free?" said Elspeth. "I don't know what you mean."

"Under nobody's thumb. That's a power in itself, believe me."

"She worked hard for what you call freedom."

"Undeniably."

"I cannot understand why you want me."

"Because I love you."

"I'm not Gaddy's daughter, nor was Coll my father. I'm a mystery, James."

"Perhaps. But not to me," James said. "Come, it's been a fatiguing day. You must go to bed and rest now."

"Aye," said Elspeth obediently.

James opened the door of the dining room. "Will you require a maid?"

"I can manage fine on my own. I always have."

"I've had a lamp put in your room and a small fire lit to cheer you."

Elspeth stopped and reached up to kiss his cheek. The kiss was polite but had no warmth in it. James preferred it so. In time, perhaps, she would become more expressive, grateful for all that he would give her and she would come to need him, need him on his terms, in ways that would not deprive him of power.

After the kiss Elspeth said goodnight and climbed the stairs to the bedroom in the first floor of the house. In the hallway below James lingered, watching her, until a pair of servants appeared from the gloom of the kitchen passage.

He started, as out of a trance, and told them, "Aye, you may clear table."

He went down the passage and along a short corridor into a narrow, board-panelled room in which he kept documents related to commercial dealings and, securely locked in an iron-bound chest, certain personal papers folded into his accounts ledger. No servant, save Tolland, was permitted to enter here and Tolland had no key to fit the chest. It was a chamber set aside for business of the most private kind.

From a decanter on the desk top Moodie poured a glass of

whisky. He added fresh water from a jug that Tolland had topped up that very evening. In the low, iron-basket grate coals glowed. By taper, James Moodie lit an oil-lamp. He seated himself in the room's only chair, an unquilted ladderback, unbuttoned his waistcoat and put his heels on the desk. He sipped the spirits then let his head tilt backwards.

Over his head the boards creaked. Moodie smiled and in his eyes there was a sudden flooding, sentimental warmth.

"God!" he whispered. "God, she's here at last."

The noises of movement were light and delicate and restless. Aye, Moodie thought, it would be difficult for Elspeth to find sleep tonight. He understood night trouble well, the nocturnal sorrows, guilts and anxieties that came with the snuffing out of the light, with the laying of the head on the pillow, as if all one's deeds and misdeeds had left a sediment which stirred cloudily in the brain.

Moodie sipped whisky then, on impulse, put the glass aside and swung his feet to the floor. He knelt before the chest, took a key from his watch-fob and inserted it into the heart-shaped lock, twisted it and softly lifted the lid. Without fumbling he put his hand straight to the ledger in its worn roan binding. He opened the book with his forefinger and gently lifted out the sheet he had trimmed, many years ago, from the parish register; "his" sheet, a page covered with oddly boyish script, neat enough though and legible.

One entry; he placed his fingers straight to the line.

November, 11th Day Thereof, 1791
To pay for a coffin for a poor starved woman,
Who was a stranger......................6s 8d.

Elder Moodie had followed the traditional phrasing and had entered the cryptic record without compassion – or so he had believed at the time.

Now James Simpson Moodie stared at the page as if to rebut the lie he had penned all those years ago, the lie he had built a life to deny. Should he destroy the sheet? After all, what need had he of it with Elspeth secure under his roof. Should he not crumple the page and place it on the coals and watch it burn into grey dust? He hesitated, sighed, and re-inserted it precisely into the ledger and closed the tome with a snap. He put the ledger back into the chest and closed the lid.

On his knees, he listened. No sound came now from overhead. He strained his ears, staring up at the ceiling beams. Silence, her silence, induced an unreasoning panic to which Moodie succumbed. Hastily locking the chest, he rose and hurried out of the private room and along the corridor to the bottom of the stairs.

What did he care if the servants heard him and laughed at his anxiety? Damn them, they might gossip their tongues ragged. None would dare smirk in his presence or slight the young woman who would shortly become his bonded wife and their mistress. After the marriage the maids would have more to ruffle their fantasies than mere noises on the stairs. He had her now and he would never let her go, even if it meant that he lost face, had to brazen out whispered scandal, exchange one form of mortal sin for another.

A solitary candle burned in the bracket in the hall. Carefully James Moodie extracted it and carried it up the staircase between finger and thumb. He had climbed almost to the broad landing before he caught sight of her. Breath caught in his throat in a kind of awe, for she sat still and pale as a ghost on the seat under the tall, lead-paned casement which, uncurtained, looked out across garden and grazings to the swart breast of the moor.

She was dressed in a shift, a shawl loose about her shoulders, her legs and feet bare.

At that instant she reminded him of another girl.

Uncertainly he said, "Elspeth, is it you?"

"Yes, James."

"What – what is it? What's wrong?"

"I canna sleep yet."

Though James Moodie stepped on to the landing, he did not dare draw close to her.

Draught from the open window bent the candle flame and carried sharp autumnal fragrances into the house. In a corner of the window he could see the great, round, butter-muslin moon. A harvest moon was a lovers' moon, so folk said; but it was a moon to dream by too. Elspeth's dreams would never be fulfilled as his had been. He could

378

not be sure that he would not destroy her. He loved her too much to make promises; too much, too selfishly. How could he embrace reason after twenty years of guilt and hurt and awful secrecy?

"I like a breath of sweet air before bed," she said. "See, James, see how bright the moon is tonight?"

"Almost too bright for comfort," he said. "Don't sit too long in the cold."

"I won't," said Elspeth. "I promise."

"Goodnight, dearest."

"Goodnight, James."

By the way she looked at him, shy yet expectant, he sensed that she needed his touch, his kiss of comfort and reassurance. He could not bring himself to give it, did not dare. He gave her another curt "goodnight" and, turning, went quietly downstairs again, leaving the young woman alone with her dreams.

In the hall, he swung his head and, almost furtively, studied her by the silver shine of the moon. No, he need have no fear of Elspeth, of her least of all. He was safe now. No man, no woman shared the knowledge that he possessed. No man, no woman would ever share the shame of the long-forgotten crime or of the crime that was yet to come. Yes, now she was his and ever would be for, at last, James Simpson Moodie had brought his daughter home.